THIS WICKED CURSE

A Realm of Monsters Standalone

AMANDA AGGIE

THIS WICKED CURSE. Copyright © 2023 by Amanda Aggie. All rights reserved. Printed in the United States of America. For more information, please visit www.AmandaAggie.com.

Designations used by companies to distinguish their products are often claimed as trademarks. All brand names and product names used in this book and on its cover are trade names, service marks, logos, and registered trademarks of their respective owners. The publishers and the book are not associated with any product or vendor mentioned in this book. None of the companies referenced within the text have endorsed this book. This book is a work of fiction. All names, places, characters, and events are products of the author's imagination or are fictitious.

Library of Congress Cataloging-in-Publication Data

Names: Aggie, Amanda, author.

Title: This Wicked Curse / Amanda Aggie

Description: First Edition. | Book Dragon Publishing, 2023.

Audiobook Published by Podium Audio (https://podiumaudio.com/)

Printed by Kindle Direct Publishing 2023

Cover Design Copyright © November 2022 by JV Arts

ASIN: B0BND4W73Z (ebook)

ISBN: 9798860011274 (paperback)

To the girls who fall hard for the brooding, fictional villains with a heart of gold

Trigger Warning

This book contains triggers! You will find some adult situations and language intended for individuals 18+ years of age. If you believe magic and sorcery is the Devil's work, please close the book now. This book is for those who like a bit of spice with their fantasy plot, but the plot comes first.

As for major content warnings, please see the list below:

Gore, murder, blood, skeletons, dead bodies, death of a pregnant woman (not on the page), trauma, PTSD, loss of a loved one, abuse (not by the love interest, but happens off page to the main character in the past), forced pregnancy and severe pregnancy complications (main character's mother, not on page but talked about), witchcraft, witch trials, prisoners, beast attacks, animal attacks, graphic sex scenes, choking, bondage, biting, shadow play, monsters, misuse of magic, violence, and other disturbing images that might not be suitable for all audiences.

With that said, if you're family—*talking to you, Mom*—and you have to sit around the dinner table with me at Thanksgiving, you've been warned. If you can't handle the heat, stay out of the kitchen because what you're about to read might make you look at me awkwardly from here on out.

Also, please be sure to review! Honest reviews help so much with getting my books out there in front of new readers, so if you can, please leave one. Even if it's only a star value. :)

Thank you for picking up the book and I hope you enjoy the story!

Now... Be a good little reader and turn the page/scroll on. ;)

Prologue

Twenty-Three Years Ago

The oracle's gem-laden fingers graze just above my navel, and the icy texture of his magic swirls through the pit of my stomach, making the child within it somersault. It takes everything I have to remain calm. There's too much depending upon this test to not, but the nerves creep up my spine, daring the tears to fall from my eyes. I will not cry. I can't. The best thing I can do is power through.

I was supposed to have another week. One more week and the baby would've been born. I could've used my magic and cast an illusion. The king would've had an heir, making my future within this castle secure.

Sure, illusions are temporary, and eventually, I would've been at the mercy of my child revealing the truth, but by then, I might've won the king's heart. At the least, I might've found a way to make the spell permanent. No one would've known what did or didn't reside between their legs.

If only the king had waited...

The king's impatience shattered that possibility. He doesn't want to wait for the birth of our child. He wants to know now and has summoned the oracle to get the answers he craves.

The sightless man in front of me licks his dry, colorless lips. Where his eyes used to be are now long, molten scars, and the golden striations within them reflect the candlelight. Did the gold protruding through his flesh make him blind, or was it added after the fact to make his otherwise haunting face more pleasant to look at?

If so, it didn't work.

His frigid hands circle my stomach again, and I cringe. I should be grateful, not all oracles are humanoid, and some don't rely on their own magic or senses to deliver prophecies. Instead of having to endure the man's touch, it could be something slithering down my throat, and for that, I am blessed.

"Well?" a rough voice snags my attention. The King of Solaria, dressed in his finest robes, has entered the chambers. His blond hair dusts across his shoulders as he draws closer, and I can't help but smile when his eyes meet mine. "Will I have an heir or not?"

That question has haunted me for the last few months. If our child is a boy, I'll be named Queen. My life here will be permanent. I'll never want nor need anything again, and the starving teenage mage who entered this palace, begging to become one of the king's surrogates, will be a long-forgotten memory.

If it's a girl... Let's just say my fate is much more grim.

Some still think I'm mad for doing this, but family was a luxury I lacked since my parents swung from the gallows. They were thieves with quite a reputation amongst the villagers. Not even the whore houses would hire me when they learned of my last name.

Due to my gift, the royal mages would look past my heritage, but I wasn't old enough. My power hadn't fully surfaced and until it did so, I was useless to them. I'd been given up hope when I heard of the king's decree, stating the first woman to give him an heir would be named his queen. Suddenly, I had a way out of my fleeting life, and faced with the choice of becoming his surrogate or starving, the choice was easy.

The king almost didn't accept me. I was too skinny, malnourished, younger than he'd have liked, but old enough. My soul was clinging to my bones by a thread. Sometimes, I wonder if that's the only reason I'm alive now.

The other four surrogates chosen with me weren't impregnated naturally. It was through a procedure he refers to as science. The babies had been tampered with in the womb, their essence mixed with that of other species. He'd do anything to override the curse placed on him by his first wife–the one preventing him from having an heir.

I was supposed to help him as his assistant until I was healthy enough to undergo the procedure myself. Except, the king has a thing for mages, specifically those who look like me–raven-haired and young. It's precisely why I'm carrying his child now. I wasn't healthy enough for his science, but that didn't stop him from taking me to his bed.

I'm just glad that whatever creature we've created is small—normal, for the most part. After he learned that I was with child, he made his tweaks with potions and spells, cursing me the entire time for waiting so long to tell him. Apparently, it limited what adjustments he could make.

Honestly, I feared telling him sooner would earn me the same fate as the other surrogates, and he'd treated me so well…. It was as if I'd already been crowned. I was living in the same chambers as him and given the authority to run the castle staff as I saw fit. I didn't want anything to change–still don't. Perhaps it was naïve to believe it wouldn't, and something about this meeting with the oracle gives me the sense it already has.

The sightless man sits back, wiping the anointed oil off his hands with a rag. "I'm afraid not, your highness. I don't sense the presence of a male." My gut spins as I lock my jaw. I'm utterly helpless, and my only hope is that I've formed enough of a bond with the king for him to show me mercy.

Stealing a glance over my shoulder, the king's face is pale. Those blue eyes were once full of longing. Now, they're just hollow.

Shit... "Check again." I turn my attention back to the oracle. "You're lying."

He has to be...

"The oracle can't lie, love. You know that."

I jolt the moment a hand settles on my shoulder. "Then we try for another." Craning my neck, I meet his vacant eyes. "Your way this time."

For a fleeting moment, I catch a glimpse of the man I've come to know, but it vanishes. The color of his eyes fades into pure white, and I feel a tug on my power. This isn't the man who whispered sweet nothings, who made me feel loved when I've only ever been an inconvenience. Standing before me is the ruthless King of Monsters from the legends–the mimic druid who can harness anyone's power and copy it for himself. And now he has mine.

Why wait until now? He's had months to take it, and had he asked, I would've given it willingly for a chance to stay in this castle–to stay his.

Mimicking is the rarest form of druidic gifts, and as far as I know, he's the last of his kind. It's kept him in power all these years, and it's also what allows him to hold my life in the palm of his hand–for him to save or take as he sees fit.

I stare at him, desperately waiting for him to say something–anything–to soothe my weary soul. Just as I'm about to drown in the anticipation, he finally answers. "Perhaps."

Something in his voice prickles my skin, raising gooseflesh, and an icy shiver traces my spine. The king bends to press a soft kiss to my lips. When he draws back, I keep my eyes shut until his thumb tenderly strokes my cheek. Gathering the courage, I meet his gaze. Those blue eyes are hardening by the second as if it's the last look he'll get.

"Even though it's not an heir, our child will serve this kingdom well."

It's assuring to hear him say that, but I'm keenly aware of what it means—of what our child will be expected to do.

"In marriage, you mean." My words are hardly a whisper. I've seen the king's gauntlet once. I know it's a tradition meant to unite the clans within our realm. As brutal as it may be, that's what it takes to make monsters fall in line. Without the gauntlets, and without the clans swearing fealty, it would be chaos. The realm would go to war.

"There's more, my king," the oracle hisses, drawing out the last syllable of each word.

"What." The king steps away, lifting his chin in a show of strength.

"This will be your last child for at least two thousand cycles of the hell flame. Until then, they'll be dead before they draw breath." The oracle crooks a finger toward my stomach.

"Very well. Your services are no longer required."

The oracle nods and he's escorted out by one of the royal mages guarding the door.

"Vezler, grab the healers." The king spins to face the young druid still left in the room. He's new, and barely made the age to join the royal guard last month. Why do we need the healers?

"Is someone hurt, my king?" The young man's gaze pans around the room, concern creasing his brow.

"No, but we do have a baby to deliver."

I nearly snap my neck, furrowing my brows as my mind whirls to understand what is happening. He can't truly be considering... Dropping my gaze to the marble floors, I search for a possible explanation, something other than the one rearing to the front of my mind. The pit in my stomach settles deeper when I come up empty-handed.

"It's early. I won't be full term for another week," I say, trying to keep my breath calm and collected even though every sense has heightened.

"We've delivered healthy babies sooner." The king doesn't so much as look at me as he moves toward the door.

"You don't have to risk this. You heard the oracle, my king. There won't be another viable child for two-thousand cycles of the hell flame. Why rush to the experiments now?"

He halts in the archways, pursing his lips before finally giving me his undivided attention. "I'm not, but I have no need for you. Should you wish to be a surrogate again, you can in twenty years. It would be pointless to do so now."

My heart plummets as the fragile grip I have on my composure breaks. Tears flood my eyes as I lurch from the chair, only to be snatched up by the healers who file past him. Their steps are in unison, echoing off the vaulted ceiling. The king doesn't stop them, nor does he show a single thread of remorse.

"Who will raise our daughter?"

"I have a staff for that. She'll be raised like all the others have been."

Shrugging off the hands that try to drag me toward the bed, I straighten my shoulders. "I thought you cared."

"You needed to believe I did."

The room is deathly silent except for the shuffle of footsteps as the healers and magic users gear up for what comes next. The two who tried to drag me away are all but frozen on either side of me.

"I didn't need anything from you except for food. I was starving because you made me an orphan."

"No. Your parents did the moment they stole from the castle. You've fulfilled your purpose, and now it's time that you move on. That is what you signed up for. Whatever fantasy you've concocted is just that."

"You kissed me." I take a step forward, closing the distance between us. "You held me in your arms at night, allowed me to oversee your castle...I've been your queen in every way but in title. It's not a fantasy or some twisted dream. If it was all a lie, then you pretended to care for months. Why?"

"It was an experiment."

I halt, cementing my feet to the marble, innately aware that the healers have moved closer along with me. "A what?" My voice cracks and my stomach flips as I swallow down the urge to scream.

"I thought perhaps distress or a lack of affection was what I was missing. I thought it would get me a boy. Now, I know it has no impact."

He won't let me go. I'm not stupid enough to believe otherwise. The offer he made to the public has had women flocking to the castle, ready to sign up. If they knew what they were subjecting themselves to, his experiments would be over. Which means I know too much for him to just let me go.

Before I can respond, the king slips into the hall and leaves me alone with the healers. One gently nudges me toward the bed and the harsh gesture eats away the last of my fuse. Throwing my hands up, the man takes flight and slams into the wall hard enough to knock the clay mask off his face.

"I'm aware of my purpose, but I will do so on my own accord," I snap as I stalk toward the bed.

If this is going to be the last thing I do, I'll do it with dignity. The king will remember me. If not for the time we spent together, he will when he looks at our daughter. I won't leave this world without ensuring so, for nothing and no one is more scornful than a witch with a broken heart.

1

SCARLET

My head slaps into the duck feather-filled pillow, stunting the breath from escaping my lungs. I don't think I've ever come so fast before. Clearly, my impending fate is having some effect on the man positioned between my legs. It shouldn't, but it does, or else he wouldn't be here. Not today.

His forehead rests against my collarbone, and the warmth of his ragged breaths heats my skin. This isn't the first time we've slept together. Honestly, I've lost count, but we both have things at stake if our secret was to get out. It would be both of our death sentences.

Zelix is a shadow shroud, or in more vulgar terms, an assassin who makes whoever my father tells him to disappear. Such a job required an oath of both allegiance and celibacy, and that's precisely why I've allowed him in my bed.

As a Princess of Solaria, chastity is a must. My father enchants his daughter's forbidden places to keep unwanted visitors out. Except magic doesn't work the same on me...

and breaking such enchantments has become my favorite pastime, second only to our secret trysts.

"We could run."

Zelix pushes up, his honey-ringed eyes meeting mine before he leans in for one last kiss. I cringe internally, but let him have his moment. We typically have a no-kissing rule. Kissing is emotional, and knowing what my future brings, we shouldn't be. Yet that didn't stop him from falling, and today is ruining him with every second that ticks by. Poor guy... His heart never stood a chance.

"And if we ran, you'd be dead by morning. I wouldn't be much long after." I hold up his wrist, flashing him the metal cuff around it. It's enchanted, and my father uses it to control the creatures in our realm. He can shut off their magic with a whispered incantation and kill them just as quickly. "No one runs from this, nor would I want to." Dropping his hand, I grip the sheet and pull it around my torso as we sit up.

"It's worth a shot."

"Maybe to you. I like my head attached to my shoulders and my organs seated in their proper spots."

He snorts, twisting to sit on the edge of the bed. In pure silence and stealth, he bends to retrieve his trousers from the floor.

"Ironic, considering most of your sisters end up in pieces. Your father is running out of room in the crypt. He's started consolidating the bones. I believe his exact words were, we don't need an entire casket for an arm. Yet, you're acting like this tradition is a privilege."

"It's my duty... It's what I was born for. I won't run from my responsibilities. Not when my kingdom is relying on me to do what's right."

The layers of muscle along his back tighten before he peers at me over his sun-kissed shoulder. "Right? Your father is as wicked as they come. The only reason he still wears that crown is because your kingdom is terrified of who he used to be."

"We don't speak of it."

He glances around the room. "Last I checked, it's just you and me here. We don't need to lie. Your father is nowhere close to as powerful as he used to be when he became king. He's absorbed too many abilities over the last few decades, now he can barely wield any of them with precision. If it weren't for Asmodeus and his 'chosen sons' protecting him, he wouldn't be on the throne anymore."

"His power remains in his name and those he surrounds himself with. He doesn't need to deliver the killing blow if he has enough men beneath him who would do it in a heartbeat or enchanted wristbands that could force someone to do it in seconds. That's all that matters."

"You still talk about it like it's Sunday tea in the garden and not impending death." A growl sounds from his throat as he threads his arms through his shirt. "Excuse me if I'd rather see you live."

"What would you expect me to do? Like I said, I can't run from it. I don't have a wristband, but my father would find me, eventually. I can't harm him. I'm biologically incapable of doing so. Even then, there's more at stake than my life. If I don't go through with the ceremony, people will die. The peace within our realm will be shattered, and where would I be then? The clans are fighting as is. The gauntlet has been long overdue, and it's the only thing that will bring them together for the next ten years."

"Sure, except the king had a twenty-year dry spell. Do you think one gauntlet is going to hold off war until your younger sisters turn of age? Even if it does, the cycle will repeat itself. When does it end?"

"I don't know... but it's too late to change that now. We both knew this day would come, just as we both have obligations that are bigger than us."

The frown he gives makes me avert my eyes. I gather the bedding closer, wishing I could shrink beneath it and avoid the rest of this conversation. If only dreams did come true.

"What happens when they come to check?" he asks, clenching his jaw as if to prevent grinding his teeth.

"To see if I'm still sanctified? Don't worry about it. I have it handled."

"You're forgetting that we're both caught up in this. If they find out you're not a virgin—"

I swing my legs over the edge of the bed and storm toward the bedroom door, taking the sheets with me. "I hate to break it to you, but it'd be a hell of a lot worse for me. You'd get to slip off into the night, no one the wiser, because I wouldn't tell a soul who defiled me. I, however, would get fed to a fucking beast that also happens to be my half-sibling. Now, I'll say it again. I have it covered."

His boots clap against the marble floor as he closes the distance between us—now fully dressed—and upon reaching me, he cups the side of my face in the palm of his hand. "I don't want to have to watch you die."

"Then close your eyes. It's in the fates' hands now, and should their spirits let me live, I'll wear someone else's last name by morning. Either way, this is the end of us."

He nods his understanding, pressing his lips together before placing a gentle peck against my forehead. As much as he wants to savor this moment, I have to pay off a witch doctor before meeting my suitors in the ballroom.

"I'll see you in there," he says, dropping his gaze to the floor as he takes a step back.

"It better be by my father's side and not because you pledged to enter the gauntlet."

"We'll have to see." With that, he's out the door, sneaking down the hall without a single witness.

I watch him go, the silence of his footsteps soothing me as his form disappears around a corner at the end of the hall. The sun has set now, casting long shadows across my room. A breeze drifts in through the window, carrying the scent of sweetgrass and lavender. I inhale deeply, letting the fragrance calm my racing heart.

Even as I close my eyes and try to find some peace, I know that Zelix's words have stirred something within me. His questions about the future, about the endless cycle of violence and death that seems to define our realm—they are ones that have been on my mind for quite some time.

And yet, I have no answers.

I let the sheet fall to the floor, my body still humming with a strange mix of desire and fear of what is to come. I wonder if anyone else in my family has ever had doubts about the traditions we uphold, and the sacrifices we make for the sake of peace. Perhaps they have, but they never voiced them. Not that they would've had a chance to. As soon as a gauntlet is announced, the promised daughter is separated from the rest of the king's daughters. We're not allowed to speak to one another until after the wedding.

Biting my bottom lip, I try to push those thoughts aside. There's work to be done. Slipping on a thin gown, I make myself presentable and don a thick cloak, pulling the strings tight around my throat. The nights get cold here, and the fabric might offer me some discretion should I run into one of my sisters, or worse, my father in the hallways. They'd suspect something if they caught me visiting the healers without a valid reason, and here, an accusation might as well be a conviction.

Moving down the hall, I wind through the labyrinth of stone walls and stairwells, until finally, I come face to face with Amara's door. Knocking quietly, I wait for the rustle of feet and the click of the lock, but she doesn't bother to invite me inside. Instead, she slips a note through the cracked door. I take it, feeling something other than paper wound up inside of it.

I don't dare open it here. Amara's hand waits for me to fill it with the sack of gold coins, and once she's been paid, the door shuts without a word or a mumbled goodbye. Shoving the folded note in my cloak pocket, I return to my room, and no sooner do I make it inside, I'm ripping the note open without care.

'Here are the herbs. Put them in your tea. It will last for one tick of the sun, so use it right before they come to check. I'll miss you. -Amara

She'd been one of my closest friends before joining the healers. We used to spend hours talking, strolling through the gardens, or getting lost in the castle library. Once she joined the Bekorium Order, she wasn't allowed to do such things. It didn't stop us from exchanging notes, though, or from her helping me now.

Rolling the sachet of herbs in my hand, I bring it to my nose. Amara has never steered me wrong before, and I hope that won't change. The pungent aroma fills my nostrils, making me grimace. It's amazing what a simple concoction can do, and this will supposedly make it appear as if I'm just losing my virginity, rather than having lost it years ago to Zelix. That is, assuming I survive to see the examination. The odds aren't great, but I'd rather be prepared.

The truth is, I have no idea what will come of tomorrow. The only thing that is certain for me is this has to happen. And if I'm going to play the part of sacrificial lamb, I might as well maintain some dignity and not spend my final moments chained to my throne.

2

HOOK

Smee's sharp whisper jolts me from my trance. I nearly drop my spyglass into the sea below, jostled by the rolling waves that rock our ship.

"Looks like we've got company," she says, her dark curls whipping in the wind.

"It would appear so." I wipe away the saltwater beading on my brow, but it's pointless. With the choppy waves crashing against the hull of our ship, everything above deck is covered in it.

The sharpness of her glare bores into the side of my face as if it's the tip of a dagger, and when I meet it, her lips purse. She's out for blood today.

"I know that look." Pushing off of the wooden rail of the Jolly Roger, I shake my head. Nothing good could come of this conversation, not when she's in a mood, ready to lecture until her tongue goes numb.

"You know nothing."

"Is that so?" Raising a thick eyebrow, I halt and Smee plows into my back. For as talented as she is with a sword, by the gods, she's obnoxiously clumsy.

I love my half-sister with all of my being, but she's more brazen than what's good for her. It doesn't matter who you are or what your title is, she'll tell you exactly what she thinks. It's led to me having taken more lives ending fights she started, than I have in the years I've served as the second mate of this ship. I can commend her courage, but that mouth of hers will be her undoing one day.

Smee rights herself and takes a step back as I slowly turn to face her. Those hazel eyes don't even flinch, challenging me as she clears her throat and crosses her arms over her chest. The motion causes my gaze to drop, and I immediately regret it. Clenching my fists and grinding the hinge of my jaw, I glue my eyes to the caps of the waves.

Would it kill the woman to wear a proper shirt?

I could've gone my entire life without seeing the bite mark bruise she's wearing with pride on the curve of her breast. Smee is a grown woman who can handle herself. She doesn't need her big brother floating every man that dares to touch her. For the most part, I try to stay oblivious to her... endeavors, but sporting things like that test my patience.

"Look, it could be months before we have another opportunity. We know they have the compass, and they're alone with no fleet to protect them. It'll be an easy grab," she says, standing her ground.

"Exactly." Continuing down into the skin of the ship, I hear her pattering footsteps keeping pace.

"That doesn't answer my question." Smee grips my arm, forcing me to halt or risk pulling her off her feet. Again.

"What is a merchant ship doing outside royal waters on its own? They always travel in fleets or squadrons outside the Solarian Bay. That's a trap if I've ever seen one."

Smee rolls her eyes hard enough to crack a socket. "Please. There's nothing wrong with the ship. You're just too chicken to board it."

"Chicken? Really? That's what you got?" When she doesn't answer, I twist and continue through the passageway.

"Sebastian," she groans, using the same tone a mother would with their child. "You need that compass. It's the one thing that can lead us to Pan. Do you want your shadow back or not?"

Smee skirts around me to stand in the middle of the passage. Something tells me she'll cling to the walls if I try to move her, and when Smee puts her mind to something, she doesn't stop until she gets it.

I wish I could say my will is stronger than hers, but she's the only person that can make me cave. Call it sibling love, but it's impossible to resist her when she bats those long eyelashes. I hate it.

Her lips twist as she pokes my sternum. "If I didn't know any better, I'd think you're scared to find it–to be whole again."

Of course, I want my shadow back, but Pan is hiding out on the mainland. Even with the compass, we'd never reach him without risking capture and execution. We step foot in Solaria and all it will take is someone to recognize us. They'll turn our whereabouts in for the price on our heads. We might put up a good fight, but one crew won't last against the entire king's guard.

"There's never going to be a more perfect time to get that compass. It's either now or never," Smee says as a hand clamps onto my shoulder—one I know far too well. I'd recognize those tattooed knuckles anywhere.

"She's right, son." My father moves to stand beside us, scratching his dark beard with his metal hook. "No better time than the present. Who knows when we'll see that ship again, and from the rumors circulating in the Lunaries, I'd say our ticket to the mainland is coming sooner rather than later."

If that's so, then it's news to me. We're pirates, criminals of the seven realms, and wanted for a whole list of crimes by the Solarian crown. Porting anywhere on the mainland is asking for trouble.

My father, the captain of this ship, brushes past us, surfacing on the deck. He doesn't waste any time barking orders, and the crew scurries topside to prepare for the ambush. They're beyond eager, not that I blame them. It's been weeks since we've taken a ship, and our pockets are growing thin. Then there's everything we could take back home...

Merchant ships are always packed full of food, supplies, clothes, and goods to trade with other ports along the Arcadian coast, not particularly gold or treasure. Though ones like this tend to have some precious items on board, like the compass I need. Our people rely on these heists, and if our stores are running low, I can't even imagine how those back on the island are wavering.

Smee meets my gaze with fire in her eyes as she smirks and climbs the stairs back to the top of the ship, leaving me in the passage. She lives for this, and normally I do too, but something settles in the pit of my stomach. It's as if the shadows around me have grown weary of what comes next just as much as I have.

As I let out a long exhale, I climb the steps and surface in time to see my father take the helm. His red leather coat swishes around his legs and the lapels flip in the wind. Taking my place beside him, I catch the corner of his lips tip up.

"Come to your senses, have ya?"

"I suppose," I say, looking out at the sea.

The merchant ship looms closer now, seemingly oblivious to our presence. It does little to settle the unease building in my chest, but I'm steadfast. The black sails with the red skulls unfurl just as figures appear on top of the enemy deck. Our men take up arms, gearing up for the approach.

"Brace!" I roar as we careen into their side with a mighty crash. My legs jolt, but I maintain my footing.

Grappling hooks fly and our men swing aboard, steel singing as it meets steel. I leap off the deck and onto one of the ropes, gripping hand over hand until I clear the rail of the merchant ship and drop down onto the metal surface near Smee.

She slices and jabs, leveling the men with lethal grace. I wish she'd use more when she walks, but I suppose if she was going to have it, now is better than never.

Pulling my cutlass free, I lunge into the thick of the chaos, matching Smee stroke for stroke, two entities bound by blood. As we fight our way across the deck, the shrill battle cries echo out, only to be swallowed by the roiling sea around us.

"We gotta get to the cargo hold!" I shout to her over the metallic clatter of swords. The nod she gives is the only response I need.

The merchant crew is skilled, but they're cut down faster than I anticipate, and before Smee even makes it to the door, that leads to the companionway, the deck falls eerily silent. The six crewmen who came over with us await orders, their chests heaving as they catch their breath. Something about this isn't right.

There are fifteen bodies littering the ground. It would take ten times that to smoothly operate a ship this size. Where is everyone?

I give the signal for the others to board before finding Smee waiting with her hand poised and ready to open the door to the companionway. Blood splatter and sweat beads on her dark skin.

"Go ahead." I step closer, and she wretches it open.

A grizzled man with a scarred face appears on the other side. His ax swings at Smee with a speed that belies his bulk. She parries, but the ax comes again, and she hits the deck, rolling before the curved blade can stab into the place she just laid. I surge forward, my blade a blur as I drive him back into the rope lining the outer edge of the deck. Before I can deliver a deadly blow, he stumbles and careens into the deep, disappearing beneath the black waves.

Smee gets to her feet, dusting off her shirt like it will dislodge the blood staining it, then adjusts her headband and picks up her discarded sword.

"Keep your eyes peeled. There have to be a couple dozen below deck." I stride down the companionway steps until I hit the next level.

A dimly lit room comes into view, a passageway on each of the four walls. Fixed tables and benches fill the space, littered with flipped and discarded trays. Whoever was eating left in a hurry. Reaching the nearest table, I grab the edge of a plate and pull it closer.

"The food is still hot," a muffled voice says to my right. Nelvin—the most experienced swordsman on this crew—leans against one of the tables, trying to stuff an entire bread roll into his mouth. "In case you were wondering."

Is it odd that I can understand the gibberish he speaks? No. In fact, I've become rather used to it. No matter how wealthy the man gets, he always eats like a pig. It's no more unusual than the rabbit's foot he's rubbing between his fingers. He never takes it off. Not even to bathe.

Twisting my neck, I arch an eyebrow at him. "Can you leave the food alone?"

"Well, someone's gotta eat it."

"That someone doesn't have to be you," Smee says, poking him in the ribs with the tip of her sword.

Nelvin rolls his eyes, grabbing another roll off a tray and shoving it into the pocket of his harem pants. "Fine. I'll eat them later, but I call dibs on all the ones without a nibble." Brushing his long blond hair behind his pointed ears, he makes eye contact with the others, like he knows they'll try to steal them, anyway.

"Let's split up. Groups of two. If you find the cargo hold, you know what you're looking for. If you get it, you head back to the ship. Don't linger." I pluck a green bean out of Nelvin's hand and eat it, enjoying the way he frowns at me. "You're with Smee. I need to know you won't eat your way to the bottom of the ship."

His silver eyes fall flat, but the moment Smee moves between us, his demeanor changes. His gaze turns hungry, and his smile is all teeth, widening even more when he catches a glimpse of her chest. I think it's safe to say he's admiring his handiwork.

"Eye-fuck my sister again and I'll feed you to the fish," I growl, shaking my head when he snaps to attention.

As the group pairs up, I pull Zephyr with me. He's shit with a sword, but beyond skilled with a needle and one of the best healers on the Jolly Roger. As an elemental, like me, he can control the air, but his ability is nowhere near strong enough to be a weapon. It can't even fill the sails when the winds die due to him being part orc.

The magic in his blood is diluted, but it doesn't stop him from becoming useful in other ways. He can stitch you up in seconds, and when we need to send messages long distance or to the rest of the crew on heists like this, he can whisper it and the wind will carry it where it needs to go.

He follows me into one of the passages and down the stairs to the floor below. It's a berthing, where the crewmen that serve on the ship sleep. Much like the mess hall above, it's empty and hauntingly silent, which does nothing for the anxiety knotting in my gut.

The doors on both ends are open, but otherwise, everything looks as it should. I motion for Zephyr to help check the bunks, ripping open the curtains to the three-tiered racks of beds. Not a single soul is present.

Using my gift, I search the darkness, letting it bend to my will to reveal the secrets hidden within it, but the room is empty. I sense heartbeats present on other floors, likely my crew, but none on this one. It's as if the ship has been abandoned. The vessel creaks as it lolls with the waves.

Grabbing Zephyr, we go deeper, continuing down to the lowest level of the ship. The companionway ends at a door. Locked, but not by magic. Touching the tip of my finger to the keyhole, a trail of smoke-like darkness forms around it, threading inside until the lock pins click open.

Turning the circular handle, I crank until the hatch releases and the hinges whine. Every hair on my body seems to stand on end, and I lift my wrist to get a better look, furrowing my brow. A sulfuric scent leaching into the air, burning its way down my windpipe.

"Something isn't right." No sooner do I get the words out, power gushes through the opening. It slams into me as the darkness swarms around my body and I'm thrown back. I hit the bulkhead and a ringing explodes through my ears, but my shadows soften the blow.

The force was so strong, so unexpected. It takes me a moment to register the pain that sweeps over me, making every muscle in my body scream. I gasp for breath, clutching at my chest. A burning sensation settles deep as if a bolt of energy burrowed into my sternum.

Lifting my gaze, I find two robed figures. Though most of their faces are obscured, I can see their wicked smiles, along with their blackened teeth and gums.

Fucking witches… It's a trap, just as I'd feared, but there's no way I'm turning back now.

"Zephyr!" I call, hearing a groan to my left. Forcing my neck to turn, I see a lump of green flesh on the stairwell move. As my eyes focus, the twisted dark horns that arc over the shape of his head come into view. He pushes up, holding a hand over the gash in his head.

He's breathing and moving. That's a good sign.

The figures step forward, spreading their fingers as they chant in a language I don't understand. My sword lay on the floor near the hatch door, but I'm far from unarmed.

The air vibrates with their sickly magic as I push up to my feet and I summon my own. Thick black tendrils of smoke roll around my skin, the edges of my being blurring with the pulsating darkness. It coils around my arms and power thrums through my veins. With a flick of my wrist, the shadows dart forward. They collide with the figures, wrapping and constricting around them, depriving them of air and draining the life from their forms. Their skin pales and cracks form along the surface until the figures explode into charred embers and gray ashes.

Zephyr limps closer, his eyes widening as he takes in what's happened. "Are you alright?"

"I should be asking you that," I say, nodding at the gash on his head.

"I'll be fine... They can't say the same."

Stepping closer, being mindful of the burning embers, I enter the cargo hold, Zephyr in tow. "None of this makes sense. Why are blood witches here? The king won't let the marked join the guard. Even he thinks they're vile."

It's one more reason for me to believe the ship was abandoned. They must've taken up residence and decided to feast off whatever was left of the crew.

"Who knows, but the sooner we get what we came for, the sooner we can leave." Zephyr starts thumbing through the items on the shelves, archives by the look of it. Boxes upon boxes of them. "They're empty. Almost all of them. Look."

Grabbing a box, I lift the lid and find the hollow bottom. "Fuck..."

Ripping box after box from the shelves, I form a pile of them until finally, I find one with something in it. A note scrawled in blood for ink, and with it, the compass.

'Congratulations Captain. Hopefully, this token of my appreciation can let us become allies, assuming you can forgive and forget. Maybe having your shadow will help with that. - C'

The Crocodile. My father's sworn enemy. Suddenly, everything makes sense. He's the only slimy creature that would do business with blood witches. He and his crew of freakish misfits likely pillaged this ship and left a present, knowing we'd find it once it floated into our waters. But it still doesn't explain why he called me captain. I'm certain it was me specifically since he brought up my missing shadow.

He's planning something. I just wish I knew what.

Zephyr lets the others know to head back to the ship and when we reach the deck, the grapples await us to slide down like a zipline. Smee goes first, hooking her sheathed sword over the rope and gliding down. The other men follow after, one by one, giving me a moment to take in the sight.

The Jolly Roger is a mess. Arrows are lodged into the spars, and holes are shredded into the sails. What happened? Where did they come from?

We cleared the deck of the merchant ship and the others only found stranglers below. So, who shot the arrows?

Whisking down the line, my feet touch down on the familiar planks of the Jolly Roger, but Smee jerks me toward the captain's quarters before I can get my bearings or question further.

"Something happened." She tugs me faster by the fabric of my shirt.

"You don't say."

"I'm serious, Sebastian!" she snaps, whirling to face me. Her face gives me pause, the tears in her hazel eyes. She never cries.

"Who?" I ask, dreading whatever name leaves her lips.

She doesn't answer as she pushes open the door to our father's room. No. It can't be. But the truth confronts me without mercy.

My father groans as the men force him to lie down. Zephyr is already hard at work, examining where three arrows have pierced my father's torso, but the look he gives me tells all. The thick scent of hemlock in the air means they'll be fatal... Even with an antidote, his odds of survival are slim, but without one it's impossible. There's nothing Zephyr can do, but like a loyal friend, he'll try everything he can.

I fall to my knees beside the bed. My father's face is pale, his breathing ragged. Still, he manages to spit out a string of curse words at Zephyr.

"It's alright," I say, nodding to the orc. His own head is still bleeding and needs tending to still. With a curt nod, he bows his head, his long dark hair falling forward as he takes a step back and exits the room.

"Did you get it?" my father breathes. "The compass. Did you get it?"

Pulling it from my pocket, I show him, and a smirk tilts his bloodied lips. "Well done, my boy." He grips my hand and it's impossible not to notice how cold it is.

"Save your strength," I urge him, though I know it's a losing battle.

No one can convince the infamous Captain Hook to do anything he doesn't want to. Smee gets it honestly... She kneels beside me, her hand wrapping around both of ours.

My father closes his eyes, exhaling long and deep. "The tips were dipped in poison."

"We know," Smee says, pressing her lips together as the tears slip down her cheeks.

"The Crocodile knew we'd be here. He must've rigged the ship. I swear they came out of nowhere, but they all flew at me like they were spelled to do so. I thought for sure that the compass wouldn't be there. At least I won't die for nothing." I'm not sure if he's trying to convince himself or soothe our souls, but he smiles big and cups his free hand over Smee's.

"We did it," she says, trying to grin through the tears, but the smile never reaches her eyes. "We'll get his shadow back. I promise."

With the last of his strength, my father lifts the captain's hat from his head and places it upon mine. "She's yours now. Take good care of her. Promise me the two of you will take care of our people. They need a Hook just as much as they need air."

"We will." I don't dare to meet his eyes. It's not just this ship he's leaving us, it's the entire island. Those on the Island and in the Luminaries will depend on us to protect them from the king's voyagers. They'll rely on us to bring them the goods they need to survive. They always have.

Smee leans forward, placing her lips on his sweat-beaded forehead. She lingers for a moment, her chest heaving as she strains to contain the tears.

The steady tap of blood dripping off the saturated bed turns into a steady stream and, as she sits back, I realize why. She's spared him... Hemlock poisoning is no glorious way to die. It's ruthless and by the time you get your foot in the afterlife, you want it to end. She's given him a quick way out.

My father's hand squeezes one last time around mine before his eyes drift shut. Captain Hook is gone.

I sit in silence for a long moment, hat in hand. This changes everything. But it cannot be undone. When I rise and step out of the captain's quarters, the crew is waiting on the deck, hats in hand.

"Sebastian..." Zephyr says, his voice barely audible even though he's merely a foot or two away. "Your father. He made me write this down before he'd let me treat him. It's about a gauntlet. He thought it would get you access to the mainland."

My eyes skim the paper, penned in rushed lines but legible. Swallowing the thick lump in my throat, I fold it carefully and put it in my pocket, feeling the cool metal of the compass. Pulling it free, I examine its face while Smee wraps her arms around my waist.

"Do you really think it will work?" she asks.

I clench my fist. "It has to."

"We'll find him, Sebastian. I swear it. I made a promise and I plan to keep it with my dying breath."

3

Hook

Turning over the glass vial in my hand, I pull the cork and gulp down the metallic liquid. It's sour upon my tongue, but the sweet contrast of magic makes me grimace more.

Normally, I shy away from witchcraft. It's different from the elements some of my crew wield, me included. Even the king's royal mages don't use it. Our gifts originated at birth. They were blessings from the gods that came before us.

Blood witches, however, use sacrifices to fuel their spells. Some of which can be derived from plants and animals, while others cost a steeper price, and whatever it can't take from the sacrifice, it takes from the caster. It's what makes their bones rot from within and causes their skin to shrivel. They're vile, despicable creatures who are power-hungry, and so much so they're willing to die for it.

Yet, we paid one of those wretched souls to make this glamour... to brew us up a batch to maintain our facade while we're on the mainland. It was all I could think of to carry out my father's wishes. In a world where beasts hide around every corner, sometimes it's necessary to conspire with darkness, even if I despise the creatures that speak it into existence.

Circumstances like this, for instance... Walking into the belly of the beast, it might be the one thing preventing the guards from snatching me up and hanging me from the highest arch in this castle.

My father believed this gauntlet was the way forward. The king hasn't announced one in over a decade, but coincidentally enough, my father managed to catch word of the event before he died. One of the king's daughters has come of age and this gauntlet is his way of celebrating. A fight to the death between the men in our realm brave enough to enter. Only one will emerge victorious, but that one will be crowned a chosen prince.

Since the king is incapable of providing an heir to his throne, this is his way of securing his legacy, but for me, it'll be what gets me, and my people, pardoned. The king will be forced to wipe my slate clean to save face, paving the way for my crew to search the mainland for Pan without constantly looking over our shoulders.

"It will last for a couple hours, Captain, but you'll need to take another before the moons smother the hell flame," Zephyr says, adjusting the lapel of his leather jacket.

The glamour didn't just change his face, but his clothes, too. Where he used to have sage-toned skin and dark, twisted horns, and ivory tusks, he's more humanoid now. His long, dark hair is still present, but everything else appears like a man of nobility. Rich, dark leathers embezzled with rubies hang from his form, and it makes me wonder how much the glamour has changed my appearance.

Brushing a hand through my hair, I don't notice a significant difference in length or texture. It's still shaped closely to the side of my head and wavy up top, landing just above my eyebrows. From what I can see, it still holds the same dark color, too. My clothes, on the other hand, are much different.

Instead of the loose shirt and leather pants I'd worn here, the glamour made them appear like something a prince would wear. Knee-high leather boots end into white pants, belted around my waist. A fitted black shirt, made of some of the finest fabric I've ever laid eyes on, tucks into them. A long black coat that splits from the waist down rests on top of it where my father's red one used to be, though the color still remains in accented swirls and jeweled buttons.

Clenching my fist, I test the stretch of the leather gloves, hating the way they constrict around the rings on my fingers. It's why I usually cut the finger sections off, leaving the leather to cover the thicker part of my hand but allowing my fingers to maintain full mobility. It's perfect for dealing with the ropes on a ship, and for handling my sword if needed.

"Well?" Zephyr says, holding his hands out. "Are you going to tell me I look pretty?"

My lips tip up at the corner for a short moment. "It's better than before."

"Aye, I'll take it. Let's hope you can be smoother for the princess, though." He swipes a hand over his eyebrow as if to slick it close to his skin. "If you can't be, then this plan is dead in the water."

"I don't need help in the art of wooing."

"You don't? I can't seem to remember the last time you went steady with a lass. In fact, I don't think I've ever seen you with one for more than a night. You don't get to throw around your title here, Captain. You actually have to make her like ya, and with your chipper personality... Good luck."

"Thanks for the pep talk." Rolling my eyes, I step out from the alley between merchant shops and head down the cobblestone path. "When we get to the castle, stay low. I don't want any surprises. I promised I'd bring you back in one piece. Don't make a liar out of me."

Zephyr nods, crossing his arms over his chest as we come to the bridge connecting the marketplace to the island in the Solarian Bay. The bridge dead ends into the castle courtyard, but the sheer size of it is both breathtaking and morbid.

The colossal pillars are constructed from the remnants of dragon skeletons, left behind from when the mad king eradicated the species from our realm. The wing bones loop around the sides of the stone platform to form a rail and the curved ribs create arches every so many feet overhead.

We approach the castle steps, feeling the scrutinizing eyes of the royal guard watching our every move. I just hope the glamour holds, and that the spell is as strong as the crooked lady who sold it to us suggested.

The castle stands tall with towers reaching into the clouds. Sand-colored stones make up the walls, but moss has overtaken most of the exposed surfaces, dampened by the humid, salty air. We climb the steps and enter the arched doorway, hearing the faint bustle of music.

Once inside, I break away from Zephyr and head for the great hall. The noise only grows louder and the crowd thicker until a grand room full of flickering candles and polished gold surfaces takes form. The marble floors seem to echo, and the heightened ceilings carry the sounds far and wide.

I note each exit, the double door hidden amongst the sea of windows on the right wall, leading to some sort of private garden. The hall to the left of the thrones and lastly, the one I came through. It's always wise to be keen on every way out of a room. You never know when something will go wrong, and it's better to be prepared and not need the knowledge than to need it and not know.

Guards are stationed along the wall and entrances, with a handful surrounding the king in all his glory, standing in front of his golden throne. All of them are clad in silver and gold armor, and like the flags and tapestries hanging from the ceiling and walls, they too are accented in a bright crimson red. The Solarian crest, dire wolves circling each other, is apparent on every single one.

The crowd is a mix of monsters and men, but a few women are present. Most are from the king's staff, but that's expected. Most lords wouldn't bring their wives—assuming they have them—to an event like this. Maybe to the gauntlet itself, but this is more for the pledges entering than your standard social gathering.

The men aren't here to form compromises between the clans or even to make eyes with the princess, though she'll be marrying one of us. Tonight is for them to suck up to the king and beg for his favor. My hope is everyone will be so busy kissing up to him that they won't spare a second thought when I try to talk to the princess.

With every gauntlet, the king picks a favorite pledge, and gives his advantage to one, blessing them with the opportunity to change a rule before the game begins. It can be anything except the location of the event. You could choose for no one else to have a weapon but you, or even for the king to suppress the other pledges' magical abilities. The possibilities are endless.

Under normal circumstances, it'd be wise for me to try to earn the king's favor, but I've got my eye on a different course of action. While everyone else plays inside the box, I'll be playing outside.

The king clinks something silver against his goblet and the roar of voices dwindles to an uncomfortable silence. "Welcome, brave souls, and thank you for coming." His gaze sweeps through the crowd. "I'll now begin accepting pledges, but please, enjoy the feast, the ale, and the wine, for tonight is a celebration after all."

One by one, creatures line up, and the crowd segregates into two sides. One made up of pledges awaiting to see the king and the other of those who came to witness. The musicians begin to sing again once the king has taken his throne, but I don't rush to get in line.

Leaning against the wall at the back of the room, I watch pledge after pledge say their oaths and swear their fealty to the crown. They give the king their word that should they win, they'll be at his beck and call. It's just their word, though. Words can be skewed, and oaths can be broken. Pirates are only loyal to their own and any oath spoken outside of that means absolutely nothing.

Movement draws my eye. The crowd is still mostly parted, the king front and center having stepped away from his throne, but the streak of white hair... It's impossible not to notice. She's stunning, in a form-fitting crimson gown.

The corset bones form to her waist and long sleeves hug her shoulders, flaring wide around her wrists.

Even with her face obscured by the lace veil, she's breath-taking. Yet, no one notices or so much as stops to pay attention as she takes who should be the queen's throne. It irks me that a magnificent image like that would go unrecognized, but it's for the best. If I hold any chance of talking to her, the less attention she garnishes, the better.

The man currently pledging his oath glances at the princess, stumbling on his words before stopping his pledge altogether. "Why would we risk our lives for a princess if the king won't let us see her face? Is it that bad you feel the need to hide it?" he asks, and the king frowns.

"Do you question my honor? Would you think so little of your crown to mislead you?" The king steps toward his daughter as her younger sisters file into the smaller thrones lined up behind her. He grips the lace of the veil and rips it off her head, scattering strands of white hair across her face. "I can assure you my daughters are just as beautiful as ever."

I set my jaw, watching as the king tosses the veil to the floor as if it means nothing. The pledging man doesn't waste a beat, stammering over his words to finish his vow.

My gaze lingers far longer than it should, fascinated more than anything. Hardly any of the princesses live past their wedding night. Usually, the winners of these events are savage creatures who know nothing more than bloodshed and couldn't care less about the prize, only that they've earned the title for their clan.

Whatever pledge prevails will become one of the king's chosen princes, earning a spot in the final trial. Should the king die of natural causes, the chosen—or their living legacies—will be allowed to fight one last time and the winner will be crowned king, but that's just the beginning. Once the gauntlet is over, the winner's clan or village will be treated like royalty. Their people will be regarded in the highest manner, and the king will see to their needs before the rest for ten years.

It's why most didn't even spare a glance at the princess when she emerged. She's a part of the prize, but she's not what they came for... Well, except the sorry fool who asked to see her face. Clearly, he's interested.

It's been this way for centuries and because of it, most of the monsters who win either kill the princess to rid themselves of the responsibility of caring for her, toss them in the forest, and let the beasts within do it for them, or worse... For some of the more brutish creatures who enter, they kill them trying to complete the wedding ritual. Regardless, only a handful of the king's daughters live to see twenty-four.

Yet, as I stare at the woman in red, she doesn't look like someone facing a near-certain death. She sits tall, holds her chin high, and is a face of silent strength. I'm not sure I could do the same in her circumstances.

Someone nudges my shoulder and I jolt, finding Zephyr chuckling to my right.

"I told you to stay out of sight," I grit, letting my heartbeat settle back to a normal pace.

"And I did."

"Then why are you here now?"

He snorts, crossing his arms over his broad chest. "To make sure you're not getting cold feet. You've stood here for far too long. I thought that the potion might've turned you to stone."

"I'm learning my enemy." Regrettably turning my gaze away from the princess, I scan over the pledges, looking for signs of weakness. Anything that might give me a leg up. A limp, or a favored hand...

Zephyr doesn't relent in his stare. "Surely you don't expect me to believe your enemy wears a corset and crown?"

"Not her, no, but if I'm going to convince her to help me, I need to know her tells too. Except she doesn't give anything away... It's as if she wants to be here rather than escape."

"Hmmm." Zephyr watches her for a long moment before clicking his tongue. "I suppose you're right. So much for the I'll-save-you-from-your-fate bit you had worked up. How will you convince her now?"

"I'll come up with something. I have to."

"Captain…" Zephyr trails off, drawing my attention.

"What?"

"Maybe you should talk to her before you pledge. If she doesn't get on board, we can find another way. We have other options, like searching for Pan in a smaller group and using the potions…"

"It could take us years at that pace."

"Maybe so, but it's better than dying. We don't have much use of your shadow if you're not alive to claim it. If she doesn't side with you, then you should walk away and live another day."

My lips tip into a teasing smirk as I meet his misfitting human eyes. "You don't think I can win without her help?"

"Not saying that, but the odds wouldn't be in your favor. There's talk of beasts, those who aren't here tonight because the king deemed them too uncivilized to attend, having pledged. A troll and one of the ogres."

"All the clans have sent someone. They all want the royal treat for the next ten years. It doesn't surprise me they would, too."

"And what happens when a pirate wins, huh? Do you truly think the king will drop the charges against us and let us live in peace instead?"

"Well, it's cheaper for him than providing for all of us for ten years, and it's not a permanent pardon."

He sighs. "Fine… How is the cuff holding up?"

"It's fine. You did a great job."

"Good, because mine has almost fallen off twice now and I haven't been fighting, not like you'll be in a few hours."

The king has placed magical cuffs on all his subordinates, allowing him to turn off their gifts and abilities or enhance them if he wishes. None of us pirates have them, but Zephyr and Nelvin were crafty enough to create realistic-looking replicas to help us avoid suspicion.

"The pledge line is growing slimmer." Zephyr lets my cuffed arm drop, clearly having passed his assessment. "You might want to untie your tongue."

"My tongue's fine," I snap, knowing damn well I've been stalling for far too long.

"Then what are you waiting for?" He waggles his fingers, and I catch his wicked grin out of the corner of my eye. "Woo her. Don't make me have to do it for you. She's... not my type, but at this point, I'm wondering if a gay man might stand a better chance at seducing her."

"I know what I'm doing."

"Then cross the bloody room. At this rate, the moons will be out before you so much as take a step."

Growling low in my throat, I send him a glare and make my way across the great hall.

4

Scarlet

I hate this room... Not once in my short life have I ever entered the great hall and felt at ease. Every morning, my father insists on my sisters and me joining him for breakfast here, and every time, my skin seems to crawl. A wooden table usually occupies the stretch of floor from the platform where the thrones sit to the far wall, topped with an elaborate food spread. It's always over the top and far more food than the handful of us could ever put away, but it was a tradition, and my father will carry his traditions to his grave.

Perhaps my body knew before I did what would happen here... that my last meal would be eaten within this room. It doesn't matter now, though.

Guards are stationed along most of the walls, standing post at all the exits, but I can feel Zelix's eyes on me... He's here somewhere likely mingling with the crowd like the rest of the shadow shrouds and a handful of the royal mages. I slightly regret not giving him the affection he desperately needed from me, but it's for the best. I care about him, but I don't love him, and telling him otherwise would've been a lie.

Shoving him from my mind, I do as I was taught, zoning my gaze out on the crowd. I thought when I sat on this throne and listened to the pledges, that my fingers would tremble, that I'd feel the nerves creeping up my spine, anticipating what's coming, but all I feel is numb. I've spent days worrying about this night, and now that it's here, it's as if my brain has become desensitized to the chaos... to the worry. Oddly enough, I'm grateful for it.

Man after man bends the knee before my father, reciting vows and oaths that have been voiced by thousands before them in this very hall. A ghoul with stone-like skin is next, easily five times my size, with dark wings tucked close at his back. His long talons curl around his sword as his haunting red eyes lower.

Behind him waits a dryad, a creature whose part tree, but instead of his bark-ish skin being brown, it's charred as if he's been struck by lightning. His eyes lay within hollows of his oblong-shaped head, and his limbs are long and thin, but I know better than to underestimate his strength. They're some of my father's most lethal soldiers, and the vines they can wield and create are stronger than any rope we can forge.

According to my father's tapestries, his kind has taken out legions of men in past wars, but that's not what scares me. Dryads are also known for being cannibals. They'll kill and consume any creature that crosses into their lands, and when they run low on trespassers, they sacrifice their own. If he wins, I don't doubt that I'll become dinner...

At the least the ghouls would kill me first before doing heinous things. The dryads prefer their food live.

Behind them is a line of beasts of various species. Some are dire wolf shifters, harpies—a weird mix of bird and man—and mermen. Others are of a demonic nature, but I'm unfamiliar with which clans they hail from.

Something moves in the corner of my vision. At first, I shrug it off as being someone in the crowd, but when I catch it again, it's close enough to the thrones that I could reach out and touch it. Whoever it is, isn't aware of our customs—or doesn't care about them. Regardless, it's an unspoken rule to not approach the throne platform unless invited.

Yet, I don't move to see it. Whoever it is, should they continue, the guards will escort them away as they have before. Keeping my gaze trained on a ceramic pot along the back wall, I suck in a breath as someone clears their throat.

"Pardon me, princess..."

I discreetly pivot my gaze, finding an elven man unlike any I've encountered before. He's... peculiar, with short dark hair instead of long, fair locks. The elves believe cutting their hair breaks their connection to the moon and the magic it grants them. It's why the fairest tend to be of noble bloodlines. To them, it's a sign they were blessed by the goddess. Even though the dark elves in our realm were exiled from their kingdom, they typically still keep to their religious traditions.

According to my father, the elves believe in keeping their bloodlines pure. They don't sanction inter-species relationships, since doing so would cause the magic within their familial lines to diminish over time. For an elf, cutting your hair is akin to soiling the bloodline. Maybe cutting it changes the color the same way their skin grays when they sin.

Beyond his hair being short along the sides and long on top, it's messy as if he's driven his fingers through loose waves. Messy hair doesn't set him apart as an elf, but it does from the rest of the people in this room. Everyone has dressed up for the occasion, even those most would call monsters. They've put their best foot forward to appear as royalty for the night, where this man looks like he's just rolled out of bed.

His clothes are nice, though. They fit in if you look past the wrinkles in his shirt and the scuffs on his boots. Rubies sparkle from the buttons of his jacket, and those aren't cheap in Solaria. Any sort of gemstone would cost a small fortune since the mines don't exist in our realm and we're forbidden from crossing into the next. All we have was here before the boundaries were erected and since then, the price of stones like that has only been driven higher as time passes.

The man bows, making a show of it by holding one hand out to the side and tucking the other against the hinge of his body.

"I'm sorry to startle you, but if you're willing to give me a moment of your time, I promise to make it worth your while." He stands, a crooked smirk flashing across his full lips.

My gaze darts to the guards, but they haven't moved an inch. "I'm not allowed to talk to you."

"Well... From where I stand, your father seems quite busy." He leans in a bit closer, dropping his voice to a whisper. "I won't tell if you won't."

His green eyes darken as he loops his hands to lace together behind his back. They're a stark contrast against his greyish-blue skin, but that doesn't make me pause nearly as much as the rogue dimples that form when he smiles. It goes against every hard line of his face, from the strong, sharp edge of his jaw to his straight nose. Even the thick curve of his eyebrows is masculine, yet his long eyelashes and those dimples could get him away with murder. It makes the virile man before me look cute, and I'm not sure how to process that information.

Suddenly, his eyes dart past me and widen as he takes a quick step back.

"Scarlet." My father's voice is unmistakable, and much closer than I would've anticipated.

I meet the king's gaze and offer a sweet smile, hoping it'll spare the fool from being carried away by the guards. Considering the reason we're here, I shouldn't care what happens to the man, but my mind is still trying to wrap around his... everything. The contrasts. The mystery. It's caught my curiosity in a way I can't describe.

"I told him to approach," I lie, watching the realization wash over the elf. He looks as stunned as I feel. "I believe he wanted a dance."

"I see," my father says, glancing at the dark elf. "Are you pledging?"

"Possibly." He doesn't give away a shred of emotion, having locked down his features.

My father cocks his head to the side. "You're unsure? I'd advise you to figure it out. Most men come into my castle knowing whether they plan to risk it all for what they want. How do you plan to win if you're not even sure whether you want what you're fighting for?"

The elf doesn't waver for a moment, tearing his gaze away from my father to send a razor-sharp smile at me. "I know what I'm fighting for, my king. I wouldn't be here if I didn't. The only thing I'm wavering on is whether the princess could learn to love me when I win."

My father's laugh echoes off the walls of the great hall, cutting through the silence of the now-hushed crowd. "Scarlet, my dear, give the boy a dance."

The king resumes his place at the front of the line, accepting pledges. For a moment, it's like I've forgotten how to move. The elven man arches a brow, giving me a closed-lip smile and flashing his dimples. He slowly closes the distance between us, and when he reaches my throne, his chin lifts and he extends a hand out to me.

My cheeks heat as I set my hand in his glove and he squeezes it. It takes everything I have to fight the strain of my cheeks as I try to hide the smile and maintain the facade of stoic beauty.

I've never understood why we're taught to look numb and react to nothing... It's like happiness is a weakness. Yet, for the first time since this gauntlet was announced, I have hope. Maybe there's a chance of surviving this after all.

"I never got your name," I say, letting him lead me to the empty area in front of the musicians.

"Sebastian." He turns, looking at something or someone behind me and nodding slightly. Craning my neck, I find someone watching us, leaning against the wall, but the man quickly turns his gaze away the moment it locks with mine.

Sebastian grips my hand while his arm wraps around the small of my waist, pulling me closer. His hand is warm against my spine, despite the multitude of layers of fabric between my skin and his. He lets out a long exhale and I can feel the air against my skin, drawing my attention back to him. I'm acutely aware of just how close his body is to mine and the fact that he stands a solid foot taller than me. I should be nervous, but I'm not. His presence is almost familiar, or perhaps I want to be because if he enters and wins, I can let myself think about what comes after.

"Was that your friend?"

"Aye—yes, princess." He clears his throat as we begin to move in a slow, gentle motion, his palm at my back guiding me. Sebastian watches our feet as we move, like it's an unusual act for him, even though he moves with grace.

"You don't have to correct your natural tongue for me. Believe it or not, I feel like the formalities are obnoxious most of the time." I can feel the tension leave him as his grip on my hand and the muscles of his stomach ease.

"That's good," he breathes, glancing up at my face for a moment before continuing to watch our feet glide over the marble floors.

"You don't dance often, do you?"

"What gave me away?"

A smile pulls at the corners of my lips, and this time I allow it. "Everything."

He laughs, and it's all I can do but listen to it. The sound is captivating and surprisingly comforting.

"Truth be told, I avoid it like the plague," he says, spinning me out and beneath his arm until my back is pressed to his front. His breath caresses the shell of my ear, making my heart thud against my ribs. "Is it something you enjoy?"

"Sometimes. It depends on the circumstances."

"And what might those be?" Sebastian spins me out until we're face to face again.

"I'm not a fan of all the eyes watching, but alone... I'd enjoy it."

His lips press into a line as he nods. "I see... Then I'd learn to enjoy it for you."

I feel the blood heat in my veins as I stare at the necklace he wears. An orange stone of some sort. I've never seen one like it, but it's a welcomed distraction. On either side of it are smaller milky white ones.

"Are you going to tell me the real reason you wanted to talk to me?" I spit the question out before I can lose the courage to ask.

"Hmm." The noise comes more from his throat than anything, but coupled with the dimples staring down at me, it's the sexiest sound I've ever heard. "Pretty and clever."

"So, there was a reason beyond wanting to know if I could stand you." His lips turn into a wolfish grin as we stop moving.

"There was, but I'm curious about the verdict you came to." Sebastian leans closer, lifting my chin with a gloved finger. "So, what will it be, princess? Do you think you could learn to love me?"

Could I? He seems interesting enough. He's handsome and has a sense of humor. Does it matter, though? Someone like him seems like a much better option than being eaten by a tree, and since he hasn't pledged yet, whatever I say could steer him away from entering at all.

I'll need to be careful... I need to give him the answer he wants to hear. His stormy green eyes flicker between mine as if he can read my thoughts like a book.

"Yes. I could."

He snorts, squinting at me for a moment as if he doesn't believe it, but is willing to bite. "Then let me make you a deal."

"For what?"

We start moving again and Sebastian glances around the room like he's making sure there are no witnesses to whatever he's going to disclose.

He bends down, putting his mouth close to my ear. "Help me win, and I'll ensure you have a good life. You'll never want or need for anything. You'll be safe."

My eyes widen as I lean back to stare at his face. "How could I possibly help you?"

He lifts a single eyebrow, giving me a knowing look. "All the king's daughters have had extraordinary abilities. I might not be keen on what yours is, but the few of your sisters who lived outside these walls have all been looked at like goddesses for their power. Even now, I can feel yours. I'm not sure what you can do, but I'm sure with power like that, you can do something."

My father would slaughter me on the spot for interfering with his gauntlet. Sebastian isn't wrong. I could help him win with my gift, but at what cost?

"If I was caught helping you, we'd both be dead."

"I hate to be the one to break it to you, but if any of the other pledges win, you'll likely die, anyway."

"True, but it would be with cause."

"And what cause is that?"

"My life would end, but most of the clans would be united for the next ten years. If I help you cheat and get caught, the gauntlet would be for nothing. My father would have to publicly execute me. There would be no wedding and no chosen prince. The clans would go to war because the oaths spoken here tonight would be null and void."

He pushes a lock of my hair behind my ear. "You're a smart girl. I'm not asking for a miracle or for you to fight for me. I'm asking for you to help where you can."

This might be the only way for me to live and fulfill my duty. It's my one shot, but if I mess up, it's over and my family will pay the price.

"I have a duty... and if I turn my back on it, it won't only be me paying the price."

He sets his jaw and forces a smile to his lips. "We forge our own paths in this life, Scarlet. You shouldn't let others choose it for you. Outside these castle walls, there are places unlike anything you can imagine. I've seen them and I still can't fathom their beauty. Haven't you ever wondered what it's like?"

"Of course, I have. I've dreamed of it. I've stared out the windows for hours wondering what could be had I not been born into a golden cage, but this is reality. I've accepted it, and I've renounced myself to seeing the world through my books."

He laughs silently. "Books? They'll never compare."

"It's what I have."

"Then let me give you more." Sebastian stops us once more, taking my hands between both of his. "Let me show you."

I'm not sure how long I stare at him, but the longer I do, the more I want to say yes, but the more I need to say no.

I've wanted nothing more than to know what lies beyond the ocean outside my bedroom window. If he's telling the truth, he could show me. Maybe if Sebastian won the king's advantage, he would stand a chance. I don't have to risk more than I have to…

"Fine, I'll help you, but only if you win the king's advantage. You're a dark elf. He's been looking to form a permanent alliance with them for years. Use that when you pledge."

Sebastian grins so wide, that I see every white tooth of his smile gleam. "I will. Thank you."

"Don't thank me. I'll expect you to hold up your end of the bargain when it's over."

"Have you considered what your choice of arena will be?"

"Do you have a suggestion?" I'm not sure why I ask. Clearly, he does or he wouldn't care where I choose for the gauntlet to take place.

"Something open. The fewer hiding places, the better."

I cock my head to the side. "Why?" How could that possibly help him?

"Because I don't need to hide and I hate surprises."

"You're willing to face an ogre and troll head-on, with no cover? I might not be trained in the art of war, but I can recognize stupidity when I see it."

He snorts, blinking at me like a man who's been struck, but he doesn't seem upset about my insult. In fact, he almost seems intrigued by it. "Do you trust me?"

"No."

Sebastian smiles, letting his head drop forward for a moment before meeting my gaze again. "Can you try?"

"Perhaps."

"Then choose somewhere open."

"Fine... Poseidon's Punch Bowl it is."

"That's perfect." He beams at me, reaching for my hand. "I suppose I should go pledge then."

I give him a curt nod as his lips brush my knuckles. "Until we meet again, princess."

"Scarlet," I correct.

"Scarlet..." The sound of my name rolling off his tongue shouldn't excite me. Given the circumstances, I should be shaking in my heels, but it doesn't change the fact it does. My stomach explodes with butterflies, but I try to smother the feeling before I can get my hopes up.

He lets my hand drop and starts to step away, but I grab his wrist, demanding his attention once more.

"Sebastian," I say, stopping him in his tracks. He tosses a look at me over his shoulder, but I don't miss the intrigued look in his eye. "Be hard to kill."

5

HOOK

I nod as I slink past Zephyr, joining the line of pledges while Scarlet returns to her throne. She's nothing like I expected, which both terrifies and intrigues me at the same time.

Oddly enough, she reminds me of my mother. Even in a realm where women are expected to look pretty and stay silent, she never shied away from speaking her mind. It's a strength I admire in Smee too.

Reaching the front of the line, the guard ushers me forward. "State your clan, your full name, and speak your vow."

"Understood."

The king has taken a seat on his throne, his face emotionless as he watches me approach. It's only when I kneel before him that he stands as if to give the illusion of towering over me.

"Did you enjoy your dance?" he asks, squinting down at me.

"I did."

"Hmm." He steps a bit closer. "What are you from?" His face may not give away his thoughts, but his tone sure does. It's okay. I wouldn't trust myself either.

"The Western Isles," I say, being careful to not lie. The king is known for his gift of sniffing them out, so I make sure everything I speak is the truth but twist it to hide my secrets.

My mother is from the Western Isles, but I don't believe there are many dark elves there. Hopefully, he buys it.

"I see... You've journeyed far then to pledge. It's a blessing that you evaded the pirates—despicable creatures they are. I wish my merchant ships would share your luck."

"The gods must be watching over me. I'm lucky to be standing before you in one piece."

"I wasn't aware there were elven settlements outside the mountains. Are you of high standing where you're from? Do people listen to you?"

"They do. I haven't been given a lordship by the crown, but my family protects our village and feeds them when the crops die out."

"Interesting... Alright then, make your pledge." He adjusts his stance, watching as I pull a dagger from the sheath hanging from my belt.

I bow my head. "I, Sebastian Octavius, leader of my clan, swear fealty."

The warrant on my head refers to me as 'the dark one' due to my gift, otherwise, the crown only knows my relation to my father and what I look like. They're oblivious to my first and middle name. Only my last will be significant to them. Combined with the new face the potion gave me, I should avoid any suspicion.

Using the blade to slice my palm, I let my blood drip to the floor near his feet, along with the rest of the pledges from the day. "I bleed for my kingdom, and should the fates deem me worthy, I will rise as your heir."

"I accept your pledge." The king touches my shoulder, telling me I can get up.

Once on my feet, I glance at Scarlet, who's staring at me from her throne. Her lips are pressed into a fine line, and the stoic expression she wore earlier is nothing but a memory. I wait a moment, hoping she was right about her father—that he'd give me his advantage in hopes of an alliance with the dark elves—but his silence is deafening.

He nods to the guard to let another pledge through, and I twist my lips. I'd hoped the king would give me his blessing so I could alter a rule, but I knew it was a shot in the dark. It's why I wanted to establish a deal with the princess.

I got ahead of myself.

Disappearing into the crowd, I find Zephyr talking—more like flirting—with a guard. I've seen him bat his eyes enough times to know. Looping my arm with his elbow, I drag him away before he can say goodbye to his newfound friend.

"What part of stay low didn't make sense?" I hiss through my clenched teeth.

"Excuse me." His voice pitches as we weave through the guests toward the exit. "I am staying low, but I'm also trying to make sure my best friend doesn't die tonight."

Releasing the air in my lungs, my nostrils flare as I stop and turn toward him. "You can't help me."

"I can and I did. The ogre is missing his right eye. It's a blind spot, and the troll will rely heavily on his weapon. The dryad's left leg is rotting, and the harpy recently broke one of its wings. It's healed, but it'll have lost mobility. As for the wolves, they're all from the king's guard. They'll likely hunt in a pack and use formal tactics out of habit."

Blinking, I raise my eyebrows. "I stand corrected."

Zephyr's eyes soften as the tension leaves his shoulders. "I might not be able to pick up a sword and help, but I'm still going to do what I can. Besides, I think Smee will kill me if I return to the ship without you."

"She'll understand."

"I'm not so sure." He shakes his head. "She carved my name into a small wooden box that apparently is for my testicles if you die."

I can't help but chuckle. That sounds like something she would do. "Smee's just scared. We just lost our father a few months ago. I'd imagine she's in no rush to lose her brother, too."

"Well, I'm still going to try to get you back to the ship in one piece. My body parts don't want to be her punching bag."

The king calls for any final pledges and the conversations in the room dwindle to a low hum. There's a sharp click of metal against the twisted goblet in his hand and everyone turns to the throne.

"Thank you all for coming. At nightfall, my mages will start to set the boundary for the event. Which begs the question..." he trails off, turning toward Scarlet. "As usual, my daughter will decide where the gauntlet will be held. Have you made your decision?"

Scarlet nods and her eyes find mine through the crowd. "Poseidon's punch bowl, my king."

"Fantastic choice." He grins at her before turning back to the crowd. "As for the event, the rules stay the same. The last man standing will win my daughter's hand in marriage and be named an heir to my throne. In the event of my natural death, they will be allowed to fight amongst the other chosen princes for the crown." He folds his hands behind his back as he paces in front of his daughters. I don't think the younger ones seated behind Scarlet have even blinked. "Every gauntlet, I choose one pledge to give an advantage to—someone I believe will win. To this day, I've never been wrong. They're allowed to make one amendment to the otherwise short list of rules. Tonight, I'd like to grant Sebastian Octavius, of the dark elves, with that advantage."

My heart lurches, slamming into my ribs as my eyes flare wide. Scarlet smiles at me from across the room, but I can barely breathe, let alone return it.

"Please step forward and state your wish," the king says and Zephyr pushes me, urging my legs to move.

Reaching the front of the crowd, I bow my head. "Thank you, my king."

"Your rule? Choose your words carefully. They will be followed exactly how they are spoken."

"No weapons, neither physical nor magical, will be permitted during the fight for those wearing one of the king's cuffs."

Lifting my gaze, I feel his scrutinizing stare boring holes through my being.

"You realize you wear one of my cuffs?"

"I'm aware of my cuff, yes."

"Then you understand the rule would apply to you as well?"

"I will follow my own rule as if it were yours, my king."

"Very well. The mages will set the perimeter." He looks at the crowd, dismissing me. "The gauntlet will commence at sundown. All pledges please meet on the bridge."

As the king and his daughters file out of the room, the crowd starts to disperse. My heart is pounding as I follow the other pledges toward the bridge, leaving Zephyr behind. We wind through the halls and out the front doors until we can huddle on the bridge.

The guards in front of me gasp and when I follow their stares, I immediately see why. On the far end stands the troll who has entered. Zephyr was right. One of his eyes is hidden behind a patch, secured tight behind his head. A large club covered in spiked shards of metal rests against his shoulder. I'd hate to be the man to tell him he can't use it.

The other pledges file onto the bridge until there's hardly enough space to stand without bumping into one another. I don't think any of us know what we're waiting for, other than that we have to. Will our names be called?

Guards pushing some sort of cart with a large bell appear from behind the castle, parking it just at the base of the stairs leading to the front door. I glance at the sky, wondering how long we'll be out here and whether I should drink the potion again. I'm not quite sure how my magic will respond if I do, but if they discover who I am before the gauntlet begins, I'm not sure how the king will react, either.

I know they'll find out soon enough. I can't stay disguised forever, nor do I plan to, but what I do know is the king won't stop the gauntlet. Once it starts, there's only one way out. Win. After that, it won't matter. The king will have to pardon me or risk uproar from the clans.

Deciding to chance it, I wait, watching the balcony of the king's observatory like the others. It's a weird dome at the top of one of the towers, made up of glass planes and crystals. The soft sound of the waves hitting the pillars of the bridge stops, followed by a rumble that grows louder by the second.

The pledges shuffle as their heads swivel, trying to place the noise. It's not until I spot the line of hooded figures along the rocky edge of the mainland that I put it together. It's the mages. They're pushing the water out of the bay. Pressing my hands to my ears, I try to muffle the noise, but it's too loud. My eardrums scream as the water builds into a single wave and gushes out of the bay, leaving jet-black sand behind.

Stone lifts at the opening of the bay into the sea, blocking the water from coming back in. I peer over the bone railing. The sea floor is riddled with skeletons and saturated plant life, but it's open. There aren't many places to hide.

I've heard of Poseidon's punch bowl, but I never would've expected it to be this. I thought it might be in the marshes, some sort of canyon maybe, but not the entire fucking bay.

I swallow hard, wondering how we'll get down there. Steps? A ladder? Are they going to toss us? More importantly, how does one get out?

As if on cue, stone slabs shoot from the cliffside, creating a staircase into the canyon and the pledges at the far end of the canyon begin to descend. The troll doesn't even bother with the stairs. He simply jumps from the edge, landing with a thud strong enough to shake the bridge.

"The torches along the castle walls have pierced the night for years since my father sparked them into existence. They ignite in the dark when the hell flame's light can no longer reach them. Not a moment sooner. There are some along the ridge of the mainland, but they are not to be used as weapons. You may not bring physical weapons into the arena with you, but you're welcome to scavenge for something to use as one once you're inside. Magic will be prohibited for anyone with my wristbands during the fight."

He must use magic or something to project his voice because it echoes through the cavern, reverberating his every word. The hell flame is almost gone now.

I step down the floating slabs of stone, careful to keep my balance until my boots sink into the black sand. It crunches beneath my feet like glass, and it's now that I can truly appreciate the size of this place. The cliff stretches up over a hundred feet high. It's been eroded by the water, but I can still make out the ancient markings carved into the edge.

The vertebrae and dragon skeletons swirling around the thick pillars of the bridge are larger than I expected, having only seen them from up top. I thought it was magnificent before, but now, seeing what was hidden beneath the w ater... It's incomparable. A single rib bone is taller than I am, and the entire rib cage of one could be made into a small ship. The skeletons of the pillars are staged, like the dragons were petrified mid-battle, climbing up the pillar to scorch their enemies.

Skulls from gauntlets in the past peek through the sand at my feet. The hollows of them are tangled in the vines of the sea life that now lays limp against the ground. I wonder if swords and discarded weapons might be hidden there as well.

People from the villages line the cliffside, ready to watch the bloodbath. As the last pledge hits the sand, the rock ledges disappear seamlessly back into the cliffside like they were never disturbed.

It's hard to see much in the dim light, but I catch motion near the ledge at the base of the castle. Thrones come into view, and as the torches light, I see Scarlet and her sisters resume their seats. She lifts a hand ever so slightly, as if to wave to me, and something about it makes me chuckle. It seems rather mundane for a time like this, but I'll take it.

Her father appears at her side, branching a hand on the back of her throne, and her expression turns to stone, zoned out on the horizon like the rest of her much younger siblings. It's like he requires them to be porcelain dolls.

The king lifts a chunk of crystal to his lips as if to speak into it. "This tradition was made to unite us, and it has for decades. Let it unite us again tonight. May the fates sew in your favor, but if they don't, know your sacrifice will allow our realm to prosper. My daughter—your prize—will ring the bell and upon its toll, the gauntlet will begin."

The king nudges Scarlet out of the golden chair, her crimson dress swishing as she makes her way toward the bell. Frantically, I look around the edge of the cliff, searching for Zephyr, but he's nowhere to be seen.

The wind picks up, swirling around me before carrying on. "Behind you, you fool." Zephyr's voice is plain as day. Spinning, I find him sitting along the edge of the cliff, far away from the crowd. "You don't truly believe I'd let you enter a fight to the death on your own, do you? I'll watch your back."

My skin prickles and I suck in a breath. The magic holding my disguise together is waning. It won't be long before it fails. The prickling grows stronger and stronger until the glamour gives and the bell tolls. The gauntlet has begun.

6
Hook

With my glamour gone, my true face is revealed. Silence falls over the crowd, gathered around the top edge of the cliffside. Not even the other pledges move, mouths agape as they stare at me like they've seen a ghost. For a breath, it's as if time itself stops.

The only sound is the distant sea breeze and the suction breaking on my boots with each step I take. The wet sand will make this difficult... Whispers from the crowd gathered around the top of the cliff become static.

They can't possibly have anything nice to say about me. My family has sunk the Solarian merchant ships for decades, bleeding them dry. I'm sure the king's people blame us for their lack of trading goods, but stealing them is all we can do. It's not our fault these people chose to stay here and accept the king's leashes while on their knees. My people might be pirates and traitors to his majesty's crown, but we're not weak. We do what is needed to survive, and if it means crippling the king's ports, then I consider that a win-win situation.

Those living in the Luminaries–my people–stood up for themselves. They were forced to flee and settle on the islands far off the mainland. They rely on the pirates to protect their shores from the beasts that live in the sea, and to bring back what they can from the king's ships. It's a matter of survival for us, but to them, I'm nothing more than a thief.

"It's the Dark One," someone breathes to my right. Twisting my head, I find one of the king's men, a dire wolf shifter from his royal guard. The moment my eyes connect with his, he bolts, heading straight for the island the castle is perched upon as if he'll find a place to hide there.

"Coward." My lips curl in disdain as I glance up to where the king and Scarlet are perched, regal in their thrones. Her little sisters are nowhere in sight now. Perhaps the king does have a heart, letting the small children stay innocent of the slaughters we're all about to witness.

Scarlet's eyes soften for a fleeting moment, a hint of a smile playing on her lips, but it's swiftly replaced by an icy facade. It's different from the emotionless mask she wore in the great hall. There's a flicker in her eyes, an indecipherable emotion. Is it hope? Fear? Or the weight of our shared agreement?

I just pray she'll follow through. Even if she doesn't, I don't suppose it would change much. If I die today, then that's it. And should I win, I'll be married to her by sunrise. Either way, I'm not sure I'd blame her for being scared. She might be my enemy's daughter, but she's a pawn in this scenario, innocent, and blindly following her father's lead.

If our conversation in the great hall was anything, it proved to me that she's doing this out of duty. Still, she's smart enough that if I were to pull the wool out of her eyes, she'd see her father for who he really is. I can work with that.

The pledges stand fast. They haven't moved an inch like they're waiting for something. If no one else is going to be man enough to make the first strike, it'll have to be me. I have places to be and a god to confront. There's no time to twiddle our thumbs. The moment Pan catches word of my visit, he'll hide. Not only that, there's more than just my life riding on me winning now. Scarlet's is too.

My fingers twitch, and darkness leaps at my command, snaking towards the fleeing dire wolf. I tug back with a clenched fist, and the element obeys, yanking the coward to me by his throat. A loud crunch breaks the tense silence. I hadn't intended to end him so quickly... Honestly, I'd planned to make a show of his death, but the bell tolls anyway, marking the first casualty.

The noise seems to snap the other pledges out of their stupor. They clash amongst each other as I creep toward where a skeleton peeks out of the ground a few feet away. The glint from the hilt of a sword shines through the black sand, calling my name. One down, eighteen to go. The metal is rusted, but it's better than no weapon, I suppose.

I test the weight of it in my palm, flexing my fingers as I survey the other pledges.

The troll is having a grand Ol' time mocking the demons as he punts them across the arena, his rotting teeth on full display. The serpent-man's tail crashes with ferocity, knocking wolves down left and right, while the birdman takes to the sky, launching surprise aerial attacks. He scoops in from above on his prey, using his talons to snatch up another demon and drop him from the air–high enough to snap the creature's bones upon impact. The bell rings twice.

Make that sixteen.

Darkness erupts from my outstretched hands to ensnare the serpent-man. With a jerk of my wrist, I send his body smashing into the troll. They collapse into a tangle of scales and gnarled flesh. The birdman shrieks, wings beating hastily as he swoops to snatch up a dire wolf. Seconds later, a blob of fur smashes into the ground beside me and the bell tolls again.

Fifteen.

My shadows give chase, catching up to the harpy mid-flight, sending him hurling to the ground. The sand ripples as his large body slides across it, wings bending at an unnatural angle as he drills into the sand. His body comes to an abrupt stop the moment he hits something hard beneath it. The dirt settles and the birdman goes limp.

Fourteen.

"Behind you!" Zephyr's warning chimes in my ear as the wind picks up, flooding my nose with the briny ocean air and the thick scent of seaweed. I whirl as a demon lunges. His large horns make up half the size of his head, and his talons extend his arm's length by half a foot. He's strong, fighting me tooth and nail as my shadows wrap around him. Dark lines trail up his face as his red skin pales to a colorless gray. He crumbles to dust at my feet. This is almost too easy.

The bell rings again. Thirteen.

The sword in my hand is dull. I doubt it would cut much without putting my entire weight into it. It'd cause more blunt-force trauma than anything. Stabbing might bode well though... I test the balance of it as the wolves circle me, deciding I'm the bigger target–the bigger threat. Their black, ratted coats are full of sand, and their eyes are hollow and empty. Blade-sharp teeth clash as they snap at the air between us, searching for my weaknesses. They're a well-trained pack, hunting as a unit. Just as Zephyr warned.

One wolf finally takes the leap. I pivot, the blade stabbing into fur, using its own weight against him. I tear the sword out sideways, ripping flesh, and a pained howl cuts through the air as the wolf cowers against the ground.

"Which one of you is next?" I joust my sword at them, making one of the wolves sidestep. Then another rushes for my legs, I kick out and my boot collides with its head, hitting at just the right angle to snap its neck. Another jumps at me and my shadows jolt up, snatching it out of the air. It anchors the wolf to the black sand, and I drive my sword into the base of its skull.

Two more wolves still circle, watching and waiting as I pull my sword free. Deciding to make the first move, I throw my shadows out, coiling around one of the wolves like vines and sucking the life out of him. The other wolf tries to sneak up behind me, but I sense it. Spinning on my heels, I grip the blade of my sword with both of my hands as the wolf slams into me, knocking me onto my back. It snaps, saliva dripping from its bloodied mouth, but I lock my arms, holding it away. Darkness coils up my arms, wraps around its throat, and squeezes until the bell tolls. My nose fills with the scent of copper, the musky perfume of wet dog mixed with the fishy aroma of sea sand. I knock the creature away and get to my feet.

Pledge after pledge falls until the number dwindles to five. The serpent, dryad, troll, a demon, and me. I glance at the thrones, finding Scarlet with her fingers wrapped around the armrests of her throne, knuckles bleaching white under the strain of her grip. Our gazes meet across the distance. For the life of me, I can't tell what she's doing to help, if she's doing anything at all. Did she change her mind?

A sickening snap rings through the air as the dryad is torn to shreds by the troll. I can't look away. His muscles flex as he growls, tearing the dryads vines from his limbs. Their vines are supposed to be stronger than any rope or chain in existence, yet the troll just cleaved them from his body like it was nothing.

Fuck...

"Watch out!" Zephyr's warning comes too late. Something hits me from behind, hard enough to send pain shooting through my entire body. Luckily, it didn't feel like a sword. It was something blunt. My head rings as I try to focus my vision, but I'm seeing double as I roll over.

Anytime now, Scarlet. I didn't sign up to do this solo.

The serpent man comes into view, holding a large piece of driftwood. He must've clubbed me with it. He tosses it onto the ground, his forked tongue lashing out between his lips. He bends and in a moment of clarity, I know exactly what he's going for. My sword.

Darkness bolts from my hands, snatching up my discarded weapon before the serpent can take it.

Screw the princess. If she's not going to help, then so be it. I will not die here.

The serpent hisses, fangs bared and dripping venom. Rolling out to the side before he can pin me to the ground, I get to my feet. He lashes out with his claws, and I parry each strike. There are only four of us remaining for a reason. He's fast and he won't go down easily.

The death dance continues for far too long as strike after strike is deflected. Something juts through the sand, a skeleton, and I almost lose my footing. The split second is all the serpent needs. He snaps at the air, and though I canter, his venomous fangs tear through my shirt, ripping open my shoulder.

I growl, wincing as pain shoots through me. My mouth goes dry, and before I can move, the serpent's foot collides with my thigh, knocking me to one knee. His tail swirls around me like he plans to squeeze until my bones break. My element explodes around me and the serpent man vanishes from view. It's only when his tail nearly dissolves around me that he stumbles backward. The darkness clears as I stand, blood dripping down my arm and onto the sea floor. The serpent wails, crawling backward as he struggles to get away from me, but the damage has already been done. I lift my sword, thankful that he didn't tear open my right arm, but my less dominant left. Suddenly, it's like my vision narrows until the only thing here is me and the serpent man missing his tail. I swing, holding nothing back. Even with the rusted edge of my sword, the blade embeds into his throat, almost taking his head off.

Tearing my blade from the man, agony drips through me like fire in my veins as the venom takes hold. I stagger back, vision swimming, and clench my jaw. My shoulder is so warm... I can feel my heartbeat in the wound he made.

The demon's steps shake the ground as he nears me, but this time I feel it in my feet. I wait until the last second, spinning and throwing my darkness out toward him. His form is blocked out by the haze, but I can hear snap after snap of bone. It's only when I let up that I find him in a misshapen mess, his form no longer humanoid. Helpless, he shrieks, spitting curses, coming in and out of consciousness. I cross the distance between us and plunge my blade deep into his chest. A fatal strike. His blood leaches into the sand.

The bell rings out. Only one pledge remains.

The venom throbs in my veins, burning like acid. My leg shakes, nearly giving out with each step as I turn to face my final opponent.

The troll grunts, revealing yellowed, uneven teeth as he rips flesh from the fallen in the arena. Did he stop for a snack in the middle of a blood bath? As if hearing my thoughts, his beady eyes snap toward me, gleaming with bloodlust as he sizes me up. He roars, not even bothering to finish the half-eaten limb in his teeth. He's far too eager to crush my skull between those ham-sized fists.

Tossing his meal, the troll charges. I step into the shadow of the island, emerging in another near the pillars of the skull bridge. He spots me and I hold steadfast, letting him gain ground. I wait until he's just a few feet away before stepping through the shadow to another nearby, popping up behind him. Lifting my sword, I leap and drive it down the exposed flesh of his back, but it doesn't so much as scratch him. He whirls, eyes filled with rage.

Fuck...

Ten feet of muscle and tusk towers over me. His arm lashes out and I drop, rolling across the sand to evade it. His fist smashes into the sand, sending black specks flying. I close my eyes, trying to keep it from getting in them. He apparently wasn't as wise. The troll thrashes his head from side to side, his fists rubbing into his eyes. Gritting my teeth, I gather my shadows and hurl them at him, but even blind, he bats them away as though they are mere insects. My shadows scatter into nothingness.

So much for that.

My vision swirls due to the venom, and I stumble a step to the right, trying to regain my balance. Before I can register that he's crossed the distance, something slams into me and I fly through the air.

7

SCARLET

I can hear the beat of my heart. It's battering into my ribs as I watch the chaos unfold below us. The gauntlet has always been brutal, but this... I didn't expect this. Each pledge is out for blood, fighting for a title they'll likely never be able to use. It's pointless to be named an heir if the king is immortal–at least in my opinion.

My father's on his throne to my left, chewing on his fingernails. Even he is uneasy, eyes narrowed into slits as he takes in the scene before us.

"Did you know?" His voice is calm and controlled, but his bouncing knee and his antsy movements say otherwise. I don't answer him, sure he must be talking to one of the guards. "Answer me, woman." Maybe not...

"Know what?" I ask, playing dumb. He's asking about Sebastian, but I won't disclose anything I don't have to. I straighten my shoulders, being mindful not to turn my head away from the fight. We're not supposed to, but it doesn't stop me from seeing his head swivel toward me, revealing his cold gaze.

As a princess, we've been taught to be seen and not heard, and not to speak unless spoken to. Our entire lives we train for this day, when we're supposed to stay silent, look pretty, but remain numb. Sadly, nothing has prepared me for reality. Everything has changed and nothing is what I expected it to be. Not even Sebastian.

Turns out, he's humanoid, just like me. From here, I can see his messy dark hair, still the same as before, even though whatever illusion he cast has dissipated. Except where his skin held a grayish tone, like the dark elf he presented himself as, it's now beige. His dark linen shirt hangs over his form, bellowing out around his middle and tucking in at the waist of his leather pants. The sleeves are rolled up to his elbow and the neckline plunges, revealing dark inky lines of tattoos across his chest and arms. The linen is torn in many places, but still covers more of his torso. Whatever he is, it's clear he's an elemental, due to his magic, and that he's not wearing a cuff.

He's clearly not noble, based on his clothes and messy appearance, but his power would have granted him a high standing in the king's court. My father would've jumped at the chance to have him on the royal guard, yet I've never seen his face before. I'd remember it if I had.

He's... a mystery. I'd say handsome, but that doesn't even begin to cover it. Though lethal is the word that sits on my tongue.

"Scarlet, are you listening?" My father's voice cuts through the fog settling in my mind.

"Yes. I'm sorry, there's just a lot going on."

He snarls, grunting as he leans into his chair. "Despicable. I should have you lashed for that. I asked if you knew who the man you danced with was? Did you know he was deceiving me?"

"No. I didn't. He seemed nice and genuine. I don't even know who he is now or why he had to pretend to be an elf."

My father pinches the bridge of his nose before sitting back up. "He's the Dark One. A pirate."

Cocking my head to the side, I let that soak in. A pirate? "Like the ones who protect your fleet?"

"No. The kind that sinks them. Not just any pirate either. He's their god-awful leader." He tossed his hand toward Sebastian, effortlessly slaying the wolves with an air of confidence that sends shivers down my spine.

"How do you know it's him?" I ask, trying to keep my voice steady despite the unease writhing within me.

My father rolls his eyes as if it should be obvious. "There's only been a handful of elementals capable of controlling darkness."

I can't tear my eyes away from Sebastian as he continues to fight, his movements swift and graceful. A mix of fascination and dread washes over me. This man, this criminal, has somehow managed to insert himself into my life with the promise of adventure and freedom, but how can I trust him? He's already deceived me once about who he was, and he did so in a way where he never truly lied, just omitted the important parts.

I never anticipated living after today, since not many of my sisters have after their wedding night. Yet, Sebastian promised me a good life full of the adventure I've only dreamed about. What if that was just to get me to help him? If he truly is the Dark One, what if he intends to use me to get at my father?

Honestly, I'm not sure it even matters at this point. The dire wolves are dead. He just slaughtered the last of them. I'm not even sure why they bother pledging. They've never made it to the final five, but they'd have been the only creature other than Sebastian in this arena that might not kill me the moment we're married. At this point, trusting in our deal is worth the risk.

"If he's your enemy, what will you do if he wins?" I ask before I can think better of it. If my father means to kill him the moment he exits that arena, then it doesn't matter if I help him or not. It's not even worth thinking about. It'd just mean my father would host another gauntlet and I'd be given to someone else.

My father weighs his head from side to side. "I can't simply arrest him. The clans are watching, and if I break my own rules—if I don't honor the tradition and let him take his prize—then the people won't want to participate in future gauntlets. Not to mention, I gave him my advantage... I never thought I'd be rooting for my enemy, but here we are."

The king's advantage is everything to the clans. They practically bribe my father with gifts, vows of trade, or services in advance to sweeten him up. He's never given his lead to a losing pledge before, and it's partially why the clans and pledges jump through such hoops to earn it or to sway his favor.

I nod, understanding the gravity of the situation but still feeling a sense of unease as I watch Sebastian fight. He's dangerous, yes, but there's something about him that draws me in, something that makes me want to trust him despite everything.

"We're just in a big fucking pickle..." my father says, resuming his nail-biting as he watches the show. "A big pickle indeed."

For better or worse, my fate quite literally is in Sebastian's hands, and only time will reveal what he intends to do with it.

A serpent man and Sebastian clash. I'm not a warrior–I've never even held a sword–but I do my best to anticipate attacks. It's easier said than done, though. More often than not, I'm hardly using my gift in time to keep Sebastian from being hurt.

The serpent man lashes out and I'm barely able to tilt him off kilter from this distance, but it's enough to make sure his fangs only scrape Sebastian's arm. It's better than sinking into his throat, though, and that's where they were heading.

The roar of the crowd and the clash of weapons fill the air. My father's words still echo in my mind, and I can't shake the feeling that this entire situation is a precarious house of cards, ready to collapse at any moment.

Sebastian skillfully dodges attack after attack, killing the serpent and a demon after that. Still, I find myself holding my breath as I watch.

My father rises from his seat, leaving me to my thoughts, and under the protection of Zelix, who's standing guard near the thrones. I'd recognize him anywhere, even beneath his thick cloak. Slowly, he sneaks closer until he's right next to my throne. I can sense the tension in his posture, the way he stands just a tad bit too tall, his spine rigid. Paying him no mind, I watch Sebastian discreetly using my magic to make his opponent misstep or stumble to give him the advantage.

After the fourth or fifth time of intervening, Zelix clears his throat. "Why are you helping him?" Apparently, I wasn't being discreet enough. However, that might be because he notices absolutely everything, including things others wouldn't pay mind to.

"I don't have much of a choice. I can either help him win or become the troll's toothpick. I think I'll take my chances with the pirate." My gaze remains fixed on the brutal fight.

"He's your father's enemy. Do you truly believe he'll be much different? If your father catches you helping him, he'll feed you to the beasts."

"He better not catch me then," I say with a sigh.

"You danced with him..." It's a statement to himself more than to me. "What did he offer you?"

"A life. A chance to see the world outside these walls. It sounds a hell of a lot better than being monster food."

"And you believe he'll keep his word?" Zelix's dark brown eyes meet mine from beneath his cloak's hood. "Hook is a murderer. If he wins, I wouldn't be surprised if he sends you back to your father in pieces, just for the pleasure of it."

I wince at the image, my lungs tightening in my chest. Yet, I can't deny the truth in Zelix's words. I'm witnessing firsthand how ruthless Sebastian can be, but I have to hope this won't be it for me.

I want more. I want to live, and Sebastian can give me that.

"Has he seen it?" Zelix asks, leaning closer as if sharing a secret. "Your mark? Does he know?"

I scoff. "Of course not. Why would you ask that?"

"Because the Dark One hates blood witches. He's killed dozens just for existing. What would he do if he found out about you?"

My breath catches in my throat, and for a moment, a sense of foreboding coils inside me, seizing my heart like a vice. I force myself to remain calm, schooling my features. "I'll just have to make sure he never finds out."

"You're playing with fire, princess," Zelix warns, his voice low and serious.

"Do you blame me? If that troll wins, I'm as good as dead," I say, my voice wavering despite my best efforts to keep it steady.

"Not true. There's a chance the troll might trade for you if he was offered enough."

"And you have that kind of gold?" I ask, and Zelix's gaze drops to the ground by his feet. "I didn't think so. No one else will make that deal."

For a moment, silence hangs between us, heavy and suffocating. Zelix's gaze bores into the side of my face, but ultimately, he says nothing more.

My eyes are glued to the troll advancing on Sebastian. It's just the two of them left now. Each footfall shakes the ground, and its massive fists swing, narrowly missing Sebastian multiple times. My breath catches in my throat as the troll lands a hit, sending Sebastian flying through the air. As he crashes into the cliffside, shadows wrap around him, cushioning his fall. He faces the troll again, but he's lost his sword in flight. The troll now holds it, making it look like an eating utensil in its large, meaty hand.

The troll closes in on him despite my magic slowing his movements to give Sebastian time to recover. He crawls across the sand, eyes locked on the ax near a fallen demon.

The troll, still looming over him, seems to be preparing for another strike. I can't let that happen, but this distance... My gift has a range and he's just at the edge of it.

Right as the troll reaches Sebastian, it bends, jaws open like he plans to swallow him whole. Sebastian's fingers stretch for the ax handle, just out of reach. He snags the demon's arm, pulling it over his head as the troll chops down with the sword, severing the limb. Sweat beads on my brow, but I manage to keep him from swinging harder, sparing Sebastian's head by a sliver of space.

I glance at my father, who remains oblivious to my interference. The paranoia gnaws at me, the fear of being caught growing heavier with every use of my powers.

Sebastian, now holding the severed arm of the demon, whips it up and smacks the troll in the face with the dead hand. It's an odd sight, but effective—enough to make the troll pause so he rolls enough to get ahold of the ax.

Come on, Sebastian...

Facing the troll once more, he draws the ax to him, but the troll is faster. Its hands wrap around Sebastian's throat and yank him up. His feet dangle in the air as he thrashes, his shadows trying to hold him up. His darkness is practically useless against the creature.

I prepare myself for whatever comes next. Forcing my nerves to calm, but that's easier said than done when our lives are on the line. One misstep, one slip of focus, could lead to disaster. I can see the desperation in Sebastian's eyes as he tries to hang on to the ax in his hand.

As if sensing my inner turmoil, Sebastian's eyes lock onto mine for a brief moment, determination flaring within them. With a subtle flick of my wrist, I use my gift to loosen the troll's grip just enough for Sebastian to swing the ax, using his shadows to propel it forward.

With a swift motion, Sebastian's ax drives deep into the troll's thick neck. Black blood sprays as the creature crumbles to the ground.

The bell tolls.

He won.

My cheeks burn, trying to hide the smile that threatens to split my face. There's a chance for me. A chance at life. A chance at love. A family. A chance at adventure and to see the world...

Bodies litter the ground, blood seeping into the sand. Amid this carnage stands Sebastian, the last man standing. His breaths are heavy as he gets to his feet and holds up his ax. Sweat and blood coat his skin, his wounded shoulder still dripping.

Despite the chaos surrounding him, there's something undeniably attractive about his disheveled appearance. He bows sarcastically to the crowd and my father, and I can't help but smile. Even with the disguise gone, he's still the same sarcastic man I danced with, and it fills me full of hope.

Silence blankets the crowd as the royal mages line up along the cliffside, and work to replace the stone-slabbed stairs. Sebastian glances toward the far side of the cliff, where an orc man sits. Is that his friend? Did he wear a disguise too? When the man's fist pumps the air, I get my answer.

The crowd goes silent as Sebastian climbs up the stairs, the tension in the air palpable. One of the mages at the top hands him his sword, and he discards the ax he used during the gauntlet.

My gaze follows him, unable to tear my eyes away. He runs his ringed-clad fingers through his sweaty hair, and a sudden panic grips me, remembering what comes next.

"Come," my father says, nudging me from my seat. "The spell will last until the next nightfall. After that, assuming your heart is still beating, you'll have to figure out how to hide it."

My mark... he's talking about my witch mark. The curse my mother placed on me. It's intended to mark mages that use sacrificial magic—blood witches—and glows to warn others when they use their gifts.

I'm of mage blood, but I'm not a blood witch. My mother thought marking me as an infant would keep my father from offering me up in his gauntlets. Obviously, her plan didn't work. I've had to hide it my entire life, but I can't help but feel like hiding it is about to get a lot harder.

Sebastian smirks at me, locking his gaze with mine as he crosses the bridge with long, sure strides. The creatures crowded on it split to either side, making a path for him.

I shouldn't want him, yet part of me is intrigued… It's entranced with the aura that surrounds him and craves to bask in it. I barely know the man, yet he's convinced me to break my father's rules for him, and all it took is one conversation.

My father's hand presses to my back and I feel the warmth of it through the lace of my dress. He leads me over the bridge, meeting Sebastian in the middle. Not once does his gaze leave me.

My father lifts the crystals in his hand as we stop, and when he speaks, his voice projects across the cliffs, enhanced by magic. "The Dark One has won!"

A wave of unease ripples through the crowd. If they knew who he was before the gauntlet, they must be terrified now that they've seen him fight.

Sebastian drives the tip of his sword into the bridge just a couple of feet away from my father's feet. He bows respectfully, but his gaze is still on me. At this moment, I can't deny his rugged beauty.

"Your Majesty," he says, but my father doesn't so much as look at him.

"You have some gall showing your face in my kingdom. Had it been in any other way, your head would be decorating the cliffside pikes." He breathes out deeply, crossing his hands in front of his body. "I only hope it means you'll start leaving my fucking ships alone."

Sebastian snorts, glancing at my father with a smug grin playing on his lips. "I won fair and square, Your Majesty. I'll accept a ten-year truce in exchange for my ten years of riches." His green eyes shift back to me, his smirk turning suggestive. "I'll claim my prize now." And heat floods my cheeks.

8
Scarlet

The priestess splits the crowd, her crystal headdress standing out amongst the sea of my father's subjects. The light from the moons above shines brightly, reflecting off the patches of her silver scales, and scatters along the ground. Her body takes a humanoid shape, but she's lived long enough to witness our empire rise from the ashes of the great fall. The king smiles, revealing every blade-like tooth in his mouth as she nears.

"Let's get this over with, shall we?" my father says while I chew the inside of my cheek. Sebastian stands to my right, his arm mere inches from mine. Even with the venom in his system, he's stoic, his strength unwavering. It's commendable, but he reeks of copper and the sour stench of venom, and who knows how much of the blood on his skin is his. He needs a healer... and a bath.

The oracle stops next to my father, who's a few feet ahead of us now, barking orders at his staff to prepare for Sebastian's stay. I'm not sure what there is for them to do at the last minute. It's not like they have a room to prepare. From what I understand, he'll be staying in mine.

"I think that's our cue." Sebastian's voice is in my ear, still holding that dark, mysterious tone it held before. I jolt away, craning my neck toward him, only to find that he's leaned closer. His dark eyebrows arch up, drawing my gaze to his striking green eyes. They're gorgeous. I've never seen eyes like his, like the color exploded in the rings, creating a thousand different shades. "Sorry. I didn't mean to startle you, princess."

"You didn't."

The corners of his lips tip up as he takes off his necklace and pockets it. Must be a pirate thing. "Sure, I didn't. I must've imagined it."

My father waves us over, his arm cast out, but his gaze stays put on the priestess.

"That's definitely our cue." Sebastian's hand grazes my shoulder blades, urging me forward. My spine straightens and he quickly drops it, sensing my unease—I think—and we stroll forward.

When we reach her, the priestess's vacant eyes seek us out. "Will there be a blood oath?" She tilts her head, awaiting Sebastian's response. Her movements are almost sinister, exaggerated, and slow. Then again, she's over a thousand years old. It wouldn't surprise me if the time had taken its toll on her mind.

"Does the princess want one?"

Years of training fly right out the window with that one spoken question. My head snaps to the right, my eyes widening. Most men would have answered yes or no. I never anticipated him asking what I want, or even caring about what I have to say.

He smiles, looking at me out of the corner of his eye. "You have to use your words, Scarlet."

Shaking myself out of the confused trance, I turn back to the priestess. "Uh, yes."

She doesn't react, just stares at Sebastian, needing him to say the final word.

"You heard the lady," he says without missing a beat.

The priestess holds out her hand, drawing her dagger from the sheath on her hip. The cool blade meets my flesh and she pulls. I gasp and my entire body tenses as the sting settles in, but my blood quickly beads and starts to roll off the sides of my hand.

The blood oath binds one soul to the other. It's a mate bond for non-shifter beings, and like shifters, there's only one way to end a bond like that. Death. If he plans to hurt me, the bond will make him feel every ounce of agony I experience. And if I take it, then I will feel as he does too. The fact he's willing to make the oath in the first place is a good sign, but Zelix's warning rings loud and clear in my head.

Sebastian hates witches...

If he were to find out I'm marked, I might have to protect myself. I'm not a warrior. There's no way I'd be able to fight through pain. If I had to stab him, I'd crumble and he might not even bat an eye. That much is clear by the fact he's wounded now and barely showing it. It might not be wise for me to participate, but having him do so would be in my favor. He might hesitate if he'd feel it, too.

When the priestess is finished collecting my blood into the goblet, she hands it to my father before repeating the same thing on Sebastian's hand. Once our blood is mixed, she speaks in a tongue I don't understand. Her hands wrap around the goblet and something inside of it starts to glow. She dips her fingers into the mixture, our blood taking on a luminescent hue, and her white eyes turn toward Sebastian. "With this, you'll be linked in more than just spirit. Do you wish to be bound, not just in soul, but in mind?"

"Yes," Sebastian says, lowering his head so she can touch her fingers to his forehead, drawing a small sigil.

Moving to me, she dips her fingers again. "Do you wish to be bound by both soul and mind?"

"No..." I feel the air change. This is my only right. The only choice I'll be given in this ritual. I don't want to believe he'll go back on his word or hurt me, but just in case, any advantage I can get is a must. "No, I don't."

"Very well," the priestess says. "The Dark One will feel as you do. He'll know every emotion, but you will not share his. Are you sure?"

"Yes." My eyes drop to the ground. I can't bring myself to see how Sebastian reacts. He won't understand... not unless he's been in my place, seen the things I've witnessed.

The priestess grabs both of our hands after giving the goblet to my father. "You have my blessing." Her grip tightens around us, and a sigil burns beneath my skin on the top of my hand, forming a reddened circle in my flesh with quirky letters, and a star overlapping it. At each point of the star, there's a symbol for the elements. Air, water, earth, fire, and spirit.

I've been taught what to say for this ritual, over and over, for as long as I can remember. At this point, it's second nature. Standing up a bit taller, I look at the priestess. "Under the spirit, I vow. A union of souls."

Sebastian repeats the phrase, his voice steady and calm at my side.

"Under the spirit, you are wed," the priestess says, smiling like she's giving us our happily ever after and not binding us under grim pretenses. "You must speak your vow to the other elements. Once they're all complete, and you've consummated, your claim to the throne will be solidified, and your marriage will be permanent until your souls pass into the next life."

Sebastian dips his head and, against my better judgment, I look. He eyes the sigil on his hand, the spirit symbol glowing a bright orange hue.

"Please tell me that goes away," he whispers.

"It does," I say, offering him a smile.

When his eyes lock on mine, I almost forget that an entire kingdom is watching us. For just a stitch in time, I'm not the princess who will die on her twenty-third birthday. I'm the princess who finally gets to live.

It doesn't last long, though. We're quickly ushered inside the castle, through the winding stairwells and long hallways until we come face-to-face with my bedroom door. My father hands Sebastian a sachet, grumbling something under his breath. He doesn't even say goodbye before leaving us in the hall.

"I hope you'll be okay with your father never approving of your husband," Sebastian says, watching the king move down the hall until he disappears into the stairwell.

"I don't think he ever approved of me as his daughter. I'm sorry if you expected otherwise."

"Oh, no... You misunderstand me." He meets my gaze, reaching around my body to open the door. "I don't care what he thinks. He could burn and the world would be better for it."

"I'd hold your tongue while you're within these walls. He let you marry me, but it doesn't mean he won't arrest you the moment you commit treason under his roof."

Sebastian grumbles, drifting inside the room. He turns in a tight circle, nearly losing his footing on the spin. "This is yours?"

"No, it's the maids," I say, leaning against the doorframe. Sebastian pauses, staring at me. I don't think he picked up on the sarcasm. "Of course it's mine."

He moves to my vanity, fidgeting with the things on top of the desk and the frills on the side of the pillows resting on the seat. I step inside and let the door swing shut.

"I think congratulations are in order." I'm not sure what else to say to make this less awkward. Suddenly, I don't know where to put my hands, or where to look, so I train my eyes to the floor and link my fingers behind my back, just as I was taught.

He doesn't look too enthused as he thumbs through the spines of the books stacked on my nightstand.

"Are you not pleased? You won. It's a–"

He cuts me off, turning on a heel to face me. "I did. No thanks to you. I almost died in that arena twice, and I'm not sure why you didn't follow through on our deal. Regardless, I think we can both agree that it doesn't matter now. However, what does matter is you telling me to take the blood oath and then refusing it yourself."

"You wouldn't understand." I take a step forward, meeting his gaze.

He sets his jaw, nodding over and over. "I'd like to think of myself as an intelligent man. Try me."

"Most of my sisters are buried in the crypt beneath the castle. You didn't tell me who you were, and after finding out that you're a pirate, I was worried you'd ship me back in a box to get at my father. The blood oath might make you think twice, and my refusal gives me a chance to defend myself if you choose that route."

"So it was self-preservation?"

"Yes," I say as he closes the distance between us. "I want to see the world. Why would I provoke you without reason?"

He eyes me, the heat of his gaze traveling from my head to my toes. It takes everything I have to stay still, hands behind me, and not squirm beneath his perusal.

"You should bathe. You're wounded."

"I'll heal." His fingers grip the hem of what's left of his shirt and work it over his head, careful not to move his injured shoulder as much as possible. The moment it's gone, I catch the venom tracks surrounding the deep scrape, but also the fact it's partially healed. Elementals don't usually have accelerated healing, but I've also never met someone with an infinity like darkness.

Watching me with an intensity I've never experienced before, not even with Zelix, he unbuckles his belt, pulling the leather strap from the loops, sword sheath and all, then thrusts it toward me.

"I trust you won't stick me with it?" he says, and I take it from his hands, shaking my head no. "Good. Now, where's the tub?"

I nod toward the door leading into the bathroom and he takes my cue. Setting his sword down on the dresser, I follow after him. Sebastian spins to close the door, only for me to smack into the middle of his chest. His hands find my shoulders, standing me upright and keeping me from toppling.

"What are you doing?" His voice somehow becomes darker, and I force down the word vomit that threatens to leave my mouth.

"Helping?"

"Do I need help?"

"My father won't allow the maids to disrupt things, so there won't be anyone to help you get the water or towels. Don't you want towels?"

He takes a hesitant step back, letting me in. "Are you used to the maids helping you?"

"Rarely." I grab the things he'll need, making haste so I don't keep him waiting.

"I don't have maids. It might be something you have to get used to."

"I think living is enough for me. I'm just grateful to not be on a troll's dinner plate right now."

Sebastian snorts, and I turn my arms full of items he'll need, but I nearly drop them when my eyes connect with enough skin to know he has no shame.

"How does this normally work? Do I just get in? I'm not familiar with the royal way of... Well, everything. You'll have to teach me."

I let the air out of my lungs, blinking long and hard before training my gaze on the floor. "You just get in and I'll set this stuff down and pump the water into the tub. It's up to you if you'd like to be in it when the water comes or not."

There's a squeal of skin against porcelain as he steps inside, leaning back against the edge and letting his arms rest along the lip. That's as much as I'll allow myself to notice.

"What now?"

Lifting my gaze, I find him relaxed back against the edge of the tub, arms resting on the curved lip of it. I feel my cheeks turn beat red before I can stop them–honestly, I doubt I could–and Sebastian's mouth warps into a toothy grin.

"You're the most awkward woman I've ever been naked and alone with."

"Sorry." I set the things in my arms down on the small table near the tub and move to the foot of it, where the handle to pump the water is. The metal whines as I start to pump, trying harder than ever to not look at him, even though my eyes keep deceiving me and drifting.

"It's okay, you know," he says, but I don't respond. Instead, I start pumping the water in faster. "Scarlet, look at me."

Halting, I let out a breath and prop my hands on my hips, turning only my head. "I suppose it's going to happen at some point."

He chuckles, turning his head ever so slightly to drag his fingers across his jaw. "We don't have to do anything you don't want. But if you pump that handle any harder, it's going to break."

"You don't have to lie to me. I know what is supposed to happen tonight. I've been schooled my entire life for it." Allowing myself to look, I take in the dark inky lines on his chest and arms. Ships, skulls, and various other symbols twisted together into a delicate web. The hard planes of muscle they wrap around... I've never wished to lick a man, but I have this odd desire to trace those lines with my tongue.

This is a problem.

My gaze drifts lower.

A big problem.

I resume pumping the water, locking on to the dimple in the wall paint like my life depends on it. I shouldn't have looked. There are some things in my life that I'll have to say goodbye to and sex will be one after tonight.

The spell to conceal my mark takes a coven of mages to cast. I won't have one to replace it when it fades. I have three days until the moons block the hell flame again, and then my mark will be visible. Looking, allowing myself to daydream, wanting... All of those things will just get me in trouble. I will do my duty, but nothing more than what is required of me. Doing anything more than that will only make me crave his touch again. Which can't happen if I don't want him to see my back.

The water sloshes and a flash of skin appears beside me. I close my eyes. He's too close...

"You should be bathing."

"Keep pumping like that and I'll drown in here."

"Very well..." I step away from the pump, but as I start to link my hands behind my back, he catches my arm, yanking me closer. My arms flail as I try to regain my balance, latching on to him for support. "What did you do that for?"

"Don't pretend to be my wait staff. I don't have servants or maids. I don't expect my women to play the role either. I'm more than capable of taking care of myself. Now, why won't you look at me? Do I not appease you? You had no issues doing so when we danced. Do you just prefer elves?"

My eyes meet his as my eyebrows scrunch together. "No, none of that. I don't care what you are and I'd be lying through my teeth if I said I wasn't attracted to you."

"Then why won't you look at me?" His head tilts to the side and the gentle stroke of his thumb reminds me that he's yet to let go of my arm.

"I'm trying to be respectful of your privacy."

"Don't," he whispers, his hand dragging down my arm until his fingers wrap around my wrist. He places my palm on his chest, still crusted in dried blood, though most of it has washed away, tinging the water red. "You're forgetting that we–that I–took a blood oath. I know there's more that you're not telling me, but I can feel your unease. I know you're nervous. This might be new, we might be strangers, but I won't do anything to hurt you. My body, my mind, even my soul are yours if you want them."

He brings my knuckles to his lips, squeezing my hands for a moment before letting it go. "I don't know how to respond to that."

"Just promise not to abuse my pieces like you did that handle."

A laugh escapes me, and the tension eases in my shoulders. "I won't. I promise."

"Good. Now, if you're going to help me, then it's only fair that I get to help you bathe in return. Deal?"

I nod, and he sits back down in the tub. Who is this man?

9
SCARLET

The dim mage light on the wall casts a soft glow across the bathroom, its reflection dancing on the warm water inside the clawfoot tub. I can barely make out the ocean outside the window, but it doesn't matter; my attention isn't there. Not tonight.

Most nights, I sit in the tub, looking out at the dark-capped waves rolling in and out of the bay, dreaming of what lies beyond the line where the world ends. Now, I couldn't care less what's out that window. My mind is focused on the naked stranger in my tub. Sebastian's form relaxes into the bath, his wounded shoulder half-submerged.

"Let's get some candles going, shall we?" I say, trying to sound casual. I think that might've been a losing battle to start with.

It's impossible to keep the shake out of my voice. Not when he's... exposed. He doesn't seem shy about it in the slightest, yet the first time I was naked in front of a man I trembled until my eyeballs rattled. It took weeks of seeing

Zelix to get over the nerves, and I'm getting an odd sense of Déjà vu.

I strike a match and light a few candles around the room, their crackling flames licking off the wooden wicks, casting shadows that seem to move with every breath. Grabbing a jar off the table, I scoop the bath salts and drop them into the water. The scent of lavender and eucalyptus fills the air. That scent... something about it makes me feel lighter. It calms me from the inside out.

Delivering the second scoop, my arm bumps into Sebastian's hand. It's been resting on the edge of the tub since he's gotten in, but I hadn't intended to touch him... just leaned too far, I guess. It doesn't stop him from twirling his fingers through a strand of my hair, though. Sebastian watches his ringed fingers like it's the last thing he'll ever see.

"Does your shoulder hurt?" I ask, trying to stay busy so my mind doesn't drift. Eyeing the raw wound on the side of his upper arm—where the serpent man's talons tore through the flesh—I notice the venom tracks have faded significantly. It still looks painful, even though it's healed some.

"It'll be fine," Sebastian says nonchalantly, muscles tensing slightly. "I heal quickly, and the venom's effects are gone. It's just a matter of time before the wound closes up."

I sigh, letting out the air in my lungs. He drops my hair and moves his arm inside the tub as if he's worried I'll do something to it.

"You don't have to pretend around me. If it hurts, I can help." Considering the fact I turned down the blood oath and he tried to hear me out and understand, the least I can do is help where I can. I'm not a healer, but I know my way around the medical arts enough to know how to close a wound.

Sebastian's eyes soften, and he studies me for a moment before nodding.

"Would you like something for it?"

"Like what?" he asks, a crease forming between his brows.

"I can go get something for the pain from the apothecary." I start to lift from the stool, but he puts his hand over mine and water drips between my fingers.

"No. I'm fine."

"Alright. I probably have sutures in here somewhere." He lets me up this time and I scurry about the room, searching drawers for the kit I left in here... somewhere. Two drawers later, I find it and work on threading the needle.

"Why would you have sutures?"

His question stops me cold. "Well, some call it clumsy. I call it a curse. I fell."

He snorts and I spare a glance at him over my shoulder, getting an eyeful of his scrutiny.

"If there's one thing I've learned about since we met, it's that you're graceful. You nearly float when you move. Someone like that isn't clumsy. Would you like to try again?"

Tucking my chin to my chest, I roll the needle between my fingers and turn to rest my backside against the dresser edge. "Well, if you must know, I was trying to climb out a way through my window. The lattice that covers the sides of this tower isn't friendly."

"Sneaking out, huh?"

"More like trying to escape." Stepping closer to the tub, I sit on the stool, getting as close as I can so I can gently clean the wound.

"You were running away..." It's a comment for himself more than for me.

"Trying to, yes. Except I'm terrified of heights and the lattice doesn't go all the way around the tower. The only way off it would've been to go in the water and I can't swim, so I climbed back up. Had my room been in the other tower, you might not have met me."

"And what a shame that would've been."

I breathe out a laugh, prodding at his skin to figure out the best way to close it. Little does he know it's not the first time stitches have been given in this bathroom. Neither was the lattice incident.

Sebastian's skin is so warm, and the art that covers it is a masterpiece. The detail of his tattoos must've taken so long... I want to run my hands over it and trace the contours of muscle in his arms. My cheeks flame as I try to force myself to focus on the task at hand.

"Thank you," he murmurs, his voice rough and low. The baritone of it sends heat coursing through me in ways I didn't know existed.

"Of course." I purse my lips, tying the last knot. The man didn't even flinch throughout the entire procedure. His pain tolerance is impeccable... and slightly scary. "I'm afraid it'll likely scar still, but hopefully it'll heal faster this way."

"In case you haven't noticed, it wouldn't be my first."

Oh... I noticed.

His hand runs over the long-jagged mark beneath the tattoos on his chest, and I want to ask what made it, but don't. If he wanted me to know, he'd tell me. Then there's the two short ones on his ribs. Multiple small ones on his arms. I'm afraid to look elsewhere.

I pull up on the thread to cut it. "Sorry," I murmur, feeling a pang of guilt. I'm sure tugging on it doesn't feel great.

"It's fine," he assures me with a tight smile. "You did better than I expected, actually."

"Is that supposed to be a compliment?" I raise an eyebrow.

"Take it as you wish." His lips twist into a grin before pulling wide enough to reveal his white teeth. I always thought pirates would look scraggly and dirty, nothing like him.

Before I can stare for too long, I pull the chain to empty the tub, then start to refill it with fresh, warm water. I motion for Sebastian to sit up, intending to use the bucket to gently pour water over his head to rinse away any lingering blood and grime, but he bats me away.

"Just pump the handle. I can get this part."

"Alrighty, then..." Pumping the handle, a stream of warm water cascades into the tub.

Sebastian dips his head beneath the flow, and as he sits back up, he flips his hair back, and streams of water dribble across every hard plane of his body. My mouth goes dry. His dark locks cling to his face, framing his striking features, and I open my mouth but fear I've forgotten how to speak. What I wouldn't give to be a bead of water right now... I snap my mouth shut, watching the rivulets roll over his body.

"Time to strip, princess," he says, smirking as if he's caught on to my thoughts. But before I can protest or argue, he adds, "You promised. Now it's my turn to play maid."

"I—Um, okay," I concede, and he stands from the tub, grabbing the towel I placed on the table nearby. Water drips from his body, and I turn away, letting him dry off without prying eyes.

His gaze lingers on me, and I can feel it in my soul. The room feels a degree warmer, or maybe it's just the heat rising to my cheeks. While I fidget with the fabric of my dress, he steps closer, the towel wrapped snugly around his hips. Sebastian lifts my chin with a curled finger and my breath catches.

"Are you alright?"

I nod, my voice lost somewhere in my throat. My heart races in my chest and I swallow hard. He gives me a knowing look like he can tell I'm the furthest thing from being okay.

"Are you nervous?"

"Yes," I answer honestly. "I've, um, never done something like this with someone before."

"I heard the king promising virgins, but I didn't think it was true."

"I'm not... I mean, to my father I am. I cheated the physical inspection, but you've been so nice to me. It doesn't feel right to lie about it to you."

Sebastian smiles, his eyes searching mine, but I have no idea what he's looking for.

"Breathe, Scarlet. It's okay. I don't care who you've been with. I care even less about what your father thinks, but we'll have to see each other naked at some point. I'm a man of my word."

"I thought pirates were only loyal to their own?" The question is out of my mouth before I can stop it.

He chuckles, helping me to my feet. "True, but the moment you were bound to me, that applied to you, too. I have no intention of hurting you, Scarlet. I promise. Do you trust me?"

"Not a chance," I whisper, taking a deep breath to steady myself.

His voice is warm–enchanting even–and every time he smiles I have this odd urge to do it too. "Turn around."

I spin on my heels and pull my hair over one shoulder. "You just untie—"

"I'm fully aware of how a corset works, but thank you."

My entire body is blushing at this point. Knees and all.

He pulls on the strings, loosening up the corset tie and layer that goes over it. The first layer slips over my head and he tosses it onto a chair on the far side of the bathroom. His rough fingers brush against my skin as he finishes untying the corset strings, and I can't help but shiver at his touch. He's gentle, despite his rugged persona, and I'm reminded once again of the many layers that make up my husband.

There's the kind, gentle, charming man I danced with, that I'm here with now. Then there's the obnoxiously lethal man I saw in the arena today, the one who'd likely kill me if he ever discovered my mark. I'm still not sure what to do about that. Regardless, my brain doesn't know how to process that both of those people can be the same man undressing me now.

Sebastian tosses away the boned corset and gently slides the stretchy neckline of my slip over my shoulders until it starts to fall down my arms. It doesn't plummet to the floor, but it's enough to expose my shoulders and enough of my back that the mark and my scars would be visible had my father and his mages not concealed them.

Warmth flutters over my shoulder before his lips press to the crook of my neck. It causes the air to become trapped in my lungs, but I twist my head, giving him better access anyway. It's heavenly... and it's so mundane. He carefully pushes the dress down my arms, sending goosebumps rising to the surface of my skin.

"You still have to get in the tub, Scarlet. I'm not sure this will work with you out here," he teases, his voice low and seductive.

I laugh nervously, acutely aware of my growing attraction to him. "Right, of course."

Taking a deep breath to steady myself, I step into the warm water, feeling it rise around me as Sebastian follows suit. He picks up a sponge, lathering it with soap before gently starting to wash my hair.

"Close your eyes." His lips brush against my ear as he speaks, and I comply, feeling the tension begin to drain from my body as his fingers massage my scalp. Holy... fuck. This is the meaning of bliss. I'm sure of it.

"Your hair is beautiful." Sebastian runs his fingers through the length, setting my long, white locks over my shoulder as he goes. "I've never seen anything quite like it."

"Thank you," I reply, my cheeks warming with a blush. "It's not exactly common."

"Neither are you," he says, and I can hear the smile in his voice.

Only my family has snow-white hair. Not even the elves do. The lightest theirs gets is silver. My father claims it has to do with his experiments. That altering our genetics causes the phenomenon. I don't have much choice but to believe it, seeing as my father's blond and my mother's was dark.

I chuckle, opening my eyes to meet his gaze. "You're quite the charmer, aren't you?"

"Only when it's warranted." There's a playful glint in his eyes. "And with you, I have a feeling it most certainly is. Let's just say, I can feel it in my soul how nervous you are. And for some reason, that settles a bit when I speak."

"I think it's your voice."

"Are you telling me I'm not romancing you right?"

"Didn't say that...but there's something about your voice that makes it feel like I can breathe." For all that's holy, please tell me I didn't just say that out loud... I just met the man. I can't say things like that. Yet, he's the only person who's ever shown me kindness and treated me like a person and not a sacrifice. It's hard not to revel in it.

"I'm sorry that your own family has treated you this way."

"What do you mean?"

"All day you've been treated like a lamb being led to slaughter. I mean, they inspected you before offering you up on a silver platter to whoever wins. It's wrong."

"Yet, you competed."

"Not for you. I did it for a pardon or a truce. My people need to find something important on the mainland. They couldn't when there's a reward on our heads. Not just for criminal charges either, but because we don't wear one of your father's cuffs. Whether you were offered to me or not, I would've entered. It still doesn't make it fair for you to have been paraded around a ballroom like a prized possession. What would you have done if that troll had won?"

"I would've fulfilled my duty. The gauntlets are the only thing keeping the clans from war. One person's life doesn't mean anything when it's compared to the hundreds and thousands that would die if the realm went to war again amongst itself."

"So, you would've just played the part of sacrificial lamb?" His fingers twirl around my hair as he watches the way the ends of the strands fray when they're submerged in water.

"Yes. I'm glad it didn't go that way, though."

Sebastian's eyes widen slightly, taken aback by the revelation. "It's barbaric."

"Unfortunately, it's the reality of being the princess," I say bitterly.

"Well, it won't be your reality anymore." His stool is seated behind the tub, allowing him to rest his chin against my shoulder.

"I hope not. Forgive me for not getting my hopes up just yet."

We fall silent as he rinses the soap from my hair. Once I'm clean, I step out of the tub, gripping his hand for support. His fingers brush against my skin as he wraps a plush towel around my body, making my heart skip a beat.

"Careful now," he teases, his breath warm against my ear as he pulls me close. "Wouldn't want you to slip."

I roll my eyes playfully while trying to ignore the tingle that runs down my spine.

"You should know I've climbed out of that tub on my own hundreds of times."

"Yes, but that was before someone made your knees weak," he says, grinning devilishly. "You're forgetting that you made me take the blood oath."

"I didn't make you do anything."

"Still, I can sense everything. It's how I knew you were nervous. I don't typically feel much, so it wasn't hard to put together that it was coming from you."

"Is that what you've been doing, then? Learning what makes me tick."

"Maybe." Sebastian allows me to turn to face him. "I think I've learned a lot."

"Like what?" I'm not entirely sure how the blood oath works, but I know it doesn't just spell things out. The feelings are vague, and their emotions act as your own. So, if I'm sad, he'll feel sad himself and have to figure out if it's him or me having that feeling.

"For starters, you don't like talking about your father or whoever the man you slept with is. You're nervous about sleeping with me or doing anything remotely intimate. At first, I thought it might be that you weren't interested, but then I touched you and I discovered that it's clearly not the case. That leads me to believe you're inexperienced—maybe a one-off fling? How close did I get?"

"He wasn't a fling." Maybe I was wrong... Somehow, he's able to differentiate between my feelings and his like they're black and white. I'll need to be more careful going forward.

"Don't do that," he says, kissing my shoulder and making butterflies spin in my stomach.

"I'm not doing anything."

"You're shutting down. It's not a bad thing to feel... I think some people take it for granted."

"I think we have some vows to say." Changing the subject, I step away, pulling the towel tight around my middle.

I exit the bathroom and the cool air hits me like a wall, making me shiver as I open my wardrobe. Pulling out a nightgown, I slip it over my head and let the satin slide down my body. Then it hits me... There's nothing for him to wear.

"I don't need anything," he says, beating me to it.

"What will you wear tomorrow, then?"

"The clothes I wore here. I have clothes on my ship. I'll change when we get there."

"Your shirt is in shreds."

"Then I won't wear a shirt. I'll be alright. I don't usually sleep in clothes, anyway."

It's so vulgar. Everyone sleeps in clothes... right? Maybe it's just the people in the castle.

Sebastian, still with the towel around his waist, crosses the room. The sachet my father gave him is in his hand. My heart races as I watch Sebastian's expression shift from playful to something more serious and introspective. He seems to be studying me, taking in every detail of my face with an intensity that makes me feel both vulnerable and exhilarated.

"Vows," he says softly, reminding me as he reaches out to tuck a loose strand of hair behind my ear.

"From the air," I begin, raising my hand to reveal the sigil the priestess gave us. "I vow, a union of souls."

"From the air," Sebastian echoes, his voice steady and strong, as he displays his own matching sigil. We continue with the other elements—earth, water, and fire—each time pledging our union of souls to one another.

With the final vows spoken, I can feel the weight of our commitment settling upon us. We stand before each other, strangers bound together by fate and circumstance. There's only one thing left to do...

He smirks at me, a look I'm starting to realize might be his true superpower. That single look, the way his dimples flash, could make me do unspeakable things. My walls shouldn't crumble this quickly around them, yet all it takes is an instant and he has them turned into rubble.

Sebastian drops his gaze to the sigils on his hand. It glows with power, reflecting the strength of the elements we have invoked. "When will these sigils disappear?"

"Now that we've completed our vows, maybe an hour or two."

His eyes narrow thoughtfully. "It doesn't require consummation?"

I swallow hard, unsure where he's going with that question. "It's not required to marry us, but it is for you to be named a prince. My father will send someone to check in the morning."

He steps closer, his figure towering over me. "I won't force you into anything, Scarlet. I want you to know that, but I need to ask. Seeing as you're not a virgin, will that be enough?"

A mixture of relief and uncertainty swirls within me. "I don't know. I'd assume so, but I can't know for sure." I hesitate for a moment before adding, "The choice is yours. If it's not enough, then you won't be named a prince, and your right–your truce–will be void. My father could arrest you."

Despite the seriousness of our conversation, Sebastian's eyes soften, and he shakes his head. "That doesn't change anything. If you don't want to, we'll find another way."

His words send warmth spiraling through my middle. "Thank you," I whisper, my voice trembling with emotion. "That means more to me than you could ever know." My mind whirls, taking in the gravity of the situation.

I reach up to cup his face in my hand. His eyes search mine, and I see a flicker of surprise before they fill with warmth. "Are you sure, Scarlet?" he asks, placing his hand over mine on his cheek. Before the surge of courage can fade, I kiss him.

10

Hook

How am I supposed to react? I don't kiss women. I mean, sure, some want it and that's all fine and dandy, but I've never yearned to kiss someone before. Not like this. I physically couldn't stop myself from touching Scarlet in the bathroom. Even now, every ounce of my being desires to be closer until it's impossible to be anymore.

My body relaxes into hers, our lips moving in tune. Is this what it feels like to be whole? To have emotions? If so, I understand why some call them consuming.

Without my shadow, I essentially have half of my soul. I still feel, but the sensations are muted like my emotions are trying to go through a barrier. I only get to experience what slips through the seams. At least that was the case until the blood oath.

It's trouble.

Scarlet is trouble.

I knew the moment she danced with me that this woman was going to wreck my world. From the way her dainty hand fit in mine to the way she held nothing back...

Maybe a small part of me wanted her to. I just didn't know what to expect.

Scarlet's skin is so soft beneath my fingers. Even as I dive them into her silky white hair, I can't stop myself from deepening the kiss. I want more. I'm just not sure if it's her specifically I crave or the feeling I've been deprived of for as long as I can remember.

I'd been just a little boy when my shadow was taken, and I hadn't realized what I was missing until I knew what it was like. Now, it's like a drug I can't get enough of. It's a new experience I want to explore and push the limits, to test and see what variables elicit different sensations.

In a way, I'd already started doing that without noticing it. Every time I changed the subject of our conversation in the bath, every time I touched Scarlet in a different way, a response rippled through our blood bond, as if I felt it myself. It's both terrifying and exhilarating at the same time.

The scent of lavender floods my senses and my nostrils flare, but the scent is nothing compared to the way she tastes. I hold her to me, kissing her while trying to stay gentle. She's so fragile in my hands…

Scarlet knows what I'm capable of. She's witnessed it, yet not an ounce of her soul is worried. She trusts me not to hurt her, even if she won't admit it. I won't break that trust. Not tonight, not ever. Except, a part of me knows this won't last forever. It won't be safe for her on the

Jolly Roger, and I don't think she'll want to stay in the Luminaries. It won't be safe for her anywhere else without me, though, and if I want to get my shadow back, I'll have to leave.

Letting my hands roam down her slender throat, over the delicate curves of her shoulders, and the satin slip of her dress. I bend, hooking my hands behind her knees and lifting her up so her legs can twist around my torso.

Scarlet links her arms behind my neck as I blindly feel for the bed. As I set her down, she nips her teeth into my lower lip, and I swear my brain short-circuits. A growl reverberates from deep within my throat and I push her back onto the thick comforter. My towel slips from my waist, pooling onto the floor as I climb onto the bed and position myself between her legs. Just as I bend to kiss her chest, she stops me.

"Your shoulder," she pants against my lips, worry flickering in her gaze.

"Healed," I lie. Finding the hem of her nightgown, I slip it up her thigh and my mouth waters at the thought of kissing her there. I'm desperate to hear the sounds she makes and to feel her shake in my hands, and for the life of me, I don't know why. I've never been this out of control before.

"Sebastian," she whispers, though her hands clench my hair at the base of my neck.

"Yes, little lamb," I trail kisses along her jaw, down the delicate column of her throat. Her pulse leaps under my lips and I groan.

"I want to do this. You need that title, and I'd be lying if I told you that I wanted you to stop."

I smile down at her and a wave of lust rolls through our bond. "I know…"

"Be gentle with me."

"I will. As much as I can be."

Her hands tighten in my hair, and she arches into me, guiding my mouth back to her throat. My hands explore, lifting her gown until it's bunched above her tits. I pull her up off the bed just enough to yank the stain over her head.

"You're so godsdamn beautiful, Scarlet… and all mine." She sucks in a sharp breath, but she doesn't protest when I lower my head again, cupping her breast in my hand. "Mine to touch," I breathe, and her eyes darken.

Need spills through our bond. Something about my voice… That's what she said earlier, but she forgot to mention that it didn't just calm her, but that it turns her on too.

"Mine to please," I say, kissing the valley between her breasts. "Mine to make scream my name while you come…" I groan, sitting back to take in the sight of her. "I've been dreaming of that sound since I laid eyes on you."

Heat pools low in my gut, but Scarlet blushes and averts her gaze, likely unused to admiration. I cup her cheek, forcing her to meet my gaze. "Look at me, Scarlet."

A shiver rakes through her, and she stares up at me, full lips parted. I bend my head and kiss her, slow and deep. Her hands roam over my shoulders and back, gently scratching my skin. I moan against her lips, desire burning hot in my veins.

Breaking the kiss, I travel lower, kneading her breasts one by one and teasing her nipples into peaks. She arches into my touch, hands fisting the sheets.

"Sebastian—"

"Shh." I kiss my way down her stomach and settle between her legs. "Just feel, Scarlet." Biting the inside of her thigh, I chuckle when she jolts. "Do it for me."

And then I taste her.

Her hips buck at the first lash of my tongue, and I wonder if she's ever had anyone ravish her this way. She's not a virgin. She told me that much and that only one man has ever been here, but have they done this?

She cries out, back arching off the bed as I swirl and flick. I devour the most intimate part of her, drunk on the scent and taste of her pleasure, and driven by the need to claim her in the most primal way possible.

I won't stop until she comes apart for me. Slipping my hands under Scarlet's thighs, I tilt her hips up for better access. Her hands fist my hair like she's torn between pushing me away and pulling me closer.

As her thighs tremble in my hands. She's close, so fucking close I can feel her muscles tense and coil. I can taste it on my tongue. With a low moan, Scarlet shatters. Her back bows, hips jerking against my mouth as she rides out the waves of pleasure. I don't stop, drawing out her climax until her head falls back against the bed, and her chest heaves.

Only then do I raise my head, lips, and chin glistening with the evidence of her release. Scarlet blinks at me through half-lidded eyes, cheeks flushed, and mouth parted. She looks thoroughly sated, but I can still feel her desire burning in my veins. It mixes with my own, and I can't wait any longer.

"You're not done yet," I say, voice low with need. I climb up her body and settle between her thighs, the head of my cock nudging at her entrance. Her eyes widen, pupils blown with lust. "Are you ready?"

Her slight nod is the only answer I need. With a groan, I thrust into her and we both cry out. The blood bond flares to life, stronger than ever, until the pleasure nearly becomes euphoric. It's... otherworldly.

Scarlet won't be able to know this drug-like state since she refused the oath, but fuck... Zephyr understated what this felt like. Maybe that's because his is a true mate bond where ours is magically induced, but I don't care. Nothing and no one will ever compare to this, not anymore. Our desire spins through me on loop and I bury my face into the crook of her neck, inhaling lavender as I try to steady myself.

After a moment, I push up, dusting the stray hair from Scarlet's face. "You fit me so perfectly."

I kiss her lips, long and deep as I start to move. She moans against my lips and my eyes roll back into my head. Fuck, I could suffocate on those noises...

"More," she whispers, lifting her hips to take her pleasure.

"You want me to make you scream, little lamb? To ruin you for anyone else." The challenge in her eyes, the emotion roiling through the bond says yes, but I want to hear her say it.

"Please," she breathes, and I straighten, gripping her hips as I drive into her. She cries out, fisting the bedding as her eyes close and her head falls back. Those perfect pink lips of hers part on a moan and I grit my teeth, biting my tongue between them to keep from coming right here and now.

"Come for me, Scarlet. Show me how pretty you are when you fall apart." Angling my hips, I hit that spot deep within her. She shudders, inner walls clenching down on me until it's nearly impossible for me to move. With a sharp cry, Scarlet comes undone, convulsing around me. She doesn't hold back, either, letting her moans ring out in the air. A part of me wants to smother them, to keep them for me and only me, and the other wants to try to make her come louder.

My name is on her lips as she comes down and I slam home hard. The slap of our bodies fills my ears as I take what's mine, and I chase my own release.

Scarlet looks up at me, those bright hazel eyes locked on mine from beneath her long, dark lashes. The sight sends me tumbling over the edge after her, pleasure exploding through me as I bury myself deep within her dripping core and empty myself with a groan.

Catching my breath, I bend to kiss her, mustering up the energy to move. I want this moment to last, to savor it. She holds me to her chest and I nuzzle her throat, pressing soft pecks against her fluttering pulse.

"What have you done to me?" I rasp, not realizing I've asked the question aloud until Scarlet stiffens under me. I raise my head to find her wide eyes watching my every move. "I wish you could understand what that felt like."

"It felt amazing," she says, releasing an airy laugh.

"I can assure you, the bond made it more so. I've been with plenty of women and nothing has ever felt like that." I swallow the lump forming in my throat and force a smirk, trying for nonchalance.

She squints at me. "So, my husband is a whore?"

I gasp, feigning offense. "I am no such thing."

Rolling onto my back with an exaggerated groan, I pull her against my side. Scarlet stands, not bothering to dress before she slips off to the bathroom, leaving me alone. When she returns, her white hair is bundled on top of her head, but the baby hairs frame her face in a messy way. A gown hangs from her shoulders by tiny straps and there's something positively stunning about the sight that has my insides stirring into a frenzy.

She crawls into the bed, joining me beneath the covers, resting her head against my chest. Unsure of how this works, I settle my arm around her. I don't think I've ever cuddled with someone before, but I don't want to let her know that.

Within minutes, her breathing evens out and the steady rise and fall of her chest lulls me toward sleep. As darkness claims me, a single thought surfaces, reminding me that we'll be sailing home in the morning, where I'll be leaving her behind. She'll be safe there, and taken care of, but she's going to hate me for it...

11

SCARLET

The hell flame casts a warm glow over my bedroom, scattering an orange glow on the stone walls. The healer finishes her examination with a nod. As she replaces her cloak, she pulls the hood over her red curly hair and glances at me. "I'll inform King Midicious that the marriage has been successfully consummated."

She doesn't wait for a reply before ushering out of the room and leaving the bedroom door open. Sebastian slips inside from the hall, leaning against the frame as I sit up.

"Well, did you pass?" he asks, arching a dark brow. He crosses tattooed arms over his bare chest and toys with the stone pendant on his necklace, but the smaller white stones that surrounded the larger orange one are gone. He's taken them off at some point. Maybe they're like wedding rings to pirates? Regardless, his shirt was torn to shreds in the gauntlet, so he'll be leaving in only his leather pants and long red coat.

"What do you think?" A smile hints at my lips. Of course, he knows I'll pass.

His dimples flash as he pushes off the wall. I swing my feet over the edge of the bed and the moment he's near, he tips my chin. "I think we should get going."

I can't help but steal glances at him and reach out to place my hand on his chest, feeling the steady thump of his heart beneath my palm. "I've already packed," I say, pointing to the chest near the door.

The memories that echo within these walls are both dark and bittersweet. This was my home, but it never offered me the warmth and love that a true family should provide. I'll miss my sisters... I don't think I'll be offered a chance to say goodbye to them, and seeing as Sebastian isn't keen on my father, I don't think we'll be coming back.

He fingers the maroon fabric of my dress. It's casual, but still billows out at my hips and swishes around my knees. The sleeves are long and loose, and Sebastian traces the scooped neckline. "I like this," he says, taking a step back to give me a once-over. "Come on. We'll send up some of the guards to bring down the chest."

I take Sebastian's outstretched hand and he helps me to my feet. The castle halls illuminate as we head toward the stairwell and down to the bottom floor. We barely make it out the back door and into the courtyard, before a squeal slices the air. There's a pad of little feet against the concrete and something wraps around me from behind. Twisting, I find a mop of white hair, just as wild and unruly as the little girl it's attached to.

"You're alive!" Her words are muffled by the skirts of my dress.

"Eva Midicious! You know better than just to—" One of the maids rounds the corner of the castle and stops dead in her tracks. "Miss Scarlet. I didn't... I'm sorry if she's bothering you. We'll get her—"

"She's not," I say, picking her up and hugging Eva tight. She's barely four years old. She, like the rest of my little sisters, who aren't much different in age, will undoubtedly have questions. I did at their age with my older siblings.

"I'll miss you, Scars."

My back stiffens. None of my little sisters have seen my witch mark. My older siblings, yes, but they're in boxes now. Honestly, it started with her not being able to say my full first name, and the nickname sort of stuck. On any other given day, I wouldn't have batted an eye at the endearment, but in the presence of Sebastian, it's risky.

I smile gently, ruffling her hair. "I'll miss you too, but just know I'll be going on an adventure."

Her eyes light up. "Do you think you'll see the beasts of the deep?"

"Those are just tall tales."

Sebastian scoots closer, his voice changing. It's innocent and sweet. "Actually, they're real." He takes his arm out of his coat sleeve, revealing a jagged scar on his forearm. "One tried to bite me once."

Eva's eyes widen, and her mouth drops open in shock. "Really?"

"Really." He grins, flashing his dimples. I set Eva down and she runs back to the maid and is ushered to where the others play in the courtyard.

"Would you like to say bye to the rest?" Sebastian asks, but I quickly shake my head no.

"I think it's better that I don't. I don't want to lie to them and tell them I'll be back. Eva is different. She understands more than the others."

Sebastian studies me for a long moment, his mouth opening and closing as if he's looking for the words to say. The guards interrupt, dropping my chest behind us and making me jump.

"In that case, I think our ride is here, anyway." He points to the ship in the bay.

In the distance is a ship. Its sails whip in the wind, full and proud. But it wasn't the size or grandeur of the ship that caught my attention. It was the flag. A stark, black canvas with a white skull and crossbones. From the worn wood of its hull to the battle scars etched across its side, it looks just how I envisioned it would.

Sebastian leads the way, guiding me toward the island's edge where a small rowboat is tied. An orc holds the paddles, beaming at us as we approach. I recognize him from the gauntlet. He'd sat far off of the crowd along the cliff by himself.

"I was starting to think I'd never see you again," the orc calls as we near.

"I'm a bit harder to kill than that." Sebastian smiles, helping me into the rowboat. It rocks and wavers, and I quickly take a seat. For a moment, he leaves me to grab my things, disappearing around the courtyard wall.

"I'm Zephyr, by the way. I don't think we met." The orc holds out his hand. I take it, eyeing the twisted horns on top of his head and his jade-colored skin. He holds almost an ethereal beauty to him. Strong, yet perfectly chiseled features make up his face and his dark brown eyes are bottomless.

"Scarlet," I answer. I'm not sure anyone has ever offered me a handshake before. Most people bow or curtsy, primarily to the king, but they normally look past his children like they're statues. It's nice—different—and something I could get used to.

"It's lovely to meet you, and I hope Hook wasn't too much of an ass. I tried to teach him to be civil, but sometimes the pirate in him runs a bit too deep." His full lips curl around short tusks.

"I'll have you know," Sebastian says, setting my trunk in the boat and dusting off his hands before stepping into the boat. "I was a perfect gentleman."

My cheeks flame when Sebastian winks, his bright green eyes locking on mine. "Is he always this charming?" I ask, speaking to Zephyr even though I don't look at him.

The orc belts out a laugh, pushing us off the pier so he can start rowing us into the bay. "Not in the least. I was about to ask what you did with him? Is my real best friend stashed in that trunk or something, because I've never seen him so much as smile twice in a given day?"

"That's enough." Sebastian sets his jaw, his face going blank as he looks off toward the ship.

The waves lap against the sides of the small boat as Zephyr rows. There's a rhythmic creak of the oars filling the silence. My life, as I know it, will never be the same. The large castle I've called home grows smaller, the towers still disappearing into the clouds above. This place might've been my prison, but it was also the only place I've ever called home... and now I'll never return to it.

Sebastian sits across from me on the wooden bench, Zephyr behind him. I have to squint against the light bouncing off the water's surface and until yesterday, I never knew just how deep that water went. After seeing the bay emptied for the gauntlet, I know just how far I'd sink if I went overboard.

The hell flame casts a haloed light around Sebastian's form, growing stronger as the moons move out of the way. In reality, they're not truly moons. They're islands, but a permanent boundary hangs between them and us. It locks our realm off from the other six and even though the dragons are extinct within this realm, they still thrive outside it and those islands are their home.

I suppose if I were a dragon, I'd want to stay near the hell flame too. I'd want to bask in the warmth of it. Sebastian, though silent, must sense my awe and wonder. I catch him staring at me with an air of curiosity.

Dragons have always fascinated me. I thought at first it was because they were the things my father hated, and I loved them out of spite or rebellion, but the more I read, the more my curiosity grew. Really, the only thing that rivals my interest in the winged creatures my father stripped of this land is the plants and the magic that filled the void their species left behind. The ecosystem is fragile, and magic never truly disappears. In their absence, our world adapted, putting their magic into something else.

Zephyr's strong arms make short work of the distance and before I know it, the wooden ship is towering over us. The black sails are filled, arching away from the mast, but the ship stays in place despite the current. Elemental magic... They must have an air elemental onboard, ensuring the ship stays still long enough for us to board.

"You ready to take your hat back?" Zephyr's gruff voice breaks the silence. I doubt he's talking to me.

Sebastian smirks. "Anything interesting happen while I was away?"

Zephyr weighs his head from side to side, twisting his lips. "Depends how you look at it. Nelvin may have gambled away a date with Smee and she almost floated him overboard for it."

"Floated?" I ask. I've never heard that word used as an action before.

Zephyr nods. "In simple terms, she almost threw him overboard."

"That sounds like something my sister would do," Sebastian says, laughter resonating in his voice. I didn't realize he had a sister... I suppose there's a lot I have to learn about him.

As we approach the ship, a rope ladder is thrown down, and I can hear the boisterous voices of the crew, their excitement palpable. They missed their captain, that much is clear.

"He's back!" someone shouts from up top, and a resounding cheer echoes. It's dozens of voices strong as people rush to the railing.

Zephyr is the first to climb up, his movements graceful. When he reaches the top, he lowers something down, a platform of sorts, and Sebastian loads my trunk onto it so it can be raised up and moved onto the ship. Returning to my side, he offers me a hand, silently helping me move to the edge of the rocking boat so I can reach the ladder.

"Based on your lattice climbing, I think it's safe to assume you can make it to the top by yourself, yes?" His hand is warm against my back as I grip the rails.

"Yeah, I'll make it."

"Good, I'll be right after you."

With a deep breath, I begin my ascent, each rung of the ladder bringing me closer to my new reality. Upon reaching the deck, the sight is nothing short of overwhelming. Pirates of all shapes and sizes, in varying states of revelry, watch as Zephyr steadies me. Their mouths gape as they size me up. The white hair is typically the giveaway, but I'm starting to think they just might not be used to a woman on the ship.

Sebastian steps up behind me. Something changes in their expressions, creating smiles wide enough to reveal teeth and lively eyes. Someone whistles and it breaks the haze. His crew jumps and leaps, rushing forward to offer Sebastian claps on his back and singing his praises. It's evident that they feared he wouldn't return, but more so that they don't just look at him as their leader. The tears that leak down some of their faces tell me they're more than a crew. They're his family.

Sebastian takes my hand, guiding me through the crowd. Our intertwined fingers feel oddly comforting amidst the chaos. Someone busts through a door, coming from somewhere below deck. A woman. She shares a striking resemblance to Sebastian, but where his dark hair is made up of loose waves, her's is in tight coils, bound into a thick braid. A red bandana frames her face like a headband, revealing an oddly shaped ear, like someone has quite literally taken a bite out of it. This must be the sister, so there are differences too. Where he's tall and muscular, she's slender and barely over five feet. Where he has green eyes that are bright and stand out against his naturally tan skin, her skin tone is slightly darker and the color of her eyes matches with undertones of amber.

The woman's teary eyes stare at us. She doesn't move, even as Sebastian leaves me to close the distance, his arms held out, waiting for a hug. He stops halfway and I catch the tremble in her lower lip as she sprints toward him and barrels into his chest.

"You're a fucking idiot, you know that?" she seethes, loud enough for the crew to hear. They chuckle in response. "When I said we'd honor him, I didn't mean for you to enter the bloody gauntlet."

"I know," he says, smoothing her hair as he holds her to his chest. "But I'm here, Smee. I'm home."

She pushes off his chest, meeting his gaze. "And you're never leaving me again. Where you go, I go, from here on out."

He hooks a hand behind her head, dragging her closer so he can kiss the top of it. Suddenly, she looks past him and right at me.

"Is this her?" she asks, her gaze unwavering as it travels from my head to my toes.

"Scarlet. Her name is Scarlet and she's my wife." His sister pushes away from him and starts toward me. When she gets a couple feet away, she bows, bending at the waist like a man would. In fact, she's even wearing men's pants and boots by the look of it. Her shirt is far too revealing and skintight to not be a woman's top, but it still holds a masculine feel to it.

"It's lovely to meet you, princess," she says, standing back up. I can't pinpoint the emotion in her voice, but I don't think it's hostile.

"It's lovely to meet you too," I curtsy, realizing I'm still not quite sure what her name is. Smee is what Sebastian called her. Is that her name or an endearment?

Sebastian's voice cuts through the tension. "Smee, make sure she's comfortable." An elf with long blond hair comes up beside him. He's obnoxiously tall, easily a foot taller than Sebastian, which is saying something. His long legs cross as he props his elbow on Sebastian's shoulder but immediately removes it the moment a death glare is shot his way. The elf straightens in a snap and folds his hands together in his lap, but Sebastian maintains his glare a moment longer.

"Who's that?" I ask, and Smee turns, propping a foot out as she crosses her arms over her chest.

"That would be a rat."

"A rat?" I ask as my face twists. I've never heard of rat-shifters and definitely not that are elven decent, too.

"Not literally, he's just on my shit list. His name is Nelvin."

"Ah... I see."

I jolt when Smee's arm loops around mine, hooking at the elbow. My eyes dart to where her skin touches mine. These people, the pirates, are so informal about the way they greet others. I've barely touched anyone beyond my sisters or my father and even then, our physical interactions have been limited. I just met this woman and yet she acts as if we've been close our entire lives.

Smee leads me to what would be my quarters, going through the door she came out of. According to her, this is called the companionway and leads to the lower levels of the ship. We travel through a narrow hallway, composed of wooden walls like the hull of the ship until we reach a door with an odd symbol engraved on it. Pushing inside, I find a room that's cozy and small. It's private, with a large bed in the center and a wall dedicated to enclosed bookshelves. Glass window panes cover them, likely to keep things from falling off the shelves while at sea. Pictures and artifacts litter the shelves and a handful of books.

"Is this where Sebastian stays?" I can't see him staying here. Things hold too much of a feminine ring to them, especially in the trinkets and bedding.

"No. He'll be in the captain's quarters, but he wanted you to have a space to call your own for the time being. You're new to all of this and the pirate life can get overwhelming at first. He wanted to make sure you could escape it if you wanted to as you settle in." Smee adjusts the pillows and smooths the comforter.

"Is this yours?"

"Aye, yours now, though. I'll be in the next room over with Nelvin until you're ready to move in with my brother."

Nelvin and Zephyr appear in the doorway behind us, dragging my chest inside the room and placing it at the foot of the bed before leaving us alone. Smee doesn't waste a moment, popping the latch on the trunk and craning open the lid.

My fingers slide over the glass plane in front of the books. "You have a good collection." Eyeing the well-worn spines, I don't recognize the names.

"We spend many nights at sea. Those stories are the only escape I get most nights."

She appears at my side, opening the cabinet to pull out one made of dimpled, blue leather. She hands it to me and I'm surprised by how heavy it is.

"This one's about the sirens of the North. My favorite."

"Educational or fiction?" I ask, resisting the urge to open it up.

"Fiction—definitely. I don't think I'd survive reading anything else. I'm more of a romance person, and let's just say the sirens don't lure men to their death in that one."

I press my lips together, nodding my understanding before placing it back on the shelf and closing the door. "Sounds captivating."

"Oh, it is. Do you read?"

"All the time," I say as I stand to pull my things from the chest. "Mostly adventure stories. Some have romance too. I've never been outside the castle and the courtyards, so anything that tells me about the world surrounding it typically grabs my attention."

"Well, in that case, you're about to see quite a bit. We're porting in the Luminaries first, then if you go with us, we'll be heading back to the mainland. We're supposed to port near Mortys."

"For what? Why not go there first? It's closer." I pause, setting the dress in my hands onto the thick fur comforter.

"I don't ask those questions. I'm sure Hook has his reasons."

"He mentioned you were looking for something important. Is that in Mortys?"

"We hope so. My brother has waited a long time to find it."

The ship creaks and the floor rocks slightly. "What was that?" I grip the edge of the bed and Smee laughs.

"We're leaving the bay. Or rather, the anchor has been pulled so we can. It's alright." Her smile meets her eyes as she takes the dress, popping open a hidden door on the wall that leads to a shallow wardrobe.

I stand, moving to a port hole in the wall that gives a view of the ocean. The castle looks so small from here, like a replica someone has built on a table instead of the imposing towers I've wandered through. The trunk lid shuts with a smack and I turn to find her opening the bedroom door. The sound of music and raucous laughter filters into the room.

"Come on, princess, let's show you around."

"Scarlet," I remind her. Smee smirks, like my rejection of the title suits me. I might be a princess by blood, but the moment I married Sebastian, I knew I'd have to adapt. Part of that is being neutral on whether I stand with or against my father. So, in the meantime, it'll be best if I try to see through their eyes and find common ground.

Smee takes me down the hall, rattling off the names of those living in the rooms around mine. I don't think I'll ever remember all of them. At least not anytime soon. She shows me where the bathrooms are, which are shared, along with the showers. Next, we go up the stairs to the mess hall, which is where the cooks on the ship will serve food for meals and where the drink taps are. It's the first floor below the desk and spans almost the entire ship in length. My room is directly below it.

"I'd take you to the bottom levels, but it's not very interesting down there. It's mostly storage. Besides, this is where everyone spends most of their time, anyway."

She's not kidding. As she pushes open the door from the stairwell, the room is alive. Dozens of men are drinking and playing cards. A handful play instruments on the far side of the room, and others dance and sing along with it. Mugs clink and laughter fills the air. The warm glow of flames in lanterns paints everything and everyone in a golden hue.

Sebastian's commanding presence draws a crowd as the men gather around him, asking questions and demanding tales of his fight. Some of the other crew members cast me side glances as Smee drags me toward the wooden barrels. Odd metal pegs jut from the curved surface.

"Whisky, wine, water, or beer?" She spins, handing me a mug.

"Um... water I guess."

"Wine it is." She nudges my hand toward a barrel and pulls up on the metal spike in the side. A metallic purple liquid spills into the glass. It's not just any kind of wine. It's fairy wine. I've seen my father drink it, but I've never been granted a taste. It's a delicacy and reserved for only the most precious moments in the Solarian castle. Even then my father hoards it like there will never be more made. There's got to be at least a dozen or more barrels of it.

"How..." I breathe out the word before I can stop myself.

"What? The wine?"

"Yes, the wine," I say, letting the sarcasm flow. "It's rare, isn't it?"

"Not where we're from. It's just as common as anything else. Have you ever tried it?" I shake my head and she pushes up on the bottom of the glass, silently telling me to drink up. "You're in for a real treat, then. Just be careful. It's strong."

12

Scarlet

I lift the glass to my lips, letting the fairy wine fill my mouth. My senses explode and I moan at the taste. It has a magical sweetness to it, swirling with hits of wild berries that give it a tart aftertaste. It's heaven in a bottle—or in this case, a barrel.

"Told you it'd be good," Smee says, but I'm already taking another sip, letting my eyes close, savoring the taste. "Come on. Let's go find the boys."

She leads me toward Sebastian, the elf—Nevlin—and Zephyr, but others I don't know yet are with them at a round table. As we near, I eavesdrop, taking another sip of the fairy wine.

"Glad you didn't die, Captain. Smee would make a horrendous leader," the elf says, winking at Smee and flashing his teeth. The top of his tongue runs along the point of one of his incisors.

Smee punches him in the arm, making him grimace. "Keep it up. You'll be sleeping on the deck."

Still, it doesn't stop Nelvin from pulling her into his lap. I stand awkwardly, not sure what to do with my hands or what to say, so I keep sipping. Sebastian chuckles, lifting from his seat to offer it to me. "Relax, Smee. He just doesn't want to be floated."

"Why do you call it that? Since I heard it earlier, I've been trying to figure that out." I set my cup down on the table and start to lean back against the chair, only to realize it's a stool and my shoulder blades meet Sebastian's body. He stiffens for a moment but rests a hand on my shoulder.

Smee smirks, eyeing her brother while answering my question. "It's what we do to blood witches when we throw them overboard. The ocean rejects them. They don't sink. They float until some beast decides they're dinner."

I swallow hard. So Zelix was right. They do hate the blood witches, so much so that they turn them into fish food. Lifting my glass to my lips, I attempt to use the fairy wine to hide my shock. "How do you know if they're a witch?"

"They rot," Nelvin says, his voice angelic, every syllable perfectly executed. He holds a dark glint in his eyes. "Blood witches rot from inside out. It's impossible to predict how much of a sacrifice they'll need to cast their spells, so their bodies often have to pay the rest of the price. It starts with their teeth and eyes. Then, well, the whole hag transformation follows—"

Sebastian interrupts him, glaring over my shoulder. "We make sure, Scarlet. Always. We've never floated an innocent."

From the crowd, someone bellows, "We float them ugly bitches, don't we!" The crowd roars, but Sebastian sighs, drawing out a long exhale as if he's had enough already.

I force a smile, though it feels more like a grimace. He doesn't know I'm a witch, and I can't help but wonder how he would react if he knew the truth. The laughter of the crew rings in my ears, their drunken words echoing like a taunt. Two days. I have two days to figure out how to hide it or to ensure no one sees it. Ever.

Sebastian's hand squeezes my shoulder, his thumb drawing lazy circles. "Easy," he whispers, having bent to put his mouth next to my ear. His voice is low and comforting. "You're not one of them. You have nothing to worry about, and I'll make sure you never have to see it."

Zephyr's fingers intertwine with the man's next to him. A druid by the look of it, which makes my heart ease a bit. So, it's only blood witches... Mages and druids are okay with them. They just don't want those who use sacrificial magic.

His eyes meet mine and he gives a slight nod, silently letting me—or maybe Sebastian behind me—know he understands and changes the subject. "Soon, we'll get your shadow back. You must be antsy now that we can look on the mainland."

Shadow? I crane my neck, glancing at Sebastian. His jaw is set, and his eyes are narrowed at Zephyr. Apparently, that wasn't the subject change he wanted.

"You don't have your shadow? But I saw you control the darkness..." I whisper.

"They're different. One's an element and one is part of my soul." His eyes never leave Zephyr. "Thanks for that."

My mind races, but before I can ponder too much into it, Smee nudges my glass. "Drink. I think you're going to need it."

The fairy wine is unlike anything I've tasted and its warmth spreads through me instantly. After a few sips, the world seems a bit brighter, my senses heighten. As the pirates chit chat and I finish the glass, I'm very aware of the euphoric feeling that settles over me. The noises drift in and out, the room blurring in a way, yet focused in another.

Sebastian shakes his head as if he too is experiencing the same mind-fog. Reaching for my glass, he pushes it away from me. "That's enough of that. Come on." I take his hand and my head swims the moment my legs stretch, like a blood rush, or maybe it's all left my head.

"Where are ya going?" The man holding Zephyr's hand says, a crease forming between his brows.

"Taking my wife to her room."

A flurry swarms through my stomach at the mention of Sebastian calling me his wife. It shouldn't—I barely know him—but it does all the same.

"Not without a dance, you're not. It's a rite of passage when someone gets married. We even made Zephyr and Lorian do it."

I notice the rings on their fingers. They're married. Lifting my hand, I school my features before they can give away my thoughts. It's not customary for a royal wedding to have rings. It's a commoner thing, yet a part of me wants one.

"Fine, one." Sebastian loops his arm around me, guiding me toward the group of pirates playing music. "Are you alright?" His bright green eyes search mine as he turns me toward him.

"I'm fantastic," I lie. "I've never been drunk before, but I've seen others. My tongue doesn't work. My feet are numb, and I can feel my face."

He snorts out a laugh, dropping his head forward as he lines up our feet. His hand laces with one of mine and his other presses against my spine, smoothing down the curve of it until it presses to my lower back. When he lifts his head, his smile nearly stops my heart. It's so genuine… and so much more significant than I realized.

I've learned about shadow loss. My father experimented with it a bit and, oddly enough, science was the only thing he'd willingly talk to me about. It's what kept me calm when he tried to figure out how to remove my mark. Some of his tactics were easier to endure than others, but somehow, learning new, fascinating things kept me grounded. It kept me sane.

A person's shadow houses a part of their soul. It can be powerful if it's harnessed properly, but the loss of it steals away the host's ability to feel any emotion on an intimate level besides pain. Everything is muted in a sense. They still feel things, like how a person can feel a ghost pass through them. It's faint, but there, and nothing like it would be if they were whole.

Does the blood oath even work with someone without a shadow? Since he took it, I thought it could. There were moments that he seemed aware, like when they were talking about the witches, but what if I'm just not as good at masking my emotions as I thought? What if he's just perspective?

"You're spiraling." His breath is warm against my neck. "Are you sure you're up to this?"

"We're here, aren't we? We might as well stay in your crew's good graces."

He straightens, watching me for a moment as we drift in gentle circles. If it weren't for his strong, steady form holding me up, I'd be tripping all over the place. The music fades into the background and I become acutely aware of every point of contact between us—the heat of his palm against mine, the steadying grip of his other hand on my waist, the brush of his thigh against my leg. Our eyes lock, and for a moment, the world around us seems to disappear. We're not in a room full of pirates. It's just him and me.

"Is this about the room?" he asks.

I force my gaze to steady, even though everything whirls with every turn we make. "No... I understand that."

"Then what is it you don't understand?" He stops us even though the music continues to play. "Did I do something?"

"No... It's just the wine. I think I've had enough festivities today."

He leads me through the crowd of the mess hall and down to my room. Once inside, I sit on the trunk, hinging at the waist to slip off my shoes, but his hand swats me away.

"We'll need to get you better shoes. These won't work here." He unclasps the tiny buckles of my flats. "You need something with soles. I'll check with Smee in the morning and see if she might have some you can borrow."

His touch is gentle, each movement considerate. "Thank you," I say, closing my eyes to block out the vertigo. He holds out a hand, helping me to my feet.

"Spin," he commands, and I turn my back to him. He makes quick work of the corset strings, loosening it enough that I can slip it along with the layers of my dress past my hips and step out. I stumble the second I lift up my foot from the ground, but his arm wraps around my bare stomach to steady me. "Rule number one of being on my ship, don't drink your weight in fairy wine."

Blinking hard, I arch a brow as I spin to face him. I'm immediately aware of how clothed he is and how not I am. "There are rules?"

"There are now." His voice is stern, but I can see the smile in his eyes, the way they crease ever so slightly at the corners. It dissipates the moment his gaze dips to my chest.

I chuckle silently as his throat bobs. His tongue darts across his lips, wetting them as he drinks in the sight of me, and it turns my insides into knots... I only have two days. After that, I might never be able to be with him like this again, unless I can find a way to hide my mark. My gaze travels down his throat, along the unbuttoned edge of the top of his shirt. His coat is long gone, his sleeves rolled to reveal his dark tattoos.

Before I can stop myself, I reach for his necklace, turning the dark amber stone over in my hands. Its raw edges are rough against my skin, and he watches me intently. "What is this?"

"It's sea flame." Sebastian reaches behind his neck and unclasps the necklace, then places it in my hand. "When exposed to water, it acts as a beacon. My father gave it to me when I was little."

"So he could find you if you went overboard." I finish the thought for him, holding the stone up to the light.

"Yes. I've had it ever since."

I hand it back, but he shakes his head. "Until we get to port, you should keep it." He walks to the hidden wardrobe door and pops it open, just like Smee did, and grabs one of my nightgowns. Fishing my arms through the straps, I let him tug it on.

"Will you help me?" I ask, gathering my hair and pulling it over my shoulder so he can clasp the necklace on. His hands linger on my neck. I shudder when his fingers trail over my collarbone and down my arm. "Why didn't you tell me about your shadow?"

"And now the truth comes out," he says, chuckling beneath his breath. "I knew it was something."

"How can I know if the blood oath works for you without it?"

He presses his lips to my pulse and I fight the urge to close my eyes. It feels so good when he kisses me like that... I feel wanted—desired. Needed. "Ask any of my men. I think all of them will tell you I'm different than I was before I left. I've felt more in the last day than I have in the last twenty-four years."

My head snaps to the side as I glance at him. "You're only twenty-four? You're only a year older than me."

There's an airy humor in his tone. "I'm twenty-eight. I was four when my shadow was taken. I don't remember much about before, but I can tell you that since we've been bound, I'm starting to remember what it was like."

"How so?" I twist and sit on the edge of the bed. His boots thud against the wooden floor as he steps closer, pushing my hair behind my ear.

"You already know the answer to that. The oracle said as much. I feel everything you do. Under normal circumstances, it's diluted, but to me, since I don't feel much at all, it's stronger... You should get some rest."

With a curt nod, I settle down into the bed, pulling the thick fur blanket up to my shoulders. It's soft against my skin. Sebastian leans down to kiss my forehead.

"Thank you for everything," I say, snuggling into the pillow.

"Don't mention it, darling," he whispers as he steps back into the shadow being cast along the floor by the lantern hanging on the wall. The darkness wraps around him and he disappears.

13
SCARLET

The moment my boots hit the dock, the harsh ambiance hits harder. The cold stones, slick with something I hope is just seawater, make for treacherous footing. The coarse laughter of sailors, the grating sound of ropes strained to their limits—it's all so jarring. But nothing prepares me for the raw crystals jutting up from the ground. They're huge... Each splits light into a riot of colors and pulses through the land and from beneath the water. The waves hold a blue iridescent glow as they roll off the black sand along the coast as if the stars themselves had come to rest here. I've never witnessed anything like it before.

"Welcome to the Luminaries, Scarlet. Your new home," Sebastian says, helping me down off the dock.

I tear my gaze away from the crystals to take in the bustling port. A magical mix of creatures fills the streets. Mages, merfolk, and elementals, I'm sure. Some are light elves, like Nelvin with pale skin and hair, and other various shifter-like creatures or non-humanoid ones like Zephyr. The buildings are a blend of architectural styles, some elegant and regal, others are quaint and charming. It's mesmerizing.

"Let's go bitches," Smee says, catching up to us. "I've never been so happy to be home. Just wait, Scarlet, you're going to love it here."

We make our way through the labyrinth of cobblestone streets, leaving the lively port behind. There are shops and bars, a bakery, and so much more as we pass. It's a city…but it's also a city filled with rebels and their descendants. As I take in my surroundings, I'm also very aware of the glares I get as we pass. My hair is a dead giveaway of my lineage and, clearly, Sebastian's people weren't enthusiastic about him becoming a prince. Or maybe they just aren't about him being married to me.

I can feel their stares, the unease that ripples off the villagers as we pass. If I didn't know any better, I'd think I was on my way to be executed. Shaking my head, I try to dispel the nerves that seem to spark with warning. Even my body knows I'm unwanted here. It makes the hair on my arms and the nape of my neck stand on end.

It isn't long before we arrive at their family home, tucked away in a quiet corner of the island. Its exterior is made of wooden shingles, painted a nautical blue, the roof from some sort of metal that's covered in moss and carpeting flowers. Where the other homes we've passed have been placed side by side, their home has a small section of land around it. The grounds are landscaped with some sort of iridescent moss I've never seen before, but it lights up beneath the canopy of trees surrounding the small structure.

"Home sweet home," Smee mutters, rushing up the two steps of the front porch and pushing open the heavy, wooden door.

As I step inside, I'm struck by the beauty of the place. Tall windows let in streams of sunlight, illuminating dust particles that flurry through the air as we move. Sheets cover most of the furniture, but it's the mementos of Sebastian's father that truly make this house feel alive. It's like stepping into another era, one where Captain James Hook's presence is as palpable as the air itself. His legacy is everywhere—in the form of frayed maps, trinkets, pictures, and more.

"Sebastian," I say softly, turning to him. His eyes hold a dark ring to them. The usual kaleidoscope of greens now is barely separated from the dark pupils in their middle. It's nostalgia... Something tells me he's no longer with us in the realm of the living. Between Smee's teary eyes and their frozen stares, I don't need a blood bond to feel their heartache.

Sebastian shakes his head, blinking long and hard before offering me a forced smile. "It's been a long time since we've been here," he admits, his voice barely audible. "But it's your home now, just as much as ours."

"Ours," I echo, the word feeling both foreign and familiar on my tongue. In this house, surrounded by memories of a life I never knew, I can't help but feel like I don't belong. This will take some getting used to. And I just hope Sebastian's people will come to accept me the way his crew has. His friends had no problem introducing themselves and making me feel included, and though I didn't get a chance to talk to many of the crewmen on his ship, since it only took us a day and a half to sail here, they weren't hostile either. The people we passed on the streets, though, looked like they wouldn't have any problem putting me in the gallows.

Sebastian and Smee begin to peel back the sheets on the furniture, and each uncovers beautifully carved pieces that only a master woodworker could make. The couch and chairs are lined with blood-red velvet, the floors a dark wood. Even the windows are unique, made of textured glass panes that someone has cut and shaped into images of a mermaid and the sea, but they're still clear.

As we walk deeper into the home, Sebastian points out various portraits lining the walls, but I can't look away from one in particular. His father. The man in the painting looks fierce, with piercing eyes and a confident, almost arrogant stance. I can see the resemblance between him and Sebastian, both possessing an air of authority and a magnetic charisma.

"Was he good to you?" I ask, curiosity getting the better of me.

Sebastian hesitates for a moment before answering. "He was a complicated man, but he loved us in his own way. He never hurt us, if that's what you're asking. He was just a captain first and a father second."

"Sometimes that's all we can ask for." I trace the ornate edge of the frame with my finger. There's a little boy in the photograph with him, just a toddler, but there's no doubt that it's Sebastian.

Each room we stepped into reveals another piece of the puzzle which is my new husband. I find myself drawn to the smaller details, like the intricate carvings on the wooden banisters and the worn pages of books that must have been read countless times. Ship models sit on wooden bookcases, intricate maps marked with Xs and cryptic symbols adorn the walls, and a table stands in one corner, cluttered with sealed letters and trinkets.

"Quite a collection, isn't it?" Smee catches me taking in the relics in the living room. Her boots clap against the floor as she moves closer, reaching for a black feather the size of my forearm. "He was quite the man. He swore this was a feather passed down through generations of our family, that it belonged to the Devil himself. I'm pretty certain it was a lie. He used to threaten to summon him with it when me and my brother would act up."

She hands it to me and I run the smooth edge over my palm. "Where do you think it's from then?"

"My guess? A bird or something, but as kids, we didn't question it."

"Sebastian... he must have looked up to him, huh?" I hand the feather back and she places it onto the shelf.

"More than you'll ever know."

Sebastian emerges from the hallway, his gaze falling on me as I pretend to study the map on the wall. He needs his space.

"While I'm gone, make this place feel like home for you. I'll make sure your trunk is brought by," he says, his boots thudding against the wooden floors as he starts toward the front door.

"You're leaving?" Hustling after him, I catch up in the foyer.

"Yes. Smee will ensure you're taken care of and she'll be here if you need anything." He steps closer and leans down to press his lips to mine. They taste of salt and sea, with a hint of fairy wine. It makes me almost forget that he's leaving, which I hope is just him saying he's running an errand or something.

"Ugh, get a room," Smee says, and as we pull apart, I catch the end of her eye roll. "You can't seriously be benching me? You promised."

"I'm sorry, but it's too dangerous for Scarlet to go." Sebastian's voice is firm. "You're the only person I trust to keep her safe."

"Get Zephyr to do it. Lorian might have to stay too, but finding your shadow is as important for me as it is for you. We agreed. It was Father's last wish. I need to help you do this." She pokes a finger at his chest and his eyes glance at it, but nothing else moves.

"You are by making sure Scarlet's protected and taken care of."

"How long?" I ask, trying to ease the tension between them.

Sebastian closes his eyes and lets out a long breath before glancing at me. "I don't know, but I'll come back as soon as I can. I promise."

"You can't just leave me here. This entire island is filled with people who despise my father. What happens when one of them decides to take out their grudges on me?"

"No one will dare touch you. They know who you belong to and they respect me and my family too much to cross us in that way."

"That's not enough," I say, shaking my head. "You underestimate how much revenge can impact someone."

"I know the feeling personally. Trust me."

He turns to start toward the door, but I rush to get in front of him, blocking his exit. "It's not that I question you, but I don't trust them. Don't leave me here. You promised me I'd get to see the world, not take a boat ride."

"I'm sorry, Scarlet." He disappears before my eyes, using his shadows to escape. I sprint to the windows, finding him walking down the pathway toward the cobblestone street. That asshole...

"Damn him," Smee mutters under her breath, her eyes narrowing at the place where he stood just moments ago.

"We have to go after him." Stalking into the foyer, Smee blocks my path.

"I'm sorry, but I won't defy my brother. He's the captain, and what he says goes."

"Fine then, don't." I mosey back into the living room, arms crossed firmly across my chest. "The least you can do is tell me where the bathroom is."

"Down the hall. Last door on the left."

Following her directions, I disappear into the dark hallway, not bothering to light the lanterns mounted there. Once out of sight, I use my mage magic to subtly light up the space. There are hooks at the end of the hall, holding up coats and hats. At least what I think are hats? I've never seen any like these before, not in Solaria, but on the way here I saw multiple people wearing them on their heads on the streets. I'm not sure why they've chosen to wear their overly-sized socks like hats, but it will do. If I'm going to follow after Sebastian and not draw attention, I'll need to hide my hair.

Snatching it from the hook, I slip into the bathroom, coiling my hair on top of my head and placing the sock over it. It's the same creamy white color as my flesh, and if it weren't for the knitted fabric, I wouldn't know where my face and the cap begins. As is, I can barely see with it on. It hangs close to my eyes, rubbing against my lashes.

This is absolutely ridiculous... Folding up the edge of the stocking up so I can see, I stare at my reflection for a long moment. I look like a feminine penis with eyeballs. Scoffing, I try to wipe the image from my mind. This is what his people dress like? Why? Who decided this was okay? I can't live in these conditions.

Flipping the latch on the window, I gently push the pane up until the hole is large enough for me to fit through. With a jump, I hoist myself onto the sill and leap down to the ground, dusting my hands off on my dress.

Here goes nothing.

Staying here is a death wish. I don't know Smee, I barely know Sebastian, but I know enough to believe if I stay here without him, someone will try something. Smee is only one person. She can't face an entire island. Not alone.

Granted, it'd be easier to hide my mark if I stay here. No one has to see me without clothes, but what good is that when it's not my witch mark they care about, but the blood running through my veins and my maiden name? I know my father isn't the best man. He's done things—unspeakable things in the name of kingdom and country. Who knows how much he's harmed these people?

I move swiftly through the streets, keeping my head down but staying vigilant. My heart races, fueled by both adrenaline and determination. Tracing our steps from the port, it's only a matter of time before I spot the ship along the docks. Sailors shout and the glowing water laps against the wooden sides of the boats in port.

They've erected a tent near where the Jolly Roger is moored, and a line of pirates carry things down the ramp from the deck while another is bringing things aboard. Convincing Sebastian might be out of the question. He's already made up his mind and he doesn't seem like the type to change it once it's made up. However, if I'm already on the ship, I doubt he'd turn around to bring me back...

As stealthily as I can, I inch closer, peeking between the canvas flaps to ensure no one is inside. I won't be able to walk up the ramp and board. Anyone with eyeballs would notice, but there might be something here I can hide inside of.

The tent is filled with storage items, trunks, and crates, providing me with plenty of options. I choose one of the larger trunks, testing the latch and breathing a sigh of relief when it opens. It'll do. I can fit inside. I'm just not sure how I'll close it from within it and if they see the latch open, they might check inside.

"Scarlet," Sebastian's voice calls out, startling me. He stands at the entrance of the tent, his green eyes narrowed as they find me crouching next to the trunk. "You were supposed to stay with Smee."

I chew my lip, rising from the ground. "How did you know?"

"She told me."

"I just got here myself. There's no way she'd have beaten me here when she didn't know I left."

"She's an elemental. She used her gift to tell me that you escaped. What if something would've happened to you?"

"That's exactly it," I say, stomping forward. "You leave me here and something might. Anyone with an inkling of a brain knows they could use me as leverage against my father. They just don't realize he wouldn't care enough to take the bait. Don't put me in that position. Please." I hadn't intended to beg, but I'm out of options.

Sebastian thrusts his ringed fingers through his hair, leaving it disheveled. "I'm sorry…"

"You bastard… Why let me live if you were just going to let me die here while you're off doing gods know what? I am your wife. We had a deal. Either honor it or take me home."

He steps closer, his jaw set as the muscles at the hinge flex. "I honored it already. I told you I'd treat you well and make sure you had a good life. I promised to show you the world outside your castle. Now, where are you?"

I take a step back.

"This isn't Solaria, Scarlet. Have you been harmed since your life fell into my care? No. I kept my promise despite the fact you didn't. Despite the fact, that I could've died in that arena. Don't push me. A pirate ship is dangerous and no place for a lady. Now, I'm going to go get Zephyr so he can—" he pauses, watching me as I dig through the chest I'd intended to hide in.

Ironically enough, it had his name on it. I dig through the clothes until I find something that works, then begin to untie my dress. Working the fabric off my body, I shove my arms through one of his shirts, kick off my boots, and begin to shove my legs through a pair of his leather pants.

"What in the hell are you doing?" He blinks rapidly before tearing his eyes off me and scanning the tent, likely making sure we're alone.

"Not being a lady." I tuck the excess fabric of his shirt into the pants that fit decently around my waist, but I have to roll the length up multiple times to get them to rest right on my boots. I finish doing the buttons on the shirt as I turn back to face him. "Are you going to gawk all day? We have places to see, Captain." I rip the hat off my head, tossing it and my dress in the trunk before shutting it and storming out of the tent. He's on my heels in seconds as I climb the ramp to the deck.

"Scarlet!" His voice is stern, yet it sends a thrill through me in the most inappropriate ways. "Scarlet! Stop!" I keep walking until I clear the rail of the deck. His hand latches onto my shoulder, forcing me to turn around. "You're insufferable. If I tell you to stop, you stop."

"What are you going to do? Leave me here? Kill me? Well, get in line!"

He's still for a moment, our bodies so close the tension feels like electricity—like power—rolling over my skin. My face is inches from his and the wind whips my hair with the breeze. Sebastian's teeth grind as he glares at me, anger flashes in his eyes strong enough to burn my soul, but I don't dare look away.

I lived. I'm breathing. I'm grateful to him for making that so, but I'm in no rush to put myself back on death's doorstep. It's high time this princess took her fate into her own hands, and I will not be left here. His gaze is unwavering. It takes everything I have not to shrink away from him.

"What would it look like if someone harmed your wife while you were gone? If they sent her in a box to the king or worse, used her like some salon whore for a power trip? You wouldn't be here to do anything about it. They'd think you're weak." I step closer. "Even kings fall when their people don't think they're strong enough to protect them. If you left and something happened to me, it'd only be a matter of time before they turn on y—"

His hand is around my throat faster than I can comprehend. He doesn't squeeze, but it's there–a reminder of what he's capable of. No matter how hard my fingers pry at his, they don't budge. Sebastian puts his face in mine, his nostrils flaring as he walks backward and I stumble, trying to keep up. Suddenly, the feel of the wood beneath my shoes changes. It's not rough and staggered. It's smooth. I look down with only my eyes, glimpsing the water below on either side in my peripheral.

No... He won't... He couldn't.

I catch the sight of the coils of darkness wrapping around his limbs. I feel it dancing over my exposed skin like it's testing me, or gearing up to strike, to drain the life from my body like I've seen him do a dozen others.

"Say it, princess. Go on now. Tell me all about how the people you just met will revolt."

My foot slides back as I feel for the end of the plank. The air whirls around us, shaking the thin platform enough to make my heart hammer into my ribs, hard enough to crack bone. If I go overboard, who knows how deep that water is... I doubt it'd be deep enough to accommodate a fall that far. Even if it was, I can't swim. I'd drown right next to the shore. I know I should look down, but I don't want to see it. Instead, I cling to him, desperate to not go over the edge.

Sebastian pulls me forward until his breath fans my face. "What, now fear has your tongue? You seemed so brave a few seconds ago, little lamb..." His eyes take on a menacing tone, yet the smirk on his lips scares me more. "Anyone who dared to question my ability would only do so for a second. Then their heart would cease beating and I'd get another shadow for my collection. But if you're so worried, perhaps I should rid myself of the burden."

"Please don't." I hate the desperation in my voice, but I don't want to die today. "I can't swim."

I could use my gift, demanding him to step back, but it's only a temporary solution. I'm still on this island with people who hate my very existence, and I can't control him or his crew forever. Certainly not long enough to get back to the mainland. If he saw me as a threat, he'd order to have me killed—assuming he doesn't do it himself. I've never controlled more than a handful of people at once. If it comes to that, I'd have to make sure it's enough to make the most feared man in the realm scared of me.

"Give me one good reason I shouldn't drop you off that edge." Think, Scarlet. Think. "Make it good. Your life depends on—"

I kick off the sliver of the plank beneath my feet and crush my lips to his. He stiffens but quickly gives in. I put everything I have into it, hoping his newfound emotions will be enough to distract him, enough to remind him that if I die, he stops feeling again.

Sebastian's hand loosens on my throat, moving to cup the back of my neck, holding me to him. He leans into it, kissing me like I'm the air his starving lungs need. It tilts my weight onto my heels, which are barely on the edge. Just as my heart begins to settle, just as I start to believe he'll spare me, he breaks the kiss. The clasp on the necklace he let me wear releases and he lets go.

My arms whirl as I try to reclaim my balance, but it's too late. I slip off the edge and a scream tears through me, loud enough to rupture my eardrums as I plummet toward the water. For a moment, time seems to stretch indefinitely. My heartbeat slows to a strong, steady rhythm as the wind rushes past my face. I stare up at Sebastian, crouched on the edge of the plank with a smirk on his lip. The necklace dangles from his hand as he watches me fall.

This is it... My last moments and those godsdamn dimples still get to me.

I close my eyes, knowing the ground can't be much farther, but as I let go, I'm snatched from the sky. My body is launched up before I fall again, each bounce losing momentum. I'm in something, some kind of web. I suck air into my lungs, my eyes shooting wide as I push myself up, finding a rope net all around me, stretched taut from the ship to the dock.

Sebastian chuckles up above and I scowl up at where he now sits on the plank. "Memorize it, darling. That sinking pit in your stomach as you fall toward the unforgiving waves... Remember it next time you want to test me because there won't be a net to save you. I don't have to honor my end of the deal. You didn't. I'm doing this out of the kindness of my heart, but if you continue to be difficult, I won't."

He stands and hops onto the deck, disappearing from view.

This mother fucker... My breath rakes in and out of my lungs as I flip and crawl off the net. I storm up the ramp and across the deck. The crew on board freezes in place, watching me as I stalk up to him. Sebastian's back is toward me. Either he's oblivious to the fact I've re-boarded or he doesn't care and thinks I'm not a threat.

Regardless, he's going to find out that he's sadly mistaken.

I yank his arm, spinning him around to face me. My ears are hot, my nostrils burning as the salty air scotches through my windpipe. His eyebrows lift, but that's all he gets to do before I lift my hands, angling my fingers toward the ground, and start pulling strings. Every man on board except for Sebastian snaps straight. Their motions are erratic as they fight to regain control. I make them step toward the rail, specifically the side of the Jolly Roger that lacks a net.

"I... helped... you..." I seethe between breaths, continuing to move the men slowly toward the edge. "I made sure you lived." Stepping forward, Sebastian matches my movement backward. "If it weren't for me, that serpent would've ripped out your throat." Taking another step, I halt his crew along the banister, leaning their weight over the rail. "If it weren't for me, you'd have a sword through your face. Must I continue to name every way in which I assured you won?"

Sebastian's eyes are flexed wide as he watches in horror. His crew teeters on the edge of the rail. One push and they'll all fall. Slowly, he turns those green eyes back on me and swallows hard. "No... That's enough."

"Good. I'll be boarding this ship. You'll need to send someone to retrieve my things." I let the magic fall and the crew jolts back from the rail, scattering like roaches in the light. "Do you understand now, Captain?"

Sebastian cranes his neck to look me up and down. "What are you?"

I narrow my gaze at him as my body trembles from the adrenaline. "I don't know, and it doesn't matter. I'll be in my room."

Without a glance back, I hurry to the companionway and the crew scatters as I near, giving me a straight shot.

14

SCARLET

I thrust my fingers through my hair and huff, staring at the lines of text that all seem to blend at this point. My back aches, my eyes burn. I've been at this for hours, and not once has that insufferable pirate captain darkened my door.

Not that I want him to.

It's been a day since we left port and I've avoided the man like a plague. Mostly, that's consisted of spending the day helping the only person on this ship who doesn't shrink at the sight of me. Smee's been tasked with logging inventory in the storage bay, the lowest level of the ship, and though the air is musky, it's better than running into him.

The soft scratching of our pens against parchment fills the silence. For the most part of the last three hours, neither of us has bothered to strike up a conversation. We let our minds entertain us as we get the job done, at least that is until I find her staring at me through the open void on the shelves. Her honey-colored, brown eyes narrow and when I try to ignore the feeling of being watched, she reaches through the shelf and yanks the pen from my hand.

"You can't avoid him forever." Her head ticks to the side as her glare deepens. "This is my quiet time. This is where I escape from the men and their antics. At this rate—seeing as you've been working circles around me—I won't have an excuse to slip away to work down here."

"He pushed me off his ship. He's dead to me."

She snorts. "Dead to you? I don't need a blood oath to see the way you look at him—or how he looks at you. You're both fucking smitten, knee-deep in the Cupcake Phase. He's nowhere near dead to you. I'm pretty sure if he batted his eyelashes at you from the doorway, you'd swoon."

"What is the cupcake phase?" I ask, shaking my head at her as if it'll help me understand. Is that a commoner thing? A pirate thing? Sometimes I feel like she speaks a foreign language.

"Dear gods... We need to get you out more. Your innocence is showing." Her eyes roll before they glance back at me. "The cupcake phase is when two people first get together. Nothing else in the world exists but the two of them. They have this uncontrollable urge to touch each other at all times and can't stop staring. It's obnoxious, but I get it. The blood oath really sped things up for y'all on that front."

"And you think we're in this? Have you seen him?" I set the wooden placard I've been using to write on down, along with my paper. "I might've agreed with you a couple days ago, when we first got to the ship, but I barely recognize him now. It makes it seem like I didn't know anything about him at all."

"That's because you didn't. The both of you have been thrust onto this collision course and shaken up with magic. Nothing is normal, but it has only been a handful of days. My brother hasn't felt much of anything in years and now he's been hit with every emotion you feel. It wasn't right, what he did...but he's also going through more than any of us can understand."

"You shouldn't make excuses for him. Noble men own their decisions. They think before they act. I'm not a toy that he can dangle off a ship to get a rise out of and he didn't respect that."

Smee gives me a knowing look. "Says the girl who would've died three days ago."

My body stiffens as I zone out on the floor.

"Look," Smee says, her voice softening. "I didn't mean it like that, but you have to understand, your version of 'noble men' and mine are different. The men on this ship might not be swimming in riches, but they're good men. You pushed him and he had to make an example."

"He could've found another way." I pick at the hem of Sebastian's shirt. He never did bring my things. They were in too much of a rush to get ahead of the incoming storm to send someone back for them. I haven't ever not worn a corset around people, yet there's something freeing about it.

"You told him, in front of all his crew, that the people would mutiny. Do you not realize how big of a deal that is? Threatening mutiny is usually a death sentence. Had it been any man on this ship who'd spoken to him that way, Nelvin or Zephyr included, they'd be dead. He spared you."

"I didn't threaten to mutiny him. I simply stated his people would if he allowed someone to hurt me." My head dips, watching the fabric fray between my fingers.

"It's the same thing, Scarlet."

"Well, it's cruel."

"It's the same customs your world shares. If someone made a similar comment to the king, do you truly believe your father wouldn't have them hanged or executed?" I don't answer. "Exactly. They have to make an example because all it takes is one seeded thought and more start to think the same way."

"It wasn't my intention. I just didn't want to be left behind."

Her lips quirk up into a wry smile. "If it makes you feel any better, the captain's been sulking around all day. I think he's waiting for you to yell at him." She stands and rounds the end of the shelf between us, peering down at me.

My nails bite into my palms. "He'll be waiting a long while, then."

"Just talk to him, Scarlet. He's dense, but he means well." I arch a brow, unconvinced. Smee sighs, throwing up her hands in defeat. "Think about it. It's not like you're married for life or anything." She twists and starts to make her way toward the door. Her boots thud against the floor and the sword at her hip clinks with every stride. "I have to go check on the rigging. Don't stay here too long, or you'll start growing barnacles."

"Ha ha," I respond dryly, rolling my eyes as she leaves the room.

Something moves to the right of the door like it's hidden in the air... or the shadow there. My face falls. How long has he been hiding?

"Are you going to show yourself or continue eavesdropping?" I ask, hoping I'm not going mad but also not really wanting to see him either. Maybe it was just the porthole light or dust. The longer I stare at the shadowed space, the more of the outline of the man I see. "Stop it. It's rude."

Sebastian steps out of the shadow and his form takes shape. He's leaning against the wall, arms crossed over his broad chest. Striking green eyes track me as I try to maintain my business-as-usual appearance and ignore him as I stand and carry a small box to the appropriate shelf. In my peripheral, I can see the muscles of his jaw feathering. He looks about as enthused as I feel.

"Well, aren't you a vision," he purrs, pushing off the doorframe to drift closer. "I nearly snapped one of my men's necks because he tied a rope wrong. Considering I couldn't care less how shit is tied as long as it holds, I thought I might have you to thank for that." His eyes drift over me before returning to mine. "Clearly, I was right."

I scowl harder when he flashes those dimples, hating how it sends a wave of heat through my body as if on cue. "What do you want?"

"I want many things, love." He braces his hands on the desk behind me, caging me between his arms as he leans down. "But for now, I'll settle for a smile. It seems if you're not happy, I'm not happy and I can't do my job like this."

His scent envelops me, like the sea and something darker - something tempting and forbidden—and a hint of fairy wine. I wet my lips, struggling to form a coherent thought.

"What? Want me to apologize? For what? I did nothing to you that you didn't provoke."

"For avoiding me." Sebastian's eyes gleam with something predatory. Hungry even and it takes everything I have to look away from it. My brain can't function properly when he looks at me like that. "You can't ignore me forever."

I clench my jaw. "Watch me."

He chuckles, the sound rumbling in his chest. "I think you'd rather me do more than watch, little lamb."

"Stop calling me that." I scoff.

"But that's what you are." His lips form a mischievous smirk. "My stubborn and absolutely insufferable sacrificial lamb."

"It's not helping your case." My breath hitches as one of his hands slides down to grip my hip. My body tenses, as if it's warring between fury and desire. I try to shove him away, but he doesn't budge. "Let me go."

"Or what?" His brows arch. "You going to pull my strings? Go ahead."

The dim lanterns cast everything in a murky glow, including him. Yet, somehow, the amber lighting seems to accent his chiseled jaw, and his long dark eyelashes. It draws attention to every inky line peeking out from beneath his linen shirt. It's wrong... all of it.

Having lingered for too long, I tear my eyes away. It's an impossible predicament. He's everything I should hate, yet he can give me everything I want. I'm starting to think I've been cursed twice. Once by my mother and once by the gods or whoever put our fates on a collision course. I should've let the troll eat me. Had I, I wouldn't feel betrayed right now. I wouldn't feel anything, for that matter.

I grip the edge of the desk tighter, not wanting to admit butterflies are spinning inside my stomach. My heart is pounding. Sebastian's presence fills the room—it fills the very air I breathe—yet I can't hide the shiver that races down my spine.

"What do you want?" I ask, trying to maintain my composure.

"You... to stop being angry," he says, his voice low and seductive. The tension between us is palpable, like a live wire ready to spark.

"Pushing me off that plank was the most diabolical thing you could've done." I shoot back, glaring at him.

He sighs, leaning away from me to run a hand through his dark waves. His eyes soften as he resumes his position, trapping me against the desk. "I knew the net was there, and I get that you're angry, but you also need to understand my side, too. Just as Smee said, I had to do something. I've killed men—good men that were beloved on this crew—for talking to me like that and spouting out ideas of mutiny. Had I not, the men you puppeteer'd on the deck would've thought of me as a hypocrite. I would've floated their friends, but let you do the same thing without consequence. I knew that net was there, and I'll never tell you to hold your tongue about something that doesn't sit right, but please, refrain from doing it in front of my crew."

The sympathy in Sebastian's eyes is almost palpable and it unnerves me.

"I think it's best if you leave," I say, my voice shaky.

He hesitates, clearly not wanting to be done with this conversation, but I'm not ready to share anymore. I seize my window to slip out from between him and the desk and remove the stopper to hold open the door, signaling for him to exit. To my surprise, he doesn't budge.

"Scarlet, we need to talk about this," he insists, his voice low and commanding.

"Maybe later, but not now."

"Fine," Sebastian says reluctantly, stepping closer to the door. But instead of leaving, he smirks and slams the door shut again. The lock clicks into place, trapping us inside until Smee returns.

"Sebastian!" I yank on the handle, but it doesn't budge. His dark eyes hold a hint of amusement as he watches me struggle.

"Give it a rest, Scarlet," he says with a sigh. "We're not getting out of here until Smee comes back."

"That's not true. You can use your shadows."

"I could... under normal circumstances. However, do you see the runes on the walls?"

Reluctantly, I follow his finger, finding strange markings carved and burned into the wooden planks. I thought they were some sort of pirate hieroglyphics or something, not runes. They seem cavemen enough for it to be believable.

"This is our storeroom. It's where we keep the important things. Things people want to steal, so those runes allow people to come in magically if they wish, but they can't leave until they use a door."

"So, no shadow hopping..."

A grin stretches across his lips. "No. None of that."

I cross my arms with a huff. "Well, isn't this just perfect?"

Sebastian leans casually against the wall to my right. "Could be worse company to be trapped with." He gives me a roguish wink.

I roll my eyes but can't help the hint of a smile tugging at my lips. Insufferable man. Shaking my head, I stroll toward the bench near the desk and take a seat. Picking up the quill pen, I start to draw on one of the blank parchment papers, waiting for Smee to come back and let us out. The silence hangs heavy, the gentle waves hitting the ship the only sound as we fall into a stalemate.

Sebastian sighs. "Are you really not going to talk to me?"

I glance up, meeting his intense gaze. "I was planning on it, yes."

He pushes off from the wall, prowling closer. "You have met my sister, haven't you? Believe me, I know how this works. You ignore me until I apologize, yes? Well, I'm sorry Scarlet."

"You have to mean it."

This close, his presence is overwhelming. I can smell the sea and sweet-scented wine on him... Feel the heat radiating from his body. My traitorous heart quickens.

"Why are you so stubborn?" he asks, tilting his head.

"Why are you such a hobgoblin?"

He stands up, a crease forming between his brows. "What the fuck is a hobgoblin?"

"It's a green little hunched-back creature—nevermind." Resuming my drawing, I tune him out.

Sebastian lets out a deep exhale, storming around the edge of the desk and jerking the bench I'm sitting on to the side so he can crouch in front of me. "I am sorry, Scarlet. I should've believed you helped me in the gauntlet, and I shouldn't have pushed you over that edge. It was wrong. Can we please bury this?" Sebastian moves even closer until his legs brush mine. "I need you to understand something," he says, his voice low. "I felt it when you were scared. I know why you're upset, but I didn't have a choice. Had I done anything less drastic, the crew wouldn't have believed it."

He takes my hand, his thumb grazing over my knuckles. The contact sends a little thrill up my arm.

"What are you saying?" I ask breathlessly.

"I'm saying, I care about what happens to you. More than I should." His eyes burn into mine.

My heart is racing now. The air between us feels electric. He leans in slowly, giving me time to pull away. But I don't. His lips meet mine, firm and insistent. The kiss deepens and I slide my hands up his chest, tangling them in his hair. He pulls me tighter against him with a low, throaty groan.

Heat pools in my core and spreads through my veins. I fist my hands in his hair as his tongue slips over mine, tasting and claiming.

"I've missed kissing you," he growls against my lips.

"It's only been a day or so. Don't be needy," I tease, as his hands slide underneath my shirt. His calloused fingers leave trails of fire on my skin. I arch into his touch, need pulsing between my legs and growing stronger by the second.

"Tell me to stop." He nips at my jaw, and my neck, and kisses away the sting. "Tell me you don't want this, and I'll stop."

Tonight's the moon phase... It might be the last chance we get before my mark returns. When I don't, triumph flashes in his eyes. His hands latch onto the thickness of my thighs as he hoists me from the bench and sets me on the edge of the desk. Sebastian doesn't waste a moment, claiming my mouth in a bruising kiss as his hands work at the buttons of my shirt. I fist the fabric of his and he chuckles, breaking the kiss just long enough to rip it over his head.

The warmth of his skin presses against mine and I melt against him, feeling his hands roam down my sides with a feather-light touch. The hard evidence of his arousal strains against his leather pants. I rock my hips against his and his jaw flexes.

The button of my pants gives and his hand is there, drawing the heel of his hand over the more sensitive part of me. It's not enough. I need more.

"So wet for me already," he rasps, biting my lower lip. "Just from a kiss? And you call me needy."

His fingers stroke teasingly, circling that sensitive spot that makes sparks explode in my vision, and sends a jolt of pleasure through me. I gasp, digging my nails into his shoulders.

He kisses me again, tongue tangling with mine as he slides two fingers into me. I cry out at the intrusion, at the fullness, and clench around him.

"That's it," he praises, pumping his fingers slowly. "Take it all, darling."

The pet name only makes the ache coil tighter, like molten desire flooding my veins. He curls his fingers, stroking that spot deep inside, and white-hot pleasure erupts through me.

I moan his name, rocking against his hand, chasing that feeling. His thumb finds my clit, rubbing quick, tight circles in time with his thrusts. The dual sensations spiral out of control, pressure building and building at the base of my spine.

"Come for me," he growls into my mouth.

My release crashes over me in a tidal wave of ecstasy. I cry out, convulsing around his fingers as the pleasure rolls through me, endless and deep.

Sebastian doesn't stop, drawing out my climax until I'm boneless and limp in his arms. Only then does he slide his fingers from me, bringing them to his mouth. His eyes close as he sucks them clean, a low groan rumbling in his chest. My mouth gapes. Did he...?

"Delicious," he purrs before kissing my cheek. "I'm not sure I'll ever get over the taste of you."

Which is why we don't hear the door open.

"Oh!" Smee's startled voice breaks through the haze. "I didn't realize you two were... Wow."

Sebastian's cheeks take on a pink tinge as he smiles at me, running his tongue over his lower lip like he intends to savor every drop. My entire body has become a statue and when Smee clears her throat, I jolt, buttoning the buttons of my shirt and quickly putting myself back together. I scoop up his shirt from the floor and toss it at him, then plaster on my best smile as I turn to Smee.

"I'm so sorry," I say. It's all I got.

"The door locked," he explains casually. "We were just passing the time until you got back to let us out."

Smee raises an eyebrow. "Yeah, I can see that." Her gaze travels over our disheveled state.

I smooth my rumpled shirt self-consciously.

"Well then," Smee says after an awkward pause. "I'll leave you to... whatever that was." She grabs the stopper and props the door open before stepping back into the hallway, but Sebastian stops her.

"I should go," he murmurs to me, stealing one last searing kiss.

Without another word, he walks past Smee, still shirtless, and she gives me a knowing look.

"Don't," I say, holding a hand up and closing my eyes. I don't want to see the judgment in her stare.

"Oh yeah, he's dead to you alright." She laughs and her boots click against the floor.

Heat floods my face. I clear my throat and smooth my hair, unable to form a response.

15

Scarlet

The witch mark burns like fire on my back. I grit my teeth, my knuckles going white as I grip the edge of the built-in cabinet below the mirror.

"Fuck..." I breathe, but the sensation is over quickly. With frantic movements, I undo the buttons of the black linen shirt I'm wearing and pull it down enough to see between my shoulder blades in the mirror. The twin circles have returned, an inky black marring my pale skin—a reminder of the monster I could become and that others would condemn me for on the spot.

What am I going to do? I shake my head and yank my shirt back into place, exhaling a shaky breath. Before I can fully process my predicament, there's a sharp rap of knuckles on the door and I startle.

"Scars?" Sebastian's gruff voice filters through the wood. Every nerve sparks at once until I remember that he heard Eva call me that before we left Solaria. "May I come in?"

My heart leaps at the sound of his voice, warmth flooding my veins. I smooth my hair and clothes, checking to make sure he won't suspect anything, then answer the door. He's in loose trousers today. Not the usual leather I've seen him in prior. His hair is wet like he's just come from a bath, slicked back with his fingers. Two plates are balanced in his hands and the aroma wafts over me and my stomach rumbles in response.

"I thought you might be hungry," he says, nodding at the food. His gaze lingers on me, a flicker of concern in his pale eyes. Concern that he has no idea how much is warranted.

I force a smile and let him in. "Starving, actually."

We sit on the edge of the bed, shoulders brushing as we eat. The contact ignites sparks along my arm. I glance at Sebastian out of the corner of my eye, watching as he scoops a bite onto his fork.

He pauses, eying me in return. "What is it? Is everything alright?"

Heat floods my cheeks at being caught staring, but my guts twists. He's so intuitive—more so with the bond—how am I ever going to keep this from him? I shake my head, focusing on my meal. "Nothing. The food is delicious, thank you."

"Hmm." He doesn't sound convinced but lets it go, turning his attention to his flask. He unscrews the cap, and the scent of sweetness and berries catches my attention.

Fairy wine. My mouth waters at the memory of its taste. Sebastian lifts the flask, offering it to me. I reach to take it, but he pulls it back slightly.

"Sparingly, please. I don't think I could be the 'perfect gentleman' as Zephyr calls it if you end up naked and bent over a bed again. Not after earlier."

My cheeks flame. Poor Smee... She shouldn't have had to walk in on that.

"Rule number one," I say, letting him know I won't let it happen again.

He chuckles, taking a swig himself, and then hands it to me. "I'm pretty sure rules just sound like challenges to you."

My lips twist into a sly grin as I let the sweet, berry-filled wine slip down my throat. Heaven in a bottle...

With every bite and sip, the ache in my stomach eases. The tension in my shoulders lessens like I'm not trying to hide half of who I am. For a few moments, I can forget about the mark and what it means. I can simply be here with him, soaking in his presence and the peace it brings.

If only it could last. From here on out, I have to get creative. There's got to be a way to hide my mark with a coven. I just have to figure it out.

I set my fork down, staring at the remnants of potatoes on my plate. The worry begins to creep back in, dark tendrils that slither into my mind and wrap around my thoughts.

Sebastian sets his flask aside, giving me his full attention. "What's wrong? For real this time."

I hesitate, unsure of how much to reveal. But I can't hide the truth from him forever, no matter how much I might want to. I just won't be revealing it tonight. "How long until we reach Mortys?"

His gaze drops, a furrow appearing between his brows. "There's been a change of plans. We're altering course for the Western Isles instead."

"Why? What happened?" Alarm trickles down my spine as my mind races with possibilities.

"One of the villages was attacked," he says grimly. "We received a distress call. They need our help. Once everyone is done eating, we're dropping the sails. We'll be there in a few hours."

My mouth goes dry. "Attacked? By who?"

"The blood witches. Under the Crocodile's, and your father's, command."

The words hit me like a blow. I jerk back as if struck, blinking at Sebastian in disbelief. "But... the war ended. Years ago. The treaty—"

"The treaty was a farce. Your father has been attacking us for years, using the Crocodile and his witches to do his dirty work. All the while claiming peace." He shakes his head. "The treaty never truly existed."

I stare at Sebastian, stunned into silence. My father lied? Why?

Sebastian misreads my reaction, mistaking the shock for fear. He reaches for me, grasping my shoulders. "Don't worry, darling. I won't let anything happen to you." His eyes are intense, burning into mine. "You're safe with me. I promise."

I force a weak smile. "I know. It's just... a lot to take in."

He searches my face as if trying to discern my thoughts. Finally, he nods. An awkward silence falls over us as I stare down at my plate, appetite fled. After a long moment, Sebastian sighs, grabs my nearly empty plate, and sets it aside. Before I can protest, he pulls me onto his lap. His arms wrap around my middle as his lips press against my pulse, searing and demanding. Heat explodes inside me, and I melt into him, the world falling away.

He deepens the kiss, roughened hands sliding under my shirt to graze my back. Panic spikes as his fingers creep higher to my mark. I jerk back with a gasp.

Sebastian's eyes narrow. "What's wrong?"

My pulse races. I scramble for an excuse. He wouldn't be able to feel it, right? For the most part, it just looks like a tattoo, but it lights up the moment I use magic in a fluorescent orange glow. Would he know if his fingers settled over it?

"Nothing," I say quickly. Too quickly. I clear my throat, trying for a more casual tone. "I just... we should take things slow."

I hold my breath, praying he believes me. For an endless moment, he simply watches me, gaze inscrutable. Then he nods.

"As you wish." He kisses me softly, then helps me to my feet. "Come. There's something I want to show you, anyway."

Sebastian leads me above deck under the velvet night sky. A million lights wink overhead, scattered like diamonds across the inky blackness. I know it's not endless, but it always appears it is. In reality, there's an end and on that ceiling, there are crystals of every color of the rainbow reflecting the light from down here back at us. The air is crisp and cool, salty to the taste.

Sebastian lays down on the deck, folding his hands behind his head. "Lay with me." After a moment, I join him, and he points up at the sky. "Look."

I follow his finger and I gasp. There, hanging low and luminous in the sky, are the three moons: one pale gold, one silvery blue, and one deep amber. Together, they block out most of the hell flame, leaving nothing but a faint, shimmering ring of light around them, as if they're glowing from an inner fire. And there, just visible against their edges, are dark shapes or winged creatures, swirling in the sky. Dragons.

I rub my eyes in disbelief. "It's beautiful..." I breathe, mouth parting as I watch them with such fascination I forget to blink.

"I thought you might like it."

I glance at him, eyes round with curiosity. "How did you know?"

Sebastian chuckles, smiling so hard that his dimples show. "You were drawing them earlier today. When we were in the storage bay, remember?"

Heat floods my cheeks. He saw my sketches...

"You pay close attention," I say softly.

"To you?" His eyes glint silver in the moonlight. "Always."

"I wish my father hadn't killed them here... They're such magnificent creatures. It's awful to believe that they're all gone."

"But they're not."

I nearly snap my neck to glance at him. Did I just hear that right?

"Most of the dragons are gone, but not all. They're shifters and there's no way to test everyone in this realm. I've met one. He's a rebel and I'd imagine any others would be too. I doubt they'd stay in Solaria, but it doesn't mean they aren't hiding in plain sight elsewhere."

"You've met one?"

His smile widens until I can see the pointed tips of his teeth. "Aye, I have."

We stay there for a long time, watching the sky. By the time Sebastian walks me back to my room, I can barely keep my eyes open. He pauses at my door, bracing a hand on the frame as he towers over me. Green eyes toggle between mine for a moment before he kisses me deeply. I lift onto my tiptoes, wanting everything I can't have—not ever again. At least for now.

When he finally pulls away, we're both breathless. "Sleep well, Scars," he whispers, brushing his lips over my forehead.

"You too, Captain." He smirks before twisting the knob and nodding for me to slip inside. Closing it softly, I press my back to the door and breathe a sigh of relief. It takes a moment before I hear his footsteps leave, but my heart is so full it feels ready to burst. He saw my drawings... then gave me an experience I never thought I'd ever be able to witness.

The dragons were so close. From the Solarian castle, they look like pinpricks in the sky, but here, they were huge... the size of my thumb or bigger.

16
SCARLET

The Jolly Roger cuts through the morning mist like a phantom, eerily silent as we approach the Western Isles. The crew stands, impatiently waiting for the fog to clear, to glimpse what we're sailing into. The tension hangs in the air and the mast creaks. A gust of wind whips the sails as the hell flame casts long shadows on the deck. I inhale deeply, my nose wrinkling at the acrid scent of fire, burning something I don't recognize. Whatever wood that is, I'm almost certain it's rotten. Grey and white flecks fall from the sky, and I shiver as the wind cuts through the thin linen shirt I'm wearing.

Sebastian stands to my right, eyes staring past the bow of the ship. My body trembles and I catch him tip his head at me and take a deep breath. He jostles, drawing my attention, and shrugs off his long, red leather coat. Before I can protest, he gently wraps it around my shoulders, holding it up so I can slip my arms through the holes. It's so warm... It takes everything I have not to sigh.

"Thank you," I say, tucking the jacket tighter around my frame.

He doesn't answer, just crosses his arms over his chest and resumes his stance, waiting for something. I just wish I knew what. The ship bumps into something and the crew shouts, gearing up to dock. Peering over the edge of the rail, I spot a charred pier, and the burnt remnants of a once-thriving village spread out before us. A blackened structure on the sand looms, still smoldering, and odd statues litter the edge of the ocean, jutting from the sand.

I study them, a crease forming between my brows. They're humanoid... like someone tried to depict people running to the ocean. "Are these supposed to commemorate the war or something?" I ask, tearing my eyes away from the sculptures to look at Sebastian.

He shakes his head, a grim expression on his face. "They're not statues."

"Then what are they?" I take in their slight amber glow, maybe made from some sort of crystal?

"They're people," he replies in a low voice that sends goosebumps flooding the surface of my skin, despite the jacket he's given me.

"The blood witches did this..." I whisper, horrified.

Sebastian shakes his head again. "Those are the blood witches."

My stomach churns. What did this? I squint as the ship comes to a stop and the loud rattle of chains fills the air as the anchor is lowered. There's a slight waft of smoke rising from the nearest figure, and my eyes widen.

They were burned...

"I want you to stay on the ship. It's safer. Do I need to give you a babysitter?" Sebastian's voice is firm yet gentle.

I can see the worry in his eyes, and for once, I don't argue. "No... I'll stay."

He nods before stepping away from me and shouting orders at his crew. "Take your weapons! We don't know what's waiting for us on land. We move out in ten." He turns to the group of men a few feet away from us. Water elementals, I think. "Make it rain. We won't be able to see shit in the fog."

The crew jumps into action, their movements tense but efficient. Sebastian grips my hand, cutting through the madness as men scatter across the deck to lead me to my room. "I'll be back as soon as I can. If anything goes south, I'll shadowwalk and get you, but until then, stay on the ship so I know where to find you. It'll rain, so you'll want to stay below deck."

"Alright," I whisper, feeling strangely relieved. Gods forbid they find a blood witch alive. I don't want to watch.

He opens my room door and swings me inside. "Promise me, Scars. I need you to say it."

"I won't leave the ship."

His green eyes soften as he cups my jaw, giving me a quick kiss before shutting the door and jogging down the hallway. I rush to the porthole, straining to see through the thickening fog. There are dozens of petrified figures along the water's edge, making me shiver despite the warmth of Sebastian's coat.

The rhythmic lapping of the water against the ship's hull is the only sound that pierces the stillness and rain lashes down. Slowly, the fog starts to lift. The haunting silhouette of the Western Isles emerges - jagged cliffs stand sentinel, overshadowed by tall, darkened pines that sway to the rhythm of the sea breeze.

I watch the crew disappear into the fog that remains low to the ground, each step taking them closer to danger. As the last of them vanishes from sight, a knot forms in the pit of my stomach. My hands clench around the edges of the porthole, nails digging into the cold metal. All I can do is wait and hope nothing goes wrong. It's better this way. If I was with him, he'd be worried about me and not watching out for himself.

A flash in the sky draws my attention. My heart leaps as the unmistakable figure of a dragon cuts across the sky. Enormous wings beat against the sky as fiery scales glint in the light. My eyes round and my mouth gapes. A dragon... It's everything I envisioned and more.

Propelled by wonder, I pull Sebastian's coat tighter around me and burst from my room. I'm supposed to stay on the ship. I can do that, but I want a better look and

I couldn't care less about the rain or getting soaked. Not when there's something like a bloody dragon to witness.

"It's beautiful..." I can't tear my eyes away from the beast as it speeds through the sky.

The dragon swoops lower, its enormous wings casting shadows over the water. Rain pelts my face, cold and relentless, as I watch the dragon draw nearer. Its deep red scales glisten, a stark contrast to the gray sky that surrounds it. The creature's sheer size is breathtaking and nothing compared to the skeletons that line the bridge near the Solarian castle. Its trajectory shifts as it curbs the air, heading towards the Jolly Roger, and my heart hammers in my chest.

It picks up speed, getting closer, but it doesn't pull up. It's aimed right at me. My lungs seize as I take a small step back, then another. This isn't just a show of grace and power; this is an attack.

Running out of time, and in the dragon's sights, I reach for my gift. My fingers curve toward the ground as I pluck string after invisible string, but it doesn't let up, it doesn't so much as shift an inch off course.

Panic sinks into my veins, as my body trembles and adrenaline floods through every nerve. I try again, but it's futile. Shaking out my hands, I try to use my magic, mumbling a spell to shield myself as it opens its jaws and sparks flick across its tongue. I force my voice to be still, speaking the short spell and thrusting my hands forward.

A purple aura surrounds my hands, then fizzles out. Again and again, I try to no avail. My hands shimmer with energy, but the magic dissipates just as quickly as it appears.

I'm running out of time.

The dragon's body swells as it inhales, arching its neck as its wings start to lift, slowing its descent.

I should retreat, but I can't. I'm rooted to the spot. I can't tear my eyes away. The dragon's gaze locks onto mine, predatory and cunning, and its talons extend. I brace myself, ready for the impact that will decide my fate.

"Scarlet!" a voice roars, but I can't look. I'm in fear's deadly trance. "I swear by the gods, woman. You're going to be the death of me!" Someone lunges in front of me, flailing their arms in the air. "Not her!" he yells again, but it's too late - the dragon already unleashed a torrent of flames.

My heart twists at the anguish and time slows to a crawl. I brace myself for the searing pain that is sure to come, but instead, there's only a sudden, violent gust of wind. The heat of the flames dissipates around me, leaving me unscathed.

My back collides with something and my eyes snap open. Sebastian's face is looming over mine, his breath hot and heavy against my face. His shoulders relax as the darkness fades from all around us until I see the fog and the mainland... We're on the beach and that solid surface at my back is the sand.

"Are you okay?" Sebastian's voice is laced with both concern and fury as he tightens his grip on me protectively. His intense gaze searches mine for any sign of injury.

I nod, still in shock. "Yeah, I... I think so."

"Good." He exhales deeply, and pushes up, lifting his weight off me. "Don't ever fucking scare me like that again."

I bite my lip, processing what just happened. In the span of a heartbeat, Sebastian had risked everything to save me. He'd thrown himself into danger without a second thought. I'm breathing because of him.

"Thank you," I say, unable to tear my eyes away from his as I sit up in the sand. "You saved my life."

Sebastian's grip tightens on my hand, pulling me to my feet. Our eyes meet and rain drips from his hair and slides down his face.

"What were you thinking?" he asks. Each word is pronounced with deliberate weight, the reprimand evident.

My eyes drop to the ground. It's my fault... He could've died trying to save me and, had he not, I'd be gone. "I... I just wanted to see the dragon," I admit quietly, feeling foolish for my reckless behavior. "I didn't think it would attack me."

Despite his evident anger, Sebastian's concern shines through as he brushes a strand of wet hair away from my face with gentle fingers. His eyes search my body, lifting the lapels of his coat to see for himself that I'm not hurt. Satisfied, he lets his jacket go and I tug it close around me.

Relief floods his expression, and he pulls me into his chest, holding me there as the rain continues to pour down on us. The warmth of his body and the steady beat of his heart soothes my soul, but something catches my eye.

Beneath the blackened sand, a metallic sheen hits just right, blinding me for a short moment. I press gently against Sebastian's chest and he releases me, allowing me to investigate what it is. Carefully, I bend down, dusting the sand away, and my heart seizes in my chest. My hands tremble as I retrieve the charred doll, its once-vibrant colors reduced to ash and smears of black. Tears fill my eyes as I try to imagine the child who once played with this toy, now lost to the horrors of war.

"Who would... Why would my father do this?" I ask, looking around at the carnage before us.

"Because he wants those in the outer realm islands to accept his cuffs," Sebastian says, his voice tinged with bitterness. "The Crocodile doesn't attack often, but when he does, he can level villages like this under your father's command. Anyone who doesn't bow and pledge fealty to the king is executed. The children and women are rounded up and are never seen again. Who knows where they take them or what they do? Some say the kids are raised elsewhere to be his castle staff. Others say the witches get to keep the innocents for their sacrifices. No one knows about the women. Regardless, it's likely not good."

A mixture of sorrow and fury washes over me, and I clench the ruined doll tightly in my hand. How could I have been so blind? I'd have given my life to kingdom and country. For what? I'd be uniting the clans beneath a man who would watch it burn before him and feel nothing.

"Scarlet," Sebastian murmurs, touching my arm lightly. "You didn't know."

"I do now." Struggling to hold back tears, I lock my jaw.

A memory flutters through my mind as I stare at the melted face of the doll in my hands. I'd asked the maid who raised me where she was from. She cried and left me alone in the library. She was the one that had gotten me into reading. It was days before I saw her again. When I did, she told me her family were considered traitors, and the king had shown mercy by allowing her to serve him. I watched that woman become pregnant. She'd volunteered to be one of my father's surrogates. A few months later, I never saw her again.

The weight of my father's actions crushes me, and my legs give, becoming too weak to hold me up as the tears spill from my eyes. I loved her... She was the only mother I knew and all this time, all those years, she'd been imprisoned along with me in that castle. Rounded up like an animal and shipped off to wait on the king and his daughter's hand and foot...

Sebastian sits down beside me on the damp, charred ground. "Scarlet," he begins, his voice low and gentle. He doesn't touch me and, quite frankly, I don't blame him. I'm ashamed to be related to such a monster. "Do you understand now? This is the reason they see you, your hair, your lineage, and act as they do. It's not your fault. You had nothing to do with this, but when they see you, they see him. Eventually, they'll understand, as I do, that you're kind and considerate. That you're nothing like him."

I swallow hard, nodding as I sniffle.

He wraps his arms around me, pulling me close. I bury my face in the crook of his neck, smelling the salt from the sea and the cologne he wears. It's soothing, but nothing will ever take away the sting left behind from knowing I descend from someone so wicked.

"I don't expect you to forget your family," he tells me, his breath warm against my ear. "I don't wish for you to hate them, either. It's why I wanted you to stay on the ship. But I knew at some point you were going to have to face who your father truly is. I just wish it hadn't been today."

I catch Zephyr's form as he approaches, his leather satchel slung over his shoulder. His head hangs, giving me a full view of the horns that wrap back over his head.

"Any survivors?" Sebastian asks, his voice low but firm.

Zephyr shakes his head as he nears. "If there were, they're not here."

A sudden gust of wind stirs behind Zephyr, and I scramble behind Sebastian as the enormous red dragon who just tried to kill me lands on the ground with a heavy thud. The dragon shifts, its form shrinking and changing until it becomes a naked man. He speed walks toward us, apologizing faster than I can comprehend the words.

"Sebastian, I'm sorry," he says, running a hand through his tousled brown hair. "I saw her and thought the worst. I was still clearing the island when you approached."

Sebastian's jaw flexes as he stands, taking me with him. "It's okay. No one was hurt."

"Zephyr," Sebastian continues, "tell Lorian to stop his spell for the search. If he hasn't found anyone yet, he's not going to. I don't want him getting burnt out. Let's recall the men to the ship."

Zephyr nods and leaves us, taking the naked man along with him. Once they're gone, Sebastian turns to me, his gaze searching. "So, you're a mage."

I pale, suddenly aware of how much I've revealed. Glad I had his jacket on. It was likely the only thing hiding my mark when it glowed. "I... I'm not sure what I am." My voice wavers, and I can't help but feel exposed. "My father experiments on all his children in utero. It's why our hair turns white."

Sebastian's eyes darken, a mix of concern and anger. I can tell he wants to say something, but he holds back, choosing his next words carefully. "What do you mean by experiment?"

I exhale, gathering my thoughts. "The king has been trying to override the curse placed on him by his late wife for decades. He mixes our DNA with other species in hopes it will give him an heir one day, since the curse prevents him from having one."

Sebastian's eyes narrow, concern evident in their depths. "I see..."

"I know I'm a mage because my mother was one and my father is a druid, but I have no idea where my puppeteering ability came from. Mermaids can control people through song, so... it could be related, but it's still different."

We reach the base of the ramp leading up to the deck, and droplets of water cascade down its wooden surface. Sebastian smirks, attempting to lighten the mood. "So, mage and mystery. Got it. Just don't go to the dark side and we'll be just fine."

I smile weakly, trying to fake a laugh at his joke, but my heart clenches inside my chest.

"Hey," Sebastian says gently, lifting my chin with his finger so our eyes meet. "It was a joke. I'd know by now if you'd practiced sacrificial magic. You'd be marked by it in one way or another. I've seen every inch of you and can confidently say you have nothing to worry about."

Sucking in a breath, as we continue to make our way up the rain-slicked ramp and onto the deck of the Jolly Roger.

If only he knew just how wrong he was...

17

Scarlet

The witch claws at the metal grate as the pirates shove her into the prison hole. Her wail slices through the gentle creak of wood and rope like a sharpened blade, making my teeth ache. I'd hoped this day wouldn't come. Now here we are, and I don't think I'll ever be able to close my eyes and get the grotesque image of this woman out of my mind.

Above the grate, a curly-haired man shouts a stream of curse words. His arms wrap around her middle as she kicks, keeping the others from helping him. As soon as he knocks one of her feet off the ledge of the hole to which she clings to, the other catches, and she regains leverage. It's all he can do to twist the witch's body until it bows so tight, I fear her spine will snap in two.

She knows if she goes in, it's over.

It's not supposed to be like this... Mages and druids weren't intended to wield sacrificial magic. No creature was. Sorcery is supposed to have its limitations. It's why magic users can only channel so much of their soul's power before they need to let it recharge. Anything more than that requires a price.

I've heard the royal mages speak their motto enough times to know it by heart. You honor balance, and nature honors you. It means mages can regenerate their magic as long as they don't deplete their souls of it entirely. It's when the mages and druids cross that line that it becomes a problem. Physically, they'll live, but their shadow and spirit—the two halves of their soul—disintegrate, leaving behind an empty shell, void of morality and emotion. They lose everything that makes them who they are. All they want, all they need, is power and no amount will ever be enough...

At some point, the magic users of our realm discovered they could draw it from sacrifices. They learned how to drain the souls of living creatures to avoid tapping out their own, but they underestimated how addicting it would become. All it takes is to overdraw once... The soul disappears and then creatures like the one struggling before me are born. They're no longer blood witches at this point. They're shades. The person who dwelled within them died a long time ago. They don't rot because they perform blood magic. They rot when they no longer have a soul to make them heal. They deteriorate bit by bit until there's nothing left.

It's why my father trains his druids and mages extensively, teaching them the limitations and how to work in covens to make up for what one can't do on their own. It's also why the people in this realm who are caught dabbling in sacrificial magic are marked as blood witches. It's a warning to anyone who sees them that they're compromised morally—that they might no longer possess their soul.

The woman's gnarled fingers snap as she digs at the crew's hands. Five of them now try to shove her in, but she manages to claw her way out before they can shut the grate. Her body isn't strong enough to endure this sort of fight, though... Not anymore.

Blood drips from her wounds, staining the deck crimson, and my stomach somersaults at the sight. Her pallid skin is covered in an intricate web of dark veins—the signs of death trying to claim her. Even if we don't throw her overboard today, she won't live much longer. Once those show up, a shade's days are numbered.

Her deep-set malevolent eyes are clouded as if she's void of sight. She was beautiful once... Her features would be perfect if it weren't for the rotting flesh, broken teeth, and dark oozing gums. Skin is missing on her shoulder where she's tried to cut out the witch mark placed on her. The one that matches mine.

The harsh black lines of two circles and quirky symbols stand out against the raw, reddened layer of wounded flesh. She realized the same thing my father did. There's no way to remove it. Not by cutting it away or scarring the flesh above it to obscure the mark from view. It'll always shine through and even if it doesn't right away, it'll burn to the surface the moment you use magic.

Once marked, the only way to hide it—besides covering it up with clothes—is to use a glamour. Even those are only temporary though and require a great deal of power to make. I'm still not sure how Sebastian managed to get his hands on one the night he pledged to enter the gauntlet.

It took the power of twenty-seven mages and druids to hide my mark for the wedding. If it weren't for that, my father would've had to disclose my mark, and no one would have pledged. They'd have thought I meant to sacrifice them or was rotting on the inside. And believe it or not, even ruthless monsters have standards in who they'll take to bed.

I swallow hard, trying not to look away or draw attention to the fact I'm about to hurl.

"What do you plan to do with her?" Trying to keep my tone indifferent, I do my best to act as if watching them torture someone is an everyday occurrence.

"Float her the moment we're far enough from the isles." Sebastian is at my side, his face an impassive mask as he presses a hand against my back. Gently, he slides it up and down the length of my spine, like he's trying to soothe me, likely sensing through the bond that I'm barely keeping it together. I lean into the comfort he offers as the ship lurches away from the dock, sails billowing in the wind thanks to the air elementals and their gifts.

Sebastian clears his throat, pulling me closer so I can hear him over the waves. "Why don't you go below deck? Smee will keep you company."

His sister glares at him, standing a couple of feet away from us. "Why do I have to babysit?" She turns to me, flashing me a forced smile. "No offense, just this is my favorite part."

"None taken..." I should probably see this, anyway. I should know what'll happen if they find out about me.

Luckily, he doesn't push me to leave, just leans against the rail of the deck and watches the island shrink as we sail farther out to sea. It's not until the Western Isles are nothing but a sliver on the horizon that the pirates haul the witch from the hole. They drag her by the iron cuffs that suppress her magic and the woman bucks, fighting harder than before. Her bones start to snap and pierce through her flesh as the men drag her toward the railing.

What's left of the woman's red hair swishes in the wind as they secure a long pole to the shackles on her wrists and attach some sort of reel to it. One of the men cranks it once and the pole telescopes, growing longer with every twist.

"Smee, get her out of here." Sebastian grips my shoulders and slides me toward his sister. I start to protest, but he shoots me a knowing look. "Trust me, Scars. Go downstairs."

Straightening my shoulders, I watch, refusing to leave. I need to know... I have to know.

The crewmen drop a section of the railing around the deck and attach the plank, then make quick work of lining the witch's heels up with it. Slowly, they turn the handle of the real, making the witch step back. Little by little, she inches toward the edge, toward death. One more turn and—crack. The woman plummets into the unforgiving sea.

They don't miss a beat, as if they didn't just condemn someone to a true death. She'll never be reborn. Her spirit will never cross over because it died long ago. For a breath, there's silence, nothing but the jingle of chains as they take the unhinged shakes off the pole. They must've been rigged to release when she fell.

A scream tears through the air and I rush toward the rail. Misjudging my momentum, my stomach folds over it and a steady hand grips my shirt to pull me back before I can go over.

"Careful, love. I'm in no rush to get rid of you," Sebastian says, letting me go once my feet are on the ground.

I spot the witch floating on the surface of the water, tossing with the waves like a buoy. Her shouts are drowned out with every wave that dips her head below the water.

She's alive... and she's floating...

I'd assumed it was just a term they used for walking someone off the plank and condemning them to the deep. I thought by floating they meant treading water, but she's... floating like a leaf in a puddle, hovering at the surface of the water as if she's full of air.

Her arms flail, desperate to keep herself balanced, and I spot a large shadow in the ocean's depths, growing bigger by the second. It's moving right toward her. I open my mouth, but the question I planned to ask dies on my tongue as a blue-scaled, reptilian head emerges from the sea. The roar of water shatters the silence as its jaw gapes wide enough to reveal row upon row of dagger-like teeth. The witch's sightless eyes stretch wide as she mumbles something incoherent and scrambles to get out of its mouth.

She's too late.

The beast surges upwards, launching her over twenty feet in the air. She lets out a bloodcurdling scream, but the sound is abruptly silenced as its jaw snaps closed. Blood explodes into the air like dust, and it disappears.

I lean against Sebastian to stay upright, my knuckles bleaching as my fists clench. Bile climbs the length of my throat at the thought of drowning in that thing's gullet, or my flesh and bone crunching between its teeth.

Sebastian continues to stroke his hand up and down my back. "I told you that you didn't want to see this. It's not my intention for you to think I'm a monster, but you saw what she did to those people. I might not have been able to stop it, but I can give those poor souls she killed justice."

I flinch away from his touch, nausea roiling through me. He frowns, eyes glinting with something dangerous. I get what he's saying and honestly, I believe that woman deserved to die. What unsettles me is the fact that will be my fate... Will he hear me out when the time comes? Will he listen when I say I was wrongly marked, or will he condemn me on sight? I honestly can't say which way he'll lean, but what I do know is keeping my mark hidden for as long as possible is the only way forward.

"I'm fine. I promise," I say, dropping my gaze. The last thing I need is him thinking I care about that soulless creature.

Sebastian studies me for a long moment, but when he finally speaks, it's not me he talks to. It's Smee. "Take her to the mess hall and keep her mind off it."

His sister's face falls, but she doesn't protest. Her arm snakes around mine, linking at the elbow as she leads me to the companionway without a word.

My body feels numb... It's like a piece of me died along with the witch. Innocence, maybe? Or perhaps it just made me finally understand how real the threat is.

18

Scarlet

We barely make it below deck and into the mess hall before I push away from Smee, beelining for the closest trash can. Bracing over the metal edge, I lose my breakfast.

"Don't worry, princess. The first time is the worst. After that, it's significantly easier to watch, I promise," Smee says, wrinkling her nose as she peers into the trash. Her hand smooths over my back, hovering over my mark through the linen shirt. If she knew what was beneath it... I'd have joined that woman today.

"I hope so." I feign strength, collecting myself, and Smee nudges a flask toward me.

"It's fairy wine. It'll settle your stomach. Wait here," she says, leaving me for a moment to rummage through an only crate.

I take a swig from the flask, letting the sweet liquid drown out the sour taste on my tongue. Closing my eyes, I try to calm my racing heart. They don't know... I remind myself. You're safe.

Smee clucks her tongue, drawing my attention back to her as she twists a deck of cards between her fingers, holding them up for me to see. "Ever played?"

"I guess that depends on the game."

Her brown eyes narrow as if I'm speaking in a foreign language. "You say that as if there's more than one."

"Because there is…" Arching a brow, I take a seat at the closest table, and she slides into the chair across from me.

"But there's only one right one." She winks, making me chuckle as she starts to mix the cards up. I'm not sure what game she's setting up. I've played many, but not once have I seen someone separate the deck by color after placing a few face up, in a coffin shape.

Surely, she'll explain… right?

Smee shuffles the two stacks, keeping the colors apart. "Do you want to be red or black?"

"Surprise me." Apparently, that was the wrong answer.

Her brow arches, sassy as ever, while she hands me the red stack. "I suppose red fits you. It's Solaria's color, after all." Smee adjusts the coffin cards, which are a mix of red and black numbers and letters.

"What game is this?"

"King's Coffin. It's an outer realm thing."

By that name? Yeah… I'd say it is.

Smee points to the cards face up on the table. "Each card is a nail in the coffin. Your job is to make all the nails turn your color. When it's your turn, flip the top card of your deck. You can either lay it over its matching counterpart on the table—try to turn the black numbers red—or discard."

"So, if red is Solaria, then the black cards are the rebels, like the Jolly Roger's flag." I trace the ship design on the back of the cards with my finger, waiting for her to make the first move.

Smee nods, picking up the first card on her deck and placing her black two over my red one in the coffin. "One nail in."

"Can I change it back?"

"Of course, but only if you have a two." She flashes a wicked grin. "I'll have you know, I've never lost a game, and I have no intention of letting you win out of pity."

"Pity? Why would you pity me?" I draw a card. It's not a match, so I set it aside.

"Because anyone with eyeballs can see you're not a killer, Scarlet. You stared at that witch like you could save her with empathy alone, but it's okay. You'll harden up with time. We all did. It's inevitable, and the more you see of their wicked ways, the more you'll want to float them yourself."

I purse my lips. Maybe I should've gone below deck when Sebastian warned me to...

Smee pins two more nails before I can turn one red. Before she can make a snide remark, something hits the deck above us hard enough to make us both jump. Smee opens her mouth, but I don't hear what she says over the bone-chilling scream that rends the air.

We freeze, cards dropping to the tabletop. I surge to my feet, heart pounding, and we race to the porthole. A man splashes in the water before he's yanked beneath it by something with golden scales. Pressing my fingers to my lips, I can't move... I can't speak.

What just happened?

"Stay here," Smee says, yanking a knife from the holster on her thigh. With a graceful flip, she snatches it out of the air by the blade and pushes the hilt toward me. "I mean it. I'm not sure what's going on out there, but my brother will never forgive me if you get caught up in it."

Hesitating, my fingers wrap around the dagger's hilt and she lets go. Someone else screams as they fall from the ship, the sound silencing immediately as they splash into the ocean.

"Stay. Here. Nod, or something, to tell me you understand." Smee grips my arm and I swallow hard. My head jerks in a quick nod and then she's off, storming up the companionway and leaving me alone... With a knife I have no clue how to use.

I've used blades for rituals and spells, but never to defend myself. I've never needed to. My hands shake as I clutch the dagger to my chest, looking around the room for somewhere to hide in case I need to. There's nothing but tables and full barrels.

Think... I promised not to leave, but I could wait by the stairs to the lower decks. If someone came down the companionway, they'd have to cross the entire mess hall floor to get to me. It'd give me time to run and there are plenty of places to hide on the lower levels.

The commotion on the deck only grows louder as I debate what to do. My mind whirls, trying to come up with backup plans for every possible scenario. Then I hear the door to the companionway whine on its hinges.

Someone is coming.

My knuckles scream as I grasp the dagger tight enough for the hilt to leave indentions in my palm. The footsteps aren't dainty, and Smee speeds through everything. She doesn't leisurely stroll down steps, she all but runs.

Then there's the breathing... There's nothing feminine about it, but it might be Sebastian. I don't blink as I stare at the opening of the stairs, leading from the deck to the room I'm in now, and as the tip of bloodied, well-worn boots come into view, I have my answer. It's not Sebastian. This is someone else.

My eyes widen as I quietly suck in a breath. Time to go.

I tiptoe down the stairwell before whoever coming down the companionway can see me. Hitting the floor with the crew's quarters, I sprint through the open birthing and down the narrow hall of single-room cabins, where the higher-ranking sleep. Me included.

I couldn't imagine having to sleep in the open, bundled in the stacked hammocks that are three high. My luck, I'd fall out of one and right on top of the person below me. If Sebastian has given me anything in our marriage, it's my own room and the peace of mind of knowing I'm safe within it.

Reaching my room, I don't waste a second. I burst inside, closing the door behind me. I know Sebastian enchants it at night to ensure only he and I can enter the room, but I'm not even remotely sure how it works. I haven't bothered to test it. I haven't had the time to. All I know is when he leaves me here, the lock latches and the scent of magic fills the air. Even when we weren't speaking, I'd hear his boots in the hallway and him lock the door.

I could try to spell it shut myself, seal off the outside until Smee or Sebastian come for me. I've studied tomes upon tomes and know most by heart, but my mage magic has never been strong. During my one-on-one sessions, training with the mages to learn how to use my magic, I was never able to weave a spell tight enough to ward off a magic user. All it took was for them to pluck one translucent strand and the entire ward came down like a house of cards. It's how I know my puppeteering ability is different and unrelated to it. I don't think I lack the necessary magic in my soul to weave. I just don't know how to release it.

Still, I have to try. If the person coming down those stairs is mortal, my spell will hold. If not, at least I tried.

Turning to the door, I flex my fingers and exhale slowly to center myself. "Lacklyte Gravitas," I whisper, my voice barely above a breath as my power sings through my veins.

I extend my hand out, fingers splayed wide. Imagining the energy coursing through me, I curl each finger into my palm one by one, beginning with my pinky and ending with my thumb, drawing the power inward. As my hand forms a fist, I feel a subtle warmth emanating from it, a testament to the barrier ready to expand. Twisting my wrist hard, threads shimmer into existence, crossing and knotting together like a dream catcher.

To most, they'd be invisible. To mages and druids, we can see them—pluck them—and feel for weaknesses. Just as we know the strength of a spell by how complex the webbing of translucent lines is. The one in front of me, stretching over the doorway, isn't the best ward out there, but it'll have to be enough.

Dagger in hand, I move to the chest at the end of my bed, skimming my hand over the golden nameplate. It's the trunk I intended to hide in while we were in the Luminaries. Sebastian had it brought into my room when he couldn't spare the time to get my things from his house.

Lifting the lid, I grab the clothes he gave me from inside it and toss them behind the pillows, making sure no one will see them at first glance. Just in case…Climbing inside, I shut the lid. It's dark as I huddle my knees to my chest.

I breathe in deeply, smelling the cedar and Sebastian's cologne while I try to settle my breathing. The sound of every inhale and exhale echoes in the small space, making it appear louder than it truly is.

To anyone on Sebastian's crew, it's not a secret that I'm living in this room. I'm not naïve enough to believe that if someone was truly looking for me, specifically, they wouldn't find me here. However, we're on a pirate ship. No one can stay hidden forever and if someone truly wanted to find me, they would. This is all about buying time. Whatever is going on up on the deck isn't good. I saw the worry in Smee's eyes as she gave me the dagger. Someone like her doesn't worry unless there's a reason to.

For all I know, it could be mutiny, or maybe The Crocodile and his witches followed us from the Western Isles. Who knows? Hiding in here will buy Sebastian and his crew time and keep me out of it.

The echo of boots sounds from the hall, and I bite my teeth into my tongue, closing my eyes tight in a desperate attempt to stay silent. A rattle sounds as someone tries the knob of my door. I don't think they stopped at any of the other rooms. I didn't hear it if they did. Whoever it is, they're looking for me, which can't mean anything good.

A knock sounds on the wooden slab. "It's alright, princess, the captain sent me. You can open up. You're safe."

Opening my eyes, I sit deathly still. Do I trust it? Anyone on this ship would know mentioning Hook would draw my ear... and if I were an enemy, I'd want my prey's guard down. Pretending to ignore it, I stay put.

"There's a mutiny, princess. It's not safe for you to stay there." The man knocks again, gently rapping his knuckles to the wood.

Clearly, it's safe enough or he wouldn't be asking me to open the door.

"Fine," he says, and something bursts, causing bits to hit the chest and tumble along the floor.

Okay... Definitely not mortal. Elementals can't weave and pluck magic... Their gifts are blessings from the gods that have been passed down through generations, not true magic from the soul, like mages and druids. They can overpower wards with strength, but it doesn't smell the same. Whoever is in this room is either a druid or a mage, and their magic is potent, almost syrupy sweet to the point I have to force back a gag.

My mind whirls, thinking over every face I've seen. I've made it my business to know their abilities and there are quite a few mortal men on board, the elementals... only one man of druidic lineage comes to mind. The man I saw holding Zephyr's hand. The cook, I think.

What was his name? I've barely said two words to the man. I'm not even sure I've heard him speak. What could he possibly want with me?

The man paces around the room and then stops next to the chest. He rests something on top of it, but it takes everything I have not to lurch out of my skin when his voice hits me. He must be crouched down, but somehow, he's aware of exactly where my head is. It's as if he's talking directly into my ear through the wooden side of the trunk.

"You can't hide in there forever."

My blood runs ice cold, freezing in my veins. Even the air stills as he taps on the wooden box. I grip the knife. There's no way I can come out of this box swinging. I've seen the sheer size of this man and he could snap me in half like a toothpick. Taking a dagger from my hand will be nothing for him. It'd be better if he doesn't know I have it... I'm not sure if it'll work, but if I don't go willingly, there's no way I can get upright and out of the chest before he attacks. Just as there's no way I can fight him with magic.

Slowly, I slip the dagger down my shirt, working it into the waistband of my pants so the hilt is the only thing sticking out. Even then, I try to make it lined up with the straight plane of my thigh, hoping he won't see it if I untuck my shirt. It's Sebastian's and is huge on me, coming down almost to my knees until I tuck the front in. The baggy fabric of the button-up might just be enough.

Just as I get it settled, the lid lifts, and ringed fingers lurch through the crevice before I can even see my attacker's face. He rips me by my throat, lifting me to my feet as I grip his arm, holding him off just enough for me to breathe.

"There you are," he coos, bringing my face so close to his that my feet dangle above the ground and I can make out every single freckle on his pale skin. His bright red hair wisps over his forehead, and deep brown eyes glare at me as if he's looking into my very soul. Black inky lines curl up his neck, disappearing beneath the collar of his shirt. Druidic symbols to enhance his magic. I've seen them in books, and I've heard of the practice of blood tattoos, but it's been a long-forgotten practice to my understanding. Then again, druids and mages can extend their lifetimes hundreds and thousands of years. For all I know, this man might have existed while they were still in daily practice.

His grip isn't tight enough to choke me, but it's strong enough that I have to latch onto him to keep gravity from doing the job for him. His lips twist into a smile that has the hairs at the back of my neck standing on end. Then the brown rings of his eyes disappear, consumed by darkness. I almost lose my grip.

He's... He's possessed?

The man sets me down, gripping a handful of my hair before I can make it a single step away. His fingers drive into my hair, latching down and yanking my head at an awkward angle. I can barely keep up with his long strides as he pulls me down the hall, toward the lower levels.

Using my gift, I curl my fingers, closing my eyes to focus as much as I can. Pain sears through my scalp, but I push through, pulsing my magic out until translucent strings connect from my fingers to his limbs. Lifting on, I take control, forcing him to let go. But he grins wider than what should be possible, and magic slams into me, knocking me back into the wall. The world swims as my vision fades in and out, darkening by the second.

"Don't worry, princess. I don't plan on killing you yet. I need you alive." He crouches down beside me, smoothing my hair out of my face. Everything rings and even his voice, though he's right in front of me, is muffled as if I'm underwater. "This man is fighting harder than I expected. He wants his body back."

Something twists deep inside me. It's the witch... and she wants me.

Somehow, she managed to teether her mind—the pit in my stomach settles deeper as I put the pieces together. She must've scratched the man that shoved her into the pit. It only takes a drop of blood and enough stored magic to cast the spell. She waited until they pushed her from the plank, while the cuffs binding her magic were off to utter the spell. She only had seconds before hitting the water, yet she did it. She possessed him and after that, she must've hopped into the druid.

Tingles spread through my body, my nerves sparking like fireworks on the surface of my skin. Slowly, my vision starts to stabilize.

We've been played... The Crocodile, my father, whoever orchestrated that attack on the Western Isles knew Sebastian would come. They wanted the witch to get captured so she could possess someone on his crew. She did what was needed to survive when her body was swallowed up, but now she's looking for the best host, and her sights have landed on me.

"What are you doing to them? The men on the deck?" I ask, plastering myself to the wall to put as much distance between the druid and me.

"Oh, just a game. This host was fun, but he's too ancient. He'll push me out soon, but you... You're perfect. You can cozy up to the captain... with the right mind, you could make him do whatever you want. Especially with that talent of yours."

The druid's hand grips my arm as his head snaps to the right, toward the companionway. Lifting me to my feet like I weigh nothing, he drags me kicking and screaming deeper into the ship. He clears the storage bay doors, warding them shut in seconds with strings so tightly wound, that I can't see the wooden planks of the doors anymore.

My magic pushes and pulls, trying to take control and force him to let me go, but it's no use. She's right, he's ancient and there's no way I'll be able to keep a hold of him for more than a second or two.

I try again, putting every ounce of strength I have into controlling him. My strings attach, my fingers curl, and I feel the energy sapping away from my body faster than ever.

The druid chuckles as he steps closer, unsheathing a knife from his hip. "Hold still. It won't hurt."

I grind my teeth, feeling my witch mark burn into my shoulder blades. Normally, the glow feels like static electricity running over my skin, but with how much power I'm using, today it feels like an inferno. I've used magic enough in my lifetime to know it won't actually burn me, but gods... It feels like it.

I cry out, holding the strings as much as I can. The druid catches the orange glow, or something behind me. And in the split second that his eyes leave my form, glancing past me, I yank the dagger from my waistband. I grip the hilt tight and drive it through the man's heart. His eyes widen and I kick out, planting my boot against his stomach.

The druid pulls the dagger from his chest, dropping, and sending it clattering to the ground as blood pours from the wound. "You're..." the witch sputters, coughing up blood as the druid she's possessing stumbles backward.

I yank the strings again, this time bringing the dagger the witch intended to cut me with to the druid's throat. With a jerk of my pinky, his arm wretches to the side and the blade nips deep into his skin. Limb by limb, his body collapses onto the floor. He's dead... and since she didn't have a chance to hop hosts, she is too. It's over...

My eyes are locked on the crimson puddle, expanding closer and closer to my feet. Yet, it's like they're cemented in place. I've seen people die. I watched Sebastian kill repeatedly in the gauntlet, just as I've stood by my father during crown executions. The only one that's ever gotten to me was that witch going overboard. It was like seeing my future play out before my eyes.

I've never used, nor have the intention of using sacrificial magic, but my mark makes me no better than her. I'm not sure why my mother gave it to me, but to everyone else in the realm, me and the witch I just killed will forever be the same.

Nothing has ever made my heart feel like this—hollow. I've never killed anyone before, but I just ended two in the same moment.

"Scarlet!" Smee grabs my shoulders, swinging me around to face her. I know she's before me. I know she's saying something, but I don't hear it. Just as I don't see her face. My mind is stuck on the image of blood seeping through wooden boards, knowing I did it. Honestly, I'm not even sure if Smee is really here or if I've imagined it.

"Breathe. It's going to be alright." She tucks me into her chest, putting her chin on top of my head. Her heartbeat... She's real. The wards must've fallen when the druid died.

Shadows swirl near the door, forming into a man in a matter of seconds. Sebastian looks past us where his friend lies on the floor. Slowly, he inches closer to me and Smee and she smooths my hair. "My brother's here. I called him. It's over, Scarlet, I promise."

It's then that I realize I've wrapped my arms around her, and tear stains darken her shirt. When did I start crying?

Sebastian pries me away from Smee and clutches me against his chest, exchanging a look with his sister. "What happened?"

"The witch changed bodies. I was on my way back to get Scarlet when Lorian hit me from behind." Smee reaches for the back of her head, lifting her fingers to reveal fresh blood. "I woke up and ran after him, knowing he wasn't in control. Lorian would've never done something like that. I was too late. She used his magic to spell the door shut."

"She was going to possess me."

Sebastian stiffens. Without warning, he wretches me backward and presses his necklace to my face. It's not the pendant he uses, but the chain. He does it in another spot as I look at him, my eyebrows flattening.

"What are you doing?" I ask, swatting at him when he goes for a third time.

"Making sure you're you." His shoulders ease before he hugs me again.

"Why would I not be? I just killed a man for gods sakes. She was going to use me to get to you. Do you thank everyone by shoving a chain at their face?"

He chuckles, still hugging me even though I've stopped hugging him. His lips press to the top of my head. "Just the ones I'm married to." Sebastian leans back, lifting the chain that holds the stone around his neck up for me to see. "It's demon ore. If she had possessed you, I would've burned."

Taking a deep breath, I try to stop my hands from shaking. "I'm sorry about your friend."

Sebastian smiles, cupping the side of my face and swiping a thumb over my cheek. "Lorian is fine. If she was going to possess anyone, he was the best option. The man has nine lives. Literally."

My head tilts to the side, my eyes zoning out. "He's not dead?"

Sebastian shakes his head. That should ease my nerves, but it does the opposite. I didn't want to hurt him and I still don't, but what if he remembers what he saw? He'll know about my mark, he'd have seen it glow... Which will make me next on the plank.

Sebastian pulls me back into his arms, holding me to him. "Hey, it's alright. You didn't hurt him. He'll be just fine. The witch is gone for good and just to make sure; we're checking everyone on board." His scent wraps around me, wood smoke and sea spray. "You're safe, Scars. I promise."

My chest shakes as the panic settles deeper. I don't want to lie to him, but what choice do I have? I don't want to die... Blinking back the tears, my arms tighten around his middle. It's futile to believe promises will save me if he were to find out the truth. But hearing him say it fills me with a false sense of hope. He's a man of his word, and maybe it'll be enough for him to hear me out when the time comes.

My breathing steadies and the tension eases in my chest. The tightness that held my lungs in stasis dissipates in seconds. I let my head rest against his chest, listening to the steady beat of his heart.

"There you go," he murmurs, brushing a kiss over my hair. "It's going to be okay."

19

Scarlet

Sebastian leads me out of the storage bay, darkness rippling around us as he transports us through the halls of the ship. He reaches for something through the dark fog. His arm twists and draws back a wooden door, revealing a spacious room. Guiding me forward, he shuts it behind us, and the shadowy haze dissipates.

It's not lavish, but well-appointed. A large poster bed is nestled against one wall, draped in deep midnight linens and fluffy furs. A clawfoot tub, similar to the one in my room back in Solaria, is mounted into the floorboards in one corner. The room itself is easily four times as large as the cabin I've been staying in, with most of the wall space shelves, enclosed in thick glass shutters.

Trinkets and oddities are scattered over the surfaces, memories maybe, or magical objects. Some shelves are crammed full of leather-bound tomes—most of them grimoires and spell books. He's likely collected them from the witches he's faced in his years of pirating. Others are full of amber bottles of various sizes and shapes. There are bundles of herbs wrapped in twine, along with a selection of glowing tonics and potions. It's like a personal apothecary.

"Where are we?" I ask, stepping away from him to get a better look at the shelves.

He steps behind me, resting his hands on my hips. "My room." He kisses my shoulder. "You've had enough excitement for one day. You should get some rest. The crew will have your room door repaired soon, but I thought with all things considered, you'd feel safer here."

"But it's just past high noon," I protest, turning in place to look at him—really looking at him. It's like he just stepped out of the gauntlet.

His hair is soaked. I'm not sure if it's from sweat or water. Random red streaks stand out against his white button-up, and his hands are covered in dried blood. Splatter paints his neck and jaw, and in some places, it's smeared into crimson streaks.

What happened out there?

There's a reason he teleported me directly to his front door and didn't let me see through his shadows. Something happened on that deck that he didn't want me to see. The witch had used the druid's magic to cause chaos... Did she turn them on each other?

Oddly enough, after everything that's transpired, I don't want to be alone. I don't want to go back to my room. I'm not sure sleep is in the cards for me, but being near him helps. It might be the last moment alone with him that I get, considering Lorian could wake and reveal my deepest, darkest secret.

Sebastian studies me for a long moment, eyes softening. "Alright, that's enough worrying for one day." His voice is gentle, his hands even more so as he guides me to his bed. "Even if you can handle more worrying, I don't think I can. So, please... If nothing else, try to get some rest for me. You can take a bath if you want, but I'll stay with you as long as you want me to."

"What about your men?" I ask, letting my hand glide over the fur blanket.

"They'll manage. Everyone has been through hell, but I'm not worried about everyone, at least not as much as I am you."

His back is to me when I turn around, shocked by the implication of his words. Shrugging the shirt off his shoulders, he opens a panel in the wall and grabs out clean clothes. Something flies in the air, and I catch it out of instinct, turning the soft fabric over in my hands.

"For you," he says, grabbing a wet rag to start scrubbing the blood from his hands. "I can grab some of the things from your room if you prefer it."

"No... This is fine, thank you." I watch him in awe as he scrubs himself clean. He dips his head into a bucket of water, lifting to let the red-tinged stream run into the bathtub. Clean water drips from the rag as he swipes it over his skin, and droplets roll down his body, saturating the waistband of his pants, slung lower around his hips.

His stormy green eyes meet mine. "Are you going to put it on?"

"Are you going to turn around?" I shoot back.

His eyebrows disappear beneath the soft waves of his hair. "I'm pretty sure that's a moot point by now, don't you think?" A wolfish smile takes over his lips, but he finishes up, then holds his hands in the air like he's surrendering to the enemy, giving me his back. "Your wish is my command."

"Thank you," I say, making quick work of the buttons of my shirt and keeping my back toward the wall. A feeling washes over me, making my skin prickle like someone is watching me. I glance up to find him peeking in the reflection of the cabinet windows. "Eyes down."

His smirk grows wider, but he obeys all the same. "I sort of like it when you're bossy."

My cheeks flame as the shirt drops from my body and I slip the new one over my head. Of course, he'd find a way to make a moment like this a chance for him to flirt.

Standing up to slip off my pants. The shirt makes a nightgown, coming down to my knees. "Do you flirt with all the pretty girls this hard?"

He turns, his eyes taking their sweet time, traveling down my body. "No."

I'm not sure what answer I expected, but I do know that one didn't make it any easier. It's impossible to fight the smirk that pulls at the corners of my mouth, and he doesn't miss it. Heat floods through me, swirling in my middle. I try to push the sensation from my mind, but Sebastian steps closer, and the feeling intensifies.

He stops in front of me, reaching up to twirl a lock of my hair around his finger. "You like it when I flirt, and it's precisely why I do it."

Still wrapped in my hair, he tilts my chin. Stormy green eyes search mine as he moves closer until they flutter shut. I shouldn't kiss him... Honestly, I should be trying to figure out a way off this ship, but I don't think death itself could force me to move. Lorian could wake at any moment. Sebastian will know and it could be my undoing, but all I want is to kiss him. All I can think about is the feel of his lips on mine, his hands on my body, the smell of his cologne, and the way he tastes of fairy wine.

Rising onto my tippy toes, I kiss him, not wanting to wait another moment. His lips claim mine, his hands diving into my hair, pulling me closer. Everything falls away — the world around us, the sounds, the distractions. There's nothing but him and me, no pirate ships, no witches, no marks, no wars on the horizon.

My hands slide down his chest, feeling the wetness of his skin. He's so warm... and his skin is so smooth. You'd think it'd be rough. Every other part of him is. His personality.

His attitude. The way he carries himself could strike fear into a man alone. The stubble on his jaw brushes against my skin as he leans in closer, his breath mingling with mine. My pulse quickens as the hand he's placed on my hip tightens its grip possessively, and the world seems to tilt on its axis.

The kiss is soft, yet demanding, and our lips move in sync, every brush and caress sending sparks of electricity down my spine. Then it's over all too soon...

Sebastian pulls back, resting his forehead against mine. He strokes his thumb over my bottom lip, cupping my face in the palm of his hand. A groan escapes his throat as he bends to place another quick kiss on my lips. "There are so many things I want to do right now... How do you do this to me?" He shakes his head gently. "I know I should let you sleep, that you need to, but if you keep kissing me like that..." He takes a step back, flexing his hands until the veins of his forearms rise to the surface.

Searching his eyes, my lips twitch up at the corner. "Ever the gentleman."

He swallows hard but doesn't move or look away. "Trust me, princess, that's the last thing I want to be."

I pull back the bedding and slip beneath the covers, and finally, Sebastian moves. He continues to move about the room, cleaning himself up before sliding into bed beside me. Looping his arm around my middle, he clutches me against his side. My head rests above his heart, and the steady thrum beats in my ear. The heat of his body seeps into mine, and my eyes drift shut, surrendering to the darkness that threatens to pull me under.

Whatever happens when Lorian wakes can't wait. For now, I'll savor this moment and hope the fates act in my favor.

20
Scarlet

I jolt awake, barely gripping the bed in time to keep from rolling over the edge and onto the unforgiving floor. The wooden beams above me wail as the walls creak and groan. My world swings along with the ship's nauseating rhythm and the lanterns hanging near the bookcases send chaotic beams of light around the room.

Before I can get my bearings, the enchanted flames within the lanterns go out, and I'm in utter darkness. My senses go into overdrive. The scent of burnt lamp oil mingles with the salty air, the masculine scent of Sebastian, and the dusty smell of books. I feel for the bedpost, gripping it hard to keep still.

"Sebastian," I call out into the dark. "Can you hear me?"

Distant, muffled shouts of men fill my ears, their panic tangible even through the thick walls of the captain's quarters. The ship drops, along with my stomach, and I dare a chance of letting go of the post just long enough to reach across the bed, finding the spot next to me empty and cold.

My gut tells me I'm alone—again—in the midst of chaos. Great.

Sebastian must've gotten up before me.

Kicking off the covers, I feel around the floor for my pants. Everything has moved... Glass rattles against the shuttered shelves and I let out a deep breath. Blinking hard as I try to focus, I feel magic pour into my veins as I mumble the single-word spell for light. My hands glow, allowing me to see the room.

Finding my clothes, I pull on my leather pants and boots, trying not to taste the floor in the process. Even with my spell, I can barely see in this place. Dressed, I push to my feet, gripping the furniture as I stumble my way toward the door. I wretch it open, only to find madness waiting on the other side. The air stills in my lungs as fear creeps into my bones.

The crew dashes across the deck, some clutching weapons, others barking orders. They're fighting something, but I can't make out what. The fog is so dense, that there might as well be a wall around the deck. The ship takes another brutal dip, making my stomach feel like it's disintegrating into nothingness. Before I can make sense of what is happening, a blue-scaled tail unravels and smashes into the wooden planks, making some ripple and snap upon impact. Men fly through the air, their screams flooding my body with adrenaline.

One of the crew spots me, standing in the doorway and skids to a stop. His blue eyes lock on mine as he points at me.

"Princess, you must—" A burst of otherworldly blue blocks the man from view. The light dims to reveal the man, still pointing at me. His body is frozen solid, enveloped in icy blue flame—alive one second and a statue the next.

My heart contracts. It can't be the witch. She's dead... isn't she?

But then the ship heaves violently again, throwing off my train of thought. The sounds of chaos multiply—the shriek of tearing wood, the splash of someone being flung overboard, the screams of terror.

Sebastian. I have to find Sebastian. The monster's thrashing is violent, more intense with each passing moment. With a force that feels world-ending, it encircles us, its scaly embrace threatening to tear us apart.

I search for him, finding three more frozen statues on the deck. Then I catch the tendrils of darkness piercing the fog. It surrounds whatever creature is trying to coil around the ship, making us jolt and slingshot left and right.

Blue scales peek through the shadows, a serpent-like face and a mouth full of sharpened teeth. It's the creature. It followed us. But why? The witch is dead. Even if she spelled it, all of her magic would die along with her.

Sebastian stands, legs braced apart, and shadows writhing around him. His voice cuts through the air like a blade as he shouts orders at his crew. They rush toward him, spears in hand.

The creature's jaw opens, revealing a glow like lightning itself living between its jaws. I open my mouth to warn them, but it's too late. A blast of blue flames shoots and the men hit the deck. The boat tilts and I slam into the door frame, gripping the wooden lip of it until my knuckles turn white. The door swings wildly and I brace my foot, stopping it before it can crush my fingers in the jam.

"Ready! Fire!" Sebastian shouts, his voice strained with urgency.

Explosions rattle my eardrums as lights illuminate the dense fog. I take a deep breath, trying to quell the panic clawing at my insides. I can't just hide while everyone else fights for our lives. I need to help, but how?

I peer into the darkened room for something thick enough to hide the glow of my mark. Sebastian's shirts, as comfortable as they may be, are too thin. The mark will shine through the linen. I need a jacket or something...

Looking back at the beast, I spot Sebastian's form. He's wearing his red coat, and considering how frugal his closet is, I doubt he has another. There's got to be something else... I could wrap a blanket around me, but I wouldn't be able to hold on to it and cast. I need both of my hands to control that thing, and even then, I'm not sure I can—not unless I'm close.

"Scarlet!"

My name pulls me from my thoughts and I look up to lock eyes with Sebastian from across the deck. In the time it takes me to blink, I'm yanked back into his room. The door slams shut with a resounding thud and something crackles behind me. I whirl, coming face to face with him, trying to catch my breath.

"Stay here," he orders, leaving no room to argue. He presses something into my hand, something bright. The boat rocks and he grips onto the shelf. "If anything happens, I'll come for you, but you have to stay here."

"Why is it attacking us?"

"I don't know. Normally, they like it when we feed them." His fingers thrust into his hair as the words fly from his mouth. "But the witch must've cast something on it before she died."

"Anything she would've cast would've died with her. There's got to be another reason." My gaze zones out on the floor. "You don't think she hopped into that thing, do you? Could she do that if it stayed close to the ship?"

Sebastian stares at me, his face falling. "I—I don't know."

"When you sent her overboard, it came from beneath the ship. What if it was following you? Is it always that one that eats them?"

The ship sways, and he steadies me on my feet. "Not always, but mostly. I can't worry about the why, right now. I have to go. Promise me you'll stay right here." I don't answer, lost in my mind. With one last lingering glance, he disappears into the shadows, leaving me alone in the dimly lit room.

My heart hammers in my chest, and I struggle to catch my breath, glancing down to see some sort of glowing ball in my hand. I lift it up, eyeing the glassy surface. Cold sweat trickles down my spine, and my hands tremble, but inside is something fluttering. A bug, maybe?

With a sickening lurch, the ship tilts almost upright, and I'm flung into the wall of Sebastian's room. The ball leaves my hand and rolls away. I grit my teeth, scrambling to my feet. Ducking down, I cover my head with my arms as anything that's not bolted down or locked inside cabinets goes flying. A chair slams into the door and busts it open as the ship continues to tilt. The tail end is being dragged beneath the water.

The sight before me steals my breath away; the crew members hang on for dear life, dangling from ropes and fixtures—whatever they can—as they try not to fall into the water.

I flatten myself against the cabinets, the wall now becoming the floor, and peer through the doorway. The hinges whine as the wooden slab dangles, and I swallow hard. We're going down... The ship can't survive this kind of torture for much longer.

My gaze is drawn to the creature. Its blue scales reflect what little light pierces the fog, forming a constellation on the deck. Its serpent-like body coils around the ship, constricting and threatening to splinter the hull into pieces. With each heave of its muscular form, the vessel groans and creaks, teetering on the brink of destruction.

Sebastian dangles from the broken mast. It's snapped in the middle, but the two halves are still held together by fragments of wood. His shadows are wrapped around the dangling piece, and other tendrils hang on to other crewmen, trying to keep them from disappearing into the deep.

He grits, his muscles flexing and straining with everything he has. Those stormy green eyes meet mine and for a moment, everything stills. Something in that stare... He knows as well as I do that in a matter of minutes, we're all going to drown unless something changes. And I'm the only one with the power to make that happen.

He's slipping bit by bit, holding on to too much for one man. Any moment now, he'll go over. My mind races, searching for some way to help, but fear holds me captive.

I have to do something... I don't have a choice. It's now or never.

Taking a deep breath, I flip my legs through the hole of the doorway, holding myself up by the frame until my back is against the deck floor. And I let go.

I slide, picking up speed as I aim for the forward mast, the smaller of the two, but it's level with the creature's head. As I slide by, barely missing it, I snatch the rope loosely coiled around it and slam to a stop. The rope bites into my hands as I swing off the wooden planks and then slam back against them. Pain roils through my arm and hip, but I don't let go.

I need my hands... Stealing a glance up, I only have about a foot or two to climb and if I can do that, I can straddle the mast, putting my body right in front of the beast's face. Turning so I can brace my feet on the deck, I walk up it, gripping hand over hand on the rope. I clench my teeth, hissing out air as I gain each inch until I can pull myself up and over the poll.

Locking my ankles around the round beam, I tie the rope around my torso. Sebastian yells my name, but I can't afford to hesitate. I have to act now and seeing his face, knowing everything is about the change, will only make what I'm about to do feel worse.

My hands tremble as I lift them up, staring into the beast's bright yellow eyes. My fingers curl into claws as power surges through me, so strong it steals my breath away. But I won't stop. Translucent threads shimmer into existence, and I start to pluck at the invisible strands. The ship starts to lower as the sea beast releases its grip. Its movements are slow and fluid as the ship settles back to a natural angle. Once low enough for me to stand, I get to my feet. My gaze never wavers or twitches from the beast's as I breathe heavily, feeling the energy within me running out like an hourglass.

My time is limited. I won't be able to keep this up forever.

Its blue-hued scales shimmer like liquid moonlight as they ripple with each movement. The fog grows thinner as I take in the thin gill strands hanging from its face, its rounded eyes full of curiosity, and something I can't put my thumb on. That is until they flash black as night.

She did... I knew killing a witch powerful enough to possess and take control of a druid like Lorian wouldn't have died so easily. The beast fights against my magic, its mouth opening to reveal the blue lightning. If I let go, it'll try to sink us again, under the control of the bitch who won't die.

The sound of feet sprinting across the deck hits my ears, but if I look away, there's no way my strings will hold. I have to focus. I have to buy them time to kill her. A boom echoes over the deck, loud enough to make my ears ring, and something flies past me and my hair swirls wildly around my face.

A silver spear, tipped with some sort of brassy metal slams into the beast's chest. The momentum knocks it backward with a jolt. It's wail breaking my heart... It didn't ask for this. It's innocent, but that thing inside it is not, and unfortunately, without her body, her host will have to pay the price.

The creature falls backward into the water, sending a wave crashing into the ship so hard I lose my footing. My hands hit the deck, saving my face from colliding with it, but the loosened nails that held the boards down stab into my palms, creating shallow wounds and drawing blood. I cry out, trying to stay put as the ship slides relentlessly sideways. It twirls, spinning us like a top until the wave dies out and the water stills.

With ragged breaths, I sit back on my heels, turning my face toward the hell flame that's hidden by the clouds. My world stills, regaining my bearings, and I cringe, trying to untie the rope around my waist.

That's it. It's dead. She's dead... and soon, so will I.

"Scarlet!" Sebastian shouts, his voice breaking. It's not concern that powers it, but true, guttural fury. I deserve it...A part of me knew I should've told him the night we were married. Just because I didn't have a choice in placing the glamour on my mark, doesn't mean I didn't keep the truth from him willingly.

I kept waiting for the right moment, but the longer I waited, the harder it was to say... and the more I didn't want to hurt him.

My shoulder blades are on fire... The witch mark is burning so hot that it feels like it'll level me to ash. Tears stream from my eyes, but I'm not scared.

I've never used this much magic at once, and I nearly depleted my soul in the process of saving this ship. I felt the very edge at which the line of no return was drawn and had it been another moment, I'd have shattered. Still, I'd do it again. I'd do every bloody second again if it meant saving him.

I was already living on borrowed time, anyway. I'd made my peace with the end before he'd ever walked into my life. But I refuse to let him die with only half of his soul. He's given me so much... so much more than he'll ever understand. I owed it to him.

In the time I've known Sebastian, I've lived more than I have in twenty-three years. I've seen places beyond the castle walls. I've seen what family is supposed to be like in the way he cares for his crew and his sister—in the house he took me to in the Luminaries. I could feel it...

He's given me a chance to care about someone more than myself, more than my kingdom, or the duty I was born for. With him, I've experienced what it's like to care about someone so strongly that you're willing to lay everything on the line. Even if it's only for a chance of them breathing for one more second.

He's the first to show me love... Even if it isn't that yet, it feels like it. No one has ever looked at me like he does.

Not even Zelix. No one has ever cared enough about my opinion to ask for it or worry for my well-being enough to be scared when it's in jeopardy. No one's ever gone out of their way to soothe my soul or make me feel safe.

I'd die for him, even if it's by his hand in which I bleed.

Blinking long and hard, I lower my face from the sky and gather the courage to glance over my shoulder. His hair and clothes are soaked, dripping water onto the deck, and the expression on his face is unreadable. Though I can tell by the way his chest heaves with every angry breath that he knows... He knows my secret, along with everyone else on this ship.

The wind whips around me, tugging at my hair and billowing my linen shirt against my body. Blood drips from my fingers, coming from the nail wounds in my hands. My heart pounds relentlessly into my ribs, like it knows at any moment it'll break. I tear my eyes away, jumping the moment his voice tears through the air.

"Look at me!" His voice strains, raw from yelling commands. It's cold, devoid of the warmth and teasing nature I've grown used to—that I took for granted. My chest tightens, the gravity of my predicament weighing upon it and making it hard to breathe.

Tears prick at the corners of my eyes as his footsteps grow closer, stopping behind me. "What did you just do?" He speaks quieter now, but it doesn't change his tone. I can feel the tension rolling off him, poisoning the air.

"Maybe it just wasn't used to seeing a lady on a pirate ship," I whisper, my voice shaky with unshed tears.

He walks around me, the tips of his boots entering my vision as I zone my gaze out on the deck. "Tell me I'm wrong. Tell me I imagined it."

"I can't..." I swallow hard.

"Look. At. Me." My hands tremble in my lap, but I do as he asks. "How long?" His eyes blaze, and I can see every muscle tense beneath his skin.

"Always," I confess, my voice barely audible.

Sebastian's anger seems to bubble over as he looks away, jaw clenching, but he says nothing. I can hear the sound of his teeth grinding. There's no going back to how things were before... All I can do is steel myself for what comes next.

"Damn it, Scarlet," he curses under his breath, gripping his jaw like it will relieve the tension there.

He gestures to his men and hands grip my shoulders hard enough to make me cry out as I'm forced to my feet. They start to drag me backward and my eyes flare wide. I know all too well that the plank exists on the far side of the ship, exactly where they're going. They're going to toss me over without asking for an explanation.

I squirm in their hands, wanting to yell that I can explain, or beg or plead for mercy, but I can't get a single sound to leave my lips. The crewmen stop for a moment when Sebastian lifts his hand, and my lungs finally expand.

Except it's not understanding in his eyes. It's white-hot fury as he storms forward and grips my chin, forcing me to look into his eyes.

"Keep fighting and I'll drop you in the fucking prison hole myself," he snarls, and his grip loosens as terror floods through me. "Do I need to bind your magic, or do you think we can be civil?"

"None of the other witches got a choice," I reply before I can stop myself, taken aback by his question. I didn't mean as a taunt, but Sebastian laughs humorlessly, his tone dry.

"None of the other witches were my fucking wife." I flinch away at his words and he waves a dismissive hand at his men. "Get her out of my sight. I need a moment."

"The grate to the hole is damaged, Captain. Should we lock her in her room?" says the man on my right.

Sebastian doesn't even look up, just shakes his head. "Put her in mine. Bolt the fucking door if you have to."

The crewmen obey and start dragging me toward the captain's quarters. As we make our way, I glance at the crew crowded on the deck. Somehow, the looks on their faces manage to cut even deeper. I'm dead to them... Even Smee.

The only thing I can hope for is that when Sebastian calms down, he'll hear me out. I need to give him a reason to keep me alive long enough for that to happen though, I just don't know what that is.

21
HOOK

The anger boils inside me, festering like a wound left untreated. This entire fucking time Scarlet's been a blood witch. How did I miss it? I should've seen her mark. I've seen every inch of her... How did I not notice? Yet there it was, glowing on her back, as she took control over that damned beast. The others saw it too. There's no denying it now.

My mind is at war with itself, trying to reconcile everything I've come to know about Scarlet with what I know about blood witches. They killed my mother, and now, the woman I'm bound to is one. It's maddening. I can feel every ounce of Scarlet's pain and heartbreak, and it consumes my every breath to the point it hurts. I can feel my heart spaz inside my chest like it's ready to stop beating altogether and I don't know what to do.

"Captain," Nelvin says, keeping his distance, but it's impossible to miss the worry in his eyes. And in his ears. They always seem to sag a bit when he's concerned. "We need to get the wreckage cleared up. Considering half the crew is gone, we really could use every hand we can get."

"Fine," I snap, grabbing a broken wooden plank and turning my back toward him.

"Are you alright?" I feel his hand on my shoulder, and I stop my pursuit.

"No, I'm not alright, and asking me that is only going to make it worse." I shrug his hand off and start walking with purpose.

"She was a witch; we're just worried about you."

Something in Nelvin's comment breaks me. It shatters the last bit of control I have. The fury builds up, and I hurl the plank across the deck, watching it splinter against the mast.

"Hey! Easy," Zephyr yells, narrowing his eyes at me from across the deck. "The only thing destroying the ship will do is strand us out here."

"Then what am I supposed to do, Zephyr?" I snarl, my hands balling into fists.

"Talk about it." Zephyr's eyes soften as he steps closer, but I hold up my hands.

"I don't want to talk about it. I want to stay busy. You should be in the med bay, anyway. That's your job." Every muscle in my body tenses as I struggle to control my fury. The revelation of Scarlet's true nature feels like a knife twisting in my gut, and all I want to do is scream at the injustice of it all.

"Sebastian," he replies, his voice firm. "I'm not leaving you like this. As your doctor and your best friend, you're stuck with me."

"Are the crew members in critical condition stable?" I ask, raising an eyebrow.

"Yes." His expression is unwavering.

"Alright, then you can stay and help." It's pointless to argue with him. I start to walk away, but I pause mid-stride, turning back to Zephyr so I can point a finger at him. "But I'm not talking about it."

Nelvin saunters over, throwing an arm around both of our necks with a lopsided grin plastered on his face. "Ah, the joys of manual labor," he quips, attempting to lighten the mood. "Just what the doctor ordered."

"Cut the shit, Nelvin," Zephyr snaps, whacking him in the sternum. Nelvin chuckles, rolling his eyes as his arms drop.

We work in tense silence for a while, each of us lost in our own thoughts. How could I have been so blind? For the first time in ages, I actually enjoy the presence of someone. Her snarky comments, her perfect lips, the way she reacts to me, the way I feel everything... I've never yearned for someone like this, yet she's all I can think about. All of it, every last piece, was a fucking lie.

For all I know, the king knew it was me when I pledged. Maybe he saw through the glamour. Perhaps this was his intention, to bind me to his blood witch daughter to distract me from his merchant ship and to cloud my mind enough to unleash the bloody Crocodile on the outer realm. I just don't know how he would've known I'd try to enter.

"It could be worse," Nelvin says, limping over to pick up a piece of wood near me. His knee is wrapped and blood peaks through the white gauze. "At least she was pretty. You don't suppose her teeth are going to fall out, do you?"

My vision turns red. I can practically feel the blood pounding in my ears. My hand shoots out as shadows coil around him, squeezing until his face reddens.

"What did you just say?" I snarl, stepping closer to look him in the eyes. He sputters, the silver rings around his pupils nearly disappearing as I back him toward the railing. "Go on then, say it a little louder so everyone can hear you."

Nelvin's Adam's apple bobs in his throat. "I didn't mean it like that, I swear."

"Oh no no no. You see, I heard you loud and clear, but I need them to hear it too, so I don't get chastised for killing a cripple."

"Sebastian!" Zephyr yells, closing the distance between us. He calls for Lorian, who's closer and his magic rushes over me, prying my shadows from Nelvin's throat one by one.

Freed, Nelvin rubs at his neck, taking a few deep breaths as he backs away, creating a safe distance between us.

"You're lucky I love you, Hook, or I might be pissed right now," he says, trying to regain some semblance of humor.

I narrow my eyes into slits, my chest heaving. I shouldn't have lashed out at him. He's just doing what he always does. Nelvin lives to get a rise out of people, and I took the bait, but it was his unique way of trying to get me to work through. I know that.

"Get back to work," I growl, turning my attention back to the shattered remains of our ship's deck.

As I pick up another piece of debris, my mind wanders back to Scarlet. The thought of her alone in that room... I can feel every ounce of heartbreak and it kills me not to be able to go to her, to kiss it away and make her forget. Since taking that damn oath, I've lived for the moments that she smiles and laughs because it's such a foreign thing to me... The way my heart swells when she looks at me.

"Damn it," I mutter under my breath, hating myself for feeling this way. But as much as I wish I could ignore it, the truth remains: no matter how furious I am or how many lies she's told, some part of me still cares and I don't think that'll ever go away. As long as our bond remains intact, as long as she breathes...

I'm in the midst of cleaning up the wreckage her kind made on this ship, that took over thirty lives today. I need perspective, to remember not who she is, but what she is and never forget it.

I clench my fists, determined to push those thoughts aside and focus on the task at hand. There will be time to sort through my emotions later. For now, all I can do is keep moving forward, one step at a time.

Just as I'm about to pick up part of the railing, heat surges through my middle, catching me off guard. It nearly brings me to my knees. I stumble, catching my balance on the mast, and brace myself with one hand.

"Sebastian!" Zephyr's voice cuts through the haze, and he rushes to my side, concern etched on his face. "What's wrong?"

"Nothing," I growl, waving him away. But Zephyr remains stubborn, folding his arms across his chest.

"It's not nothing. Now you can either tell me, or I'll get Smee."

Another wave of heat washes over me, and I tense, gritting my teeth to stifle a groan. Nelvin approaches, limping slightly, but manages to flash his signature grin.

"Alright there, Captain?" he asks, one perfect eyebrow raised. Fucking elves and their cunning nature.

I straighten up, sucking in a deep breath as I try to shake off the pressure in my chest. "I don't know what's happening," I admit, my voice strained.

Zephyr looks me up and down, his brown eyes widening as they pause, then he darts his gaze away, staring out into the sea. His dark green lips press into a thin line without a word.

Odd...

Nelvin's laugh draws my attention and I watch him twirl on his heel before bringing his mischievous eyes to mine. "I'm no expert in blood oaths, but if I had to guess, your little witch wants to talk," he says, smirking.

My stomach drops. Glancing down at my body, I curse under my breath. Screw leather pants. They keep nothing to the imagination. I close my eyes, letting my head fall back for a moment. "The gods are testing me... I will not know fucking peace so long as that woman breathes." The raw truth of it settles heavily in my chest, and I can't help but wonder how things got this complicated.

"There's a simple fix for that, you know," Nelvin says and I glare at him. I'm not in the mood for his jokes or his sly comments today. With a frustrated growl, I storm off toward my room, leaving Zephyr and Nelvin behind on the deck.

"Good luck!" Nelvin calls after me, but I ignore him, focused on the task ahead. My heart pounds as I brace myself for the confrontation with Scarlet—the witch who's managed to entangle herself in every part of my life.

Whatever awaits me behind that door, one thing is certain: nothing will be the same once it's opened. I untie the rope the men used to close the door since the latch broke, and I keep one end tied, taking the other end with me inside as I enter, ready to face the storm. I can only hope that I'm strong enough to weather.

"Do you have a death wish, woman?" The words come out like a snarl, but every emotion leaves me in an instant. I don't even get a chance to tie the rope to the cabinet as I take in the sight before me.

She's drawn a bath, having figured out the magic symbols the water elementals enchanted. It's a network that pumps seawater through a series of channels to clean and desalinate the water. We wouldn't be able to stay out here so long without it.

Steam rises from the water. She's managed to warm it somehow. But she doesn't sit inside the layer of bubbles. Instead, she's naked except for the towel wrapped around her middle, like I caught her before she could get in.

My eyes trail down the length of her throat and my mouth goes dry, reaching the delicate curve of her shoulder, and the arches of her breast, peaking over the fabric edge. Her wide hazel eyes are frozen in time, staring at me.

Fuck me... This is it. This is how I lose the other half of my soul. This damn woman has me so wrapped around her finger that a single glance at her perfect body can sap me of the anger that seemed to boil my blood moments ago.

She's standing next to the shelves, and in hindsight, putting someone suspected of being a blood witch in a room full of magical objects and grimoires wasn't the smartest move. Still, if she wanted me dead, she would've killed me by now. I'd let my guard down countless times with this woman, trying to make the best of our arrangement and see if we could truly care for one another in marriage. She had plenty of windows of opportunity but didn't. Not to mention she kept the beast from sinking the ship when she could've ridden it out of here and left us to die.

In her hand is a milky, white stone. A moonstone. The one I needed before her.

"Don't touch that," I say, finally mustering up the ability to speak.

"I'm sorry," she says, quickly placing it back on the shelf and closing the cabinet door. "It's beautiful. I'd never seen one that big—I'm sorry, I shouldn't have touched it." She hangs her head, clutching the towel close to her body.

I turn around, pinching the bridge of my nose as I try to erase the image of her from my mind. "I need you to control your emotions, please. I can't focus and if we don't fix the ship, we're all going to die out here. And for the love of the gods, don't touch the stone. It amplifies everything you feel. Which is great for someone lacking a shadow. Not so much for someone like you."

"You mean for a witch..." The defeat in her voice guts me. I don't know how to handle this. I don't know what to do about any of it. Anyone else, I'd have booted her pretty ass overboard without a second thought, but I'm stuck...

That stone was the only thing I had before her, it allowed me to feel but it's nothing like this. Even drowning in her emotions like I am, I'd much rather experience it all than be numb again. If she dies, the bond breaks and that is over.

It could take years to get my shadow back... She's all I have.

"No, I didn't mean as a..." I trail off, not wanting to say it out loud. "It doesn't matter. I can't keep flip-flopping between wanting to murder the people I love and wanting to fuck you senseless. So please, get in the bath. Splash some water on your face and get a grip. I won't put the people on this ship in danger because you feel like being a royal pain in my ass." My jaw clenches, teeth grinding together as I resist the urge to look back.

"Does that mean you don't plan to kill me?" I hear her step into the water.

My voice softens. "I don't know what I want anymore."

My heart hammers against my chest, an angry tempo matching the fury coursing through my veins. It's the only way I can think of to drown out the sadness and desire she forces upon me.

"Tell me what to do and I'll do it." Her voice breaks and I let out a deep exhale, turning around. I shouldn't have. I should've just walked back out the door. Now, staring at the tears that streak from her beautiful hazel eyes, my heart breaks for her. I bite my lip, letting the pain diminish the need I have to wipe those tears away. She's a blood witch... Her kind killed your mother... Her kind has taken thousands of innocent lives... I can say it over and over in my head, spewing every variation of how evil the blood witches are, but looking at her, not a single fucking one of them makes sense.

I watch a tear escape from the corner of her eye, making its way down her flushed cheek. Her white hair is a tangled mess framing her face, but even disheveled, she remains infuriatingly captivating. How can I feel this way about her when she's everything I've been taught to despise?

"Please," she breathes, her voice barely audible. "Tell me what you want from me."

"Fuck, Scarlet." My hands ball into fists at my sides, knuckles straining white. "I wish I knew." As I stare into her eyes, I can see the pain and confusion swirling within them. She's a puzzle I can't solve, a riddle with no answer. The more I try to understand her, the more lost I become. "I can't do this."

22
SCARLET

A sudden wave of panic shoots through me as Sebastian turns toward the door. I lurch forward, not caring that the water likely doesn't cover much. He's seen it all now, every inch. I don't have to hide anymore.

"Wait! Please," I beg him. "Let me explain. If you still think I'm the same as that thing we killed today, then fine, but at least try to hear me out. Please..."

He freezes as if his shoes have rooted themselves to the floorboards. "Why should I care how you were marked? It doesn't change what you are."

"Because I could help you. Maybe it would be enough for you to allow me to live. Even if it's just until you get your shadow." I lean against the edge of the tub, ready to run after him if I have to.

Slowly, he turns, eyes narrowed into lethal slits. "It's precarious that the woman who was so willing to sacrifice herself for kingdom and crown is now willing to beg to live a bit longer."

The blood drains from my face. He thinks I planned for this, or maybe that my father did. He thinks I tricked him, that I played a part in a setup. I'm not sure I blame him. After seeing the lengths the blood witches will go, knowing what my father does to the outer realm by hiring such awful creatures... I get it. If I were in his shoes, I'm not sure I'd see it much differently, either.

"You still don't get it, do you? I was willing to do what was required of me. I had no choice in the matter, anyway. I didn't even know who you were when you offered me that deal, but it changed everything. I had a way to live and see the world, all while fulfilling my duty to the crown. I didn't ask for any of this. I didn't ask to be marked, I didn't ask to be married off to a stranger. My father was just as shocked as I was to see your real face in that arena. Still, the only decision I made was to help you. I bet on you."

Sebastian steps closer, but I can't tell what he's thinking or even if he senses a shred of truth in my confession. My heart races as I continue, "I didn't have to go through with our deal, and I took a huge risk in doing so. My father would've killed me himself had I been caught."

His voice softens, the anger in his eyes flickering in and out. "What changed your mind?"

"You did. You didn't just promise a chance at survival; you gave me a reason to live."

He scoffs, looking up at the ceiling. "What do you want me to say... I'm honored."

"No, you donkey." I try to keep the frustration from bubbling out of me. *I'm trying here.* The least he can do is hold the sarcasm. I point at the porthole in his room. "What's out there—the adventure, the beauty, the magic... There's so much more to see than pale stone walls and golden teacups. I wanted to see it all. I never meant to hurt you. Tell me what I have to do to prove that and I'll do it." I sit back in the tub, wiping at the tears and trying to regain some of my dignity.

"Why didn't you tell me?"

I trap my lower lip with my teeth, struggling to find the right words. "I thought you'd kill me. I was warned after you won the gauntlet that you hated witches, and honestly, I didn't think you'd listen." His eyes gloss over, pain swirling in their depths, but he never sheds a tear.

"All this time," he starts, scoffing and pacing around the room like a caged animal. "I thought you were worried and scared... In reality, it was your own skin you were worried about." Sebastian stops and faces me, his voice raised. "How did you hide it, hmm? How do you look like you do?"

I look away. I have my memories, the most significant being the way he used to look at me. I don't want to remember this, the hate in his eyes, like I'm some vile creature. I'm only guilty of existing. No matter what I say, he won't listen. He's made up his mind, believing I was planted in his life to uproot it. Nothing I can say or do will change that... I won't waste my breath.

"Answer me, woman!" he yells, making me shudder.

Inhaling deeply, I summon the strength to face him with a cold gaze and flex my jaw. "I am a person. You will treat me as such."

His eyebrows shoot up in shock. "A person?" He laughs soundlessly. "No. You're a witch. You've lied to me ever since I met you. Why would I believe a single word that comes from your mouth?"

I stand from the bath, snatching my towel off the cabinet and pulling it around me. Closing the distance between us, anger boiling inside me, I steel my expression. "I'm not the only one guilty of lying. Or did you forget the fact I met you as a fucking elf?"

Sebastian leans away from me for a moment, and I'm not sure if it's because it's the first time he's heard me curse or if it's him realizing that no one is in the right here.

We stand there, inches apart, staring into each other's eyes. The tension is palpable, and I can't help but think about how we've come to this point—how the secrets have finally caught up with us.

The cold air in the room bites at my flesh as I clutch the towel. Sebastian's eyes narrow until I can see his thoughts simmering beneath their glossy surface.

"Show it to me," he demands, his voice low and dangerous as he reaches for my arm. I slap his hand away, standing my ground. His teeth clench as he sucks in a breath. "Show me the fucking mark, Scars."

"Promise you won't float me." He darts his eyes away, and I chuckle humorously. "That's what I thought." My heart feels like it's being squeezed as I realize that there's no way to make him understand. "Just like everyone else... I can plead until my face turns blue, but it doesn't matter. You're always going to believe what you can see."

I turn away from him and let the towel fall to the floor. "Go ahead, Captain. Convict me."

Standing here, bare and vulnerable, I wait for him to make a move. But he just stands there, staring at me. My breathing comes in shallow gasps, and just as I'm about to turn around, warm hands gently scoop my hair out of the way, resting it over my shoulder. He remains silent, and I know he's getting much more than he asked for. He's realizing just how real his little nickname he's stolen from Eva truly is.

His voice is barely above a whisper. "How did you get this?"

My heart races, knowing that whatever I say won't change his mind. Sebastian and his crew have been tormented by blood witches for decades, watching them burn villages to the ground. There's no accepting this for him, and I know that now. My voice is barely audible as I reply, "I'm not a blood witch. I'm a mage. I've never used sacrificial magic—"

"Enough!" he cuts me off, his voice stern and unyielding. "Don't lie to me. The evidence is right here." The words strike me like a physical blow, and I close my eyes, biting my lip to stifle its tremble. Straightening my shoulders, I say the only thing I can.

"I understand... I won't blame you for floating me. Despite everything, I truly hope we can find each other in the next life," I say, not bothering to hide the tears streaming down my face.

He doesn't speak, his fingers still lingering over the mark on my back.

"Didn't you hear me?" I say, whirling around to face him and finding him closer to me than I anticipated, putting my face an inch from his. Still, I stay the course. "Float. Me." His intelligent green eyes toggle between mine as I stare at him, tears blurring my vision. "Do whatever you need to do to feel better. I never planned to live this long, anyway."

Sebastian's face softens for a moment, and he lifts a hand to brush my hair away from my face, swiping up my tears with his thumb. He stares at me, searching for something. "Why do you want to die so badly? Were you raised to be the lamb, or did something make you want to become one?"

I turn away from him, unwilling to answer his question. I don't need his pity or judgment. He could see, plain as day, exactly what made me become one. As I stand there, exposed and vulnerable, I feel his fingers against my back again.

"Who did these?" he asks, tracing the raised lines around my mark—the ones that my mother didn't give me. "Come on, Scars, at least tell me that." His voice is calm, sweet even. But I can't bring myself to answer him.

"Someone I loved, but sadly, he turned out to be a monster too," I whisper, my voice cracking under the weight of my emotions. I don't want him to see me like this, broken and defeated. I want to be strong, but now it feels impossible.

His hands slide down the length of my arms, causing goosebumps to rise in their wake, and his lips press to my shoulder, warming my skin with his breath. I don't know what to do or what to say. I just stand here, frozen in time. Then he's gone. Turning around, I catch him slipping out the door without another word.

23

HOOK

Stepping out of my quarters, I find Zephyr waiting for me. He leans to the side, trying to peek past me, but he quickly averts his eyes.

"Tell me you didn't," Zephyr says, his tone disapproving.

Ignoring his question, I ask, "What's the gauge on the crew?"

Zephyr sighs and falls into step with me. "They're mixed. Most believe a blood witch is a blood witch and Scarlet shouldn't be treated any differently. Smee, Nelvin, and Lorian are among them. Others, though far and few, say she has never been anything but kind to them, and they're not sure where to stand."

"And you?" I ask, my voice tense. "Where do you stand?"

Zephyr purses his lips, clearly struggling with his answer. "I think we need more information before I can truthfully say."

Hearing what the others have to say about Scarlet makes my chest tighten. I care for her, more than I'd like to admit, but I know if my crew wants her gone, it's a battle I can't fight alone. I'm not sure I could fight it at all.

"Did you talk to her about the mark?"

I shake my head. "She won't answer much, but she swears she's not a blood witch."

Zephyr runs a hand through his hair, inflating his cheeks with his exhale. "That's tough... I think we have some truth tea left. We could give it to her, and force her to answer. She might never forgive you for it, though. But I don't think you'd ever forgive yourself if you shoved her off the ship, only to find out she was telling the truth."

As we cross the deck, Smee falls into step beside us, having overheard our conversation. "It's illegal, even in Solaria, to mark someone as a blood witch without proof," she adds with a scowl. "She's lying."

Pursing my lips, I shake my head. There's only one way to put my mind at ease. It's not foolproof, but it's something. "Brew the tea."

Smee rolls her eyes and mumbles under her breath before addressing us more firmly. "We need to have a meeting when you're done with your little interrogation. By then, I'll know the extent of the damage to the ship and what's fixable."

Zephyr nods and sets off to prepare the tea, while Smee and I wait in tense silence. My mind races with possible outcomes, weighing the consequences of each decision.

"Do you love her?" Smee asks, and I narrow my gaze.

"What do you think? Don't be absurd."

"I saw the way you looked at her. At least to some extent you cared, but I need to know that you understand and have wrapped your mind around what she is. Don't let her get in your head."

I cross my arms over my chest, not daring to look at her. "I'm aware, and I'll do what needs to be done."

Zephyr returns, out of breath with a thermos in hand. "Ready?"

We give Scarlet a moment to dress before knocking on the door to my quarters, the sound echoing through the tense silence. "Are you decent?" I ask, trying to keep my voice steady.

"Yes," she scoffs in reply.

Zephyr and I step inside, securing the door's rope to the cabinet. I hold another in my hand, lifting it for her to see. I prick my finger, pressing it into the carved symbol on the wall. Magic swirls around us, making the air taste bittersweet as the wards on the walls ignite. "You can either make this easy, or we can fight. But you should know, with the wards set, any spells cast inside this room while they're up won't work."

Scarlet's hazel eyes narrow at the rope in my hands but doesn't protest. Zephyr twists a metal loop embedded in the floor to lift a table from it, locking it into place while I grab the folding chairs from the wall cubby. Scarlet sits on the edge of the bed, her legs tucked beneath the tabletop, while Zephyr and I take our seats opposite her.

As Zephyr unscrews the top of the thermos, steam escapes with an inviting aroma. He sets a cup on the table, and I find myself holding my breath, watching Scarlet's reaction. Tension crawls up my spine.

"Why are you doing this?" Scarlet asks, defiance lacing her words.

"Because I need answers," I reply, meeting her gaze. "The truth, and I can't trust you'll give that to me."

She stares at me, and I can feel her worry pulsing through the bond we share. It takes everything in me not to reach out and comfort her, but I need to focus on the task at hand.

"Drink," I command, my voice firm as I hold out the cup to her.

Scarlet hesitates for a moment before taking a deep breath and swallowing down the truth tea. I set an hourglass on the table, and the sand starts to trickle down.

"Let's begin with something simple," I say as the first grains of sand settle at the bottom. "What is your full name?"

"Scarlet Elevian Micidious," she answers without hesitation, her voice betraying no emotion.

"Good. What are you?"

She stares at me for a long moment. "Mage, both my parents were magic users. But I truly don't know otherwise. My father changes his children, mixing species."

"Why?" I ask, settling back in my seat.

"To override his curse." She chews the inside of her cheek as she speaks.

"Did he know or plan for me to enter the gauntlet?"

Her eyes widen. "How should I know? I didn't know who you were. I told you that."

I raise my eyebrows for a moment. "Can't be too careful... Have you ever used sacrificial magic?" I ask, my heart pounding in anticipation of her answer.

"No," she answers firmly, locking eyes with me. "Never."

"Then why were you marked as a blood witch?" Zephyr beats me to the punch, leaning forward and cupping his hands together on the tabletop.

"I'd ask my mother why she did it, but she's dead." That time, the question struck a nerve. I can feel it, her anger rising.

"How did she die?"

"My father killed her for placing it on me after I was born," she replies, her gaze dropping to where her hands sit on the table.

"I want to believe you..." I bite my lower lip. "I want to wrap my mind around the idea you were marked without justification, but I also know it's not possible. You can't become marked unless blood stains your hands. If it were done as an infant, you wouldn't have had a chance to sacrifice someone."

"That's what I was told. It's been there for as long as I can remember. I've never questioned that someone might be lying."

Zephyr taps the table with his finger. "Not necessarily. If her mother was marked while she was pregnant, then the mark might've been placed on the child too. Scarlet would've been born with it."

"I thought blood witches couldn't have children?" Scarlet tips her head, her eyes vacant, like she's deep in thought.

"They can't become pregnant after they've been marked. It keeps it from happening, but before... Well, that's not so much the case." Zephyr looks at me, and I know what he wants to say. He always sees the best in people, and I think he wants to believe her.

As the last grains of sand fall through the hourglass, I realize I don't have much time left. "Scarlet," I begin softly, "do you hate me?"

"No," she replies, her voice barely audible. "But I wish I did."

"Then I suppose we're even."

"Time's almost up," Zephyr warns, and I grit my teeth. I need more time.

"How did you manage to keep it hidden?"

"Royal mages glamoured it, but it takes a coven to replace the spell, and it only lasted a couple of days," Scarlet answers, her voice barely above a whisper. The pain in her eyes is almost palpable, and I find myself struggling to keep from trying to soothe her.

I feel her knee brush against mine beneath the table, and I place my hand on it, my thumb drawing slow circles.

Time is running out; the truth tea's effects will soon fade. Desperate for clarity, I ask, "Do you have any intentions of using sacrificial magic in the future?"

Her jaw clenches, but her answer is firm. "No."

Zephyr intervenes, his tone decisive. "Well, it looks like you got the answers you needed." He glances at the hourglass, still a minute or so left before the sand runs out.

I want to believe her, to trust that she's telling the truth. But the stakes are too high, and I can't afford to let my emotions cloud my judgment. In the end, I know that I'll do whatever it takes to protect my crew—even if it means breaking my own heart in the process.

I focus on the warmth of Scarlet's leg beneath my hand, trying to ground myself amidst the chaos of emotions swirling within me—coming from her. With each stroke of my thumb, I feel her anger ebbing away, replaced by something more tender and fragile.

Zephyr glances between us, then clears his throat. "Well, I can see you need a moment. I'll be outside."

The door closes behind him as he takes his exit, but I can't look away from her. The scars on her back... I didn't want to say anything in front of Zephyr, but there are still questions I need answered.

"Scarlet," I say softly, holding her gaze. "Do you have feelings for me, or was it all an act?"

She closes her eyes a moment, drawing out a blink. "I didn't fake caring about you, no." My heart clenches at her words, and I stroke her leg higher, seeking reassurance in the connection between us.

I lean closer. "One last question. Who gave you those scars?" Scarlet bites her tongue, watching the sand slip away. "Answer me, darling, please." I don't mean for it to sound desperate, but whoever did that to her... They don't deserve to breathe anymore. I'm not sure if they did it to try to remove the mark, and if so, then it adds validity to the idea that she was born with it. It could've been something she did to herself too after it was placed on her... It's hard to say, but I need to know.

"My father," she finally admits. "He thought scars would cover it, but when the skin healed, the mark remained."

My fists clench involuntarily, nails digging into my palm as the other hand grips tight onto her leg. It just makes me hate the king more. The thought fills me with a rage, unlike anything I've ever felt before.

"Alright," I murmur, releasing her leg and sitting back. "That's all."

Scarlet rubs at the palms of her hands, and I spot the reddened circles where something has pierced her skin. I'm not sure when it happened, but the angry red circles around them don't give me a warm and fuzzy feeling.

Standing up, I grab one of the salves from the cabinet, twisting off the tin top and reaching for her hand. She doesn't give it, clutching them close to her chest.

"Don't make me force you, please. It looks infected." I hold my hand out, beckoning for hers. Slowly, she sets one on mine as she watches me, her hazel eyes searching my face for any hint of what might come next.

"How long will I be locked up in here?" she asks, as I work the medicine in.

"I don't know. The crew is scared of you, and I'm not sure there's anything I can say to make them believe that you're not a blood witch."

Scarlet's eyebrows furrow, determination shining through the pain as the medicine takes hold. It's Nelvin's magic. The elves are fantastic healers, and salves like this can heal superficial wounds in seconds. I watch the skin knit closed, the evidence of her being hurt is now nothing but a memory.

"I'll take the truth tea again, in front of them all if I have to," she insists.

I shake my head, knowing it won't be enough. "You could have undeniable evidence. I could brew the tea in front of them so they know it's real and they can watch you take it, but there will always be someone who thinks they were tricked." I run a hand through my hair, frustration bubbling under the surface. "I'm not sure how to fix this."

She gives me her other hand and I do the same, working the salve into the deep scrapes.

"Do you believe me?" she asks, catching me off guard. "Or do you still want me dead?"

I hesitate, weighing my words carefully. "I want to believe you, Scarlet," I confess. "But the truth tea works most of the time, and some blood witches, specifically those who used to be the king's royal mages and druids, know how to protect themselves from it. It makes me feel a little better about all of this, but it's not solid proof."

"Is there any way you'll know for sure?" Her eyes sparkle with unshed tears as she stares up at me. I want to tell her the answers she wants, but I'd rather say nothing than lie.

I swallow hard, hating the words that are about to leave my lips. "The only way that's a hundred percent accurate is to float... I can't promise you it won't come to that. But I can promise it won't be tonight."

She nods but doesn't say anything more.

"There," I say, checking to make sure I've gotten them all. I hold her hands, palms up, so she can see they're healed. "All better." She doesn't smile. She doesn't beam with light. I miss that... I'm not sure if I'll ever get that side of her back or if it's wise to try, but I can't resist the urge to comfort her. Bringing her hands to my lips, I kiss the top of each. The door swings open before I can drop them, and I meet Zephyr's wide-eyed stare. He quickly shuts the door again, and I breathe out a frustrated sigh.

"The man has impeccable timing," I say, letting go of her.

Scarlet, to her credit, manages to keep a straight face, though her cheeks are flushed. "Sebastian," she says softly, her voice barely above a whisper, "thank you."

I steal one last glance at her before leaving the room.

"What the hell was that?" Zephyr asks, speed walking to keep up with me as we enter the companionway and travel to the lower level to where the wardroom is.

"It was nothing." I try to brush it off, but Zephyr isn't buying it. Instead, he gives me a knowing look, the one that says he'll demand answers until he gets them.

"That was not nothing," he insists as I push open the door to the wardroom.

Inside, Smee, Nelvin, and Lorian are waiting for us. A large round table sits in the center of the room, surrounded by dark leather chairs. The walls are adorned with maps and weapons, and the air smells like saltwater mixed with the scent of old wood and rum.

Smee leans back in her chair, one leg crossed over the other, and Nelvin lounges beside her, lazily swirling his drink. Zephyr passes them, taking a seat next to Lorian and the druid drapes an arm casually around him. They're polar opposites, but they fit together like puzzle pieces.

This is all that's left of my crew masters. The rest are resting in the deep, but they're also the people I'm closest to, and the fact they're still breathing gives me peace.

"Alright, let's get this meeting started," I say, taking my seat at the head of the table. The tension in the room is thick, but I can't afford to let that distract me. There are too many decisions to make and not enough time.

"Well?" Smee says, her voice sharp as a knife, cutting through the silence. "What's the verdict? Is she a witch or not?"

Zephyr and I share a look, our gazes heavy with unspoken thoughts.

"I don't know, but she definitely has the mark." I rap my knuckles on the wooden tabletop, looking everywhere but at my sister. She's too intuitive for this. She'll see right through me.

Smee snorts. "It's pretty black and white."

"Scarlet claims to have been marked without conviction," I explain, trying to keep my voice steady. "I need more time to figure it out."

Laughter bursts from Smee, harsh and mocking. "That's just what a witch would say. In fact, I've heard it more than once." Her words sting, but I push away the hurt, forcing myself to focus on the matter at hand. Smee levels her gaze at me. "You can't seriously be contemplating this... Blood witches took our family from us. If she's marked, then she's one of them and deserves to share the same fate."

My chest tightens as if bound by invisible chains. I'm caught between my growing feelings for Scarlet, the renewed emotions coursing through me, and the undeniable truth that Smee is right. Letting Scarlet live, knowing what she is, would disgrace the memory of both my parents. They're likely rolling in their graves as we speak.

"She saved the ship. For that, I owe it to her to think about it before just rushing into floating her."

Zephyr nods at me. "Take your time. We trust you to make the right decision."

"Thank you," I say, my voice barely audible above the creak of the ship. "For now, we focus on the ship and its repairs. It's not going to matter if we all die out here, now will it?" I level Smee with a glare.

Smee, Lorian, and Nelvin exchange glances before giving me a rundown of the Jolly Roger's status. The damage is extensive, but fixable—though it will take at least a day or two to repair the sails. Zephyr adds that no one is critically injured, mostly minor fractures, scrapes, and a dislocation. At least out of those of us left.

I chew on my lip for a moment, taking in the report. "If we have to sit here for a day or two, we need posts round the clock doubled. The storm we tried to get ahead of when leaving the Luminaries will be heading this way and we need to be prepared to take the brunt of it if we can't get the sails up before it reaches us."

"Is there any word on why the Wysterian attacked? They don't usually mess with us," Smee says, tapping her pen on the notepad in front of her.

"I don't know. Scarlet had a theory—"

Smee cuts me off, rolling her eyes. "Of course she did."

I take a deep breath. She's just pissed, I know that. She'd grown close to her and my sister has always used sarcasm and anger to avoid feelings. It's what she does best.

"As I was saying, she thinks the witch possessed it when she stabbed Lorian." I nod at the druid, who is thankfully in one piece.

"I'd believe that," Lorian says, his voice low and deep. "She left me right as Scarlet stabbed me. I couldn't sense her presence before I blacked out. It'd make sense."

The room falls silent for a beat, but if there's one thing I'm sure of, it's that they'll trust Lorian. And with him backing up Scarlet's theory, it gives me hope that maybe I can trust Scarlet too. Just that damn mark makes me question myself and every word she says.

"Look," I say, leaning against the table. "I understand how worried you all must be, but I promise we'll be fine. We just need to get underway as soon as possible." My crew nods, understanding the gravity of our situation. As we break from the meeting, everyone separates, doing their part in securing the ship and preparing for the storm.

24

Scarlet

I lay on Sebastian's bed, staring up at the wooden ceiling. I'm not sure what I'm waiting for, but I don't think I have much of an option. I draw the blankets up over my body, breathing deeply. It smells just like him... I'm not even sure how to describe it, just that it clings to every pillow, to the blankets, and the air in this space—that it wraps around me like he's here himself.

It feels like weeks since he held me in this bed, but it's really only been a day. This place had been my personal heaven, and now it's nothing more than a gilded cage. I'm torn between wanting to stay alive, to live just a little longer, and wanting to make the pain and betrayal I see in his eyes stop. I know I hurt him, but what else was I supposed to do? Had he learned the truth sooner, he might not have given me a chance to explain myself. He might've chucked me over the first chance he had and all the moments we've shared would've never existed.

I didn't do this to deceive him. It was a means of survival.

It's been hours since Sebastian left, and I can't shake the way butterflies swarmed through me when he kissed my hand. I thought for sure I'd imagined it, but healing my palm and endearments like that... That's not the sign of a man who wants me to burn or drown. He's conflicted—and rightfully so—but it tells me he still cares, and it means there's a chance to make it out of this.

I can't imagine what he must be going through. How torn he must feel.

From where I sit, I can hear men walking across the deck. Occasionally their muffled voices filter through the damaged door from the outside. They're still cleaning up the ship and making repairs. From what I can tell, we're going to be stuck here for days. The elements tried to use magic to push the ship, but it didn't move much. Without a sail to inflate, it's pointless.

A few words catch my attention. "...it's getting dark. Are you sure?" one of them says.

It's almost nighttime... Three days have passed since I watched the dragons during the last moon cycle. I wonder what happens if the ship is stagnant by dusk. Are they worried about something reaching us? My ears strain as I quietly lift up in the bed, as if sitting will make me hear better. It won't, but I do it anyway.

"Yeah, captain's orders. The princess goes overboard at nightfall," another adds. I can taste the hatred in his tone. He thinks I'm a monster, just like that woman. How?

How can they all be so short-sighted? I saved their ship. Shouldn't that earn me something?

My heart stops and my blood turns to ice in my veins. He promised. Sebastian stood there and swore nothing would happen tonight. He told me I would be safe. Why would he lie?

Here, I've been ashamed that I've hurt him so deeply, pitying everything he must be going through. I was so sure... so naïve to believe him kissing my shoulder when saw my scars and him ensuring my hands were no longer in pain had meant something deep within him cared. But why lie? Why tell me to relax, that I'll be fine for the night if he was just going to walk out that door and change his mind? Why give me a false sense of safety? Is this some sort of game to him? Is this his form of revenge, making me feel the same betrayal?

I rub the hilt of my hand into my chest, trying to soothe the tightness growing there. I have to keep my emotions in check. I can't spiral, not now. If I do, he'll feel it and any chance I have of coming up with a plan will shatter the moment he barges through that door.

Getting up, I start looking through the cabinets and drawers, pressing on every plank of the wall to find the hidden compartments. There's got to be something I can use as a weapon if it comes to it. I might not be able to get off the ship, but if one beast was following them, maybe there's more. Maybe I could control one and it could take me off this ship.

It's a shot in the dark. I might not be able to control it long enough to get to land, but it's better than drowning because I can't swim, or floating... I pause, chewing at my lip. If what Sebastian said was true, that I could only be marked if I'd done blood magic, will I float? I still don't know how that's possible, but as Zephyr said, if my mother had been the one to do it, maybe I was born with it. But would it be enough for the water to reject me?

Shaking my head, I focus my thoughts. I can't worry about that right now. I have to figure out how to get off the ship. What if I used the rowboat? I could escape and untie it, maybe get a beast to pull me to land for as long as I can if I can find a rope. I doubt Sebastian would come after me. He has his emotions as long as I'm alive, and if I'm not on his ship to be a problem, he might just accept that and move on. I could start over somewhere else, but would need to use magic or something to change my hair. Even on the mainland, I'd stick out like a sore thumb as a Midicious.

I can work with that. I just need to make sure that come nightfall, I don't get tossed into the sea, that I can get to the boat. It hasn't been enough time, though... My magic and power are still severely depleted. It'll take days before I'm back to full strength, but Sebastian doesn't know that.

I slam the drawer, having searched the room without finding a single weapon. Seeing as he trapped a witch alone in a room with magical objects and grimoires, specifically those for blood magic, I thought he would've left something in here. Clearly, he doesn't see me as much of a threat at this point.

Taking a deep breath, I glance around the room one last time, pausing at the bed. Sebastian doesn't take risks. He's always one step ahead of everyone. When he slept beside me, all of his weapons were across the room, which means he felt safe there with me... For him to have felt that way, there would have to be something within arm's reach.

Looking under the bed, I find nothing but flat boxes of things—things that don't help me but are likely precious to him. Furrowing my brow, I slide my hand beneath the mattress, feeling between it and the platform it sits on until my fingers touch something metallic.

Found it.

Gripping it, I pull it free, eyeing a dagger. It's the length of my forearm, the blades sharp enough to cut down to the bone. The hilt is wrapped in leather for grip and etched into the blade is his name.... Sebastian Hook. This will work.

This is my way out. I might not make it to the mainland—there are still a lot of loose strings hanging in the air—but it's a chance. It's better than staying here so he can torture me and toy with my emotions, pretending to care about me only to threaten to end my life in the next breath. After everything, I can accept being locked in here and him wanting answers. I can accept his cold mentality and his need for safety. I can even accept the punishment that comes along with lying to him, but I don't deserve to be played with. I saved him and his people. I kept this ship from sinking. I deserve better than that.

I hear footsteps outside the door and before I can come up with how I'm going to escape this room and make it to the rowboat, I'm faced with the fact someone is about to come into this room. Judging by the dark sliver that peeks through the gap in the door where the latch used to exist, the hell flame is gone.

They're going to take me…

The door creaks open and I do the only thing I can. I flatten myself against the wall and wait. Sebastian's form comes into view and I lurch forward, pressing the blade to his throat. The lamplight flickers across his face, highlighting the strong cheekbones, sharp jawline, and curious green eyes I could stare into for days and never grow tired of.

"Feeling murderous, are we, darling?"

Butterflies take my stomach by storm, but I don't let them get to me. This is life or death.

"If you're planning to kill me, you're going to have to try harder than that," he says, and I narrow my gaze.

"I'm capable of a lot more than you think."

Sebastian laughs, his face lighting up as if I've just told him the best joke he's heard in years. "You're on a ship in the middle of the ocean. Are you planning to float the entire crew too? I don't suppose you've learned how to operate a ship in those books of yours, have you?"

He's right... There's an entire crew outside that door. All it would take is one person to see me escape. I can't control them all. One or two, maybe, but not the entire crew. Not with my magic depleted, There's no way I'll make it to the rowboat. I have nowhere to go. I'm trapped here with him and his crew, and the only way off this ship is to float. And to float means death.

"Is this how you treat someone who's saved you? I haven't even heard a thank you. I kept that creature from killing us all." I glare at him, my eyes narrowed into slits.

Sebastian doesn't answer me. Instead, he takes a step closer, and I tense, arching away from him with the knife still positioned between us.

"One more step and I'll do it," I say, willing my voice not to shake, even if my body is.

He snorts, eyeing where my fingers grip the hilt of his dagger, so tightly my knuckles glow white. With a smirk, he steps forward, taunting me. I have to match it backward to avoid cutting him.

My shoulder blades meet the wall. I'm not sure when the space of the room disappeared, but Sebastian leans in closer, bracing his arms on either side of my head. I'm trapped between him and the wall of cabinets. He's acting as if the blade in my hand hasn't nicked his skin, but the evidence is undeniable. I watch the single drop of crimson roll down the length of his throat.

His warm breath dances over my flesh, and I jolt the moment his lips press to my pulse, just below my ear. There's no doubt in my mind that he can feel my racing heartbeat. I shouldn't want this. I shouldn't have to fight the urge to melt against him. He's going to kill me, yet I'm flooded with an odd mix of lust and fear, so consuming I've let the knife's point tilt down toward the floor. It's trapped between our bodies now and utterly useless.

"We have to work on your threats, little lamb." He practically purrs his nickname for me.

"Oh really? I can assure you my threats are— "My voice betrays me, going silent as he tips my chin up with his finger.

"Never said you weren't. But I've taken more than one step closer and all my pieces are still in order." With a swift motion, he snatches my wrist, the one holding the dagger.

"How did you know I wouldn't...?" The panic bubbles up inside me, knowing I've possibly just pissed him off more. I should've waited, but I believed—still worry—that he planned to march me through that door and shove me over.

"If you wanted to kill me, you would've." He plucks the knife from my hand and tosses it to the floor like it's nothing. The metal clangs against the wood as Sebastian turns his attention back to me. "You would've used your magic and made me do as you wished long before now. You've had access to every grimoire on that shelf, yet they haven't been touched, and you could've cast them earlier since the wards were down. You've had countless opportunities to hurt me, just as you could've slit my throat without hesitation the moment I walked through that door. Yet, you didn't."

I don't know how to act or how to breathe. I'm trapped in awe, incapable of comprehending the whirlwind of events that have transpired today, nor the emotions that rampage through me so hard that not a single one of them is recognizable. I don't know how to feel... He believes me.

Sebastian bends ever so slightly. The rings on his fingers are cold against my skin as they slip beneath the shirt I borrowed from him like he's searching to see if there's anything else I'm hiding. Were there other weapons in the room? Did I miss them? I don't know how. I searched every shadow and crevice of this place.

"Tell me, princess," he muses, his hand still lingering beneath the hem of my dress, but they no longer roam, as if he's satisfied with his curiosity, sure I'm no longer hiding anything. "What is it you want from me?"

My body stills... He doesn't believe me. He thinks I don't want him dead because I want someone from him.

That I need him alive for some reason other than because I care.

"Nothing," I say, trying to breathe normally and doing a shit job of it. I don't want him to hear the tremble in my voice, but it's impossible to keep it out of it. "I don't want anything from you. I simply don't wish to die."

He brushes a lock of my hair behind my ear, his bright green eyes staring into mine. I couldn't look away if I wanted to.

"Luckily for you, I can't bring myself to toss you off this ship. I'm not sure what you've done to me... I'm starting to fear you've sunk your claws in too deep, or perhaps I just don't want to remove them. Either way, we're here... alone... and the only thing I want to do is kiss you."

My heart pounds in my chest, adrenaline coursing through my veins. The danger is imminent, yet despite the fact my life hangs in the balance, there's something undeniably alluring about the way he looks at me now. The curiosity in his eyes, the hunger... I want him to kiss me. I want it more than I want the air I breathe. What the hell is wrong with me?

"You won't hurt me for the same reason I can't you," he says, his gaze flicking over my face as if he's reading something there, penned in invisible ink.

Standing this close to him... It's impossible to think straight. My eyes lock onto his full lips, craving to feel them, to taste them, again.

"Now... If you'd stop trying to stab me for a moment, we have places to go."

That single sentence seems to slice through whatever spell I've been sucked into. My eyes dart to his, my heart kicking it up a notch, speeding away in my chest until my ribs ache from the onslaught.

"Where are you taking me?" I demand the answer, finding the strength to stand tall.

"Back to your room so you can have your privacy." His thumb rolls over my cheek as he cups my face. "Don't worry, princess. You're not going into the prison hole, but I doubt you want to stay here with me. As is, I can't even walk through the door without scaring you enough to get stabby. I don't blame you, but it's also the same reason I won't be able to sleep unless you're in your own space."

He steps back, pulling the rope free from where it's tucked into his belt. Holding it up, he nods at me, like I'm supposed to just give my hands over.

"I'll behave," I say, unmoving.

"It wasn't a request. People will ask questions if you're not tied up, so hands."

Eyeing him for a moment, I give, holding my hands out so he can bind them, leaving a length of the rope he can hold like a leash. Great... I've gone from witch to house pet. Part of me wants to say this is an upgrade, but it's yet to be confirmed.

25
HOOK

I escort Scarlet to her cabin, trying my best to ignore the glaring looks my crew sends her as we cross the deck. It takes everything I have to school my features to remain indifferent. Those glares cut through her and even though she doesn't show it, they flay down to the bone.

Doing my best to get her down to her room as fast as I can, I tug her along, keeping my grip gentle on her arm. She's tougher than she looks, that's for sure. I'd never know how much it fazed her without our bond. On the outside, she's numb, like nothing can bother her, but inside... Let's just say if I had this much emotion swirling through me, I'd be a fucking wreck.

We reach her room below deck and I open the door, letting her walk inside. A part of me wants to stay with her, but I know that wouldn't be wise, not when I'm still not sure what to believe. It's not just me, either. If my crew saw me treat her differently, they might think the worst. They could assume she's bewitched me, and that doesn't end well for anyone. It's one thing for Zephyr or my sister, even Nelvin or Lorian, to see me troubled, but they knew me well enough to give me time to process things before assuming anything. I stay in the hall to refrain from caving into the desire to hug her—to tell her things will be okay, that they'll work themselves out.

She turns, holding out her arms so I can untie the ropes. I make quick work of it, looping it through my belt and crossing my arms so I can rest against the doorframe. "You'll be spelled inside, so no one can bother you, but you won't be able to leave, either. Smee will escort you to the bathroom and bring you dinner. If you need her, she's in her room, so just knock on the wall."

Scarlet nods silently, her eyes scanning the room as if she's seeing it for the first time. "It's emptier than before."

I scratch my head. "My sister cleared out most of her things, but there might be some books still in the cupboard. I'll see what I can find for you to pass the time."

"Thank you," she murmurs, her voice barely audible. She stops pacing in front of me, wringing her fingers as if she's unsure what to do with them. Then she reaches for my hand and I quickly take a step away. If she touches me, I'm done for. I'm barely keeping my shit together as is, but knowing how... isolated she feels, it's ripping me apart at the seams.

"I–I'm sorry, I thought...I thought you would want me to, but I must've misread things." She reluctantly tucks her hand to her chest and turns away from me, taking a seat on the chest at the end of her bed.

"You didn't... It's not that I don't want you to. I just can't."

She nods, tucking her chin to her chest so she can tangle her fingers in her lap.

"I'm sorry..." I shouldn't have said that, but it's hanging in the air now and I can't take it back. Her hazel eyes lock on mine, so big and bright that it fills me with something I can only describe as hope. "I'm teetering, Scars–" I close my eyes, hating that I used that nickname. I understand why her sister calls her that now it kills me to know what she's been through... the way her father treated her. "Scarlet," I correct. "I meant to say Scarlet, but you have to understand. I'm barely keeping it together and I'm trying as hard as I can to wrap my mind around all of this, but it's hard when we share this connection. I can't tell where you end and I begin. I just need time to figure it out."

"I understand," she says, not looking up at me, just staring at her fingers.

I give a curt nod before shutting the door. Digging in my pocket, I fish for the spelled skeleton key to seal it shut. As I head back down the hallway, I blow out a deep breath, trying to shake off the tension. She's going to be the end of me. I can feel it in my bones.

I stop on the mess hall floor, finding Zephyr nursing a drink at one of the tables. I slide in next to him without a word, and I take a grateful sip of the fairy wine in my flask. The fruity taste does little to soothe my frayed nerves, but it's something. I drag a hand down my face, attempting to release the pent-up frustration and stress, then gulp down two more mouthfuls of the wine.

Zephyr catches me staring at him and raises an eyebrow. "Are you going to speak, or are we going to pretend each other doesn't exist?" he asks bluntly. "I'd rather know now than risk the wrath you unleashed on Nelvin earlier. I don't heal as quickly as him."

"It's nothing." We both know I'm lying. He's known me since we were toddlers—I can't lie to him. He knows all of my tells.

Zephyr snorts. "In that case, let me know when you're not feeling so murderous, ay?"

"Do you have sedatives to spare?" I ask, taking another sip.

His brow furrows as he looks at me as if he doesn't recognize who I am. "Have you gone mad? That isn't the answer—"

"They're not for me." My tone is clipped, but it's not him I should be mad at. Fuck, I don't even know who to point the finger at right now.

"Then who?" He tips his whiskey glass, arching a dark brow.

"Her. I haven't gone mad, but I fear I'm on the path to it. She's been through so much... I don't know how much more of this I can take. I thought if she was asleep, then maybe it would give me a break and I could breathe again."

"The bond doesn't just break because she's asleep, Hook. Trust me, as one of the few people on this ship who can sympathize with you, sedating her wouldn't change anything. Besides, we don't have much to spare. With the storm coming and gods know what else, we should keep it for those who need it." He swirls the amber liquid in his glass, then downs the hatch.

"How do you do it? You and Lorian are mated, which is just as strong, right? How do you stay sane when he's out of sorts?" I rest my forehead against my hands, elbows propped on the table.

"It is, and there's no way to make it easier. You just power through, but it's different. When Lorian is upset, I can help him. My presence brings him peace, so when he gets upset I just try to be there and it makes it easier. You... I pity the fact you can't. Though, I suppose in a way you already are. It's not like you were stroking her knee under the table or anything while interrogating her." He shoots me a pointed look.

"You thought–still think," I correct, "that she's innocent. So why are you upset with me?"

"You know damn well why." Okay... I do. He's worried the crew will mutiny since more than half of them believe I should've treated her like any other witch we came across, but I can't. She's my wife... and she saved this ship. I can't just ignore that.

"It was eating me alive, Zeph... What else was I supposed to do?"

He tilts his head to the side, pouring more whiskey into his glass. "That's why I didn't say anything to anyone else."

"I don't know what to do about Scarlet," I admit, scrubbing a hand down my face. "She's marked as a witch, but... I can't bring myself to do what needs to be done."

"Is that really what needs to be done?" Zephyr counters, his eyes searching mine. "Or is that just what you think you're supposed to do?" I don't have an answer for him, and the silence stretches between us. He takes a sip of his drink.

"Maybe." I couldn't stay still to save my life... My knee bounces beneath the table and my hands crave to fidget. "I don't know."

"Sounds to me that you need to figure out what you want—and what you're willing to risk for it." His voice loses its normal playful tone, dropping to something more serious.

"I can't float her. I know what she is, but I just can't do it." My hands flex on the table, making the veins in my arms rise to the surface as I try to work the nervous jitters out of my system. Zephyr raises an eyebrow, the corner of his lips tip up. "You don't have to give me that look. I know that's what you wanted to hear or you wouldn't have skipped off to get that truth tea," I snap.

"Fine," Zephyr relents, leaning back in his chair. His hands are up in surrender. "Let's state facts then. Fact number one is that you've smiled more since she's been here. More than I've seen you do in decades."

I roll my eyes, but I know he's right. Scarlet has a way of getting under my skin and making me feel things I haven't felt in years. I genuinely enjoy her company and maybe a small piece of me hates the fact that I can't do that anymore. Not in the way I've grown used to.

"Fact number two," Zephyr continues, ticking off on his fingers. "She admitted to having the blood witch mark and claims to be illegally marked as one while on truth tea. And based on the shitty firework show we saw her do to stop that dragon, she lacks the talent to ward herself from the tea. It's just not possible."

"She's talented. I don't think she performs well under pressure," I grumble, pushing away the image of Scarlet desperately wielding her magic to save us.

"Some druidic gifts are innate, like her ability to control others or Lorian's ability to fight. They don't need spells, but innate abilities are rare. What she did with the dragon, she needed a spell for. I saw her trying to cast it. She's incredibly gifted in the innate sense, but the girl couldn't cast to save her life. She can't ward her mind if she can't cast."

It's possible... and it'd make sense. She's controlled dozens of men at once and a fucking Wysterian to boot. It doesn't mean the truth tea is a hundred percent certain. Some things could've gone wrong like it not steeping the tea long enough. But for now, I can agree that she's clumsy with her magic.

"Fact number three," Zephyr says, undeterred by my silence. "If you don't take action soon, the crew might mutiny. They think you're too close to her to make the right call."

"The only thing they want, or will accept, is floating her. And like I said, I have no intention of doing that." I take another sip, feeling my cheeks grow warm from the alcohol.

"We're already going to have to operate with a skeleton crew. We can't afford to lose more people." Zephyr doesn't look at me, spinning his glass on the table.

"Well, I can't give them the answers they want. They won't accept the alternative because they think I'm too close. What am I supposed to do?" I pause, biting my fingernail as I stare off into space. "Maybe I am too close to it," I admit, my chest tightening at the thought. "Maybe I should consider passing the hat for a bit until this is figured out. Smee would respect my wishes, hat or not, and the crew would respect her decision."

"Seriously? You'd give up your position, even temporarily?" Zephyr asks, his voice laced with concern as he twists in his chair to face me. I clench my jaw, feeling the weight of the decisions ahead bearing down on my shoulders.

"I have no choice," I answer without hesitation, knowing deep down that it's true.

"Alright," Zephyr says, nodding slowly. "Fact number four." His eyes narrow with thought. "There are rumors that some of the king's daughters are part fae. If she is, then the truth tea didn't work at all."

That catches my attention, and I can't help but frown. "You think Scarlet might be part fae?"

"Maybe," Zephyr shrugs. "Fact number five is, I can see that Scarlet does care for you. I truly don't see her as a threat. If she wanted to hurt you or anyone on this ship, she would've done so by now. She would've let that Wysterian sink us and controlled something to get herself to land. Her ability makes this situation very different, and I just have a gut feeling about it."

I sigh, rubbing the back of my neck. "I respect your gut feelings, Zeph, but it'll take more than that to prove her innocence. And even more so to convince the crew of it."

As we talk, Lorian comes to sit next to Zephyr, pressing a gentle kiss to his cheek. Watching them, I see the happiness and comfort they share—something I've been craving ever since that first spark ignited between Scarlet and me. But how much of this feeling is mine, and how much belongs to her?

"Captain," Lorian says, drawing my attention back to him. "Fancy meeting you here."

"You say that every day. At some point, you have to just start expecting to find me here," I manage a smile.

"Give yourself some time to think," Zephyr suggests, as the two of them get ready to leave. "Now, if you'll excuse me. Just in case we die tomorrow, or whenever that storm reaches us, I prefer to go out with a bang." He winks at me, and the two of them disappear.

"Right," I mumble, my heart heavy with the responsibility that comes with being the Captain and harboring feelings for someone so dangerous... But I can't shake the image of Scarlet's face when she fought to save us, despite everything. She didn't have to risk her life. Yet, she did.

The mess hall empties around me, the laughter and camaraderie of my crew fading into the night. I swig the last drop from my flask, its once-warming contents now barely a memory. Turning in for the night seems like a good idea until that familiar sensation begins to stir within me—coming from the bond.

"Damn it all," I mutter as I refill my flask and head to the deck, hoping the cool night air will offer some reprieve.

I make my way to the railing, closing my eyes and letting the breeze caress my face. The scent of saltwater and fresh air fills my nostrils, a welcome reminder of why I chose this life. Granted, it was the only thing I knew. I was bound to fill my father's shoes from the first breath I took to his last.

When I open my eyes, I find myself entranced by the sight before me: the three moons hanging heavy in the sky, casting their halos of light on the dark-capped waves below. The water is mostly still, but there's a storm on the horizon–the one we outran before our detour to the Western Isles. It'll hit sometime tonight. The air is charged with it. I just hope it won't be as rough as we anticipated.

I rest my forearms against the wooden railing, watching the current. The bond tugs at me, and for the love of all that's sacred, I don't know what Scarlet could be doing or thinking about that she's turned on while held prisoner in her room, but fuck... My head drops forward and my eyes close tight. Heat blooms low in my stomach, my muscles in my stomach tightening until it hurts. My thoughts are consumed with images of her before I can stop it, making it difficult to focus on anything else.

"Get a grip, Sebastian," I scold myself quietly, taking another long swig from my flask. This bond between us has proven to be both a blessing and a curse. I've never craved someone the way I do her. It's like an addiction I can't sweat out. Not once have I been so wrapped up in a woman that I've lost sight of what's right for this ship or its crew.

Before her, I wouldn't have put them in danger because I couldn't walk away, yet she's here, living–breathing. If her ploy had been to do something malicious, keeping her prisoner instead of floating her on the spot would've been like opening up the damn gate and letting her in. Luckily, there's something else in this for her, assuming she is a witch. But I have to assume she is until proven otherwise. It's the only thing I can do to hopefully keep whatever this is I'm working through from endangering anyone else.

"Focus on the storm," I say aloud, attempting to push aside the butterflies that rampage through me. I feel fucking weightless and it's wrong. It's all wrong. Deep down, I know she doesn't fully understand the impact she has on me, and I'd prefer to keep it that way. At least for now. It torments me, but it's also given me peace of mind. I'd know if she meant to hurt someone, I'd feel it.

The storm in the distance looms on the horizon. There's no way we'll get the masts up in time. Not with how fast it's moving. We'll need to secure the deck and batten the hatches. Everything and Everyone but the water elementals need to be below deck when it hits.

I feel the tingles start in my damn toes... The only time that's ever happened is with her and only when she was teetering on the precipice, dangerously close to falling and shattering so fucking beautifully... I wet my lips, tasting the lingering wine. It's almost over. She'll come. She'll go to bed. Then I can go on about my life business as usual.

My pants are so godsdamn tight. It's like I've been edged to the brink, over and over, and denied any sense of pleasure, any form of release. It's maddening. I cherished this feeling once, before all this witch business. I reveled in it because I could bury myself in her until I was satisfied, but now it's the sickest form of torture imaginable.

I didn't know how sex was supposed to feel before this connection was placed. It felt good, sure, but not like this. Not where you forget everything and anything and the only thing that matters is the woman lying in front of you and the sounds you can coax her into making. It's like I've experienced everything from behind a window.

You can see the trees through the glass, see the grass sway in the breeze and the birds, but when you step outside, you experience it. The sounds, the textures, the taste. Once you know what it feels like to be outside, looking through that window will never be the same. You'll know too much and crave to feel it again. Scarlet is the fucking outside, and I don't want to look through the window anymore. But I can't just step outside. Not without risking everything I've built, my ship, my crew's lives, my family... myself.

The bond calms for a moment and I suck in a breath, filling my lungs until they can't hold any more air and letting it out through my nose. My nostrils flare, and some of the tension eases, but not all. I run the heel of my hand down my stomach and over the front of my pants, trying to adjust myself. There's not enough room and leather doesn't give. It constricts and suffocates and robs the blood flow, adding to the entire orchestra of discomfort that only one person can fix.

Taking another swig from my flask, I pray the alcohol will travel south. I'd much rather it be useless at this point than so hard it hurts. However, the irony isn't lost on me—seeking solace from one intoxicating substance while being overwhelmed by another.

I stand there, staring into the darkness, watching the storm inch closer. It's like it's taunting me, or maybe the purple streaks lighting up the low-hanging clouds are just symbolic. Scarlet is my storm, and fuck... she's going to rock the boat. She's already crashed into me so hard that I've lost control. All it'll take is the wind to pick up and she's going to wreck me.

Scarlet's pleasure surges through me once more, stronger than before. My knees wobble as heat drips through me until it becomes unbearable. I grip the wooden railing tighter, biting into my tongue until I can taste the metallic tang of blood. The pain doesn't even put a dent in the pleasure that consumes me.

"You've got to be kidding me." I curse under my breath, but it comes out as more of a moan. I down the last of the wine in my flask, heart pounding in my chest. My breaths come out in jagged beats like I've run a mile instead of just freaking standing here. This can't continue.

But her pleasure doesn't cease, instead, it ebbs and flows in and out, just shy of reaching a crescendo. With each wave, my frustration mounts. Unable to take it any longer,

I push off the railing and stalk down the companionway and down below deck.

Before my mind can stop me, I reach Scarlet's door, dispelling the barrier keeping her locked inside. As the door creaks open, she startles, sitting up in bed with wide eyes. The book in her hand drops onto the bed.

26

HOOK

"Are you trying to kill me?" The question is out before I can make sense of the sight before me. Fury, so pure, I can hear my heartbeat rise within me. It claws its way into my tone despite my best efforts to suppress it.

I shouldn't be here. I shouldn't be fucking tempted to be here, but I am... I'm staring into those captivating hazel eyes that haunt my dreams and make up my deepest desires, and I'm helpless to resist the pull they have on me. I've never felt more powerless in my life than I do at this moment. Not a single muscle would obey if I commanded myself to turn around, to leave before I do something stupid. Instead, I step inside and lock the door.

"Sebastian," she gasps, her voice wavering. "I'm sorry. I was reading and I've never... I didn't think you'd be awake."

I glance at the book on the bed. I've seen my sister with it countless times. It's what she calls smut, but in reality, it's soft-core word porn. I regret to say I've picked it up in the past and was surprised at just how... descriptive things can get.

My jaw clenches as I try to steady my breathing. I can't decide whether to scream or kiss her, but gods be damned if she isn't the most beautifully damning thing I've ever seen.

"Well, I am," I snap, unable to keep the edge from my words. "Now, move over."

Her eyes widen even more, and a wave of apprehension seems to wash over her. Then curiosity flickers and I move closer to the bed. The morality of the situation knots within me, but right now, the logical part of me can go fuck itself.

"Slide over, Scarlet," I command, my voice a low growl.

Scarlet shakes her head, her eyes flashing with defiance. "What are you going to do?" she asks, her voice trembling slightly.

"Put both of us out of our misery because gods, woman, you don't know how to do it. It shouldn't take an hour to get yourself off. Now move." My voice is sharp and pointed as if every syllable is a blade. My eyes narrow and my lips purse into a thin line as I rub at the tightness forming in my chest.

At this rate, it's not going to be the monsters that put me in an early grave. It'll be my wife. She's going to be the reason I have a coronary at twenty-eight.

She protests, clutching the blanket tighter around herself. "You're the last man I want touching me. I'm your prisoner, nothing more. You made that perfectly clear."

"Really?" I give her a knowing look, my words dripping with sarcasm. "Are you forgetting about the blood oath we—sorry, I swore? I'm keenly aware of every emotion you feel. It's excruciating, and lust is by far the worst. So please, move over. I'd like to actually get sleep tonight."

Her face hardens, and she scoffs, "How romantic."

"Romantic wasn't the intention." Lifting a hand, my shadows shoot through the bed, flinging her up and over into the center of the bed in a fluid motion.

Scarlet squeals as she hits the mattress, white hair flying. I quickly use my darkness to cover her mouth, smothering the noise before it could alert those in the surrounding rooms to what we're doing.

"Quiet, darling. The walls aren't thin, but they're not soundproof either and my sister is on the other side of it. I promise she won't take kindly to what I'm about to do to you," I say, pulling my shirt over my head.

She pinches her thighs together, watching me with those bright eyes, the ones so full of longing I can't look away, and a wave of lust crashes through me so hard, that I have to grip the bedpost to keep my balance.

I grind my palm down my length, smothering the groan that threatens to leave me by biting down on my lower lip. Suddenly, there's no more space between me and my pants. It's excruciating.

Crawling onto the bed, I hover over her as my shadows fade away, leaving her exposed beneath me. "Now, you have two choices: let me take care of your needs so we can get some sleep, or I tie you to the bed at four points so you can't torture me anymore. Your choice."

Scarlet seems to weigh her options, and I can't help but wonder what's going through her mind. The air vibrates between us, like lightning rolling over my skin, tingling, and pricking until you can't help but get lost in it. I want to be closer, to feel her against me, to make her small body shake as I devour it, but I won't unless she tells me yes.

As much as I hate to admit it, there's something undeniably thrilling about this game we're playing. I watch her closely, my heart hammering in my chest, waiting for her decision.

Scarlet's silence is deafening as she stares up at me. I can feel the tempest of emotions roiling inside her—desire, need, and a touch of fear.

"Use your words, little lamb," I prod, watching her intently. She blinks at me, caught off guard by my demand. Her eyes dart to my lips as the tip of my tongue slips through the space between them. "Come on, Scarlet. The gods blessed you with those perfect lips. It'd be a sin not to make use of them... one way or another."

Deciding she needs more motivation, I slide my ringed fingers up the inside of her thigh. The simple touch sends a shiver through her, and she instinctively spreads her legs wider.

"Please," she breathes, her voice barely audible.

My mouth curves into a smirk as I lower myself between her thighs.

"That's more like it." I kiss down her chest, stopping to nip her hardened peeks through the satin fabric of her nightgown. Her body bows, arching into my mouth, but I don't let her have everything. She'll wait. This is my game, and my rules, and she'll play it like the good little lamb she is.

My hands graze up her thighs, exploring her as if this is our first time. Her eyes blaze as she watches me, and I look at her as I kiss from her knee to where her thighs meet.

With slow precision, my fingers move effortlessly, gliding over her smooth skin, slipping through the most intimate part of her. I groan, closing my eyes to gather myself. She's so fucking wet for me... So ready to take whatever I give her and gods on high, I want to give her everything and so much more.

When she looks at me like this, like there's nothing else in the world but us, I don't feel broken. I don't feel like I'm missing something. Instead, I feel wanted, and needed, like she can't breathe without me, and that alone is enough to send power surging through my veins. It overcomes any shred of logic.

There's a part of me that knows there's no way this will end well. Only right now, I don't care how it ends as long as I can enjoy this moment a little longer.

I let my darkness coil around her body in thick, dark tendrils that wrap around her thighs like ropes, holding her legs open as I lower my face between them. My tongue lashes out, tasting her desire. Her hips buck, but my shadows anchor her to the spot, demanding she take it, every flick, every swirl of my tongue.

Scarlet drives her fingers into my hair, tugging me closer to her as a gasp escapes her lips. I press two fingers inside her, curling them over and over, driving her higher until my dick is so hard I can feel my pulse in it. I'm high on everything she feels, needing more. I don't think I'll ever get enough to fully satiate my need for her.

I lick and suck as she writhes against my face, trying to take her pleasure as she moans, gasping for air.

She's close—so close—and I don't relent until I feel her walls contract and she shatters to pieces, soaking my fingers. Her body trembles, and even then, I don't relent. A wicked part of me wants her to feel tormented like I did, but I'm merciful. I at least allowed her to come, a nicety she didn't give me.

As her body arches and quivers beneath me, I can't help but feel a twisted sense of satisfaction. We may be enemies, bound together by fate and blood, but right now, I am the one giving her what she needs.

I can't help but feel every sensation she experiences—the heat, the pleasure, and the building tension. It's like a living fire coursing through my veins, igniting my own arousal. The tightening in my chest and the throbbing between my legs become almost unbearable as I continue to drive her into madness. I want her to be so sated that she can't fucking think straight, to know that I made her feel this way, that I gave her something she couldn't even give herself.

My body is aching for release, the hardness beneath my pants pressing painfully against the fabric. The way her body trembles and writhes only serves to fan the flames.

I crawl up her trembling form, my eyes locked on hers, filled with an intensity neither of us can deny. "Fuck... look at you," I growl, dragging my arousal-soaked fingers up her stomach, pushing the nightgown higher.

Reaching her shoulders, I slide the straps of her down her arm, exposing her breasts. I take one nipple into my mouth, sucking and teasing it as she watches me with lustful eyes, barely able to keep them open. Scarlet's back arches off the bed, surrendering to the sensations I'm creating.

She jumps when I bite the arch of her breast, and I can't help but chuckle darkly. Her body is so godsdamn perfect that I could touch her for hours. My pupils widen. I want to prolong this, to savor every last second, every moan, and every shiver that runs through her.

Her breaths are ragged, and I can feel her need for more, mirroring my own. I'm almost certain I'm obsessed with watching her squirm under my touch. I unzip my pants to give myself more room.

"Trust me," I murmur, letting my darkness trail over her skin as I begin to work slow, small circles around her clit. Her hips start to gyrate in time with my thumb.

"Sebastian," she moans, and I'm filled with a sense of triumph at the sound. My name on her lips... "I can't... I can't come again."

"Watch me prove you wrong, little lamb," I purr, taking her challenge head-on. I increase the pace of my fingers, pausing only to slip out of my boots and slip my pants down my hips. My length springs free and I grip it tight, moving from base to tip and back again.

The sight of her and the sweet friction I've been deprived of mix together until my head feels too heavy to hold up and I moan deep in my throat. My shadows tighten around her legs as I position myself between them, glancing at her face just in time to see her wet her lips.

Slowly, I push inside, feeling her wrap around me, tight and so fucking warm... I could die here and not complain. Scarlet tilts her hips, trying to hurry me, demanding I sink deeper, but she'll have to wait. I want to feel every inch of her take me, envelop me until I can't go any deeper.

Little by little, I give until our bodies meet and her mouth falls open. Drunken hazel eyes meet mine beneath her dark lashes and I bend forward, pushing deeper as I lift her chin and crush her mouth to mine.

She stills for a beat before kissing me back. It's raw and demanding, suffocating, yet so gentle that I don't want it to end. I crave every part of her, the feel of being buried inside her to the way her lips tantalize mine. I need it. I need her more than I need air to breathe, and I don't know what to do with that information. All I know is right now, we're alone. Right now, no one else knows, and nothing else matters.

I roll my hips forward, thrusting in and out of her. My movements are languid, but I break the kiss, sitting back as urgency replaces what last bit of sanity I have. Scarlet tries to smother her moans, biting into her lower lip as she watches us connect, over and over, slamming deeper into the depths of her body until there's no going back. I can sense her getting close, but I don't stop, determined to take her over the cliff if I have to drag her kicking and screaming. As long as it's my name she says on the way down, I don't fucking care.

"Sebastian...I..." she gasps, her fingers digging into the sheets as she finally succumbs. Her body tenses, stringing so tight that she drags me over the edge with her. I sit back, spilling onto her stomach with a groan. Having lost sight of the fact I needed her to stay quiet, I quickly lean forward, covering her mouth with my hand as pleasure crashes through her. It's all I can do to muffle the sounds, hoping that no one heard them before I could do so.

Her body shudders beneath me, shaking as adrenaline and ecstasy course through her veins. I'm going to fucking dream of this sight... I just know it. I try to commit every curve of her body, every sound, every movement she makes to memory until she finally eases.

Lifting my hand, we both breathe heavily, staring at each other. It's like neither of us wants to move because if we do, this is over...

I can't help but admire her flushed cheeks and tousled hair, her body covered in the evidence of just how well we fit together. Why does she have to be my enemy? Why did she have to be marked? All of this would be so simple... Fuck, I think I could fall for her if it were. I'd like to. My fingers feather over her heated flesh, trailing along her curves as I lick my lips.

"You're so fucking beautiful when you come for me, darling," I murmur, my voice husky.

Pressing my lips together, I push up from the bed, helping her clean up as I put myself back together. I stand, staring at her for a long moment, not wanting to leave but knowing I have to. If I lay down with her, if I hold her, there's no coming back for me. There might not be as is. I came here to give us both peace, to satiate whatever was gnawing at us through the bond. I did that, but I can't force myself to walk back through that door...

Gritting my teeth, I turn around, trying not to look at her. Maybe that'll help. "Goodnight, Scarlet."

I'm ready to leave when she speaks up, her voice small yet loving... so full of emotion that it hurts. "Wait... Stay with me, please?"

My heart clenches, and I force myself to ignore the sudden longing that flares within me. "I'm sorry... I can't."

"Why? I'm your wife. That's what married people do," she stammers. I turn around, running my hands through my hair. Her eyes search mine. "I'm your wife."

"You're also my prisoner," I remind her. "You may be my wife and legally share my last name, but I have no intentions of falling in love with a witch. No matter how deliciously tempting she may be."

Her eyes fill with hurt, and it takes every ounce of my self-control not to reach out and comfort her. Instead, I force myself to open the door.

"I'm sorry," I say, my voice barely a whisper. "It has to be this way... at least for now." With those final words, I step out into the hallway, leaving her behind.

As I close the door, I nearly collide with Nelvin, who's shirtless, pants-less, and nursing a drink in his hand. His eyes narrow, then stretch wide as he glances from the door to me, taking in the fact I've yet to put my shirt on. It's still in my hand. "Did you just come from…" he trails off, pointing toward Scarlet's door.

"Keep your mouth shut," I warn, my voice low and dangerous, using the skeleton key to lock the door. Without waiting for a response, I step into a shadow, disappearing from his sight.

27

SCARLET

What just happened? I knew Sebastian could vaguely feel my emotions. It's how the blood bond works. I knew he could sense my unease, or my longing, my fear, but I was trying so hard to keep my mind blank.

That book was the only thing Smee left behind and I picked it up, thinking that getting lost in some adventure or story would help keep my mind off Sebastian, not summon him involuntarily. I wanted to forget all the things happening in the real world, to pretend for just an inkling of time that it wasn't crashing down around me. But what I found between those pages... Let's just say I've never read something like that before.

Romance books aren't foreign to me, and I read a little of everything. Almost all genres have a place in my heart and a time in which I crave them, but never in all my years have I read something like that... I could feel everything the character did like I was living inside those pages. And if I'm honest, it hit a bit too close to home, with the protagonist being a siren princess and her love interest being a ship captain. What are the odds of that?

I'm starting to think Smee left it behind to torture me. At first, I thought it might've been her way of showing sympathy, giving me something to read to pass the time, but now... I'm not so sure. I can vividly picture the way her face twisted in disgust when she discovered my mark like I was the most wretched thing she ever laid eyes on. It hurt... Out of everyone on that deck, she and her brother were the only two people I prayed would look past it. They knew me better than anyone else, but it wasn't enough.

I'd started to think of Smee as a friend. Spending time with her in the storage bay was the closest I've come to a friend since Amara joined the Bekorium Order. Sure, we still had our secret notes, but I miss having someone to confide in and talk to, or simply just be around. Smee started to be that for me, even if that time was just a blip in our lives.

Maybe this was Smee's way of torturing me. She can't hurt me physically without disobeying her brother, but leaving this book here, knowing I was coming back to this room? She picked it specifically because it would pull my heartstrings. I just don't think she understands how deep my blood oath with Sebastian runs, and that it wasn't just me she was getting at, but him, too.

Hell, I didn't even know. Not until he barged in here. I knew he could feel things to an extent, but I thought it was more of an intuitive sort of thing, not that he'd literally feel everything I do. That my lust from reading would transfer to him.

By the gods, the man looked ready to commit murder when he stepped into this room. The sight stirred something within me. Those stone-cold, green eyes sought out mine and blazed, and a dark part of me enjoyed it. It wanted to see just how far he'd go. Especially after I figured out that it was my thoughts that got him so worked up.

He'd been so... I'm not even sure there's a word to describe it. Unruly, maybe? His shirt was untucked, nearly unbuttoned halfway. His hair looked like his fingers had run through it countless times. I could smell the sweet, fruity scent of fairy wine that surrounded him and gods... I'll never get enough of it, especially mixed with everything masculine about him... It's a contradiction that could stop hearts.

Above all else, it was the way he looked at me, his gaze so intense—so predatory—it left me breathless and sent a thrill racing down my spine. I never intended to make Sebastian feel like that, so fierce and out of control. Yet, seeing him so made it that much harder to turn my thoughts away from it, my body responded to him without conscious decision.

None of that matters now, though... What I took as him giving in to his heart was truly him just wanting the urges to end.

He took something so sacred and sentimental and made it into nothing, like he couldn't care less about how I felt--Like I meant nothing to him. It was transactional and I hate him for it. At least I want to hate him for it.

He's been gone for over an hour and the weight of his words still weighs heavily on my heart. The sting of betrayal is still fresh, the sensation of his touch still haunting my skin.

The soft glow of the lanterns hanging on the wall sends a flicker of shadows around the room, and though I'm alone, each one of them makes me think of him. A naïve piece of me is waiting for him to step out of one, to tell me he's sorry, that he didn't mean it. That he was wrong, but that'll never happen. It makes my teeth grit and tears sting my eyes, making my vision blur.

I hate that no matter how furious I am at Sebastian, I can't blame him for this. At least not all of it. If the roles were reversed, I'd never sleep with someone and break their heart, but I'd be just as cautious as he is. There would be too much riding on my decision. Being wrong endangers dozens of lives in his charge, and I can respect him caring about his men enough to put his own wants aside to protect them. But he crossed a line... I wanted him; I wanted everything we did, but he shouldn't have touched me if he was going to follow it up by saying he could never truly love or care about someone like me.

I touch my fingers to my lips, still raw and bruised, and trembling with unshed tears. It felt like he struck me with more than just words, that a wound opened in my chest, that refuses to heal.

Even then, if it was just me misunderstanding, or being naïve... If I could tell myself I'd been played that it was all an act on his end or some cruel game, I'd be able to wrap my mind around it right now. I'd know I messed up and trusted the wrong person. I'd build a wall and swear to never go there again. But I can't even do that.

My hand grips into the pillow beside me and I launch it with everything I have at the wall, growling out a string of curses.

Every time I close my eyes, I see him... I see the way he looks at me and I can feel it in my soul that what he said is a lie. But how can I believe that when I watched him walk out that door with my own eyes?

How can someone be so sweet, so gentle, so loving, one moment, then switch like they've become lucid and be the exact opposite? He's so confusing and complicated, and I don't know if I want to keep trying to figure him out. Not when it hurts like this.

Fury burns through my insides, knotting every muscle until my hands clench, biting crescent shapes into the palms of my hands. I sit up, dragging my knees to my chest and wrapping my arms around them.

I will not cry for this man. Not anymore. If all he'll see me for is a witch, then maybe it's about fucking time I start acting like one. I'll get off this ship. I'll find somewhere quiet to live out my life, but I sure as hell don't need him to do it.

• • • ● • ● • • •

My dreams are torn apart by desperate shouts and the violent rocking of the ship. What could possibly be happening now?

A sudden flash of lightning paints everything in a stark, white light. The loud crack that follows pierces my eardrums as I sit up, staring out the port hole in my room. In the distance, the sea crests into mountains and valleys, and a wave smashes into the side of the ship, tall enough to drown out the round window. The frothy water bubbles and streaks until it disappears, leaving behind a view of choppy waves.

Up to now, I couldn't imagine the water level being so high. The sea always rested against the floor below me, but the storm outside is massive and tosses and turns the ship like a child's toy. It's like Zeus himself has risen, determined to wreak havoc.

Is the ship always this chaotic? From blood witch wars to possessions, to sea beasts, and now to a storm that might drag us to the bloody bottom of the ocean, it's like it never ends. Another flare of lightning illuminates my surroundings as I toss the blankets off me. Through the window, I can see the crew's shadows from the top of the ship, cast on angry waves.

Why would anyone be up there right now? We don't even have sails at the moment. Cursing under my breath, I discard my nightgown and struggle into my clothes, trying to stay upright as the ship tilts dangerously. As soon as I get my pants on, a wave slams hard into the ship, sending me flying into the wall. The port hole's window cracks and water rushes in.

"No! No. No." I hiss, rubbing my shoulder where I collided with the hard surface as I plaster myself to the far side of the room. I will not drown in here.

I glance at the door, the water rising inch by inch with every rough wave. It's sealed shut. There's no way for me to get out. Not unless someone opens that door. Frustration bubbles within me, knowing that I'm powerless while trapped inside this room. If the ship goes down, I'll sink along with it.

I have to try...

The roar of water fills my ears, and panic claws at my chest. I can hear the wind howling like a banshee, wrapping around the wooden structure. The air is charged with static as lightning crackles overhead, leaving a sharp tang on my tongue.

I raise my hands, pressing my palms to the wooden slab of my door. Steadying myself, I open my mind until I feel the threads binding the ward humming beneath my fingertips. When I open my eyes, I find glimmering strings scattered about the room, and I start to search for a weak point. Every spell has one...

Whoever cast this is skilled beyond comprehension, with each string knotted in a hundred different ways. I could pick it apart, but it would take hours if not days. I don't have that kind of time.

As if on cue, the latch of the door jiggles, and the lock clicks. The door bursts open, and I have to jump back to keep from getting hit in the face with it. Zephyr stares at me from the opening. His long black hair is soaked, sticking to his face. His clothes cling to him like a second skin. The ship tilts and he grips the doorframe to brace himself as I teeter into the bedpost.

"Get out of here, princess," he barks, his eyes serious. "Don't let me regret this." And with that, he takes off down the hall toward the med bay.

I'm frozen for a moment, staring at the open door. Zephyr just saved my life, but why? I shake the seawater out of my hair, my heart pounding in my chest. Shaking out of my stupor, I bolt down the hall, opposite of the way Zephyr went.

The storm continues to rage outside, relentless in its assault on the ship. I don't know what I'm going to do, but

I know getting higher up is the best option. If I can get to the deck, maybe I can see something, or use my magic to search for a beast—anything that can take me off this ship.

Sebastian and his men will be too busy to worry about me. This is my shot. I'm not sure how it will work exactly, but I'll have to figure it out as I go.

The ship lurches again and I grab onto the wall for support. The sound of creaking wood and splintering boards is almost deafening. Water sloshes around my feet as I try to steady myself. I near the end of the hall of cabins, stopping just outside the open birthing.

At least a dozen or so men move about the room. As soon as they see me, they'll know exactly what I'm up to and they might try to play hero. But I have to cross this room. The companionway is on the other side and if there's any hope of me finding a creature to control, I have to make it to the deck. I have to be able to see it.

I take a deep breath, steadying myself before making my way into the birthing. The room is filled with vacant hammocks, crates, and barrels, some of which have toppled over and spilled their contents across the floor. The air changes, becoming almost sour. The men stop what they're doing and stare daggers into me. A few unsheathe their swords while others start shouting.

"What are you doing out of your room, witch?" one of them demands.

"She brought this storm upon us!" another yells. "I know it!"

Five of them position themselves between me and the companionway, and I know they won't let me pass.

I raise my hands, feeling the power coursing through my veins like electricity. My fingers twitch with anticipation as I narrow my eyes on the men standing before me. I thrust out my hand, sending a wave of energy towards them. They stumble back, some clutching their chests, but they don't give up.

They advance again, one swinging a sword straight at my head. I duck out of the way just in time. My eyes couldn't be any wider as panic seeps into my bones. My eyes lift from the sharp blade, locking on the man holding it. I flick my wrist, mumbling the only spell for fighting magic I know, and his body flies across the birthing and slams into the wall. His body slips down the wooden wall and slumps to the floor, out cold.

I roll my shoulders. Okay... I got this.

The others are on me in seconds, but I can feel the magic in my veins, the steady hum of power like it's singing just for me. I thrust my hands up, fingers curled to the floor. They mimic my actions and though it doesn't keep them from spouting comments, I command them into the nearest cabin room and shut the door. I quickly snatch the rope hanging off the wall just to the right of the frame and tie it around the handle, attaching the other end to the cabin across the hall. They're not going anywhere.

Not wanting to waste any more time, I sprint through the birthing. The hammocks are attached to wooden beams that line the center walkway, each one has a plethora of hooks and various other items attached to it. I snag one of the hats, twisting my hair into it.

It won't deter someone from figuring out that it's me, but in the dark, it might take them a moment. It'll be easier to slip through undetected if my white hair isn't visible. It's a dead giveaway and I'll need every second to spare.

With the rain, it's safe to assume most of the crew will be somewhere below deck and if they're not in the birthing, it doesn't leave many options. Zephyr ran toward the med bay, so it's safe to assume some are there. I don't see why anyone would be in storage right now, but that leaves the mess hall.

I stare up the stairs, taking a deep breath before climbing them. Here goes nothing. I reach the open area to find men filling the tables. Drinks in hand, like the ship isn't getting tossed around with every wave that crashes into us.

Clearing my throat, I pull the hat a bit lower, thankful that Sebastian's clothes conceal just about everything feminine about me. My pants are soaked from the knee down, and my bare feet patter against the wood planks. I manage to make it to the other side without anyone being the wiser, but I only get one step into the companionway before I realize why everything is here. The door's blocked. I'm trapped down here... Various things have been shoved down the stairs, stacked like a house of cards. I move one thing on the bottom and all of it will topple down into me.

I grit my teeth, trying to steady my heartbeat. There has to be another way out. There's got to be. If I don't get to that deck, I'm not getting off this ship alive. At some point, Sebastian will give in to his crew's demands to see me float. He'll have to or risk them turning on him. I thought he might eventually believe me, but after tonight, I don't think he ever will...

Searching around the room, I spot the porthole. I'm just below deck. It can't be that far. Ropes hang off every inch of the side. I could climb. And it looks big enough for me to fit through...

Trying to stay inconspicuous, I move toward it, grabbing an empty wooden crate from one of the tables. Setting it down, I glance at the men a few feet to my right, playing cards. Only one seems to glance my way, but I keep my face turned and he seems to lose interest, likely assuming I just want to look outside but am too short to see.

They'll be the first to reach me once they figure out what I plan to do. I'll have to be quick. Quietly, I undo the latch, making as little noise as possible, but in a room filled with chatter, I doubt they'd hear much, anyway.

I hold my breath, then move. I rip the circular window open, gripping the ledge to pull myself up. My feet lash out, trying to find something to push on until they meet the wooden wall. It's harder barefoot, but I manage to get a hold and pull myself through, twisting at the waist as I slide into the pouring rain.

Shouts carry through the air from inside and the wind rips my hat off my head, sending it twirling through the breeze and into the ocean. I scramble, gripping the thick ropes along the outside of the ship. Rain and sea spray pelt my face, but I squint and yank, and climb until I'm just outside the window.

A meaty hand reaches through, latching onto my ankle, but I kick with everything I have, connecting with what feels like a face. Their grip releases and I climb.

I can't help but curse. None of this would be happening if I hadn't accepted Sebastian's damn deal. I should've just stuck to my fate... I might be dead, but it's better than being in some hot and cold tornado that is Sebastian Hook. The man can't make up his mind to save his life. Or mine.

His betrayal fuels me as I slowly and methodically make my way toward the railing. The ship rocks, but I cling to the ropes with a ferocity born of desperation. As long as I don't look down, I'll be just fine. I'll make it.

Finally, I manage to haul myself over the railing, gasping for breath as I sit safely against the inside of it. The storm rages around me, and I can't afford to rest for long. My fingers burn from the ropes, and I hold them up to take in the angry red welts on my palms.

The wind howls in my ears and a shiver runs down my spine. It's so cold... My teeth chatter and my heart pounds as I struggle for breath, saltwater stinging my eyes. I close them tight, trying to steady my racing pulse.

"Well, aren't you fucking crafty..." I know that voice all too well...

Sebastian... the infamous Dark One. And he's just caught me trying to escape.

I am so screwed.

28
Scarlet

My gaze locks on his from where he sits, a few feet in front of me. His back is leaned against one of the exterior walls of his quarters. Blood seeps through shaky fingers pressed, coming from a wound on his stomach, and his body trembles as he struggles for breath.

His crew just left him here...

I tear my eyes away, searching the deck for any sign of life, but there's no one. My throat tightens, but I swallow hard. Flicking my wrists, my hands swarm with light as I mutter a spell. I know what he's capable of and, wounded or not, by escaping, I stepped against him. Even if it was Zephyr who let me out. Right now, it's just the two of us, dangerously close to the edge of the deck, and all it would take is one flick of his shadows to send me flying over the rail.

I straighten my shoulders, gearing up to run if I have to, but his chuckle saps it away, draining my focus. The light fades instantly, and his vibrant green eyes slice through the night, staring up at me, now on my feet.

"Relax, princess. In case you haven't noticed, I'm in no shape to stop you from... Well, whatever you're planning to do." His voice is weak, void of his irrationally confident tone.

I glance at his wound. Sebastian's hand covers it and keeps me from seeing the extent of the damage. There's a pool of crimson around him, washing over the edge of the ship. It's too much to lose, even for someone like him.

With the companionway blocked, there's no way to get him to Zephyr, not like this. Everything he needs is trapped inside the ship and he knows that. It's likely why he's resting here instead of trying to find a way in.

Looking out at the sea, my magic searches the water. There are creatures out there, at least one big enough to take me off this ship. I can feel it. Yet, when I meet his gaze, my heart yearns to go to him, to drop to my knees and try to stop the bleeding. I might be angry with him, but I don't wish him dead.

"Why are you still out here? Why aren't you below deck with the rest of the men?" I ask hesitantly, taking a step forward.

"Too many were going over, so I sent them below until the storm passed. There's nothing much we could do up here, anyway. I'd intended to join them, but a wave came and this happened." He nods his head toward his stomach. "I can't focus enough to shadow walk and even then, there's nothing Zephyr could do. If I manage to get down there, he'd be too focused on trying to save his dying best friend instead of saving who he can."

I can't leave him like this. I don't think I could leave anyone like this... I know I should think of myself first, but the thought of just abandoning him is unbearable.

"Maybe my father and I really are alike, after all—both taken down by poison." Pain laces Sebastian's words, as he shifts uncomfortably. "Smee will get what she's always wanted, this ship, and you'll hopefully find somewhere, away from me and all of this." He throws up a hand. "It'll be okay, Scarlet. Just go. Go before I'm gone and the crew finds you. I won't be here to stop them from tossing you over."

I inch closer, squinting through the darkness to see. With a flick of my wrist, my hand begins to glow, casting light on the dark blue coral chunk protruding from his flesh. He's right. It is poisonous.

I want to scream, to shout at him, but I can't. The only thought consuming my mind is that this man, this infuriating and intoxicating man, is dying and I have to choose to either save myself or him. I can't do both. If I use my magic to heal him, I won't have enough left to control some sea creature to take me to land.

"I should let you die," I say, my voice barely audible above the waves as I glare a trail from his wound to stormy green eyes.

Bloodied brows raise, and a weak smirk tugs at the corners of his lips. "Aye. You should."

"Fortunately for you, I'm not the vile creature you believe me to be. Bite down on something."

Sebastian's eyes widen, his gaze still sharp despite his pain. "Scarlet, I—"

I cut him off, "Don't. Don't sit here and try to convince me to go. Not now. Not after everything I've been through."

His dark hair falls in front of his forehead and his lips are parted as if he wants to say something but can't. Instead, he lifts his flask to his mouth, bites the cork and pulls it free, then takes a long sip.

"I see you're as stubborn as ever," Sebastian grumbles, watching me warily. He takes his belt off, ripping it through his pants loops with one hand, and doubling over the leather strap before placing it between his teeth. Those stormy green eyes watch me intently as I look him over.

"You've got no idea." I unbutton his shirt, moving his hand out of the way so I can gently tear the fabric from around the coral. My fingers hover over the blue structure, like stone in a way, but more porous. I hesitate a moment before I grasp it firmly.

"Ready?" I ask. Sebastian nods, his nostrils flaring as he breathes heavily through his nose. "On the count of three. One. Two."

I yank hard, careful to pull at the same angle it embedded into him at. Sebastian cries out, his hands gripping his stomach. I drop the coral to the deck and blood splatters into the water.

Sebastian winces, shaking his head. "There's no way in. The companionway is blocked."

"Yeah, I figured that one out. We don't need to go down there, though." I mumble a spell under my breath to make him lighter. "Come on, let's get you to your room. It's better than staying out here," I say, guiding him as slowly as I can toward the door.

The ship rocks as we carefully make our way to the captain's quarters, the sound of rain and wind howling around us. Once inside, I lay Sebastian down on his bed, my mind racing as I scan the room for anything that might help.

"Stay here," I tell him, trying to keep my voice steady. "I'll find something to stop the poison."

Now that the coral is gone, I can see the darkened veins around the wound, almost purple in color. It's a sure sign that the poison is in his bloodstream.

"Scarlet..." His voice is weak, but it draws my attention, anyway. "Stop... Just lay with me, please." His breaths are weak, his tanned skin almost pale in the dim lantern light. "Please," he repeats, gripping my wrist. "I don't want to spend my last moments watching you worry. I'd rather just hold you."

Snatching my wrist away, I shake my head. "No... I won't. You're not dying today."

I can't help but notice the tension in his jaw and the beads of sweat forming on his brow. His breath comes in shallow, uneven gasps, and I know I don't have much time.

Sebastian groans as I whip away from him, frantically rummaging through his makeshift apothecary. My hands shake as I search, but I can't find anything on this shelf that can help him.

There's nothing to stop the bleeding or speed up his healing—my breath hitches as my eyes lock on a small pouch filled with dried yarrow leaves—an herb known for its blood-clotting properties. My heart leaps, and I hurry back to Sebastian's side.

"Here," I say, holding out the yarrow. "Chew on these. They'll help slow the bleeding."

He raises a skeptical eyebrow but takes the leaves without protest, wincing as he chews. The metallic tang of blood fills the air, mixing with the scent of damp wood and salty water. My stomach churns, but I force myself to focus.

With the immediate crisis under control, I focus my attention on finding a more permanent solution. Pulling grimoires from the shelves, I flip through their pages, looking for a spell that might save Sebastian without too much of a payment in return. I know that's asking for a miracle, but there's got to be something in here. Even if it'll only help him heal faster, just enough for his body to take over the rest.

"Scarlet," he grits, as if he's reading my mind. "Don't fucking dare."

"You can't condemn me if you're dead, can you? And that's exactly what you'll be if I don't do something."

Looking for a spell isn't an easy task; many of them require sacrifices or ingredients I don't have access to. But then, just when I'm about to give up hope, I find it. There's a healing spell that will draw on my soul, but only as long as I keep the spell going. I can stop it before I deplete it, avoiding any permanent damage to myself. But it'll help him heal without using sacrifices—not that I'd have access to anything to do one, anyway.

He spits the leaves out as his eyes narrow into slits. "You're not using blood magic on me."

"You're right. I'm not," I say, bringing the book with me. I set it down on the bed as he watches every move I make with rounded eyes.

I press my hands to his stomach over the wound, and he cringes at the pressure. My mind spirals, desperate to block out every warning bell ringing in my head, but I stay the course. Reading the scripture aloud, Sebastian tries to move, to stop me, but he's weak, and I'm able to hold him in place.

"Scarlet, don't! You can't do those without a sacrifice. You'll shatter your soul. Trust me, it's not worth it." Shadows spark around his hands as he tries to use his gift, but they fizzle out as if they were never there.

"Just shut up! Please! I can't focus with you shouting."

Despite Sebastian's narrowed eyes, I notice them fluttering, betraying his weakened state. He finally relents, removing his hands to allow me to do what I need to.

Closing my eyes for a moment, I focus on the words of the spell, allowing them to fill my thoughts. The air around us crackles with energy, and I feel the drain on my magic as the spell starts to take root, knitting the skin closed from the inside out. Poison floods the middle of the wound, the sour scent of it filling my nose as it's drawn out by the power. It's working... The spell feels like a weight pressing down on my chest, making it difficult to breathe, but I refuse to let it stop me.

"Scarlet..." Sebastian's voice is barely a whisper, but it's filled with concern. His head lolls as he tries to sit up. "That's enough! You've done enough."

I release the spell, feeling drained, but I didn't take too much. I hovered the line and my soul will regenerate. I know it will.

Sebastian's wound isn't fully closed, but the bleeding has stopped, and the poison is out. He'll live, and Zephyr will be able to stitch him up the rest of the way.

Dizzy and disoriented, I attempt to stand up, my legs wobbling beneath me. The world tilts and sways, the colors of the room swirling together. My heart pounds in my chest, its rhythm erratic and frightening.

"Scarlet?" Sebastian's voice is distant and distorted as if filtered through water.

My breath catches in my throat, and I struggle to remain upright. Knees buckling, my hands grip the edge of the bed for support. Despite my best efforts, darkness creeps into the corners of my vision.

"Scarlet!"

I can't respond; my tongue is heavy and numb. The room tilts again, and my grip on the bed falters. I crumple to the floor. A ringing explodes inside my head as I try to regain control of my body.

"Gods fucking damn you, woman," Sebastian's voice echoes through the haze, growing fainter with each syllable. The darkness engulfs me completely, swallowing me whole.

29

HOOK

The med bay is so quiet... Most of the men Zephyr and his assistant tended to during the storm have all been returned to their spaces, bandaged and drugged.

Luckily, we were able to retrieve a few of the crew that had gone overboard once the storm settled—one being the alchemist. The seas must've been rough enough to drive the beasts down deep. Two of my crew are still missing, and I know the likelihood of finding them now isn't good. In fact, it'd be a miracle if we did.

Not that anyone's life is more valuable than others, but we'd be shit out of luck without Jordi to make all his concoctions. If it weren't for him and his magic potions, as he calls them, I'd still be gimping around here like I'd be shot with a cannonball. I'm not sure how he does it, but he's managed to synthesize pain meds and anesthetics, and so much more in his little portion of the ship. It's why he has the second-hand's quarters, to make space for all his science shit.

It works though... I'll give him that. He's the reason I don't feel pain right now. Scarlet healed me enough to save my life and draw out the poison, but I still had a gaping wound by the time it was over. Even with my healing abilities, it'll take time to close up.

I felt fucking useless... She collapsed and I could barely hold my own weight to stand, let alone carry her to get help. It was all I could do, while still recovering from the poison, to crawl off the bed and drag her into my arms. I'm just lucky she didn't need immediate attention, or I wouldn't be sitting next to her, fast asleep in her cot. I'd be planning her funeral.

She shouldn't have done that fucking spell...

"How do you feel?" Zephyr asks, pulling back the curtain to come sit next to me on the wooden bench.

I shoot him a side-eye. "What do you think?"

"That's not what I mean... It wasn't that long ago that you practically begged me to sedate her. I know it's a shitty way to get a break from the bond, but it doesn't mean I'm not curious about whether it's helping or not."

Arching an eyebrow, I lean back against the wall and pick at my fingers. Blood still coats them. I haven't left her side long enough to wash it off. "What? Are you going to Ether Lorian next time he pisses you off?"

Zephyr doesn't look at me, but his lips tug into a smirk. "Not that the thought hasn't crossed my mind, but no. I believe in working through our problems, not postponing them. That and I meant what I said before. Our supply is dangerously low, and Jordi can't make more unless he has Everbloom to distill it from. So, unless you're planning to take a trip to Neverland soon, it's a last resort only."

Reaching out to hold Scarlet's hand, I bring our intertwined fingers to my lips. "Is it that bad?" I can feel Zephyr's stare, locked on the side of my face, but I don't care.

"No... She'll be alright. I gave it to her at first because I wasn't sure what was wrong, but Lorian looked her over and she's not in pain. Her soul is still intact, though she'll need time to recover before doing magic again. A day or two will be sufficient."

"Then why is she still asleep?" Stroking my thumb over the top of her hand, I can't stop looking at her. It's like every piece of me is on pins and needles, just waiting for her to open her eyes, like my brain can't relax until she does. It won't believe she's truly okay until it sees it.

"Well, like I said. It was a last resort, but it wasn't for her sake. You needed a moment to relax. I've never seen you that... distraught before. Not even when your father died. So, sure, our supply is low, but this ship needs its captain and at the time, I wasn't sure our captain was going to survive if she turned out to not be okay."

"I would've been just fine." I feel something spark inside my chest. I'm not sure what, exactly, but something.

"I'll ask again," Zephyr says, crossing his arms over his chest. "How are you feeling?"

"Honestly, I don't feel anything at all, which is precisely how it was before Scarlet was bound to me. I hate it and don't want it to go back to this. Ever."

"So, the ether does block the bond, then…"

I nod, watching Scarlet's chest rise and fall in a steady rhythm. Her white hair is splayed across the pillow like a silken halo. She looks so peaceful, so unburdened. It's a stark contrast to the chaos that unfolded mere hours ago.

Zephyr runs his arm over his forehead, wiping at the sweat beading there. He hasn't stopped going since the storm hit. "Sebastian." He grips my arm, forcing me to meet his concerned gaze. "Breathe. She's going to be okay. Lorian looked her over. She got very lucky. Her magic stores must've been high because you stopped her before it could do anything bad."

I run a hand through my hair, exasperated. "She used a blood grimoire without a sacrifice, Zephyr. We won't know the full extent of the price she paid until she wakes up."

Zephyr weighs his head from side to side, contemplating my words. "Maybe, but for now, she's okay. She's stable and can be woken up in minutes if you'd like, but she should get some sleep. And you."

"I don't need anything," I grit, but I feel him pulling at the gauze bandage on my stomach and I glare at him. "What are you doing?"

"You have to let me look at some point. You can't just slap a bandage on and say a magic word. From what I've gotten out of the little you've told me, you need stitches."

"I'll heal. I'm not leaving her. So, if you're going to do them, then you'll have to do them here."

Zephyr lets out a long sigh, digs and his pocket, and produces a small suture kit. "As I anticipated. Now can I do my job?"

Dropping Scarlet's hand, I sit back. He works the sticky part of the bandage off my skin and I hiss as it tugs on the wound.

"So, still think she's a witch?" he asks, spraying something into the gash.

I clench my teeth together, trying to ward off the sting. "What kind of question is that?"

"I'm just saying you have an entire collection of shadows in jars within that room. If she was a blood witch, she'd have used one as a sacrifice. Yet, she didn't. She used herself."

It's not something I haven't thought about. She'd have felt the power within those bottles. Any skilled mage would, let alone a blood witch. She passed right over them as if they were nothing. "I don't know if it matters to me anymore. Blood witch or not, I can't lose her. I don't want to feel like this—numb and empty. I need her..."

"She's fine, Hook. I wouldn't lie to you."

"I know... Just I can't believe it until I can talk to her, until I know that she's still in there." I drag a hand down my face, pressing my fingers into my cheekbones to distract myself from the needle going in and out.

"Then wake her up. Like I said, I kept her asleep for you, but if it's causing more distress, then it's a simple fix."

I nod, standing up from the bench before Zephyr can cut the suture string. He rushes to keep up, finishing the knot and slicing the excess off.

"Give me a moment. Please." He presses his lips together but slips through the curtain, leaving us be.

I reach for the mask sitting on her face. As long as she wears it, the ether will keep her out. It only takes a minute or two for her to slip out of the sedation.

Scarlet's face scrunches and her eyes flutter open. I hold my breath. I'm not sure what to say or do, but gods... I'm just so grateful she's not dead. I want to say that's because, without her, I don't feel, but I know deep down that there's more to it than that.

For a moment, she seems disoriented, but then she blinks in rapid succession and her hazel eyes liven up. I stay silent as she takes in the room, and finally, her gaze settles on me. I swear my heart skips inside my chest, like I can finally breathe.

She starts to sit up, but I place my hand on her stomach, keeping her still.

"Take it easy, little lamb." My thumb strokes over the fabric of her shirt. "You've been through enough. Zephyr was right. I should've let you sleep, but I had to know you're okay."

Her eyes drop down my torso, getting an eyeful of the bandage Zephyr placed just below my ribs. "You're alright... It worked."

I flex my jaw, taking a deep breath. "You used a blood grimoire without a sacrifice. You're lucky you're alive... but thank you."

Her eyes light up, searching mine like she's not sure she heard that right. I reach out to cup her cheek, running my thumb over the softness of her skin.

"You scared me," I admit, my voice cracking and I swallow hard. "Promise me you won't make a habit out of that?"

She doesn't say anything, her eyes dancing between mine. Fear spills into the pit of my stomach. She's scared I'm going to hurt her for it... I don't blame her. The last time she used her magic to help me, I locked her in a room. And despite everything—the words I've said that I can't take back—I can see why. I've never physically hurt her, but I've said things that are just as bad.

My entire life, I've been taught that things are black and white. A witch is a witch, but I'm starting to realize that's not the case.

Zephyr clears his throat, standing just inside the curtain. "Captain... I'd love to give you more time, but there are pressing things to attend to."

"I asked for a minute," I say, twirling my finger in her long, white hair.

"And I gave you one."

I didn't intend for it to be literal... I laugh humorously, bringing her hand to my lips to kiss the tip before stepping aside. "I suppose he needs to look you over."

Sitting down on the bench, I make myself comfortable as Zephyr does his exam. Once he's finished, he holds his arms out to his sides. "Was that thorough enough for you? Do you believe me now?"

My lips pull into a smirk as I drop my gaze, bouncing my knee as I sit back against the wall, arms crossed. "Yes. Thank you."

Zephyr rolls his eyes. "She needs to rest, and you are needed in the wardroom. So, do you want me to sedate her or just have my assistant keep an eye on her? Her room flooded and though the water elementals cleared the ship, everything is soaked through. So, she should probably stay here, regardless."

I don't answer him, shifting my attention to Scarlet. "Where would you like to stay? Do you want something to help you sleep?"

"Um..." She looks between us before dropping her chin to her chest. "Here's fine, and no, I should be okay."

"You heard the lady." I nod at Zephyr, swallowing the lump in my throat. He holds open the curtain, beckoning for me to take my leave. As I stand, I steal one last glance at her before heading out.

We make our way through the med bay and I spot Zephyr's assistant. I brush his arm and he spins toward me. Leaning in, I keep my voice down. "Anything she needs, but no one goes in there and she doesn't leave. Got it?" He jerks his head, nodding far too many times than what's necessary. "Good."

"You're going to scare the boy," Zephyr says as we walk to the wardroom. "Hell, you sort of scared me."

Reaching the lower level, I grip the door handle to the wardroom. "Not a word of what you saw. Please."

Zephyr drags two fingers over his lips like he's sealing them shut. I push inside, finding Smee, Nelvin, and Lorian waiting. Nelvin slips into a seat next to Smee, who gives me a scrutinizing glance as I enter. I don't sit, I'm too restless. Part of me worries about leaving Scarlet in the med bay, or anywhere that can't be magically sealed. There are people on this crew who blame her for the storm, like she caused it somehow. Just as there are people on this ship who wanted her dead long before that.

"Update," I demand, scrubbing a hand down my face.

"Things are under control," Lorian replies, folding his arms across his chest. "There are more injuries and the damage to the ship is minimal, all things considered. Most have already been repaired. Scarlet's room got the worst of it."

"My room," Smee corrects and I roll my eyes.

"Good." I ignore her comment, nodding at Lorian. "What about the sails?"

Nelvin chimes in, sitting forward in his seat. "They'll be up and replaced by the end of tomorrow. I don't want my guys on the masts until daylight."

"Is there any way to remove the blood oath?" Smee takes her feet off the table as our eyes meet.

"No, they're for life," Nelvin says, barely sparing her a glance.

"Why the hell would you ask that?" The words are out of my mouth before I can think better of it, my tone holding a lethal ring as I stare at Smee.

She scoffs, arching an eyebrow at me. "You have to ask that question? You've been off since you married her. I thought it was good at first, but since we found out about her mark, you've been making some interesting decisions."

"I'm still adjusting. It would likely be the same way if I'd gotten my shadow back—"

"That's the thing, Sebastian. Had we searched the mainland like we planned, right after you were pardoned, you might have your shadow back."

"You can't blame all of this on her," I say, bracing my hands on the table. "She didn't wreck that village or bring that witch aboard. Just as she didn't summon that beast."

"No, but her kind did," Smee purses her lips. "This is exactly what I mean." She glances at the men in the room as if she's providing her evidence to them.

"You don't understand what it's like to have my soul tethered to hers," I snap, my hands clenching into fists at my sides. "I feel everything she does, whether I want to or not. I'm starting to care about her, and yeah, maybe I shouldn't. If it was any other scenario, if I discovered a witch on board my ship, I'd have floated her in a heartbeat without a second thought. Scarlet nearly died tonight, doing a spell to save my life. She's not like the others. And when I thought she was going to die, I swear my fucking heart ceased beating until she drew breath again." My voice catches and I look away, biting back the anger that floods through my veins. "Now tell me, Smee, how the fuck am I supposed to push that girl off my ship? Even then, I don't think she's a blood witch. She's marked, and that should be a done deal for me, but it isn't. I believe her."

Zephyr's eyes soften and he sends me an empathetic smile, nodding once in my direction, like he's telling me he's proud. There's a long pause as my words hang heavily in the air. I can feel the weight of their concern and the unspoken questions they're all too afraid to ask.

"What are you going to do? Float me too?" I ask, looking at all of them.

Silence settles over the wardroom, heavy and suffocating. Smee finally breaks it with a resigned sigh. "I don't know, Sebastian. Maybe someone else should make that call."

My hands clench around the wooden tabletop, knuckles turning white with strain. I force them to relax, flexing my fingers to ease the ache. "Not going to happen."

Smee snorts. "Why the hell not? You have four capable people right in front of you."

"I'd rip their heart out before her feet touched the water," I growl.

Smee looks shocked for a moment, then shakes her head, her voice surprisingly steady. "Then I'll do it. You won't kill me," say says, crossing her arms. I glance at her, concern etched across my face. "You'd kill me? Your sister? All to save a witch?"

I don't say anything, but when I turn my gaze away from her, it's all the answer she needs.

"Shit... He's in love with her," Nelvin mumbles, standing up to pace in a tight circle.

"I'm not in love with her," I snap.

"Can he even be truly in love with someone with only half a soul?" Lorian furrows his brow.

"Well, he's in love with her, by my definition." Zephyr leans back in his chair with a casual air.

"Then that's your definition." I don't bother to hide the irritation in my voice. I don't know what I want or what I am. All I know is she can't die.

Smee whispers, "What do we do then? If she's used magic somehow to get in your head…"

I shake my head, running a hand through my hair. "I don't think she's capable of that."

"Me either," Zephyr agrees, nodding solemnly.

"She's marked as a blood witch. It's reason enough," Smee grits.

I fidget, restless, and frustrated. I don't even want to be having this conversation and it's gone on long enough. The longer I'm here, the more opportunity someone has to try something, and I doubt Zephyr's assistant is capable of stopping it. The boy is a twig that can walk.

The others exchange glances, their silent conversation clear as day. I can practically see the worry etched into their faces.

"Are you sure? How can we trust that you're in your right mind, then? How do we know if you'll do what's best for this ship?"

If my own sister is questioning that, then more are. Zephyr was right… The crew isn't going to believe me. If I don't do something, they'll mutiny and we don't have the men to lose.

I open my mouth to speak, but Zephyr cuts me off.

"You're not going to...? About the...?" He clears his throat, and I give a curt nod, confirming his suspicion. "Fuck. Okay, you are." Zephyr scratches one of his horns. The room goes silent, all eyes on me, waiting for my decision. I square my shoulders and take a deep breath.

"I think... I should step down as captain until we figure this out. You're right. I can't put the crew first when they're at odds with someone I care about. So, until we figure this out..." With a heavy heart, I grab the captain's hat from the wall and hand it to Smee. "It's all you." She starts to reach for it, but I pull it back a smidge. "Just let me make one thing clear. You're not floating my wife, unless I say you can. If you're willing to make that deal with me, then it's yours."

Smee takes the tricorn hat, running her fingers over it, then looks up at me with wide eyes. "You don't have to do this. Don't get me wrong, I've dreamed of being captain of this ship. But this isn't how I wanted it."

I let out a humorless chuckle, the weight of my decision pressing down on me. "It's not a handout, Smee. You deserve it. I'm still getting used to having emotions again and until I can get a grip on that, I won't be able to think straight. Add all the things with Scarlet..." I trail off, watching her play with the textured velvet. "Look, it's temporary, and I'm keeping my room, but until I can soundly say I'm mentally fit for it, I should step down."

Smee glances at the others, searching their faces for answers or maybe acceptance that they're on board with what I'm doing. "What about spells or our potion stash? Is there anything we could use to keep her out of his head?"

I grit my teeth, hating what she's implying. Scarlet isn't purposely messing with me. She feels like a normal being and we're in this position because I don't.

"I'm with Hook and Zephyr on this one. I don't think it's her magic he needs to be worried about. This has to do with his inability to control himself." Nelvin's grin slices his face and I already know that whatever is about to leave his mouth can't be good for me. Especially given the awful mental image I just got of the pants-less version of him in the hallway.

Smee crosses her arms, her brow furrowing. "Care to explain?"

Nelvin sits back in his seat, touching his fingertips together in a wavelike motion. "I saw Sebastian leaving her room last night before the storm hit. And then he abandoned Zephyr and me on the deck right after the beast attacked because his witchling got horny. He's like a teenager."

I grit my teeth, shooting a glare at Nelvin. My face flushes with heat, but there's no use denying it. Scarlet has wormed her way into my thoughts and desires, making it impossible for me to focus on anything else. I haven't been able to resist her urges—or whatever he wants to call them.

"Nelvin! There were so many better ways to put that," Zephyr shouts, lifting from his chair. Lorian holds his arm out, holding him back.

"It's the truth! As our new captain, she has a right to know," Nelvin says, gesturing wildly with his hands. "You all saw him. The guy popped a boner on the deck. Do you think the barnacles on the wreckage gave that to him? No."

"Thanks," I mutter sarcastically, raising an eyebrow at Nelvin.

Smee turns to me, her posture oozing attitude, "Tell me you did not fuck her after we'd just found out she was a blood witch."

I avoid her piercing gaze, instead focusing on straightening the papers on the table. "I... I did not have sex with her immediately after." I shake my head, jutting out my lower lip.

"Let me be more specific. Have you since we found out?" Smee snaps, and I clear my throat, unable to answer.

"Gods, Sebastian..." She rolls her eyes, her entire head following the motion.

I still can't bring myself to look at her when I answer, "Yes, but you gave her that book—"

"There are no buts!" Smee interrupts, silencing me with a wave of her hand. "You knew the woman was a hag and still decided to fucking play with it?"

My anger flares in an instant, and I glare daggers at my sister. "I'd like to advise you to refrain from calling my wife a hag. Her name is Scarlet, and I just told you that I believe she was wrongfully marked. So does Zephyr."

Smee stares at me, her eyes wide with shock. Then she picks up the captain's hat from the table and looks away. "In that case, I'm listening. How do you tame the raging hormones—emotions, whatever this is? I feel like that's the priority while we get the sails up..."

"Clearly he and the princess are into each other," Nelvin says, teetering his weight onto the back legs of his chair. "Maybe they should just get it out of their system. Sure, he'll still be smitten, but it's like a new toy. Once you've played with it once or twice—ten times, whatever—you still like it, but you're not as obsessed with it as you were."

Smee narrows her big brown eyes at Nelvin. "And that's precisely why you'll be sleeping on the deck tonight."

Nelvin holds up his hands in surrender, a smirk playing on his lips. "I wasn't referring to you, love. You'll always be shiny and new to me."

Smee's glare intensifies. "Oh, cram it up your arse."

He licks his lips and mutters a playful, "Yes, milady," before falling silent.

I'll never understand them or the dynamic they share. I love them both, but they fight more than anyone else on this ship.

Zephyr rubs his hands together. "I think Nelvin's right," he admits reluctantly before glancing at me. "Sorry... or maybe I should say congrats?"

Smee turns her attention back to me. "You going to comment?"

"I don't know... I'm not sure that would work. Every time we've been intimate, it's like the need becomes stronger. It's like a craving that I can't shake."

Zephyr chuckles, drawing his hand down his face. "That's because it's a mate bond—well, essentially. It gets better, but it takes time. In the beginning, you want to live, eat, and breathe your other half, but it does settle and like Nelvin tried to say, there will come a point when you just know they'll be there when you need them, and not so much like you have to do things now because you won't get a chance later."

"It's actually customary to spend weeks alone when a couple bond. You only got a night, and since then it's been chaos. And if the bond isn't reciprocated, she's not going to understand that she needs to avoid certain things while the bond is still new," Lorian says, squeezing Zephyr's hand and casting him a sideways look.

"I don't even know which feelings are hers and which are mine, but I'm starting to think they're all hers? While she was under the ether, I got to experience just mine again, and it's nothing in comparison. The only thing I can truly feel to her extent is anger. But it feels real, like they're mine. It's hard to explain." I twirl my rings around my fingers, trying to avoid their eyes as much as possible. This conversation can't get any more embarrassing.

"Give me an example," Smee demands, crossing her arms. I stand corrected. Now it can't.

"Before the storm," I begin, my mind racing back to the vivid memory, "she decided to read the book you left her and it just... Her mind ran with it. Next thing I know, I'm in her room, pinning her down with my shadows. I literally couldn't fight myself anymore. I knew going in there was going to give her the wrong impression and I tried not to, but even after things were said and done, I had to drag myself from her room. It wasn't easy. I've never had a thing for tying women up. Ever. I don't even understand why people want to do it to their partner, but for some reason..." I trail off, not wanting to finish that sentence out loud.

The crew exchanges glances as they take in my confession. I can feel the weight of their judgment in the air, just as I could the lightning from that storm.

Smee shakes her head, her lips pursed in disapproval. "Gods, help me. I swear I'm having the birds and bees talk at this point, but sometimes, people don't want to be in control. They want to just have someone else do it for a change, but they don't know how to not be in control all the time. Tying them up forces them to do so."

I stop dead in my tracks, even my thoughts cease. "And how do you know this?"

"Books," she says, as if it's the most obvious thing in the world.

Nelvin snorts from across the table, grinning and blushing as he chews his thumbnail. "Sure... books."

My vision goes red, and I point an accusatory finger at him. "I swear I will throw you off this ship," I growl.

"You're not going to float me," Nelvin retorts, unfazed. "Even then, I've never hurt your sister. I've given her what she wants. She could stop things at any time."

Taking a deep breath, I force my anger to the back of my mind and focus on the conversation at hand.

Zephyr clears his throat, drawing our attention. "So, how do we finish the bond if she didn't take it during the ceremony? If he feels numb all the time, it should help dampen whatever she's feeling."

Nelvin pipes up. "Priestesses only bind spirits for royal weddings. And yes, some spells can bind you in a similar fashion, but they have to be accepted willingly."

Lorian nods, stroking his beard thoughtfully. "It's written magic, but it's worth a shot. Nelvin would have to cast it, though. Only elves and fae can."

"Actually, it's not just written magic," Nelvin corrects him. "It requires him to sleep with her and she's gotta see stars. If he can't make that happen, then—"

I lock my jaw. Never again... Next time, I'll suffer alone. "It won't be a problem."

"Good. Then I'll get the tattoo gun. I'm going to need both of your blood and apparently, you're going to need to bring your shadows." Nelvin winks at me.

Dear gods... "Alright," I concede, my voice barely above a whisper. "Let's just get this over with."

"Fuck..." Nelvin mutters, covering his eyes with a hand. "When I said I wanted a threesome, this isn't what I envisioned."

I shake my head. "You're not touching her. You're not even going to be on the same level of the ship when it happens. It's bad enough I had to learn what you do to my sister."

Smee groans, rolling her eyes. "Fine. If you think finishing the bond will work, do it. But it doesn't solve her mark issue. We'll handle one thing at a time, and I'm keeping this until she either floats or we have concrete proof of her innocence."

"I understand," I say, locking eyes with her.

As they disperse, I take a deep breath, letting my head tip back against the chair.

"Are you sure about this? You know there's no guarantee it will work," Smee says softly once we're alone.

I nod, my resolve unwavering. "I know, but it's worth the risk. If finishing the blood oath or the bond can help me regain some semblance of control, then I have to try."

"Alright," she sighs, placing a reassuring hand on my shoulder. "Just... be careful, okay? I don't want to see you get hurt."

30
HOOK

I'm not sure how long I sit in the wardroom, but everyone is long gone by the time I gather the energy to move. Checking my bandage, I find my wound closed, and that the stitches and an ugly scar are the only evidence left. Still hurts, but it's nothing like it used to be.

I peel the bandage off, crumpling it up in my hand, and toss it into the trash on the way out of the room. As I make my way through the ship, no one speaks, but I can feel the looks being shot my way. Giving Smee the hat was the right call. I've done everything I can to keep this crew happy, during the years I served as my father's second to taking the helm myself. It's like they've forgotten that.

Something strikes me as odd though... They're not the looks of angry men. It's like they're surprised to see me, like they didn't expect me here. Their expressions are full of blank eyes and gaping mouths. And then there's the whispers... Is it because I was hurt? Are they surprised to see me up and about or—

Panic shoots through me, raw and uncontrollable, like someone's plunged a knife into my gut. My knees buckle and I have to grab the bulkhead just to stay upright. My heart races, beating away at my bones and muscle until it hurts. No matter what I do, I can't take a deep enough breath to soothe the burning in my lungs.

What the fuck is happening?

No one moves. No one so much as flinches, like they expected it. They know something. Scarlet.

I twirl my wrists as shadows burst into existence around me. Zephyr asked me not to use my gift for at least a day, to conserve my energy to heal, but that was before this--before someone got to her. I step into the closest one pooling across the floor and out of another in the med bay, sprinting toward where Scarlet's cot is.

Ripping back the curtain, my blood runs cold, and my heart stops. She's not there. It's empty. Things are knocked over and the curtain is half-torn down. She didn't go without a fight. She made noise... She had to.

I spin in place, searching out Zephyr's assistant and finding him nowhere. Fuck!

How could I let this happen? I should've been here. I should've been more vigilant--more careful. Scarlet was under my protection, and I failed her.

I take a deep breath and try to calm myself down. Panic won't help now. I need to focus, to use my gift to find Scarlet.

Closing my eyes, I extend my shadows, sensing for anything and everything that moves. I search the ship, feeling the heartbeats, steady and strong. And then, in the distance, there's the faintest whisper of fluttering, the same way mine felt. It's surrounded by more. That's her. It has to be.

I open my eyes and dart through the cabins and the birthing, towards the stairs leading up to the higher decks. I don't even have my fucking sword, but I just have to get there in time. That's all I need. As long as I can catch them before she goes over, it will be okay. It has to be.

If it weren't for the fact I nearly died hours ago, I could fucking shadow walk there. Gods... just let me find her in time.

As I reach the top of the stairs, I don't stop. I barrel through the mess hall, drawing eyes from those seated around the tables. My chest burns as I reach the deck, spotting seven of my men picking up Scarlet near the rail. Her hands and feet are bound, her mouth gagged. How did they get past everyone with her like that?

It's too dark to make out who it is, but it doesn't matter. They're dead.

"Hey!" I shout, throwing out a hand. The shadows heed my command, speeding over the deck. It snatches the two men holding her like a tripwire and they fall to the ground.

By the time the others can get their wits, I'm there. One has their blade drawn. I lean back to dodge it easily, smashing my palm into their wrist. He drops the sword, and it clatters to the ground. My shadows snatch it up and bring it to my hand.

"Which one of you had the brilliant idea? Hmm?" I point the end of the blade at them as I pace. Their hands go up and they step away from Scarlet. "Fucking answer me! I am your captain. You will speak when I ask you to!"

As the men cower, I can feel the rage simmering inside me, threatening to burst. How dare they try to take my Scarlet from me? I step closer to them, brandishing the sword and allowing the shadows to swarm around me, lending a menacing aura. "I won't ask again," I growl. "Which one of you cowards thought it was a good idea to tie up my wife and throw her overboard?"

None of them speak up, their eyes darting from me to each other in silent communication. They know what they've done is unforgivable, but they still refuse to own up to it. I can't believe it. These are men whom I've fought alongside for years, and yet they betray me like this?

I'm aware of the crowd forming behind me. The door to the companionway hasn't stopped opening and shutting since I walked through it. Yet, no one joins me by my side. Clearly, it's time to remind them exactly who and what I am.

My grip on the sword tightens as I take a step towards them, causing them to flinch back. "Well then, if none of you will confess, I'll have to assume that you're all guilty,"

I say through gritted teeth. "You know what happens to traitors on my ship?"

The shadows shift around me and the ship creaks and groans. Each of their heartbeats resonates, amplified by my senses in the dark silence. There's not even a peep from the men that have gathered behind me.

Scarlet's hazel eyes meet mine. We don't need words. I can feel every shred of terror rolling through her, pulsing nearly as fast as her heart. Hold on. Just a little longer.

One lunges. I parry, shadows wrapping around his wrist, yanking him off balance. The second aims for my ribs with a dagger, but I sidestep, forcing the blade to meet only air.

The next two work in tandem, trying to flank me, their movements coordinated but predictable. A blind lunge here, a feint there. I've trained these men. I know their every move.

Dipping low, I let the darkness beneath me seep upward, covering me in a protective shroud. The first of the duo doesn't even see me coming as I drive the blade through his thigh. He screams, a sound cut short as my other hand lashes out and grabs his throat, crushing his windpipe.

The other charges at me with wild fury. A huge mistake. I deflect his strike easily and send him sprawling across the deck with a forceful push of shadows. As he attempts to rise, I thrust my blade towards him, letting it rest just below his chin.

For a brief moment, the deck falls silent, save for the panting traitors.

The next one advances. I sidestep his first slash and, with a fluid motion, sever the tendon in the back of his leg. He howls in pain, stumbling back. Shadows wrap around him, pulling him down, squeezing, suffocating.

A quick flick of my wrist sends a tendril of shadows slicing through the air, narrowly missing the next attacker, but sending him reeling backward, eyes wide with terror.

The last man stands, looking from his fallen comrades to me, fear evident in his eyes. "Captain," he starts, voice quivering. "I—"

Before he can utter another word, my sword plunges deep into his gut. I pull it out swiftly, the glistening blade dark with his blood. He collapses, choking and gasping for breath.

The deck is silent again, except for the ragged breaths of the defeated men. The gathered crew behind me stares in a mixture of awe and fear. None dare to step forward or shut their gaping mouths.

"Any last words?" The few traitors still alive stare at me, chests heaving as they try to fight off the pain. None of them answer. They tremble in place as my shadows lift from the ground and slither around them. With a twist of my wrist, their necks snap and their lifeless bodies fall to the deck.

I stride over to Scarlet, quickly picking her up and clutching her against my chest. "It's alright, I've got you." She's trembling as her head snuggles into the crook of my neck.

"Are you okay?" I whisper into her ear. She nods, her white hair falling into her face.

Behind us, the crew starts to murmur amongst themselves. I glance at them over my shoulder as I open my cabin door.

They don't need me to speak the command. The look alone has the men scurrying and snapping out of their stupor. They rush to toss the bodies overboard as I take Scarlet inside and shut the door.

Alone, I set her on the edge of my bed and grab my dagger off the table to cut the ropes around her ankles free. Her hands are still tied behind her back, and her mouth is taped shut. I run my thumb over her lips, feeling the outline of them beneath the smooth surface.

"I like you like this... All knotted up and at my mercy," I murmur, leaning down to brush a kiss against the tape. Reaching around her, I cut the rope binding her hands and she immediately starts to rub at her wrists. An angry red line lingers from where the rough rope scratched against her soft skin. I help her remove the tape from her mouth and she winces as it pulls free from her skin.

"Thank you," she whispers, her voice shaky. A surge of relief washes through me. Had I made it a moment later, she'd have disappeared over that rail... I don't even want to think about what that would look and feel like.

Zephyr barrels into my cabin. His face is frantic as he searches the room, calming a smidge when he sees both of us alive and well. "What the fuck happened?" he demands, his eyes darting between Scarlet and me.

"Your brilliant plan to keep her safe in the med bay failed," I snap, clenching my fists. "Some of the crew tried to throw her overboard."

"Shit," Zephyr mutters, rubbing a hand over his face. "I'm so sorry. I'll make sure it doesn't happen again." He glances at Scarlet briefly, who is still trembling slightly, then turns his brown eyes back on me. "Nelvin's got what you need for the binding. He'll be here soon. I'll take care of the deck."

"Good," I say curtly, turning my attention back to Scarlet.

The nerves are still clawing at her, plain as day, even though she's trying to piece her indifferent mask together. I don't know how to make it better. The only thing I can think of is to hold her, so I gather her in my arms and lie on the bed, letting her tuck her body against mine.

Minutes pass before there's a knock on the door. Nelvin. He enters the room, holding a tattoo gun and a well of ink, and sets them on the table. Piece of paper in hand, he crosses the room to hand deliver it to me. Opening the parchment, I find the inscription I'm supposed to write.

"You'll have to add both of your blood to the ink. Just a few drops should do," he says before turning on a heel and leaving the room.

"Are you going to tell me what's going on?" Scarlet sits up, pulling the fresh blanket around her.

"I'd like you to finish the blood oath... I'm not used to experiencing the things you do, and the emotions have become overwhelming. I actually just handed over my captain's hat to Smee because of it. She'll be taking over in the morning."

She glances away for a moment, staring off into space like she's deep in thought. "I don't understand how that would help..."

"If we finish the bond, the emotional swings won't be as consuming. We'll still share our link, but our emotions won't be as entangled. I need to be able to focus and most of the time I can, but when your feelings are extreme, it clouds everything in me."

"Is that why you came to my room the other night when I was reading?"

I nod. "It's not just knowing how you feel, I physically feel what you do. I couldn't fight it anymore, and even though I wanted to, I shouldn't have. Listen, Scars... I shouldn't have said what I did. I was angry, and felt like I was out of control. I took it out on you."

She studies me for a long moment, then gently shakes her head. "Okay," she says, her voice steady, but her eyes betray the fear she tries to hide. "I should've taken the blood oath, anyway. I regret not, but we don't have a priestess onboard..."

I hold my hand out, waiting for hers. "No, we don't. We have Nelvin, and he's capable of doing written magic because of his lineage. It's not exact, but it mimics it enough." When she gives her hand to me, I prick our fingers, dripping blood into the ink.

"So, it's a tattoo..."

I nod. "Non-royal weddings have blood bonds, but they're temporary. A spell is done on the couple's blood and as long as it's on their body, they feel just like I do with you. To make it permanent, it has to stay on your skin, or in this case, in it."

"I see..." She eyes the ink curiously. "So, he spelled that?"

"Yes... Let's get you changed," I tell her, helping her out of her dirty clothes and into one of my shirts. The fabric falls around her thighs, similar to her nightgowns. She looks so small in it, but there's a fierce determination in her gaze that tells me she's anything but fragile.

"Will it hurt?" Her voice is quiet as she lays back on my bed.

"Of course, it will." My lips tug into a smirk. "It's a needle going into your skin."

Her expression turns to curiosity as she reaches out to trace the tattoos along my arm, her touch gentle, but the way it shoots tingles through the pit of my stomach... Fuck, it feels good.

"Obviously you've been victim to it a few times," she says, barely running her nails over the lines on the inside of my forearm.

My mouth goes dry, and my head falls forward. It's like a trance I can't pull myself out of. Every muscle in my body relaxes and my eyes flutter closed as she moves. I bite my lower lip, and for the first time, I realize that this isn't her feeling. It's me. It's my feeling and it's not pain or anger, but it's just as strong. It's not really lust either, but just good.

Maybe that's why it's so hard to block out her lust. It seems to be the strongest emotion I feel through the bond, but perhaps it's because it couples with my own, and if she can make me feel this, just like she is right now, then her lust would only amplify it. I still experience her sadness and terror vividly, but this... whatever this feeling is, and her lust, they're far more significant.

"I've been no one's victim, love." I raise an eyebrow. "Well, maybe Pan's, but all of this," I hold my arms up, "I signed up for it, and I like them. They hide my scars."

Scarlet tilts her head, and something swirls within those hazel eyes of hers at the mention of me hiding my scars. She looks closer, feeling across my chest. Her fingers meet the raised skin of the long scar that goes from the tip of my right shoulder to the bottom of my ribs on my left. "Like this one."

"Yes, exactly like that one. Though, I'll have to get where the coral got me redone. That was Nelvin's newest edition, too. I don't think he'll be too happy about that.

"Is he the one who does yours?"

"Aye." Her pupils are blown as she continues to trace line after line.

My gaze shifts from the tattoo gun to meet a pair of eyes that pull me in, like a moth drawn to a flame. Her pupils are blown, the bright hazel rings appearing darker than usual. They slide over my features, slow and deliberate, as if she's mapping every contour, every ridge, every shadow.

Every blink feels like an invitation, and between the way her hands feel against my skin and that look, I have to swallow back the need to kiss her, to push her back on that bed... It's not the time or place. I need to finish the bond, to regain some semblance of control, then I can do as I please. It's needed to activate the link, anyway. I just have to get through this.

That's easier said than done... Her long lashes cast playful shadows on her high cheekbones. The soft light of the lanterns paints her beautiful, fair skin in a warm glow. Her lips twitch into a sweet smile that just about undoes me.

I was worried I'd never see her smile again, at least not at me. Those first days, before I found out about her mark, I lived for those smiles and to hear her laugh. The noise alone was all I needed to forget that I'm not whole. For just a stitch in time, I wasn't missing something because she filled that void... Nothing has quite felt that way since.

My heart kicks up, watching her, drinking in every second, like it might be the last glimpse I get at the way things used to be. I find myself instinctively swallowing as her hands trail higher, over my collarbones and up the length of my neck. There aren't any tattoos there, but she does it anyway. Her fingers dust over my pulse and I suck in a shaky breath, feeling the weight of her gaze, the electric charge in the space between us.

She's so close... so close. I can feel the warmth of her body teasing my skin. My eyes are glued to her lips. I don't even know when I started looking at them, but seeing them move is the only reason I catch myself.

"What kind of man likes to be hurt?" She continues to explore, all shreds of fear gone, replaced by something that has butterflies swarming my insides. I'm never going to get used to this—her. I'm not even sure finishing the bond will put a damper on the pull she has on me. If it means being able to take my hat, though, I have to. Even then, it would be nice to not be completely at the woman's mercy, to at least be able to walk away if I want to. Just right now, I don't want to.

Fuck... I need to focus. I have a job to do, a tattoo to make, and if I can't control myself long enough to place it on her skin, Nelvin will have to. And him doing something this intimate with her? Over my dead body.

Taking her hands off my chest, I place them gently in her lap, clearing my throat. "The kind you have no business looking at like that."

"Looking at you like what?" she retorts, feigning innocence.

I chuckle, shaking my head. "Oh please. Your eyes nearly sparkled. I'm starting to think you're turned on by villainous behavior."

"Fine," she says, turning her gaze away. "Where will it hurt the least?"

"Thigh or shoulder." With the gun put together, I test it in the air, ready whenever she is to get started.

"Whichever is more discreet." She pulls the hem of the shirt down as if it's not long enough. And somehow, that little motion tells me exactly where I'll be putting this tattoo.

"Thigh it is, princess." I motion for her to lie back on the bed. Positioning myself in a chair next to the bed, I bring the tattoo gun to her thigh. I don't even touch her with the needle, just the side, and as the cool metal connects with her skin, she jolts.

"Scared, are we?" I tease, enjoying this rare crack in her armor.

"Your hands are just cold." If only she knew how adorable it is to me... She knows I can feel her nervousness leaching the bond, yet she pretends to be tough for my sake. I can respect that.

"Relax, little lamb" My voice is low and soothing. Cocking my head, I can't help but notice the tremor in Scarlet's hands as she braces herself. "Here." I offer her my flask of whiskey.

"I'd rather not," she protests, but my gaze hardens.

"Drink up, princess. It's not optional." She hesitates, but eventually, she takes the flask and swallows a gulp. Her face twists, clearly not a fan, and I bit back a chuckle. "Another. It might stop you from shaking."

"I'm not shaking," she breathes, but I know better. Gently tipping her chin up, I force her to meet my eyes. "Aye, you are. It's okay to be scared, but I promise it won't hurt as bad as you think it will. I'll be gentle."

Narrowing her eyes like she doesn't believe me, she lifts the flask once more, taking a longer sip, then settles back onto the bed.

"You never know," I say, sliding the hem of the shirt she's wearing up over her hips. "You might even like it."

"I seriously doubt that." She doesn't look at me, pinching her thighs closed. Since her clothes were soaked through from the storm, my shirt is the only thing on her body. And as much as I like it that way, clearly, she's not a fan.

Grabbing one of the smaller blankets on the bed, I drape it over her, pushing the fabric up until just one leg is exposed.

"Thank you," she whispers, but I can still feel the tension radiating from her body.

"Remember to breathe," I remind her as I lean forward, kissing the top of her thigh before touching the needle to it. The gun is powered by magic and vibrates softly in my hand as I draw the symbols Nelvin scribed. I'm hyper-aware of each flinch she tries to suppress, and my chest tightens at the thought of causing her pain.

Her eyes flick around the room, searching for a distraction from the discomfort. I can sense her curiosity mounting, the questions she wants to ask about the treasures and trinkets I've collected over the years. Honestly, I'm surprised she's waiting so long to do so.

"Breathe, love," I say, pausing to stroke my fingers up her thigh. Her legs tremble, but I don't sense fear from her, just the nervousness. It's likely the adrenaline. "Think about the fact you can float me once it's done. I'm pretty sure Smee would allow it."

A laugh escapes her as she looks down the length of her body at me. It's music to my ears. "She'd never allow that."

I raise my brow, tilting my head as I look over our progress. "I don't know... She's going to be pissed when she hears I killed those men. Especially since I just showed everyone on that deck that I'm their captain, almost immediately after handing the helm to her. She's not going to be happy with me, but I suppose she already wasn't. Part of my conditions in giving control of the ship to her was that you remain unharmed."

Scarlet lifts onto her elbows, meeting my eyes. "Why? You've been so torn about what to do with me up to now..."

"Because that's the second time you've saved my life. I don't think a blood witch would've done that. A blood witch would've let me die on that deck, yet you did literally everything in your power to ensure that didn't happen." Rolling my wrist, I get ready to start again.

"You believe me?" she breathes, her eyes rounding by the second.

"Aye, I do. It doesn't change the fact the crew doesn't, though. I'm hoping they'll listen to Smee. If I can prove it to her, the others might listen."

She nods, sitting back so I can continue. As I work on the tattoo, Scarlet's gaze wanders to the shelves.

"What's in those jars?" she asks, and that one question alone means Zephyr was right. She didn't know what was in them, and anyone crafty with magic would've felt the power they contain.

"Shadows," I say, and her gaze snaps to mine. "They belonged to traitors my father killed. He believed he could trade Pan for my soul, so he collected them, hoping the more he had to trade, the more likely the god would make a deal."

She stays deathly still, allowing me to work, but her gaze returns to the shelves. "You make it seem so transactional... Like a merchant selling goods. He couldn't truly believe that he could bargain a god for your soul."

"Hasn't anyone told you not to speak ill of the dead? My father didn't have much of a choice. Bargaining was the best option. Still might be. Not everyone on this crew can fight, and it would've taken dozens of men to even attempt to overpower Pan." As the final lines of ink take shape, I sit back, admiring my handiwork. "Done."

She cringes as she sits up, looking for herself. Swirls and twisted symbols form a line at the top of her thigh.

"How do you feel?" I put down the gun and clasp my hands in my lap in an attempt to keep them to myself and not on her.

"Like I've just been stabbed a thousand times," she replies, attempting to sound casual but failing to hide the relief in her voice. I snort out a laugh, grinning wickedly as Scarlet examines it. "It seems feminine enough. It's not like yours."

"What? You expected skulls and ships?"

She pokes at the skin around the mark, hissing as she does. "I'm not sure what I expected."

Honestly, I'm just relieved she's taking this with minimal resistance. I'm not sure how Smee and the others would've reacted if she'd turned it down. It's just one less thing to worry about and one less weight on my shoulders.

"I don't feel anything different." Her head tilts to one side as she gazes up at me.

"It's not activated yet..." I'm not sure how to explain this part. I was hoping I didn't have to, that things would just sort of happen naturally.

"How do you activate it? Say the rest of the spell or something?"

I shake my head, trapping my lower lip between my teeth. "No... You have to willingly accept it. Intimately."

Her eyes grow wide with understanding, and I fight the urge to smirk at the sudden flush of color creeping into her cheeks.

Before she has a chance to pepper me with more questions, I offer my hand and help her up from the bed. "We should talk about what happened," I say, sitting back in the chair. "Not many knew I was going to be in a meeting. The men who took you knew you'd be alone."

"What are you saying?" She cringes, tenderly running her hand over the symbols I placed.

"That someone from my meeting was in on it. They were the only people who knew I'd be there and that you were alone in the med bay. Well, all except Zephyr's assistant, but the boy looks up to him, and Zephyr's been your biggest supporter. I doubt it was him. Even then, I won't float a fifteen-year-old. He's just a kid. If he was involved, it's because someone else got him involved."

I hate to think that any of them are a part of this. Everyone at that table has been in my life for so long, I can't envision living it without them. But it's the only thing that makes sense.

Zephyr isn't an option. He's been trying to prove Scarlet's innocence from the start, and he's definitely not been silent about how he likes this new, married version of me.

Nelvin is... Nelvin. He's a pain in my ass at all hours of the day, but he's like a little brother. Though he hasn't exactly been hushed about his opinions to see Scarlet go overboard. At the same time, he's loyal. I've seen him tortured by blood witches on a heist gone wrong and he didn't so much as peep. They wanted to know where I was, and the man has the scars to prove just how unwilling he was to tell them.

Lorian, I'm not sure. He's never given me reason not to trust him and if he had intentions, I feel like Zephyr would know about them. But would he tell me? Zephyr and I are close, but if it came down to protecting him or me, I'm not sure what he would choose. Their bond changes everything.

Now that I know what it feels like to be bonded or mated to someone, I'm not sure I'd choose him over Scarlet, and we've been married for just a flicker of time compared to their years together.

Then there's the fact Scarlet stabbed him. He was possessed, but Lorian might hold some sort of malice over it. It took one of his lives. They're sacred to him.

Only his familial line of druids and mages have nine lives, and each one gives them their strength. Each time they come back from the dead, their gift or innate ability changes. Before, he was able to use magic to enhance his fighting skills. Now, he has to figure it out all over again. It could be something entirely different.

It's the equivalent of being a king whose castle just burnt to the ground. You're still you, but you have to start at the ground and rebuild everything you worked so hard to create before.

I'm not sure I can think about Smee doing this. She's the only true family I have, and we've always had each other's back. Not to mention I just handed her the ship... Out of the four of them, she's been the most adamant about floating Scarlet and I can't overlook that.

"I need to know what happened," I say, my tone becoming serious. "I can't trust anyone right now. So, you'll be staying in here with me until I know who else was involved with taking you."

"In your bed?" Her eyes widen, and she looks as if she's about to argue.

"Unless you plan to rough it on the floor, yes. In my bed with me." I arch an eyebrow, daring her to protest.

She smooths her hands over the blankets, and for the first time, she's hiding even her emotions from me, keeping her face blank. "What do you want to know?"

"For starters, who was there when you were taken? Did you see anyone? Was it just the men on the deck?" I shrug, trying to force myself to ask in chunks. I have dozens of questions but asking them all right now would just overwhelm her.

"Just the men from the deck. We didn't pass anyone on the way up to the deck except the mess hall."

Cocking my head, I try to think of who I saw there. I wasn't far behind them. "Did they say anything that would hint at who else was in on it?"

She shakes her head. "No. Nothing."

I drag a hand down my face, pinching my fingertips to try to ease some of the tension. "Alright. Thank you for telling me."

"I wish I had more to offer, but..."

Standing from my seat, I wring my fingers. They still tingle, the nerves frayed from the vibrations of the tattoo gun. "You should get some rest. You're safe in here. I'll get this stuff to Nelvin and be back soon."

I step back, looking her over one more time. Her white hair is mussed, draping over her shoulders. It's so long it nearly comes to her hips. The marks around her wrists and ankles have mostly faded, but I reach for the salve anyway, lifting her wrist to apply it before she can protest.

"I feel like I'm going to have to stock up on this stuff. It's like you're a magnet for bad omens." Releasing her wrist, I move to her ankles, letting the magic do its work. It's another one of Jordi's experiments, and though it can only heal minor wounds, it's come in handy.

"Stay here, okay?" I step toward the door.

"I have a choice? I thought I was your prisoner."

A smile tips my lips as I turn to face her one last time. "You always have a choice with me."

Her cheeks flush, breaking through his mask, and I step outside.

31

SCARLET

The door creaks open on its hinges and Sebastian steps inside his dimly lit quarters. I couldn't tear my eyes away if I wanted to... Every part of me is drawn to him, from his chiseled jawline to the roguish curve of his lips.

His mussed hair falls effortlessly over his forehead, just above his eyebrows. The dark color of it only makes his bright green eyes stand out more. Then there are the slow, steady paces of his footsteps, like a drum echoing through me, swallowing up the distance between us. His gaze is almost obsidian, the colored rings mostly drowned out by blown pupils.

I feel my heart skip a beat. All he has to do is enter a room, and his presence commands the attention of everything and everyone within it. An undeniable attraction buzzes between us, electric yet unspoken. Trying to respect the fact that I subject him to everything I feel, I clear my throat and force my eyes away. Especially since—as he put it—lust is the worst, and that's exactly what I feel pooling inside me.

Get yourself together, Scarlet. He saved you. Big deal. Sure, the entire time he tattooed me, I was explicitly aware of every brush of his fingers, and just how close he was to me. It doesn't mean I need to jump his bones now.

"I thought you might want these." His voice is like velvet, warm and inviting, and it sends shivers down my spine. I try to steady myself before looking at him out of the corner of my eye. He has books in his hands, their spines worn and well-loved.

I reach out to touch them, curiosity piqued. "You picked these out for me?"

"I did," he replies, a playful smile tugging at the corners of his mouth.

"If you're trying to swoon me, you're on the right track." I raise an eyebrow at him, my voice teasing.

He smirks. "Ask, and you shall receive, princess."

My fingers brush across the spines, reading the titles. The textured surfaces are rough, grounding me, a reminder that this is real. I haven't fallen asleep. This isn't a dream. Sebastian is standing in front of me and for the first time since I've met him, there are no more secrets.

Everything is out in the air and accepted. I'm not sure how to breathe in these conditions, even if it is a nice change of pace. My hands wrap around the stack, ready to take them from his grasp, but he lifts them out of my reach.

A teasing glint sparkles in his eyes. Mischief if I've ever witnessed it. "These are yours, but only if you do something for me."

I cross my arms over my chest. "And what would that be?"

"Promise me that you won't leave this room alone," he bargains, his gaze never leaving mine. "You're not a prisoner anymore, but the crew— "

"Deal," I cut him off, reaching for the books. The corners of his mouth twitch into a smirk as he lowers them into my hand.

"Aren't you a good little lamb," he murmurs, his tone warm and approving.

My cheeks flush at the unexpected praise, and I cradle the books against my chest.

The worn spines flex and Sebastian watches me, flipping through the pages of the one on top of the stack, like he's tracking every move I make.

He chuckles, shaking his head. "Mental note, bribe her with books and she listens..." His comment seems more for his own amusement than anything else, but I can't help the small smile that tugs at my lips.

"You're learning," I say, and his gaze sweeps over me, causing my cheeks to flame and my pulse to quicken. Yet, I don't look away. "And you say I'm the one with stars in my eyes."

"Excuse me?" he asks, cocking his head. "Would you prefer I make you see them instead?" he asks, the glint in his eyes challenging me to take him up on his offer.

My breath hitches, and I'm momentarily lost in the thoughts they provoke. He drags over one of the folding wooden chairs, sitting backward in it, facing me on the bed. There's a knock on the door, and the tension dissipates.

"Come in," Sebastian calls, not taking his eyes off of me.

Zephyr enters the room, quickly assessing the situation and ducking his head. "Just wanted to let you know dinner is ready whenever you'd like to join us below deck."

"Thank you, Zephyr," he says, his voice slightly breathless. "We'll be there shortly."

He nods, casting one last amused glance at Sebastian before slipping out of the room.

"Looks like we'll have to put the star-seeing on hold." He winks at me—winks at me—then stands from the chair. Who is this man and what has he done with my husband? You know, the one that's silently threatened to toss me overboard every chance he's had? Did that guy just die on the deck? Did the coral kill him? If that's the case, may he rest in peace. I swallow hard, taking a deep breath in a futile effort to regain my composure.

He bows theatrically, offering me a hand. "Shall we?"

As ironic as it is, he did the exact same thing when he asked me to dance in the great hall, before everything fell into chaos. It's like his way of saying we're starting over. We've come a long way since then. My outlook on life has changed, including the way I view my father and the kingdom. I doubt my corset will even fit right anymore.

Hesitantly, I place my hand in his and he stands to his full height, looking down at me. Sometimes I forget how tall he is. Usually, we're sitting down or at a distance when we talk. It's almost like a comfort thing he does just for me, as if coming down to my level is a way of implying that I'm of equal status, that he's not some high lord barking orders from above. It's weird to think of it that way, but he'd be much more intimidating if I had to crane my neck to talk to him all the time.

As we make our way to the mess hall, Sebastian intertwines our fingers, leading me across the deck. The man doesn't miss a step, his spine unyielding, like he couldn't care less about how the men are gawking at his not-so-subtle statement. It's nerve-wracking yet leaves me weightless all at once.

"Wow, public displays of affection, huh?" I waggle my eyebrows as he opens the companionway door.

His lips tug up at the corner, his eyes looking everywhere but at me. "Don't get used to it."

I chuckle, slipping beneath his arm to journey down the steps. "I wouldn't dream of it."

The mess hall is bustling with activity, the noise of conversation and clinking dishes filling the space. Sebastian guides me to a small table at the corner, ignoring the looks Zephyr, Smee, Nelvin, and Lorian give him when he chooses to set us at a table alone.

He pulls out my chair and takes a seat across from me, his gaze unwavering as he studies my face.

"What are you thinking about?" I ask, breaking the silence.

He leans forward, resting his elbows on the table. "You," he says simply. "Food. It's a pretty solemn space up there, and the two of those things sort of go hand in hand."

My cheeks flush at his words, and I bite down on my lip to suppress a grin. "Well then..."

"I can't stop thinking about what happened." His voice drops to a low whisper, and my skin prickles.

"With the men?" I chide, glancing around to make sure no one is listening in.

"Aye. I still don't know exactly who I can trust, but like I said before, please don't leave the room alone. Zephyr is safe. I know that much." He reaches across the table, taking my hand in his so he can stroke circles across my skin with his thumb.

"So that's why you're being like this..." I chew the inside of my lip.

"Like what?"

"Affectionate. You're hoping one of them will crack, that it'll clue you in on which of your friends aren't on your side."

He sat in the chair that allowed him to see the room, so he could watch them and analyze. It's not because he wants to hold my hand or touch me. He's doing it to get a rise out of someone. I take my hand back, setting it in my lap.

Sebastian's gaze darts to mine before dropping to the table. The tick in his jaw making an appearance. "I love how smart you are... but I hate that you're wounded by assumptions. Luckily, once the bond's complete, that'll subside, but until then, why don't you ask your burning questions instead of assuming answers to them?"

"Fine. Are you touching me because you want to, or because you're trying to find your mole?" I search his face, waiting for him to answer.

"Both. If it weren't for the fact you're hungry, and that it's not safe for you here until I figure out who else is involved, I'd love nothing more than to be touching you right now, but I can assure you it wouldn't be your hand. However, both of those things exist and I'm not sure I'll be able to sleep until I figure it out."

I nod, pursing my lips as I process. "If that's the case, then holding my hand isn't going to be as effective."

"As effective as what?" A crease forms between his brow as he opens his hand, silently asking for me to give it back to him.

I stand from my seat, gracefully stepping around the table. His eyes track me, drinking me in. Stepping close to him, standing between his wide-stretched legs, I tip his chin, forcing his attention.

"It's not as effective as you looking at me like you do behind closed doors. Let them see the way you kiss me. Show them that I'm yours, not a witch they should float. I guarantee someone will show it. You'll find your traitor."

His eyes gleam as he stares at me, like I'm the only thing in this room. Warm arms circle my back, pulling me closer, then his large hands slide down the length of my spine, palming my backside in his hands.

His gaze drops to my lips, and the lump in his throat bobs as he swallows hard. "Be careful what you wish for, darling. I might want you all to myself, but I'm not above letting them watch. So, if you kiss me, you better stay in control of your emotions, because if you don't, I can't promise what will happen next."

Fingertips glide ever so softly up my side before his knuckles continue the way up my neck and over my cheek. The touch is feather-light and electrifying. I feel the tingling sensation spread like wildfire through my veins, setting my skin ablaze.

He chuckles darkly. "You're already losing control, aren't you? I can feel it slipping bit by bit." Sebastian studies me for a moment, then a plate hits our table and I nearly launch out of my skin.

Clutching my hand to my heart, I find Zephyr and Lorian standing next to our table.

"Since you weren't coming over there, and it looked like things were about to go down on this table, I thought you'd like the company," the orc says, sliding two plates toward us. "And food."

When I turn back to Sebastian, his cheeks have taken on an almost pink hue, and his lips are pressed together as if to keep from grinning like a madman. "Thank you, Zephyr. I appreciate that."

Movement draws my eye and I catch Smee and Nelvin storming out of the mess hall. I guess that answers that question. It's got to be one of them, but who's going to tell Sebastian that? He's close to his sister. The last thing he'll believe is that she might be involved with what happened on the deck. He'll need to figure that out for himself, assuming it's true.

Sebastian uses his boot to kick out the seat beside him, silently telling me to sit. The moment my butt hits the chair, he grips it and slides it closer to him, handing me a fork. It's quiet as the two of us eat, and I can feel the floorboards rattling as Zephyr bounces his leg.

He jerks in his seat, adjusting his posture before twirling a hand. "Alright, I'm just going to ask. Did you finish it?"

"Not entirely, no," Sebastian says while shoveling forkfuls into his mouth. He eats like he's starving, which is kind of barbaric, but it's him and I can be okay with that.

"What do you mean?" Lorian sits forward, resting his elbows on the table. "Like you tried to finish it and it didn't work?"

"No, like I tattooed her, and that's as far as we've gotten. Gods..." Sebastian sets down his fork while I continue to eat, pretending to be too busy to listen in, yet hearing every word.

"That explains a bit. Written magic is powerful and exactly like a true mate bond. If you don't seal the deal, it can cause a mating frenzy. Ever heard those?" he asks to no one in particular and rolls his eyes with a snarl. "They're... something. And if you don't seal it within a day or so of the bond forming, you'll be finding new uses for all of these tables." His gaze falls. "Trust me."

Something tells me that's not a scientific fact. It's proven advice. I snort and Zephyr narrows his eyes at me.

"It's not funny, princess. I'm not kidding. You won't walk for days. So, just get it done, ya?" Zephyr snatches a foam box from someone's hand and places the rest of my food inside it.

"Hey! I needed that." The man starts to protest.

Zephyr flips a hand at him, holding up a single finger. "Oh, go lick a barnacle."

The man's nostrils flare, but he leaves without another word. Zephyr shoves the box at me and pops his eyebrows. "Now, get. The both of you and you better not come out of his room until someone has been properly plundered."

He jerks his head toward Sebastian. "And in case I wasn't clear, I was referring to her."

Sebastian blinks long and hard. "I got that much. Why are you rushing me?"

"Two words. Mating. Frenzy," Zephyr says, counting off fingers.

Lorian shakes his head, gripping his jaw to hide his mouth. "Written magic is fierce. If the spell has to force you to complete it, it won't just be the two of you that get dragged into the frenzy."

I furrow my brow, sitting up straighter. "You mean people will try to do things with me?"

Lorian shakes his head. "No, but we'll have men all over the ship humping tables. The pull starts immediately from the time the mark is placed and intensifies over time. Until you finish the bond, the two of you are essentially living, breathing orgy starters."

I've never given orgies much thought, but I always assumed someone had to start it. I never considered that it might be something magical. I thought someone just pulled themselves out and whirled it around, and people took note. You learn something new...

"In simple terms, you're making the men uncomfortable. Not because of the witchy business, but because their dicks hurt. Look around. If you don't finish it in the next few hours, all of those strangled faces you see won't be able to stop themselves from doing unspeakable things."

"I see," I breathe, glancing around the mess hall. Maybe that's why Smee and Nelvin left... It would make sense.

"Fine." Sebastian stands and holds a hand out toward me. "We'll go."

Great... This isn't awkward at all.

32

SCARLET

As we step inside the room, I set my food down, the appetite suddenly gone. I should've known something was off. Since he placed that mark, being with him is all I can think about.

Desperate to ease the tension in the air, I look at the books he brought me. I turn them over one by one, my back toward him. Warm arms wrap around my middle and soft lips press against my pulse.

"Thank you for these," I say, unsure if I said it before. It just feels right to do so now.

His hands start to roam, not wasting a moment, one climbing to cup my breast through the shirt and the other dipping between my thighs, teasing me over my pants. The scent of wine and mint, and something uniquely him storms my senses. It's intoxicating and dangerous, and yet I can't help but crave more.

"I picked those out myself," he says, nodding gently at the stack of books before kissing my throat again. "I thought they'd interest you. One has maps and facts about our realm. The black one is a favorite of mine. It's about a boy who finds a dragon egg. I've read it countless times."

I can't imagine him reading... He doesn't strike me as someone who'd curl up in the covers and binge a story, but there's still so much to learn about him... Who knows what else will surprise me.

"The idea of you reading it is sort of fun," he says, teasing my nipple through the fabric, determined to make it harden. "I'm curious if the story will make you feel the same way it does me."

I arch into his touch, trying to soak in everything he's saying. How is he keeping his mind straight right now?

"The last one is from Smee's personal collection. However, if you read it, at least give me some warning. Communicating is the only way we're going to survive this bond sane, so if you plan to read it, at least make sure I'm not in the middle of something important," he says, continuing his teasing.

A grin spreads across my face. "I can do that. I didn't even know books like that existed. We don't have anything like those in the Solarian library."

Sebastian chuckles, the sound warm and genuine. "That's because they're likely deemed salacious."

I twist in his arms to face him. The lantern light flickers across his face, casting shadows that only enhance his striking features.

"I wasn't sure what kind of books you'd like," he says, holding me close. "As I went hunting for them, I realized I never asked."

My heart swells inside my chest. He took the time to think about what I like, to understand me. Just like he did the night he showed me the dragons...

"Yet you managed to choose these perfectly." I loop my arms around his neck and start to play with his hair.

Sebastian's lips tug into a knowing smirk, his tall figure towering over me. "I'm glad you like them." He gathers my hair in his hand, wrapping the length around his fist. Gently, he tugs my head back and bends, putting his lips an inch from mine. "Tell me to stop and I will."

I don't speak. I can't. Slowly, I shake my head no.

Our lips meet, and the world seems to fade into obscurity, leaving us suspended in time. My heart hammers in my chest and magic thrums beneath my skin. His warm hand trails up the back of my neck, leaving fire in its wake as he holds me entirely at his mercy. Every nerve ending is awake and alive, attuned to his slightest movement, but I'm helpless. I want this. I want him. I want it all.

Kissing him steals away my ability to think or reason. It's toe-curling, and the kind that awakens every dormant sensation within me. His mouth moves with a confident finesse, a dance of lips that speaks a thousand words.

My body bows against his, fighting to stay upright. My knees are weak, my lungs breathless, and there's not a single part of me that doesn't feel the humming in my veins. I'm not sure if it's my mage magic, drawn by the connection we share, or the bond taking root, but I feel it everywhere.

His warmth seeps into my very being, erasing the boundaries between us. The very taste of him is intoxicating in itself, leaving me dizzy and wanting more. Our bodies press closer, his fingers still tangled in my hair. It sends shivers down my spine.

I respond in kind, my hands finding their way to his broad shoulders, my nails grazing his skin as the kiss deepens, fueled by a hunger that's been ignited.

My hands roam across the planes of his back, relishing the feel of his muscles tensing beneath his skin. Every point of contact ignites a yearning that only he can satisfy.

"Oh, little lamb," Sebastian breathes, pulling away just enough for our eyes to lock. His thumb strokes across my bottom lip. "What am I going to do with you?"

I laugh breathlessly, unsure how to answer such a question. "I don't know." My cheeks flush with warmth and he nuzzles my jaw.

"I'm not sure when it happened, but somehow you resurrected a part of me I wasn't sure existed anymore." The words hang heavy in the air, his admission stirring something deep within me.

Without hesitation, I lean forward to capture his lips with mine, kissing him hard enough to knock him off balance. He falls back and his hands catch us before he hits the ground. I squeal, landing half-straddling him.

Sebastian links his hands behind his head. "I'm fairly certain you've just been looking for an excuse to be on top of me," he teases, his voice low and seductive.

"And if I was?" I challenge, my fingers trailing down his bare chest as I savor the feel of him beneath me.

"Then have at it, princess. Your wish is my command."

"Too bad I don't have your shadows. I'd quite like to see you all knotted up and at my mercy," I taunt, echoing words he once said to me. His wicked smile tells me he remembers them, too.

"Is that right?" His eyes darken with desire as he lifts his hips, grinding himself into my center. I moan, unable to resist the pleasure that courses through me. Sebastian bites his lower lip, his abs flexing as he does it again, hands still trapped beneath his head.

"You don't need to tie me up," he says teasingly. "Unlike you, I listen when I'm told to do something."

"Is that so?" I challenge, my fingertips tracing the curve of his jaw, down his neck, and across his broad shoulders. I lean closer, putting my face directly above his. "Prove it."

A wicked grin spreads across Sebastian's face as he says, "Anything for you." His voice is low, sultry, and so full of promise.

I let my hands wander across his chest, trailing my fingers lower, and following the lines of his abs. He sucks in a sharp breath, but otherwise remains motionless beneath me. It's thrilling to see such a strong man lay himself bare, allowing me to take control without question.

Unable to resist any longer, I lean down and capture his lips with mine, tasting the hunger and need coursing through him. I slowly make my way down his jawline, nipping and sucking at the sensitive skin. Each little gasp and moan he lets slip only spurs me on, igniting a fire within me that threatens to consume us both.

"Scarlet," he groans, his voice rough with desire, "you have no idea how much I want you right now."

"Maybe I do," I tease, shifting my hips back so I can undo his pants.

I strip the constricting fabric away, layer by layer until his cock springs free and my mouth waters. Every throbbing inch of him is on full display and all mine. With agonizing slowness, I drag my tongue from base to tip before taking all of him into my mouth.

"Fuck," he hisses, his hips bucking involuntarily. "Don't stop."

I smile around him, lowering until he fits into the back of my throat. With each languid stroke and swirl of my tongue, I can feel his control slipping away, replaced by raw, primal need.

"Scarlet," he rasps, "I need you. Now."

My heart races as I shift closer, straddling him again. His eyes are blazing with hunger and there's an electric charge in the air that sets my body alive. His strong hands grip my thighs, applying enough pressure to leave a ghostly imprint of his hands when he releases me.

I moan, feeling the heat rise in my chest as he teases my breasts, his fingers drawing circles around my nipples before pinching them gently through the fabric of my shirt.

He starts to undo the buttons and helps me slip the fabric free. His hands are like lightning as they skim across my body, setting my skin on fire everywhere they touch. When his lips finally close around one of my breasts, the gentle pull sends pleasure rippling through me, and I bite my lip to trap the moan climbing up my throat before it can escape into the air.

My eyes roll back inside my head, giving in to him. He can do whatever he wants to me. I don't care. As long as his hands are on my skin, as long as he kisses me until my head spins, he can do as he sees fit.

"Gods... You're so fucking perfect. Every inch of you," he groans against me, undoing the clasp of my pants.

With a sudden movement, Sebastian flips our positions, pressing me down onto the floor beneath him. He takes control, yanking my pants off. He sits back, licking his lips. Placing gentle kisses down the inside of my thigh, he teases me. I raise my hips, but his hands hold me in place as he cherishes every spot but where I want him. It's torture. Blissful torture.

I'm about ready to beg when he slides his fingers over my slit. This time I let loose, moaning out undistinguishable curses.

Sebastian grins, shoving my thighs apart. "Fucking hell, woman," he growls, stopping to hold me still as I raise my hips against him. "Keep making noises like that and I'll give you whatever you want."

His fingers curl inside me, hitting just right. I bite my lip on another moan. My body is begging for attention as butterflies explode in my stomach. Sebastian holds me in place. A second later his tongue darts out, swirling and flicking against my body until every muscle coils so tight I fear it'll snap. My fingers tangle in his hair as I gasp, so close to coming that it's hard to breathe.

He bites down on my clit, just enough to make my body jolt, then sits up, positioning himself between my legs. Sebastian leans closer to claim my lips in a quick kiss. I can taste myself on his and feel the length of him twitch against my stomach. It makes me vividly aware of just how deep he'll go.

Sitting back, his hands explore my body, kneading and teasing as they wish. His touch is like fire, burning me up from within and making me desperate for more. He lines himself up and, with a growl, he buries himself deep inside me in one swift motion. My mouth falls open, my eyes flaring wide. Wave after wave of pleasure courses through my veins.

He's driving into me with a force that leaves me breathless. His lips find mine, capturing them in a searing kiss before trailing down my throat, leaving a path of fiery heat in their wake. My toes curl and my body spasms, teetering just at the brink of ecstasy.

"Fuck, that's it," he whispers, his breath warm against the shell of my ear. "Come for me, darling."

He buries himself as deep as he can go and rolls his hips, hitting every spot in unison. His thumb draws circles against my clit as I run my hands up my chest. His shadows surge from thin air, gripping my wrists and anchoring them to the floorboards. A tendril swirls around my throat, just enough to know it's there, to feel it.

"You have ten seconds, then you'll get to add my teeth marks to your collection of scars. Right there on your pretty little throat." His threat is possessive, dominant, and so vulgar, but it ignites something within me all the same. Every nerve in my body feels alive as Sebastian's pace quickens, his eyes never leaving mine.

Sebastian's grip on my hips tightens. "Ten."

"Nine," he continues, his shadows constricting as he pins me in place.

"Eight... Seven... Six." Sebastian doesn't stop, driving into me harder; I can't help but moan from the overwhelming pleasure. It's too much.

"Five... Four. "Sebastian leans down to whisper in my ear, "Tick Tock, little lamb."

The thought of wearing his marks both terrifies and thrills me, and I can barely catch my breath.

"Three... Two..." His thrusts become relentless, every movement eliciting another gasp from me, each one louder than the last.

"One," he growls, and with a final, powerful stroke, I shatter into a million pieces. My entire body convulses, my legs shaking uncontrollably as we come together. Gasping, I cling to Sebastian, our bodies slick with sweat, our chests heaving against each other.

"Fuck, darling..." Breathless, he presses a tender kiss to my forehead.

Neither of us even tries to get off the floor. We just lie here, tangled in each other's arms. Magic fills the air in a sudden burst of sweetness, and my veins hum to life. The bond... It's complete.

He peppers me with kisses, brushing my hair from my face. I snuggle into his side, my head in the crook of his arm. He's so warm... I could lay here for hours and feel right at home.

33
SCARLET

I wake slowly, blinking against the harsh light streaming through the porthole. An unfamiliar heaviness rests against my chest and ribs, which I quickly come to realize is Sebastian's arm.

His scent envelops me, sandalwood and sea salt. I turn my head to find him already awake, watching me with a lazy half-smile, eyes gleaming in the light.

"Morning, little lamb." The rumble of his voice sends a delicious shiver through me.

"You know, you're quite comfortable for a man made of granite." I trace a finger down the hard line of his jaw and his stubble pricks my skin.

Sebastian catches my hand, turning his head to press a kiss to my palm. "And you're a furnace. I may never let you out of this bed."

Heat floods my cheeks as my heart flutters. I swallow against the swell of emotion in my chest—affection, desire, joy, all tangled together.

Our bond. We're connected now, in a way I've never known.

Sebastian's gaze sharpens, a crease forming between his brows. He can sense my shift in mood as clearly as I can feel the steady beat of his heart against my side. "You think too loud. What's wrong?"

I shake my head, offering a wry smile. I know he can't hear my thoughts, but I suppose sensing my unease is just as powerful. "Just... processing."

Sebastian sighs, dragging a hand through his hair. "I know it's a lot to take in." His eyes meet mine, soft with understanding. "But we'll figure it out. The more we get to know each other, the easier it'll become."

A lump forms in my throat at the promise in his words. I cup his cheek, leaning in for a slow, deep kiss. By the time we part, my body seems to relax, and my lungs expand without feeling like they're in a vice grip.

Sebastian smirks, playing with my hair. "I should go help Smee. We need to get the ship underway before we drift into the reefs." He rolls onto his back with a groan, throwing an arm over his eyes. "But I don't want to get up."

I laugh, settling against his side. "Then don't."

"Tempting." He peeks at me from under his arm, eyes glinting with humor. "But we both know I will, and seeing as you always manage to get into trouble, I should try to get as much done while I can."

I gasp, feigning offense. "I do not cause trouble. It just seems to find me."

"Is that so?" Sebastian rolls on top of me with a fluid motion, pinning my wrists on either side of my head as he lands between my legs. "My memory says otherwise."

Heat pools low inside me at the possessive gleam in his eyes and I arch into him, biting my lip.

A knock sounds at the door and we both jump.

"What is it?" Sebastian growls, glaring over his shoulder.

"Sorry to interrupt." Nelvin's muffled voice comes through the wood. "Smee sent me to fetch the witchling for breakfast. She said she needed you and I was to watch over Scarlet while you're gone."

I roll my eyes at Nelvin's nickname. Sebastian releases my wrists. "We'll be right out."

Getting up, we both hurry to get dressed. I braid my hair, tying it off at the bottom, but Sebastian frowns, glaring at my hair like it's insulted him.

"How am I supposed to twirl it now?" he asks, buttoning his shirt.

I chuckle soundlessly. "You're not even going to be around."

"Fine," he says, kissing my neck. "As long as I get to take it down tonight."

A few minutes later, we emerge onto the deck, blending in with the crew members taking care of their morning tasks. A few curious glances are cast my way, though most seem indifferent to my presence today. It's better than the glares. I'll take it.

I know gaining their trust will be a challenge, but for now, having Sebastian's support is enough.

Nelvin waves us over from where he leans against the railing, blond hair windswept and a lazy grin on his lips. "There you are. I was about to send a search party."

"No need for dramatics." Sebastian runs his fingers through his hair, searching the deck. "Where's my sister?"

Nelvin nods his head toward the stern. "She's expecting you."

"Alright then." Sebastian starts to walk away, only to come back. "Nelvin, if a single hair on her head--"

The elf cuts him off. "Yeah, yeah. You'll float me. Got it."

Sebastian tucks his chin to his chest, then plants a kiss on my forehead before leaving us alone. I watch him leave for a long moment, unsure how I feel about spending time with someone else. Especially since he's not sure who he can trust yet.

Nelvin's silver gaze slides to me, his grin turning sly. "How was your evening?"

Heat creeps over my cheeks, but I feign a smile. "That's none of your business."

Nelvin clutches his chest as we head to the companionway. "Ouch. My heart, it's broken."

We descend into the belly of the ship and the aroma of freshly baked bread and cured meats greets us. The smell alone has my stomach rumbling.

Crewmen wander about, piling their plates high, and settling into groups at the various wooden tables. A few curious glances turn my way, but for the most part, it's business as usual. I guess Sebastian's show of power the other night was enough to settle their minds.

Nelvin steers me toward an empty table in the corner, well away from the thicker crowds. "Now, how about I get us some food so we can chat, hmm?"

"I can get my own food." I arch a brow at him. "I'm not helpless, you know."

He holds up his hands in surrender, silver eyes glinting with mirth. "My mistake. I'll leave you to it then, princess."

With that, Nelvin abandons me to join a rowdy group at the center table. Their laughter nearly drowns out the clatter of dishes. Shaking my head, I make my way to the buffet and fill my plate with slices of bread, cured meats, cheeses, and fresh fruit.

By the time I return to the table, Nelvin's already dug into his meal. He swallows a bite of sausage but doesn't jump to start up a conversation. Not until he's cleaned his plate.

Nelvin sets down his mug and levels me with a serious look. "Now, there's something you should know about this crew." His gaze sweeps the room, lingering on different groups. "We've been together a long time. We trust each other with our lives. We're protective of our own. These men aren't out for you specifically, they just don't want Hook to get hurt."

His words spark a flicker of unease. I know full well the challenges that lie ahead in earning the crew's acceptance. As much as Sebastian and I have grown closer, old prejudices die hard.

I keep my face carefully blank, choosing not to respond.

Nelvin sighs and shakes his head. "Look, I don't trust you, but Sebastian seems to genuinely care, so I'm willing to give you a chance."

"How generous," I say dryly, spearing a chunk of sausage and popping it in my mouth.

When both of us are done, Nelvin leads me to the room I stayed in below deck. "We'll grab your things and take them to Hook's room."

Nelvin turns the doorknob and gestures for me to step inside. "After you, witchling."

"I have a name, you know." Crossing my arms, I stare at him, arching a brow.

"Mine suits you more." He motions for me to go inside again, and I roll my eyes.

"Fine, have it your way. I'll only need a second."

Heading for the closet, I grab what I can in my arms, getting ready to throw it all in the chest. The door shuts and as I turn around to face it, the sweet scent of magic swarms my nose.

Dammit.

Rushing forward, I try the handle, but just as I suspected, I'm locked in. Spelled in, actually. Taking a deep breath, I close my eyes, focusing my magic. It'll be hours before Sebastian notices I'm down here, and for some reason, I'm not panicking... I've never felt this calm, actually. It's sort of peaceful or would be, if I wasn't trapped here.

When I open my eyes, threads appear, weaving into an intricate web. Since I can't panic to alert Sebastian, it's either breaking this boundary or crawling through the porthole, and from two stories below deck, that would be one hell of a climb.

Here goes nothing. With a deep breath, I start plucking threads and untying knots. It's going to be a while.

34
HOOK

The Jolly Roger creaks beneath my boots as I stride across the deck, scanning the horizon. In the distance, the misty shores of Neverland peek through the clouds, taunting me like a fading dream. If we don't get the sails up soon, the ship will get caught in the current and we'll get sucked right into the reef.

Smee stands at the railing, loose strands from her braid swaying in the wind. I near her and something in her hand catches the light. It's not until I'm at the rail next to her that I can make out what is. Her long fingers curl around the compass we retrieved from the merchant ship. The one that leads to Pan.

"What are you doing with that?" I ask, resting my arms on the wooden rail.

"Just wanted to make sure I was right." She sighs, tilting the compass face toward me. "It's not pointing to the mainland. It's pointing to Neverland."

"Maybe it's out of range. It's not a typical compass, Smee. Magic has limits. We might not be close enough to the mainland for it to work."

Smee shrugs, then shakes her head like she's at war with her own mind. "I don't know... I looked at it while we waited for you, the day you entered the gauntlet. It wasn't pointing toward the mainland then, either."

There's a possibility that Pan left the mainland. If not then, he might've after hearing I won the gauntlet. It's not like we have a tracking device on the god himself. We only knew he was hiding out on the mainland because we did locator spells that put him there. I know I haven't had Lorian do one since my father died, seeing as we've been non-stop going since. I thought it was pointless until we were ready to go after him.

"Watch." Smee moves to a few different spots on the deck, and each time the compass needle turns to point directly at Neverland.

From here, Neverland is shrouded in mist, with lush forests covering every inch of it. Towering mountains stretch towards the heavens, their jagged peaks daring to pierce the sky. It might look like a magical place, but the things that live there are far from enchanted. They're monstrous.

"Maybe Pan fled when he heard you were entering the Gauntlet," Smee suggests, a hint of sarcasm in her voice. "Or maybe someone has tampered with it. You said the witches you killed were with the compass. Maybe they messed with it."

I narrow my eyes, considering her words. They might've manipulated it somehow, but why? Especially when it seems like the Crocodile wants me to find my shadow for some reason.

Before I can respond, movement on the horizon catches my attention. A blip comes out from behind the island. My heart plummets when I see crimson sails. It's a ship, but it's not just any ship. It's the Crocodile's.

Panic surges within me, and I whirl around to face Smee, to tell her she has to give orders, to get the men ready. Only she doesn't appear to be fazed... like she was expecting him.

Slowly, she turns her gaze away from the Crocodile's ship, empathy and sadness lacing her features. "I called him here with my element. We need his help."

"Help?" I snarl, incredulous. "You brought our number one enemy to our doorstep for what? Fucking tea? I trusted you with the ship for one day, and this is what you do?"

"Sebastian, listen—" she begins, but I cut her off, my shadows flaring around me with the intensity of my emotions.

"Absolutely not," I growl. "This is reckless and dangerous. You've put us all at risk! For what? What could we possibly need his help for, Smee?"

Smee pulls a piece of paper from her pocket, unfolding it carefully. "I wasn't the only one to get a note on that merchant ship, Sebastian," she says, handing it to me.

As I scan the words, my anger grows. According to the note, the Crocodile knows where my shadow is. He's offering a deal—but at what cost? My grip tightens around the parchment, crumpling it in my fist.

"You don't truly believe this, do you?" I hiss, rage boiling within me like molten lava. "What did you offer him?"

"I didn't want to. Not at first, but then I saw the compass point away from the mainland," Smee suggests, her voice calm despite the tension crackling between us.

"Scarlet," I whisper, my mind racing with the implications of this twisted bargain. "This will involve her, won't it?"

"Sebastian, I see the way you look at her," Smee admits, her eyes softening just a little. "You won't float her. You can't. But she's marked. If she stays, we'll lose the ship. The men will riot."

"Then what do you propose?" I snap, fighting the urge to scream at her again.

"Listen," Smee continues. "The Crocodile might be willing to trade your shadow for Scarlet. She's a princess, and she's gifted. He works for her father. She might get to go back to her home in Solaria."

I shake my head, disbelief coursing through me. "What? You're just going to hand her over to those blood witches like some bargaining chip? No. Absolutely not."

"We don't have a choice. We're backed into a corner here," Smee says, tossing her arms up in the air.

"You don't understand. She's not a blood witch. Her father tortured her, trying to take that mark off. She's not going back there or anywhere. End of story," I protest, my heart aching at the thought of sacrificing Scarlet for any reason, certainly not for my shadow. I'd rather live without it.

"I'm sorry, but she's marked. There are no mistakes. You know, just as much as I do, that she had to do sacrificial magic for that mark to stick." Smee shouts in a hushed tone to not alert the others on the deck.

I growl, feeling the shadows around me churn and seethe in response to my mounting fury. "If anything happens to her, Smee—anything at all—I will never forgive you."

"We don't have a choice. Nelvin already has Scarlet, and the moment our uncle gets here, he'll be handing her over."

My heart pounds in my chest, the weight of their betrayal threatening to crush me. The danger Scarlet now faces sends a cold shiver down my spine. I grit my teeth, glaring at my half-sister.

"You promised!" I snarl, my anger boiling over. "You swore no harm would come to Scarlet if I gave you the ship!"

Smee takes a step closer, her voice ice-cold. "I promised not to float her. There's a difference. This was the best option to fix everything."

"Best option?" My voice drips with venom. The familiar darkness gathers around me like a cloak, my shadows eager for a taste of vengeance. "She's a living, breathing person."

As I get in Smee's face, my shadows explode around us, their tendrils coiling and writhing like living things. But before they can do harm, something cold and metallic clinks around my wrist.

The world narrows to the sensation of cold steel biting into my skin, and the sudden absence of my shadows. They vanish as if ripped away by some unseen force, leaving me feeling exposed and vulnerable. I glance incredulously at the cuff now encircling my wrist.

"Wha—" I begin, but Smee cuts me off.

"Can't have you losing control, can we?" She gives me a weak smile, her eyes glinting with an unsettling gleam.

"Lose control?" I repeat, the words tasting like bile on my tongue. "You can't do this. How could you cuff your own damn brother?"

"Desperate times call for desperate measures," she says, her gaze dropping to the cuff. "I'm doing this for you. Please try to understand that."

Her words are like daggers, each one piercing deeper than the last, but I refuse to let them draw blood. "I will find a way to fix this," I vow, my voice low and deadly. "And when I do, you'd better pray you're not standing in my way."

"Wouldn't dream of it, brother," she says, lifting her gaze to the ocean, watching the Crocodile move in.

35

HOOK

The salty wind whips against my face as I stare out across the choppy sea. The sound has always been calming to me, but today it's anything but. I feel a hand on my shoulder and find Nelvin standing behind me. His silver eyes are gentle and reassuring, but his part in this madness is entirely the opposite.

"It wasn't my idea," he says, talking with his hands. I spot a rope in his grasp, following it as he speaks. "However, I can agree with Smee on some things, and this honestly was the best choice we could come up with."

Reaching the end of the rope, I find Scarlet bound and gagged. Her white hair billows like a ghostly halo, and those fierce hazel eyes stare back at me. Gods, how did we end up here?

"Smee, please… You don't have to do this," I growl, keeping my voice low.

Smee stands tall, the stump of her right ear twitching slightly. "The Crocodile's coming. He'll take Scarlet to live amongst his witches. I'm not changing course." She can't even bring herself to look at me.

"She's not one of them." My words are like venom.

"You know as well as I do that an accusation is a conviction. That mark alone will have put people on edge. You add the fact she's a Midicious and the people in the Luminaries won't just want her dead but tortured. You'd feel all of it if something happened. This will get her off my ship, keep her safe—mostly—and protect you. It even comes with getting your shadow back." Smee crosses her arms, her expression betraying the fact she's trying to convince herself this is the right move, too.

"I will live without my shadow before I trade her for it!" I snap.

"Enough!" Smee locks eyes with me. "This is happening, whether you like it or not."

The sound of wood creaking and splintering heralds fills the air as the Crocodile's ship draws alongside us. It's deathly silent like they've concealed their sounds with magic.

My uncle grins wickedly, dropping the plank over the rail to board our ship, his silver-toothed grin splits his face in half.

"Look at us," the Crocodile says, arms open wide. "Family, together at last. Who knew all it took was an arrow to my brother's heart?"

My body tenses, shaking with adrenaline. Fury boils my blood until the rapid cadence of my own heartbeat echoes in my ears.

"I didn't call you here for a reunion," Smee says, her hand balancing on her cutlass hilt, ready to draw. The crew is all above deck, and judging by their wide-eyed faces, they're just as surprised as I am. She didn't tell them that she invited him.

My uncle's dressed in black, like he's in mourning, his long coat flourishing in the sea breeze. The feather in his tricorn hat waves and flicks. He might be past his prime, but he's still as deadly as they come.

"Ahh, yes," my uncle says, stepping closer to Smee. "You said you had something I'd want."

"Aye. The king's daughter. My brother won the gauntlet, only to find out that his new bride is a blood witch. She's gifted, capable of controlling an entire ship with a snap of her fingers. I've witnessed her commanding a Wysterian. She's all yours as long as you keep her alive and well. In exchange for my brother's shadow, of course."

The Crocodile scrubs a hand over his jaw, scratching at his stubble. "I didn't know the king was hiding a blood witch. Do you know how many witches of mine you've condemned? Why do you care about this one? She was arranged to marry him, right? It's not like they married for love."

A handful of his witches follow our uncle onto our ship, their dark ropes obscuring their faces. The thought of Scarlet becoming one of those... I can't fathom that.

My uncle eyes me and his gaze alone makes me feel dirty, like oil has dripped across every pore of my exposed skin. He's always been manipulative, able to worm his way into people's minds and plant thoughts inside their heads.

"Seeing as he's shackled, I take it your brother isn't quite on board with this exchange," my uncle says, propping his hands on his hips.

Smee shakes her head. I'll kill her for this... I love her with all my heart, but if Scarlet leaves with that man, or dies by his hand, I'll float her myself.

"No," Smee says, "He's not. She's bewitched him. He thinks he loves her. It's the only reason I'm willing to make a trade with you. He won't ever forgive me if I float her, so she's yours if you help me get his shadow back."

The Crocodile looks from Scarlet to me, his smile growing wider. "In love, you say? Well, that's quite the surprise."

I clench my fists, forcing my voice to remain steady. "You're not taking her."

I might not have magic or my shadows, but my sword is still at my hip. Gripping the golden handle, I pull the cutlass free. If he's going to try to take Scarlet, he'll have to go through me. I put myself in front of Scarlet, from where she sits on the ground, knees to her chest.

"Oh please, stand down, boy. I'm not here to fight ya. I do think we need to chat, though. There are things you should know, things your father refused to tell you or spelled you to forget. I wasn't the only one who knew where your shadow was. I took him there myself. That compass I gave you would lead you right to it, but I'm going to guess since you haven't bothered to use it, that you're still hoping to strike a deal with Pan."

"You're lying. My father didn't know. That's why we were tracking Pan," I say, letting my sword drop to my side.

"I assure you, he did. He just didn't like the cost. Seeking out Pan and making the deal was his way of getting around it."

"Around what?" Smee says, tossing up her hands. "If our father knew, he wouldn't have hesitated to get Sebastian's shadow back. It's all he ever wanted."

"He wasn't willing to pay the price. You see, it was my fault you lost your shadow. I was supposed to be watching you. I let you out of my sight and by the time I got there, Pan had already taken half your soul." The Crocodile paces across the deck like he's telling a story to children, drawing all the eyes on the ship.

"That's not news to us. We knew you were responsible. It's why our father kicked you off the Jolly Roger." Smee crosses her arms, her manicured eyebrows pinching together.

"It was part of the reason," my uncle says, pulling off his gloves one finger at a time. "You see, we didn't know the price. We knew a sacrifice was needed and I was willing to trade my soul for yours, but when we reached Pan's vault and entered that tomb, fate had something else in mind."

The Crocodile holds up his hand, revealing a twisted symbol that looks like it was banded into his flesh. It's long healed. It's not even shiny anymore.

"If you were so willing to give up your soul for mine, to right your wrong, why did our father hate you?"

The Crocodile's blue eyes connect with mine over the deck. "We learned three things that day. The person missing their soul has to be the one to open the tomb. You'll be branded like this." He flashes the symbol on his palm. "Your spirit will guide your shadow back to our realm. Secondly, we learned that the sacrifice must be someone you love. They don't have to be present, either."

"What was the third?" Smee asks, stepping closer.

"The person I loved was your mom," he says, looking between me and my sister.

"Which one? We have different mothers." Smee narrows her eyes, staring at our uncle through slits.

My uncle shakes his head from side to side. "You're wrong. You both have the same mother. Your father lied to you."

"My mother was killed by blood witches," I say, lifting the sword again.

"No, she was killed by me. Your father told you that because he didn't want you to blame yourself, then had a witch take away your memories of it. You were only six years old, and she was with you when her soul left her body and went into the vault. He worried that it would traumatize you for life."

I can't believe what I'm hearing... though a small part of me wondered. It seemed a bit coincidental that both of our mothers were killed by blood witches. Granted, it comes with the territory. And Smee was old enough to remember when the woman who raised us died. She was hexed. They looked so similar to one another; we never questioned it.

"Honestly, if it weren't for you, no one else would've been able to get Smee out of your mother's stomach in time to save her." The Crocodile steps closer and my grip tightens on the blade. It's not a memory I care to look back on. It's more like a nightmare. "You share a mother, but the woman who helped raise you, the woman you believed to be Smee's mom. She never had children, but she treated the two of you like her own."

"So, we're full siblings?" Smee asks, raising her voice.

"No. Half. James Hook was your father, Smee. By then, I'd been banished from the ship for what happened to your brother. The only time your parents associated with me after that was when I found out where your shadow was. Of course, your father blamed me for the loss of his wife, too."

"If James wasn't my father, then who was?" I ask, leaning away from him slightly and lifting my chin.

"You're looking at him. I made your mother a promise that I'd get your shadow back at all costs." The Crocodile holds out his hands and spins. "Pan can't open the vault. He's grown too weak since he became mortal. There's no way around the blood magic. Someone has to die for you to get your shadow back, Sebastian. Your father didn't want it to be Smee."

"No," I say, shaking my head. I won't believe that nonsense. "Then I won't open it. I don't want my shadow enough to sacrifice someone I love."

"Sadly, you won't have a choice. For me to fulfill my promise, you need to be whole. And for me to go to your mother, you have to open that vault." The Crocodile turns back to me, his eyes cold and calculating. "It's been over twenty years. I've waited, I've been patient. To fulfill that promise, you'll need to open Pan's vault. I gave your father the benefit of the doubt and let him search for an alternative. Hell, even I did, but there's only one solution, Sebastian."

As the weight of his words settles on me, my heart constricts in my chest. A part of me wonders if this is just another manipulation, another lie, but there's an eerie sort of truth behind his words that I can't shake. I glance at Scarlet, bound and vulnerable, and Smee... I can see the tears in her eyes, unshed but lingering there. She understands now...

The Crocodile doesn't do deals. He serves himself. It never made sense... I couldn't figure out why he'd help me find my shadow when he'd been my father's sworn enemy for decades. I knew there had to be something in it for him, but this? I never expected this.

Smee invited him here, but he had no intention of hearing her out. He saw an opportunity, a chance at our ship being divided. Weak. Blood witches line the deck of his ship, ready to heed his command. He came with one plan, to take me to that vault and, if necessary, force me to open it, to sacrifice one of the two women on this deck.

Considering the fact he loved my mother, he likely let my father search for another way. He let him try to find a way to open that vault that didn't involve me sacrificing her only other child. When Smee told him about Scarlet, he didn't have to worry about that anymore. There was someone else to pay the price instead.

Is that why my father wanted me to enter the gauntlet? Was it truly for access to the mainland? I never sat in on his locator spells, not towards the end. What if Pan wasn't there? What if he wanted me to marry the king's daughter so the blood oath would be enough to make me love someone else? What if it was his way of ensuring someone other than Smee paid the price? Blood oaths are only offered for royal weddings and the written magic we used to finish it is illegal, even in the outer realm.

Thinking back, my father tried countless times to get me to marry. He arranged meetings and always pressured me to start a family, but I'm a pirate and with how long we're gone from the Luminaries, it wasn't plausible. It wouldn't have been fair to the woman I bound myself to, who'd have to leave everything she knows to come with me or stay behind and only see me for weeks or days out of the year. What woman would be happy with that?

Scarlet is different. She was going to have to leave it all behind, anyway. Assuming whoever would've won, besides me, let her live. She would've been transplanted into a new culture and left to figure it out. I didn't think she'd want to stay on this ship.

I meant what I told her about it being dangerous and had I known about her mark, there's no way I would've let her board when we left the Luminaries. She would've had to stay behind... that is if I could've looked past it then.

Scarlet didn't have anything to lose by marrying me, but I didn't anticipate falling in love with her...

Even after everything Smee pulled today, I know she did it because she thought she was helping me... I can't lose them. Either of them. They're all I have left. The two of them hold me together when I feel like I'm too shattered and broken. They remind me of who I'm supposed to be with both halves of my soul.

I won't be the reason that either of their lights dims from this world. And I've faced the Crocodile enough times to know that he won't give up. He's waited over two decades for this. He finally has a chance to honor the promise he made to my mother without harming her other child. He won't stop until that vault opens and one of them dies... I can't let that happen.

I back up, inch by inch, until my leg is right next to Scarlet. She's smart... so freaking intelligent that it astounds me most of the time. I don't even have to give her a sign before she discreetly tries to fish out the dagger I keep in my boot. She's seen me undress enough times to know it's always there.

The wind howls around me as I stand on the deck of the Jolly Roger, my heart pounding in my chest. When I feel the small dagger pull free, I glance at Scarlet, wishing I could tell her everything's going to be okay. I feel her panic, though not as strong as it was before we finished the bond. It's there, rippling inside me.

She's terrified, but I know her and Zephyr and Lorian well enough to know that she'll get off this ship. I just have to make sure they have no use for her anymore. Smee won't float her after this... I know it.

"Damn it all," Smee curses under her breath, pacing back and forth as she rips the crimson bandana from her head.

A cold gust of wind sweeps across the deck, and I shiver as it cuts through my clothes, chilling me to the bone. Smee's frozen, her eyes wide with fear and realization. The Crocodile had played her, and sadly, there's no undoing this.

Smee snaps out of her stupor, rushing forward with her sword in hand. The blood witches raise their palms, but the Crocodile stops them without a word. Smee swings, but he deflects every move with such efficiency... He's been doing this for a lifetime. She won't get to him, but he's appeasing her, letting her get her anger out, anyway. He needs her and Scarlet alive so he can force me to choose.

With everyone's eyes drawn to the fight on the lower deck, I hear the ropes Scarlet's trying to slice through whine with each sawing motion she makes.

"Scarlet," I say, keeping my voice down. "I need you to know something..." She can't speak—Nelvin taped her mouth shut—but she pauses to look up at me with those beautiful hazel eyes. "I love you, and I'm sorry. You're going to feel this, and that's my fault for making you finish the blood oath, but I promise you, you'll be safe."

Her eyes bounce between mine, trying to figure out what I'm talking about, but I need to do this while they're distracted. It's my only shot. Striding to the railing, I draw the blade of my sword across my arms, making sure I bleed. The beasts will come. I need to make damn sure they won't be able to fish me out before then.

As the blade nicks my skin, Scarlet screams, the sounds muffled by the tape. My jaw clenches, the muscles hammering as my lungs seize from the pain.

The blood begins to drip in a heavy stream from the wounds as I step onto the rail. And with a deep breath, I float, giving over my soul to the deep.

36

Scarlet

My heart feels like it's caught in a vice as I look at Sebastian, teetering on the fragile edge of the ship's railing. The sea wind washes over me, whipping my hair in the wind, pulling it free from the braid I made this morning. Yet, all I can think about is how I'm never going to get to see his face again. I'll never get lost in his kisses or his touch.

The ropes that bound me moments ago now lay broken and scattered on the deck. The cool metal of the daggers still rests in my palm and my lips tingle, waxed raw from the tape that muzzled my cries as he sliced open mortal wounds. I can still taste the adhesive and feel the sting as salty tears stream down my face and over my freshly freed lips.

"No," I breathe, watching him waver on the railing. "No!" As if I've found my voice, my scream pierces through the chaos unfolding around me. I hardly recognize my own voice.

Desperation surges through me as I reach for him, fingers splayed wide. My magic floods my veins so quickly that it permeates the air. The seconds feel like minutes as my translucent threads glimmer into existence but refuse to attach to him.

I've never tried to control him... I never needed to. Even when I was Sebastian's prisoner, I trusted him. The bond... It has to be. It's the only thing that makes sense. The same thing that has connected us all this time is about the be what tears us apart and seals his fate. It's a cruel twist of destiny that the one time I wish to control him, I can't. Not even to save his life.

His foot lifts, hovering in the air for a moment as I struggle to get to my feet, desperate to reach him, to stop him, but there's not enough time.

His weight shifts and tears sting my eyes, clouding my vision, and he plunges into the dark sea below. An ache unlike anything I've felt before fills my chest to the point of bursting. All the noise vanishes along with him, except for the chaotic beating of my heart.

My heart doesn't just break—it shatters, shards of pain plunging deep into my very soul, ripping it apart from the inside. I'm unable to move, or think, or breathe. He's gone...

I've seen people float and their lives ended within a minute or two of going over that edge. It can't be true for him... I can't do this without him.

The roar of something crashing into the water hits my ears, yanking a sob from my lips. My lungs stop working. They don't expand or even attempt to draw air. They're frozen in time.

The edges of my vision blur, panic threatening to choke me from where I sit. My legs, weak and trembling, somehow find the strength to push my body from the ground and propel me forward into a dead sprint.

This can't end here. I won't let it.

"Scarlet!" Zephyr's booming voice rings out, but it's as if I'm hearing him through a thick veil. He's reaching for me, his hands stretched out in a futile attempt to reel me back. To keep from going over that edge after him. The raw force of my magic lashes out, a wild tempest, tossing aside any who dare stand in my path.

Without a final glance or a single thought, I soar over the railing, letting the wind and the waves claim me. The only coherent thought that flits through my mind is the fact I can't swim, but I don't care. All I know is if something comes to swallow him whole, he'll be helpless to stop it without me. Everything else I'll have to figure out as I go.

It's sort of euphoric, the falling. Having read a chapter in Smee's romance book, where a character goes over the edge, I can only hope that it's accurate. I shape my body as she did, pointing my toes, and keeping my arms close to my chest as I plummet feet first, toward the waves.

Pain shoots up my legs as I connect with the water, sinking deep beneath the surface. My magic crackles around me, helping dampen the blow, and I hold my breath. The moment I slow my descent, I flail, trying to move within the water but going nowhere. The dagger is still in my hand, clutched in my grip as I scramble toward the surface, lungs screaming for air.

I close my eyes and focus, drawing on the last reserves of my power to reach out into the depths of the ocean... There are dozens of heartbeats, of souls to control. So many of them I can't count. I have to find him before something else does. Daring to open my eyes, the murky greenish-blue water is thick and cloudy, but there's a light. Something orange glowing from below. His necklace... He put it back on.

My skin tingles like a thousand needles press into it, my legs the worst. I need air. My vision starts to close in, unable to hold my breath any longer, but I can't swim up to reach it. The fight starts to leave me and I fear I've made a terrible decision.

Instead of saving him, I'll be joining him in the dark depths. My mouth opens as my lungs try to inhale the water, knowing this is the end. My heart screams, battering into the bone so hard it'll bruise. I suck in deep, but it's not water that invades my lungs. It's air. I can breathe...

The prickling on my legs continues to intensify, and I kick off my boots, hoping they won't weigh me down. My fingers undo the button of my pants, pushing them off, and my eyes flare wide as I take in the scales on my skin. I'm not part siren...

I'm part mermaid.

With the clothes gone, my legs transform into a long jade green tail. The scales collect the light, scattering it around the water. I try to move, finding it easier to move within the water. It's still clumsy at best, but it's better than flailing.

Sebastian...

I search below me, finding the orange light, and dive, doing the best I can to catch up with him. My muscles burn, using pieces of me I've never used before.

Everything else becomes a blur as I focus on reaching him, my heart pounding in my ears. I swim deeper and deeper, desperate to reach him before he's lost forever.

Finally, I spot him — floating beneath the surface. His arms are loose and his chin is tipped back like he's looking at the sky above him. There's a buoyancy to his body despite gravity forcing it down, something keeping him afloat when everything else tells me he should be under by now. He looks so peaceful, even though death looms around us.

Perhaps there's something to this witch-floating business after all. Maybe it's the lack of a soul that keeps them from sinking. Maybe that's why I'm able to, even though I'm marked. Sebastian is missing half of his, and it allows him to sink, but yet maintain some stability in the water, preventing the abyss beneath us from taking him.

His hair floats aimlessly in the gentle current, his limbs weak. Blood tinges the water, painting it crimson like a cloud of smoke.

I reach him and wrap my arms around his chest, pulling his weight into me. He's not breathing, but there is still a little warmth left in him. Crushing my lips to his, I blow, pushing the water from his lungs and giving him the air he needs to survive this. He has to...

I start to kick my legs, or tail-thing, trying to raise to the surface, but I just stir the particles in the water. Large eyes the size of me blink open directly below us and I freeze, clinging to Sebastian with everything I have. Yellow rings and slanted pupils stare at us, unmoving, with an air of curiosity. I lift my hand, letting the translucent strings form between my fingers and it. It opens its mouth at my command, and I breathe a sigh of relief when I don't find razor-sharp teeth staring back at me. It's all gums... There aren't any teeth at all. I let it close its mouth, watching as it blows water through the hole in its back.

I've never seen anything like it or read about a creature like this... It's like some sort of whale, shark, beast mixture the size of a ship itself, but we can fit inside and if I can do that, I can save him...

Commanding it to open again, I pull Sebastian with me, sinking into its mouth. It closes around us, creating a sort of bubble or pocket of air as it empties the water.

It's a weird concept to be laying on a creature's tongue that can swallow me whole, but what other choice do I have? My legs return as the scales seemingly slip beneath the surface of my skin. How did I not know this? I've taken baths... Not once in my twenty-three years of life have I turned into a fish.

Shaking my head free, I focus on Sebastian. Now is not the time to worry about the gills. Do I even have those? I'd have to, right? FOCUS.

Sebastian's cold, his body pale despite his naturally tanned skin. The hollows around his eyes are dark. He's barely even bleeding anymore. He's lost too much. I slip off his shirt, tearing it into strips so I can tie them around the wounds.

Think... There's got to be something, a spell, or anything that could help him. I scavenge my brain, landing on a spell I saw for only a split second as I was trying to save him from the poison the last time he did something stupid. I don't remember everything about it, but I know the words. It's a transfusion. I spill my blood and give it to him. I could use that, then heal him with the other spell enough where he'll live. It's only been what? A day or two since I depleted myself? My stores aren't full, but there should be enough. Without the poison, like he had last time, it won't take as much out of me. I think...

I press my ear to his chest, listening to his lungs. They sound different... strangled. There must be water still. Rubbing my hands together, my magic sings in my veins, like music only I can hear.

"I'm sorry. If you can hear me, this is probably going to hurt." I place my palms just above his chest, letting the power build, then slam them down, forcing the water out. It spews from his mouth and nose, and he coughs and chokes, tilting his head to the side. It's a sign of life and I'll take it.

I cover his mouth with my own, forcing air into his lungs until he starts to do it on his own. His eyelashes flutter, his voice raw and hoarse as he tries to speak. "Scarlet," he whispers, fading in and out.

Tears prick my eyes as I smooth the hair out of his face. "It's alright," I say, kissing his forehead. "You're okay. I've got you. I'm going to fix this." My voice breaks, betraying me as tears spill from my eyes.

"I'm sorry..." His head lulls to the side as he fights to stay awake.

"Don't apologize to me! You will not die today. Do you understand?"

He weakens, losing the fight. I struggle to keep my breaths calm and collected, feeling the urge to breathe faster until I hyperventilate.

"Listen to me," I say, ripping the fabric. "You can't be the lamb. That's my job. We both can't do it. You have to stay with me, okay?" I cup his jaw, bending to rest my forehead on his as a sob rakes through me. "You can't leave me. You have to say. Just hang on."

Sitting back and forcing my lungs to take a deep breath, I wipe the tears from my eyes and get to work. Gripping the small dagger, I position it against my arm, just above my wrist. It's gotta be deep... I don't know if I can do it to myself. Regardless, it also can't be life-threatening. I can't heal him if I bleed out here, too.

Drawing in a shaky breath, I push as hard as I can, dragging the blade across the fleshy part of my arm. I scream out, clenching my jaw until the hinge aches and my teeth threaten to crack. I pant, dropping the dagger, and trying to block out the pain. It burns and stings and radiates up my arm and down through my wrist.

Blood spills from the wound and I start the spell, finger shaking. I've never controlled something and did mage magic before—let alone blood magic. But the beast doesn't fight me, either. It's almost like it wants to help, bringing us to the island I saw from the ship. I start to recite the spell, speaking in a tongue that's nowhere close to familiar to me. I've studied it, but I've never practiced it. I just hope it works. My blood spills onto Sebastian's body, running off the sides of his stomach. As I finish the first round of incantations, I watch the blood become uniform lines, snaking over the beast's tongue, Sebastian's body, and everywhere else flowing into the wounds on his arms. It doesn't take long before his color returns and I stop. Gripping two of the fabric straps I created, I tie them around my arm first, putting pressure on the wound. Then I do the same for both of his.

My body is already fatigued. The blood loss and the magic the beast pulls, along with what I've just given up, I'm running low and I need us to make it to that Island. I doubt I could swim with him for long. Not tired, not like this.

Biting my lip, I choose to do what I can, starting the spell I used before with the coral. I push the fabric up over the wound, just enough to peek at it. As the magic takes hold, I watch the muscle and tissue knit back together before my eyes. Pulling deep on my magic to ensure he has the best chance of survival, stopping with what I hope is enough to guide the beast to the island.

My entire body shakes, struggling to keep up. I will not pass out. I will get us to the island if it's the last thing I do. Curling against Sebastian's side, I rest my head on his chest, feeling the weight of what I just did press down on me.

"You're going to hate me for this. I can feel it in my gut." I chuckle soundlessly. "After everything, living with this mark, not once have I ever considered doing blood magic. I didn't care that everyone assumed the worst. I just kept it hidden, but I tried not to let it tempt me into doing spells like this." I draw my fingertips over his stomach, barely touching him. "I've used blood magic twice now and both times have been to save you. I know you're going to blame me for it... and I know it's going to come with a cost this time. But I couldn't lose you... I just hope you'll forgive me."

I'm not sure how long we lay here, but I'm impatiently waiting for him to wake up. My magic is almost gone, and I feel it start to sputter out. If I keep going, I'll lose something. A part of me. But I'm so tired... so weak. I don't think I could swim myself to shore, let alone both of us.

Just a little longer, then I'll have to do the rest. The beast starts to fight, and I take a deep breath, hitting that line of no return. I command it to open its mouth and I grip Sebastian tight. Water floods around us and I just hope he'll subconsciously hold his breath.

Luckily, we're not far from the surface. I can see the shimmering light dancing through crystal clear water. My legs form into a fin, and I push with everything I have, clumsily getting us to the surface. We break through and I struggle to keep us above water.

I'm not sure what I expected after that spell, but I know something's changed. When I jumped into the water before, I sank like a rock. This time, I was lighter and I don't think that's a good thing. It's not so much of a struggle to swim, but I don't float on the surface like the one witch Sebastian threw overboard. I suppose that's a small blessing.

I thrash my tail, still not sure how to even use it and just hoping for the best, but as exhausting as it is, we're above water and that's what matters.

Looking out into the ocean, I don't see anything. There's a harsh line where the water meets the sea but the ships are nowhere in sight. It didn't seem that far away... Maybe the beast took us to the other side. Or maybe they just assumed us dead and left. The masts were just about finished before Sebastian's uncle, or father, showed up. I'm still not sure what to think of that.

I can see the shore, the waves crashing across starch-white stones. Just as I'm about to clutch Sebastian to my chest so I can attempt to swim on my back, he coughs. His body lurches as his eyes flare open, hazy at first, but it's him.

"What did you do?" he growls, trying to wipe the water away from his eyes.

"You're welcome." Scoffing, I keep us afloat.

He double-takes at the water before reaching a hand through the surface to feel my tail. "You're a... You're a mermaid?"

"It was just as much a surprise to me, too. Though I'm glad, because I can't swim, and even with this thing I'm terrible at it, but if it wasn't there, I'd have drowned along with you."

His eyes widen as if he's remembering everything. He twists far too quickly, making me lose my balance in the water as he looks at the horizon. My head slips below the water and he practically plucks me out of it. "Where are we?"

"I don't know. I told the beast to take us to the closest land and ran out of magic. It's the best I could do."

He sucks in a breath, wading by himself in the water. Without a word, he starts to swim.

For once, I just want to be wrong... I want to assume the worst and have things turn out better for a change. He knows, and if he doesn't, he's going to. I won't keep that from him again.

Doing my best, I try to swim, but the tides keep pushing me out the moment I gain ground.

Sebastian makes it to land. Water drips off him as he turns to sit on the shore.

"You have to use your arms, love!" he yells, watching me struggle. This was surprisingly much easier in the open. "Like this!" He imitates what he did before and I try to copy it, but it's to no avail. "Gods dammit, woman." He's still mumbling curses as he stands and heads back into the water to come get me. "What kind of mermaid can't swim?"

"Oh, I don't know," I yell, trying to stroke harder. "How about the kind who didn't know she was a bloody mermaid!"

37

Scarlet

Water cascades off my hair in thick streams, splattering onto the small white stones. They bite into my palms as I try to pull myself out of the lapping tide, but my tail weighs me down, making it hard to move more than an inch or two at a time.

Everything I've read says mermaids are supposed to be graceful, yet I might as well be grunting trying to flop to get out of the water. This isn't anything like I'd pictured it... Not that I expected this.

From a distance, I thought the coast was made of sand, but its smooth marbled pebbles. Some or larger than others, or more flattened. They're slick and easy to move as I try to use my fingers as claws.

This has to be some god's sick joke. They're likely watching me now, laughing about how they made the clumsy one a mermaid just to watch her struggle a bit. My shirt clings to my body like a second skin, and as more of my body exits the water, the familiar prickling takes over, like a thousand needles dance over my flesh.

Thank the gods... If I had to be stuck like that, I'd cry.

I'm not sure where the tail goes, but my legs reform, and I'm able to crawl the rest of the way out of the water.

I cast a glance to my left, seeing Sebastian flop onto the shore, his chest heaving as he works to catch his breath. I'm painfully aware of the tension hanging in the air, only amplified by the fact he had to come get me.

It's not my fault I can't swim. I didn't even know I had a tail or could breathe underwater. Until today, I could confidently say nothing sprang free while I was in the bathtub, which was the biggest body of water I ever stepped foot in.

Sebastian turns his head toward me. Furious emerald eyes blaze from beneath his dark hair. The thick strands hang over his face as water beads and runs off his bare skin. At least he has pants. Some of us present can't say the same. Though it looks like he chose to lose his boots, too.

"How am I alive?" he breathes as he stares up at the hell flame. My heart races, waiting for him to blow up. He's furious. I can feel it in my gut. His fists are clenched so tightly, I can make out every indention in his knuckles.

I don't answer, but the muscle in his jaw starts to feather as I debate whether I should move away from him. I'm not sure how he'll take any of this...

"I vividly remember passing out beneath the water. It felt like my lungs were going to implode. Yet here I am. All my pieces are in order. I'm going to ask one more time. What did you do?"

My breaths come out uneven as I try to formulate the words to say to him, all while knowing he won't like any of it. He meets my gaze, and I hardly resist the urge to jump back. It's so cold... so expressionless.

Sebastian growls out my name between gritted teeth, "Use your fucking words, woman."

"Magic!" I push up off the ground, trying to get to my feet, scrambling to put space between us. "I used magic."

His jaw locks as he rolls himself up from the ground, the same tick still hammering at the hinge. Those enchanting jade eyes I love darken until the color is nearly nonexistent as he prowls toward me, and I stumble back, caught between whether I should run or stay. I don't think he'll hurt me... but he hasn't fully pieced together what I did.

This wasn't like before—with the coral—something has changed inside of me. I think I used too much... I'm still me, so my soul can't be all gone, but it just doesn't feel right. It's hollow somewhere deep down. Either way, I used my own blood as a sacrifice. If a part of my soul is gone, then I've become the very thing he hates. I've earned the mark on my back... He was willing to look the other way before, justifying it because he truly believed I was wrongfully marked. That's no longer the case.

His gaze trails down my body, pausing at my feet. My lungs seize and my heart plummets inside my chest. Something tells me it's not because I ditched my pants or my shoes–that it's not because I grew a tail and fins.

Daring a glance, I look from the hell flame to white stones near my feet. Something breaks inside me as I turn, hoping it just wasn't the right angle. The stones gleam as if nothing stands upon them. Not a single shadow in sight.

It's gone...

"You took too much, didn't you?" Sebastian whispers. His body is in full rigor, unflinching as he zones out on the beach. I swear he scoffs, but if he reacts at all, he doesn't show it. The hard features of his face are stone cold, save for that tick, and it has nerves crawling across my skin.

We've never truly been alone until now. We stayed in his room together, but there were dozens of men on that ship in screaming distance, as witnesses. I can picture the way he looked at me when he saw my mark for the first time, as if I'm reliving that moment every time I close my eyes. He threatened to kill me, to toss me overboard into the waves, to watch me be swallowed whole. He would've too, had it not been for the connection we shared, that I helped him feel, that I made up for the piece of him missing... Even then, my mark still troubled him.

I no longer fill that void... Without my shadow, I'll be numb, too. Sebastian can end me right here, right now... Worse, he wouldn't need a weapon to do it, only the snap of his fingers. Everyone would assume the sea claimed me because I was the fool who jumped off that ship after him.

Suddenly, I'd rather be on that wretched boat, surrounded by murderous pirates, than be the object this man fixed his gaze on.

"Don't look at me like that," I snap, fists clenching. I straighten my spine and tilt my chin up, refusing to cower. Not now, not ever. If he wants to kill me, I won't stop him, but I'll die with dignity.

One of his dark eyebrows arches up. "Like what?" His voice is deceptively calm, but I see the tension in every straining muscle of his body. The barely restrained violence simmering beneath the surface.

"Like you're imagining your darkness draining me to ash." My legs begin to wobble as he creeps closer, his strides slow and deliberate–taunting me.

His lips tip at the corner, but it's gone in the blink of an eye. "It could."

The breath catches in my throat, and my voice cracks at the first sign of pressure. "I saved you."

"Saved me?" He scoffs. "I jumped off a damn ship to keep you and Smee safe. The Crocodile has no use for either of you if I'm dead. Yet, you brought me back so I could be hunted and forced to do horrific things to women I love. That's not saving me, Scars..." Sebastian runs a hand through his soaked hair, scrubbing it down his face before he turns to me again. "That's torture."

My vision blurs as tears well up in my eyes. "I couldn't lose you..." One escapes, rushing down my cheek and dripping away.

Sebastian stops, his body inches away from mine. He's so close that he has to crane his neck to stare down at me. Fury is etched into every hard line of his body, his voice so deep and raw that it's almost menacing. "You should've let me drown."

He cradles my face in his hands, forcing me to meet his gaze. His touch is so gentle despite every rippling wave of unfiltered anger that floods through the bond between us. Thumbs stroke over my cheekbones, wiping away the tears that stream from my eyes.

Sebastian leans closer, pressing his lips to my forehead as he pulls me toward his chest. My heart stutters, unsure of how to handle this or what to do with my hands. He's hugging me... I keep waiting for the knife to plunge through my back or something, but it never comes.

My chest is so tight... It hurts to breathe. Every nerve sparks like wildfire, desperate to calm the growing panic welling inside me. I fear I'll burst from the pressure. His hands are the only thing keeping me upright anymore. Every muscle in my body has become weak and unresponsive as I fight for air, to force down the anxiousness that's taken my throat hostage.

Sebastian's fingers are buried in my wet hair, clutching my head to his chest. The strong beat of his heart drowns out everything around us. His arm is around my waist, holding me so tightly, I fear it's because he knows this is the last time we'll get to stay like this, suspended in time.

He's alive. That's what matters. He's here, he's breathing...

"I love you." My words are barely audible over the roar of the waves cresting against the beach. "I know this changes everything, and I understand if you hate me..." I trap my bottom lip to keep it from trembling.

Sebastian leans back slightly. The hand he has in my hair pulls, demanding me to look up. Every fleeting sign of his anger is gone, as if it never existed. "I could never hate you, little lamb."

"Then why does it feel like it?"

His eyes soften as he exhales deeply, pulling me back against his chest. "It's not you that I'm angry with... I hate that my own flesh and blood put us here, that it led to you losing the very thing I've spent years trying to get back. I hate that I can't... That my shadow is gone for good, because I'll never be able to bring myself to pay the price. And now yours..." Sebastian pauses, sinking his teeth into his lower lip as he shakes his head. "I've felt more alive since meeting you than I have since I lost my shadow. I lived for every smile, every laugh, every flood of joy you made me experience because of our connection. I hate that I can't get that back... That knowing me has now blackened your soul...You might've had the mark before, but I made you into a blood witch. My choices... and I hate that you believed, even for a moment, that I'd just stop loving you for it."

He leans forward, pressing his forehead to mine. I don't know what to say... All I can do is look at him, meet his emerald eyes, and within a split second, he closes the gap, his lips finding mine. This kiss is like nothing I've experienced before; it's passionate and desperate but also gentle and intimate at the same time. His hands cup my face as liquid fire surges through me.

His lips are soft and smooth and taste like the sweetest wine and salt. Sebastian pulls me closer and tightens his arm around my waist. His fingers trace soft lines along my jaw before his lips follow it. My head spins as I lose myself completely in the way he feels; our bodies are fused together to the point where there is no separation between us.

After what feels like an eternity, we pull away from each other, just enough for him to speak quietly in my ear. "I need you to do something for me."

"Anything," I say, still trying to catch my breath.

He lets me go, reaching down to the stones on the shore to pick up one. It's round, but the center of it is hollow, like something has eaten its way through the middle. Sebastian glances at me for a moment, then takes off his necklace and slides the stone over the chain.

"Turn around." He gently nudges my shoulder and I do, allowing him to gather my hair to one side and slip the chain around my neck. "Don't take this off," he says, kissing my pulse.

"I don't understand... Why the rock?" I turn around to face him, fidgeting with the cool stones that rest against my sternum.

He gives me a look, one that says I should know the answer to that question already, as he reaches out to slip the chain beneath the fabric of my shirt.

"You're a mage. Partly, anyway, you should know stones are never just stones. This is where my father got the moonstone you were touching in my room. It amplifies emotions and covers the shoreline all the way around Neverland. To a normal person, you'd be so overwhelmed with emotion you'd likely never travel deeper into the island. Without your shadow, though, it makes you feel somewhat normal. I used to wear one, but stopped when I married you."

The necklace he took off during the ceremony... He'd put it in his pocket before the priestess did the blood oath.

"Is that why I don't feel much different? I still feel things now, but we're also on the shoreline."

"Yes. Since you don't have shoes or pants, something has always been touching it. When you step off, you'll start to really experience what it's like to not have a shadow, but that should help."

I touch the stones through the wet fabric of my shirt. "What about you?"

He picks another stone up and shoves it into his pocket. "I'll be fine. I've been doing this for years. Even then, we're still bonded. It won't be as strong as before you lost your shadow, but I'll still feel through you. It doesn't hurt to have an extra though if we need it."

I glance down at my feet again, hoping this is just a huge misunderstanding, but where my shadow should stretch across the ground is empty.

"Hey, look at me," Sebastian says, and I reluctantly tear my eyes away from the ground. "It might not be gone. Your soul might just need time to recharge. You've just gotta have hope."

"I don't know if I can..."

He grips my hand, lifting it to brush his lips against the top of it. "Just try. Do it for me." He tugs on my hand as he starts to walk toward the woods. "Come on. I know where we can go."

38

SCARLET

As Sebastian and I step into the forest, I can't help but be swept away by its otherworldly beauty. The air itself seems to shimmer with magic. The vivid colors of the flora practically glow, casting a dreamy kaleidoscope of light on the forest floor. Trees stretch toward the sky, their leaves holding iridescent hues, while exotic flowers release intoxicating scents that dance in the breeze. It's like it walked straight out of one of my books, or maybe my imagination.

"If we're lucky, my father might've left a cuff here, and I'm hoping a key. I need to get this thing off," Sebastian grumbles, glancing at the cuff around his wrist. Smee put it on him to keep him from using his shadows.

The irony isn't lost on me, that it's one of my father's. He designed them and apparently forced them onto the people of our kingdom if what Sebastian and Smee have told me about the rebellion is true. I don't know why it wouldn't be. They're supposed to be impossible to remove, giving the king the ability to track them down or turn off their magic. They must've devised a way to get them off because no one on the Jolly Roger has one, or that I saw in the Luminaries.

If the Crocodile does come after us, we're in no shape to fight him. My magic is gone unless my soul regenerates—if it ever does—and with Sebastian's darkness rendered useless, our only form of protection is the sword sheathed at his hip, which, thankfully, he didn't lose when he fell overboard. Sorry, jumped overboard.

It's a small blessing, but it's something.

"I take it this isn't your first time here?" I ask, trying to step lightly. My feet don't like the ground much, and my socks are doing little to keep the twigs and bark bits from poking at them as we walk.

He smirks. "What do you think? Yes, I've been here before. This was one of my father's favorite places. I haven't been here since he died, though, and never alone or without my gift."

I bounce my eyebrows playfully. "That's a lot of firsts."

"Tell me about it." His voice is both bitter and nostalgic, stirring a mix of emotions within me.

We walk deeper into the magical forest, each step revealing more of its breathtaking beauty and lurking dangers. A sense of awe washes over me as I drink in the sights and sounds around us, the symphony of nature playing alongside our footsteps.

I spot a massive flower, blooming low to the ground despite it being large enough for me and Sebastian to sit on if we wished it. I crouch down next to it, admiring the vibrant pink petals and the fuzzy circular middle. It's beautiful. It looks so soft. Lifting my hand, I start to reach for it, to feel it, but Sebastian clears his throat, making me pause.

"I wouldn't do that if I were you," he warns.

"It's just a flower." I glance at him over his shoulder. "What is it going to do? Bite me?"

Sebastian tosses a twig, making me duck out of the way. It lands onto the frilly middle and, in the same instant, the entire thing folds in half. The petals snap shut, and the entire thing warps in front of my eyes, turning into something round and dark, oozing green goo that singes to the ground as it drips from its mouth like saliva. The petals have become knife-like teeth. My heart lurches in my chest as I stumble back in horror.

Sebastian chuckles, offering me a hand. "It might be beautiful, but don't be deceived, darling. Everything here wants to kill you." I nod, swallowing hard, and stay close.

He tugs me along and it's not until the flower is out of sight that I look forward again.

We trudge deeper into the woods. Each breath I draw in feels infused with magic, like the very essence of the forest is pulsating through the air. Soon, the ground becomes covered in moss, filled with tiny blue flowers. I've never been so thankful for something so simple before in my life. My feet need a break from the rough terrain.

The forest teems with life as tiny luminous creatures flit between the branches above us, and vines twist and curl around ancient tree trunks, creating an intricate, living tapestry.

I glance over at Sebastian. His eyes scan every inch of the woods as we walk. He's no stranger here and I'm not sure if that comforts and unsettles me more.

From what I've read, Neverland was a forgotten place. It used to be the old gods' garden, with a well for magic in the center. Except when the old gods became curses, forced into mortality, the well dried up. That magic didn't just disappear. It was absorbed. It created everything here, an entire ecosystem.

I'd read about it when I was little and asked the maids if the stories were true. They said a god lived here, one of the last alive. He was so greedy that he harbored all the magic from the well that he could before it completely dried up, storing it to keep himself young. Is it possible that it was Pan? Just like how blood witches that have destroyed their souls and lost their magic crave to cast again. Maybe he finally ran out. Maybe he started using shadows to keep him young instead.

"Are there more... plants like that one?" I ask cautiously, still shaken by the flower's sudden transformation.

"You don't want me to answer that."

"And if I want you to, anyway?"

He glances at me, arching a brow. "Then I'd say that plant is the least of your worries on this island."

"Great." I huff out a shaky breath, picking up the pace. I'm not even sure where we're going, but maybe getting there sooner rather than later is best.

"Told you." He chuckles, barely having to extend his gate to keep up with me. As is, I have to take two steps to his one.

My steps slow as we reach a wall of tall bioluminescent flowers. They stretch up, nearly coming to my shoulders. Halting a few feet away, I swallow hard, my limbs sprawling out when Sebastian nudges me forward.

"I promise, these don't bite," he says, walking around to hold his hand out to me. "Come on, I won't let them hurt you."

Hesitantly, I place my hand in his and he steps into the flowers. The stems twirl and move without a breeze, almost tickling my legs and arms as we pass through them.

"See, these are probably the only harmless things on the island." Sebastian grabs one, holding the bud out in front of my face without damaging it. "Smell it."

I stare at him a moment, unsure if I should.

Sebastian rolls his eyes. "Trust me."

Leaning forward, I inhale. It smells like his cologne... It's fresh, almost citric, but with floral undertones. I'd never smelled anything like it until I met him. Now I could recognize the scent anywhere. I've practically been wrapped in it since my soul was bound to his. Not that I'm complaining.

"There you go," he coos, letting the bud go. "See? Harmless. My mother loved them. Every time my father would come back here, I usually was with him and would get some. It's sort of my way of remembering her."

"I suppose I have her to thank for that, then. It smells amazing." I hang onto his hand as we continue forward. He smirks at me but doesn't try to take it back.

"Thank you. I think that's the first compliment you've ever given me," he teases.

"That's not true." Is it? I rack my brain, trying to think of something I've said that would be just a genuine compliment, but can't think of one.

"Relax, love. It was a joke. I don't need compliments. The way you stare at me half the time is enough."

"I do not stare... Okay, maybe sometimes." He's pretty to look at. Float me. Sebastian's smirk grows wider as silence filters in. We're through the flowers before I gather the nerves to break it. "Why does your father come here? If everything is so deadly, why come back?"

He takes a minute before he answers, watching the ground instead of surveying the woods like he has been. "It's where he met my mother."

I blink, taken aback. "I thought your family was from the Western Isles, or was that just part of the whole façade you used to enter the gauntlet?"

His gaze remains fixed ahead, but there's a softness to it now, a faraway look in his eyes I'm not used to seeing. "My mother was from the Western Isles. She was on a ship underway to Solaria, to be married, actually. A beast attacked and the ship went down. She managed to get into a rowboat and washed up here. No one else survived." He pauses, allowing the weight of his words to settle. "She survived on this island by herself for over a year before my father came, searching for Everbloom, a flower with anesthetic properties, and found her."

His voice cracks slightly, betraying his ironclad facade, and I sense the depth of the ache he still feels through our bond. "After she died, my father moved back to the Luminaries and stayed there when we weren't on the ship. He came back here once a year, just to feel closer to her."

My heart aches for him, for the pain in his past. There's a vulnerability in his eyes that I've never seen before, a crack in his confident demeanor that he wears like a mask.

"I'm sorry..." The words slip from my lips.

His head tilts, a wry grin tugging at the corner of his mouth. "About what? You didn't take them from me."

"No. But I can see you miss them, and considering what you just learned, that the Crocodile..." My voice falters, the weight of the unspoken truth hanging heavy between us.

He hasn't mentioned it much... I don't even think I can voice it out loud.

A shadow passes over his face, the playful mischief replaced with cold resolve. "That man is not my father. He never will be. I'm not sure why my mother did what she did, but James Hook, the man who raised me, will always be my father."

I nod, understanding. There are no words that can bring him comfort. Silence takes over, filled with the sounds of the forest as we walk. I'm not sure how much time passes, but it's a lot. I watch my feet, awed by the moss and flowers, the way they glow in the dark when the tree canopies grow thicker. It's incredible, and so unreal...

Before I can react, Sebastian yanks me backward into the hard plane of his chest, his hand clamping over my mouth. My heart races, not in fear of him, but of whatever forced that intense reaction. The rhythmic thud of my heart pulses against his fingers, gripping tightly, ensuring to smother any sound I make. I do my best to breathe quietly through my nose, but it's hard when I can hear my heartbeat in my ears.

Then I hear it—an eerie clicking noise, like nails tapping on stone. Sebastian plasters us against the tree. Even the creatures within it run away. I strain my eyes to see through the dense foliage, trying to find out what's making the noise—what has Sebastian so on edge. Spotting a figure, I suck in a breath.

A nightshade.

Even though it's blind, its milky eyes seem to pierce through the shadows. Its griffin-like body is a monstrous blend of avian and beast, moving with grace like a skilled predator. Its translucent wings—nothing more than a film between the long filaments and bones—stretch and fold. It's listening... waiting for the reverberations of its own call to come back.

Heart in my throat, I stay deathly still. Their bites are venomous and paralytic, and judging by the blood on its teeth, it's hungry.

Sebastian's grip on me tightens just a fraction, a silent plea to remain still. Even his breath is measured as his chest expands against my back.

With every ounce of skill and stealth I possess, I move in tandem with him. Each step is a dare against fate, each breath a whispered prayer to not be noticed. As the distance grows between us and the monstrosity, his hand slips from my mouth. We don't dare speak, not yet, not until that thing is so far we can't hear its call anymore.

It's at least another hour before we reach the edge of the trees and a clearing unfolds. A vast meadow stretches out before us, creating a blanket of green with wildflowers, like the ones we passed through, basking in the hell flame. I can feel the warmth of it against my skin as I step forward and breathe a sigh of relief. The grass is soft and dewy beneath my feet, and the air is so crisp here.

Don't get me wrong, the forest is beautiful, but I don't want to find out what other creatures lurk within it. At least not now. Man-eating daisies and bat men are enough for one day.

Sebastian glances at me, a soft grin on his lips that doesn't quite reach his eyes. I catch the shuffle of his hand in his pocket, the one he put the stone in before we left. "We made it."

My brows furrow, and I scan the clearing again. "I don't..."

Sebastian rolls his eyes, extending his hand to me. "Here, let me show you."

He guides me forward and I watch as he seemingly disappears right before my eyes. Next are my fingers, and my forearm... A wave of tingles washes over my entire body as I follow him forward until the mirage dances and warps. Then I see it.

Nestled in the heart of the clearing is a structure so extraordinary that I'm rendered speechless. A colossal skull. I can't even imagine what creature would be that big. Its hollow sockets are now windows into a home. Doorways curve into the gaping maw, the teeth covered in vines. A few of them are so long they nearly act like pillars. Luminescent purple crystals shine from the base, and they have to be at least ten feet tall.

"By the gods... What creature did this come from?" My voice is barely above a whisper.

Sebastian casts a sidelong glance, the ghost of a smile dancing on his lips. "A titan."

"A titan?" I meet his emerald eyes. The titans were the first creatures to ever walk our realm. They've been long gone, but I can't fathom creatures that big roaming about.

"Yes, that's what I said." He tugs me forward, but I've already turned around.

The mirage is immaculate. The spellwork is unlike anything I've witnessed. The threads are so tightly bound that I can barely see them. I reach out, trying to feel it, but my hand slips right through as if it's not there. I'm not sure what kind of magic this is, but it's strong.

Chuckling, he leans close, his breath tickling my ear. "Admiring my mother's handiwork?"

"Your mother's? How is it still here, then?" Wards and spells, any form of ongoing magic dies with the person who casts it.

"Elemental magic is different. With mages or druids, their magic fades with them because it's tied to their souls. But an elemental, they shape, bend, and command nature itself. It remains a part of the world, unyielding and unchanged unless willed otherwise."

"She was like you, then…" It's more a thought out loud than a question, but he answers anyway, nodding his head. I barely see it in my peripheral, too busy staring at the shimmering boundary. It casts dancing reflections around us, playing with the light.

Just as the realization dawns on me, he says my thoughts out loud. "She could manipulate light."

I turn my head, surprise written in the arch of my brows. "How? There's only been one light elemental known in existence."

Sebastian nods, guiding me toward the house. "That's why she was supposed to marry the king."

"My father?" The air hitches in my lungs. "It's been hundreds of years since the queen died. I didn't think he'd ever want to marry again."

"Well, she was special. Whether he wanted to marry her for her gift or for her, I don't know. It was going to end the war. The king signed a treaty for it, but since she was stranded here, she never made it to the wedding." He chuckles soundlessly.

"I never knew that..." I walk beside him, the skull growing larger by the second as we near.

"King Midicious chose to honor the treaty anyway, to let us live in the outer realm, out from beneath his rule and his protections. It's probably the most noble thing he's ever done. Though he's broken it through the years, we could still be at war. I'm not talking about the occasional village being attacked by blood witches, either. That's nothing compared to what happened before the treaty... Who knows, in a different world, we might not have been this." He gestures between us. "We might've been family."

As we approach the skull house, I let my gaze wander over the intricate details carved into the bone—swirling patterns and symbols that seem to dance beneath the flickering light of the boundary. The door is framed by a twisting vine that appears to have grown naturally into the shape of an archway.

"Are you ready to see where I grew up?"

I turn to him, eyes wide. "You lived here?

Sebastian nods, his eyes distant as he looks around. "Yeah. My mother and I would stay here, and my father, of course, when he wasn't on the ship."

I furrow my brow in confusion. "Why would your mother want to stay on the island? Your father could've taken her anywhere."

Sebastian's expression softens for a moment. "She lost all of her family on that ship when she was stranded here," he says quietly. "And if she left, the realm would find out she lived."

"She would've had to marry my father." I skim my fingers over the carved wooden door as Sebastian turns the knob and we step inside.

"Aye, and by then she'd fallen in love with my father. Still, this place was like her sanctuary." Sadness washes over Sebastian's features, and silence hangs heavily in the air.

"What's wrong?" My brow furrows.

"Nothing." He sighs, pulling his hand from his pocket and stepping out of the door frame so I can go in.

We step inside the skull house, and I'm instantly transported to a world of memories. The interior is surprisingly cozy, with furniture made from driftwood and various trinkets scattered throughout the space. My gaze is drawn to the titan's eye sockets, now grand windows that frame the ever-mysterious forest outside. The walls are bone-colored and the floors are made of an old dark wood. There's a fireplace on the far wall and a large bed tucked to one side of the vast room. A couch and some chairs, along with a small kitchen, make up the other portion of the bottom floor. A ladder leads to a balcony, and I can see handmade children's toys pushed along the railed edge.

Sebastian doesn't miss a beat. He jumps into action, getting the fireplace on and shaking things out. "We'll be safe here. No one can get through the boundary besides my sister. Everyone else would have to be escorted, man or monster."

I open my mouth, ready to ask what I can do to help, but he's speed-walking toward me before I can get a word out.

"I'll be right back," he tells me. "I know where I can find something for us to eat. Stay inside the house." He leans down and presses a gentle kiss to my forehead before walking out the door.

Hook

I stare at the little garden near the house. I'm not sure when it happened, but I know it had something to do with me dying—or almost dying. Maybe it was Scarlet's magic... Whatever the case is, memories have started to resurface. Memories I didn't think were real until we came into the clearing. Part of me wishes I could forget them all over again or trap them behind a wall, but I can't. I shouldn't.

My uncle was right... My father must've spelled me to forget them somehow, but he didn't only take the bad ones, like the day my mother died. He stole good ones too. Sucking in a breath, I walk through the overgrown rows of plants, stopping at one in particular, and I do my best to not think about it as I fill the bowl with ripened red berries.

Heading back inside, the creak of the door hinges announces my arrival as I step into the dimly lit room, a bowl full of berries from my mother's overgrown garden in hand. The scent of burning wood fills my nostrils, the fireplace crackling and casting an eerie glow on the walls.

I can feel Scarlet's sadness ripple through our shared bond and my heart clenches at the sight of her sitting by the fire.

She tries to manipulate the flickering light, daring it to cast her shadow on the wall. But it doesn't appear. I breathe out deeply, knowing that feeling all too well. I must've tried for weeks afterward, and each time my shadow didn't appear, it was like experiencing the heartbreak all over again.

For a moment, she stares at the flames, licking off the wood I put in the hearth. Then, in hurried movements, she swats away a tear and grips the necklace around her neck. It's like she's worried she'll lose the nerve to take it off, but she does. The moonstone glints as she holds it up, and with a shake of her head, she places it on the floor beside her.

I know what she's doing—removing the moonstone to numb herself emotionally, seeking solace in the void that's left behind. If you can't feel, then you can't cry.

Carefully, I sit down beside Scarlet on the floor. She looks up at me, her hazel eyes reflecting the orange flames. I see the frustration etched on her face, and I want nothing more than to ease her pain. But how? When I lost my shadow, no one could help me either. All that remained was anger festering inside me like a wound that refused to heal.

"Darling," I say, reaching out to hold her hand. "I know how you feel. It seems like the world has ended, that you're empty, but trust me when I say that being numb won't make it go away. Wearing that is nothing like you're used to, but you'll still be you."

Her eyes meet mine, searching for something—anything—that might offer her comfort. "I just... What if it doesn't come back?"

"We won't know for a day or two, but there's no point in worrying about what you can't control. We'll figure it out. I promise," I tell her, bringing her knuckles to my lips. "Don't turn it off. Please."

The silence stretches between us, the crackling fire the only sound filling the room. I watch as Scarlet's expression softens, and she takes a deep breath. Finally, she nods, and I pick up the necklace and slip it over her head. Scarlet pulls her hair through, and I can't help but watch it fall over her shoulders.

"Here," I say, offering her the berries I brought. "My mother loved these. Said they tasted like happiness." It's a small thing, but if it brings even a flicker of joy to her face, it's worth it.

She takes one hesitantly, popping it into her mouth and chewing slowly. A smile begins to form on her lips, and a wave of relief washes over me.

"See?" I tease, a playful grin tugging at my own lips. "Happiness."

Her laugh is infectious and sounds like music to my ears. I tug her into my lap, placing a kiss against her temple.

39

Scarlet

The warmth of the hell flame tickles my skin, shining through the windows. The blankets are wrapped around my legs, twisted in knots between Sebastian and my body as I curl against his side.

He's almost always up before me... I glance up at him, watching as his bare chest rises and falls softly, his breath gentle. He looks so peaceful in his sleep. I trace the contours of his face, committing him to memory. Everything from the way his hair lays, his long eyelashes, the tattoos on his skin, to his full lips... He's perfect, masculine in every way but beautiful.

I shake off Sebastian's robe and untangle myself from the warm sheets. The wooden floor is cold against my feet as I slide out of bed, inspecting the selection of clothes he set out for me. His mother's, from the looks of them.

Anything is better than the seaweed-smelling shirt I had on yesterday. I put them on with ease as if they were made for me. The boots fit snugly against my feet, more comfortable than the ones Smee gave me on the ship. Leather pants hug my curves. The top cascades lovely around my body, form-fitted but thin enough to not overheat, despite it being long-sleeved.

The suffocating silence inside the house is only broken by Sebastian's shallow breathing and the creaking of the floor beneath my feet. My lungs desperately crave fresh air, a respite from the oppressive stillness that fills every corner of this place.

I ease open the front door and step out onto an expansive porch. It's easy to see why his mother loved this place. It's breathtaking, with the light bouncing off the boundary and shimmering over the land.

As I step out into the clearing, I spot a fenced garden behind the skull house. It's overgrown, but still thriving despite no one being here to take care of it in so long. My stomach growls at the sight. Is that where he got the berries?

Swinging open the garden's gate, composed of large sections of twigs that have all been bound together, I enter the lush rows of vibrant blooms. It's a mix of crystals and flowers and herbs, and I tread carefully to avoid stepping on any of them.

The entire length of the fence is surrounded by the flowers we passed in the woods, the one Sebastian makes his cologne from, but within it, is a whole collection of colors. Some blooms are the size of my fist or as tiny as a pinprick.

Breathing in deep, a heavenly aroma takes my senses by storm, calming and exciting me at the same time.

I find the berries Sebastian brought in last night, picking a couple and eating them out of the palm of my hand as I explore. Plants to me are almost as awe-striking as dragons. Maybe it's because so many species of them were created when the species died out and their magic infused into the realm. Except in Neverland, I haven't seen a single skeleton of one, leading me to believe this place is still flourishing because of the destroyed magic well.

It's uncharted territory that's constantly evolving.

I've studied how to identify most of the plant species we know about, but some are unlike anything we had in the courtyards of the Solarian castle. As I walk through the rows of plants, a glint of silver catches my eye, and I kneel to inspect a small plant nestled between the tree limb pickets. Its leaves shimmer with an iridescent sheen, and I gasp.

"No way," I whisper as if the other plants can hear me. It's Leviflora, a rare plant that only grows on pixie graves. No wonder this little garden is thriving. It's been cared for by the pixies...

"Scarlet!"

I lurch upright as Sebastian's voice shatters the tranquility. He bursts through the front door of the house, still shoving on his pants. "Have you gone mad? You can't just disappear like that." His eyes connect with me over the plants.

"Come look at this!" I ignore his worry, diverting my attention back to the silver leaves. "Look what I found."

Sebastian's in the garden, hovering behind me in seconds. "Great, a plant," he grumbles, clearly unimpressed. "You do realize my uncle could be here at any moment, right? You can't just wander off without saying something."

I roll my eyes. "I never left the barrier, and it's not just a plant."

I glare at him over my shoulder before turning back to the delicate petals. Carefully plucking a leaf, I hold it out to Sebastian. "Here, eat this."

"That sounds like a fast way to die. I think I'll pass on that." He crosses his arms, eyeing the leaf warily. I shrug and pop the leaf into my mouth.

His eyes flare wide as he gasps in shock. "Don't—Gods, woman! You can't just eat things! You're as bad as Nelvin." He grips my jaw before I can push him away, trying to fish the leaf out of my mouth like a toddler who's tried to swallow a stone. "One of these days, my heart is going to fucking stop and it'll be your fault."

Managing to slap away his hands, I chew. "Considering the fact I'm the only reason your heart is still beating, I'll take my chances. It's Leviflora, and completely safe, so if you'd stop trying to choke me, It'd be greatly appreciated,"

I snap, chewing the leaf more. The last is almost sour, yet sweet on my tongue.

"You're insufferable." He tosses his hands up.

"And you're boring, yet I don't bring it to your attention every second of every day, do I?" A hiccup escapes my lips.

Sebastian closes the distance between us in one step, concern etching his features. "What? What is it?"

"Like I said," I manage between hiccups, "it's safe, and it's working." He arches a brow, crossing his arms over his chest. "It counters the effects of gravity. The pixies use it to travel long distances since they're so small." My feet begin to lift off the ground, leaving me weightless and hovering.

"What the fuck..." Sebastian lunges forward, gripping onto my shirt. I'm only an inch or two from the ground.

"It's alright. I doubt I'll float much higher. I'd have to eat a whole plant if I wanted to do that."

Hesitantly, he lets go, and I spin gracefully above the ground. He watches me with a hint of amusement as he covers his mouth with his hand, but he can't hide the smile in his eyes as he takes in my uncontainable excitement. I can't help but laugh as I float through the air, feeling like a pixie myself. For once, we're sharing a moment untainted by darkness or danger—just pure, simple joy.

Sebastian exhales as he props his hands on his hips. "I will never understand you," he says, shaking his head in mock disbelief.

"Whatever do you mean?" I tilt my head to one side.

He gestures at me, still grinning. "You call me boring, yet you're fascinated with the littlest things. Your books, books you've read dozens of times, and now, plants... You're hovering an inch off the ground, yet I've never seen you smile wider."

"You could join me, you know," I say, crinkling my nose.

"You're just like her... She'd have loved you something fierce." Sebastian dips his head, looking at me from beneath his dark lashes before bending to snatch a leaf off the plant. "Fine. You win. Do I just eat one?"

"Don't swallow it," I caution him. "Chew, and when you're done floating, spit it out."

He nods, popping it in his mouth and chewing tentatively. Slowly, his feet leave the ground, but his balance is off, causing him to grip my shoulder for support. The contact sends warmth shooting through me, making my heart race.

"Easy there," I chuckle. "Gentle movements."

"Thanks, Professor," he grumbles sarcastically, but I can see the beginnings of a grin tugging at his lips.

We float together, and little by little he gets the hang of it. Drifting through the clearing, we spread out and time seems to still as I take in the beauty of it all. From the twisted roots of the forest trees to the velvety moss blanketing the trunks, the intricate spiderwebs shimmering with morning dew... It's like a dream I never want to wake up from.

"How do you know how to do this?" Sebastian asks, finally steadying himself as he floats up beside me.

"Books." I shoot him a wink.

"Of course," he murmurs, a teasing smile playing at the corners of his lips. "My little bookworm."

"Hey," I protest, swatting at him playfully. "There's nothing wrong with being well-read."

"Never said there was," he grins and then propels himself forward with a grace that makes my heart flutter.

I'm so entranced by the enchanting scene around us that I almost don't hear it - the low murmur of voices cutting through the stillness. My breath catches in my throat, and I glance over at Sebastian, who has gone rigid beside me.

"Did you hear that?" I whisper, my voice barely audible.

His eyes narrow as he scans the clearing. "Time to go." The concern in Sebastian's gaze sends a shiver down my spine. "Stay close."

I nod, my heart racing with a sudden burst of adrenaline. It's the Crocodile - I can feel it in my bones. We move quickly, spitting out the leaves. As soon as our feet hit the ground, we're sprinting through the clearing. Sebastian takes the lead as we burst through the barrier that hides the skull house. We're not safe here, not if they have Smee. The house might've kept us safe from the creatures on this island while we slept, but it'd be the first place his uncle would look.

We round a bend in the path and break through the trees, dodging the underbrush until we hear someone scream his name. The voice is masculine and pained, but it's someone he recognizes. A lurch of terror that rolls through him and into me. Sebastian slams to a stop and I almost crash into him.

"Zephyr," he says under his breath, spinning in place and searching the forest as he draws his sword.

I stumble backward, trying to give him space, managing to avoid the pointy end by an inch. "Are you sure?"

"I'd know his voice anywhere. I'm sure," he growls, his voice low and dangerous. Something moves to the right of us, cracking twigs and Sebastian whirls, sword at the ready. "Get behind me."

I nearly trip over my feet to do as he demands, but as I look toward where the noise came from, I spot green skin peeking through the dark leaves. "Wait!" I grip Sebastian's arm, as the figure comes through.

Zephyr meets our wide-eyed stares and sucks in a breath, jerking back as if he didn't expect us. "Oh, dear gods," he curses, holding a hand to his heart.

My heart is pounding in my chest, and I can barely breathe as I swallow hard, desperate to soothe it. I've never been more relieved. Had that been the Crocodile I'm not sure what we'd have done. We lack the strength to fight him and his witches. Maybe him alone would be okay, but not more than that. Not without my magic and Sebastian's shadows. But it's still bittersweet. If Zephyr is here, the Crocodile knows Sebastian is alive and he's hunting him. We also don't know where Zephyr stands anymore, but I'd like to hope it's on our side.

Sebastian must share the same thought. He tightens his grip on the hilt of his sword but lowers it to his side. "What are you doing here?" He starts to take a step forward but thinks better of it.

"Looking for you! I should toss you over the rail myself for putting me through that. I grieved you, you asshat, only to find out you're on Neverland." Zephyr flails a hand in the air. "That's beside the point. Smee is being held captive. Your fa—uncle killed Nelvin. I don't know what to do." He lifts up a ring wrapped in fine magic threads, *A dreamcatcher.* "I managed to trap his soul in here, but his body died. It'll only last for a day or so, then after that he'll be released and allowed to pass on, but the Crocodile took Smee before she could say goodbye. I had to do something..."

I'm frozen, my jaw falling slack, as I try to wrap my head around what he's just said. *Sebastian...* I can't imagine how he feels. I'm not even sure what I could say to help, but I rest my hand on his arm, hoping it'll give him strength.

"Smee..." he trails off, twisting his neck like he can't bring himself to say it. "Smee made her bed. I can't save her from this one. Not without my shadows, but our uncle won't hurt her. He needs me to do that."

This isn't how it's supposed to be. He shouldn't have to choose between keeping me alive or his sister, but I don't know what to do. All I can do is stay here.

Sebastian scrunches his face, biting his lower lip as his eyes gloss over. "What happened?"

"After you went over, he took Smee prisoner on his ship. Nelvin tried to stop him, and the Crocodile stabbed him in the throat. Poor boy, almost bled out on the deck in front of her. He didn't last long after that, but Lorian managed to make this thing." Zephyr holds it up again and the light above the canopy of trees reflects off the silver strands.

Sebastian tenses. I can't see his face, but I feel the fury rip through our bond, consuming me as if the feeling were my own. And this is with dampened emotions... I'd hate to experience the full thing. I can see the muscles in his body flex as Sebastian tries to keep himself upright. Tears brim my eyes as a sharp sensation explodes deep within me. It's not physical pain, but an emotional agony so strong it threatens to break me apart. I barely knew him. This isn't from me... Smee though, despite everything I don't wish for her to die, or to be captured, but Sebastian is right. She put herself there and nearly killed the both of us in the process.

Something metal flips through the air and Sebastian catches it. His gaze darts to Zephyr as he rolls the metal thing in his hands. I look to Zephyr, hoping he'll make sense of it. To me it's just a piece of scrap. It's the first time I truly look at him, and a part of me wishes I didn't. His eye is bruised, nearly swollen shut. His lips are busted, but he holds his shoulders high. It's not until he stands directly in front of Sebastian that he speaks again. "It's a good thing I brought that then, isn't it?" His dark lips curl up, wincing as he attempts to smile.

Sebastian puts the metal piece into the cuff, and it releases as if it was the key. *They managed to reverse-engineer them... That's incredible.* Sebastian reaches for the small circle net, being careful not to strain the threads.

"I don't see a way out of this one," Zephyr says, hanging his head. "The Crocodile has way too many witches, and we barely have any men left. Trying to fight them head-to-head would be suicide. Smee wants you to choose her..."

Sebastian takes a deep breath and turns his gaze towards the canopy of trees, eyeing their fluorescent leaves. It's like the world is ending, and I can feel the despair slip into my chest, turning it cold and bitter.

"We're not going to fight them head-to-head." Sebastian's eyes glint as he glances at me. The breath hitches in my chest, hoping he's not making the decision I think he is...

Zephyr raises a brow in confusion. "What do you mean?"

"We're going to give him what he wants, or at least what he can't use." Sebastian shakes his head. "I have to die."

My heart plummets as I stand, stalking forward. "No. There has to be another way." It's impossible to keep the tremble in my voice out. All of this can't be for nothing. I've tried too hard to keep this fool alive. I won't let him die now. Sebastian releases a long sigh and turns to cup my face. His expression is resolute and his jaw is set.

"He won't accept anything else," Sebastian says quietly. "If we don't give him what he wants, he'll keep coming for us."

My face mere inches from his, and my entire body shakes, furious he'd even consider that an option. "Find another way."

"We might've had more time, but it didn't change the fact that my death is the only option to keep you and Smee safe. We can keep running from the inevitable, but all it's going to do is deny her the chance to say goodbye to the man she loves."

Sebastian's gaze is unwavering as it bores into mine, and his jaw is clamped shut with a firmness that suggests he won't be swayed from his decision. Then, as if someone has flipped a switch he changes, smiling until his dimples show, but it doesn't quite reach his eyes. "My mother survived on this island for a year by herself. You might share her freakish love for plants and remind me of her in so many ways, but she wasn't nearly as stubborn or strong-willed. You'll be just fine, Scarlet. I know it."

I stagger back, but before I can say anything, Zephyr steps forward. "If you die, he'll just kill Smee. She's not his daughter and seeing as your father banished him the day she was born, he has no emotional attachment to her. Smee is offering a way out. Let her help you. She'll get to be with Nelvin again."

"We don't know that... The only other way is for me to turn myself over and try to get her out first, then end it. But that's a risk I'm not sure I'm willing to take. If I'm captured, I can't stop him from opening that vault." He drives his ringed fingers through his hair, messing it up.

"We'll just have to make sure that doesn't happen." Zephyr says, glancing at me. I don't have words for this conversation, and even though I have the moonstone on my neck, I've never felt more numb.

There's no changing Sebastian's mind. I don't think there ever was a chance at it... I clear my throat, quickly wiping away the tears that have slipped from my eyes. "I might know something that can help." They both turn to me in shock. "The plants in your mother's garden. Not all of them were safe. You can try to get Smee and you out of there, but if it goes wrong, there's a plant there you could ingest, and it'd kill you peacefully within a minute."

"I knew I liked her," Zephyr says, smiling through the pain.

40
Hook

I don't like this plan... I don't like it one bit.

There's so much that could go wrong, but it's also the only one I have that can end with Smee and Scarlet safe—for now—that keeps me alive. It's not that I wish to be a martyr. There are just no other options at play. I've been fighting my uncle for two decades and he's relentless. He won't stop, no matter what the cost is, until he gets what he wants.

Scarlet and I can't run forever, though. This has to end here. I turn over the leaves Scarlet gave me in my palm, dragging the pad of my thumb over the dark red veins. Honestly, I'm not sure why she's helping me. She made it very clear that sacrificing myself isn't the route she wants me to go, but it's the only one that ends with both her and Smee alive. No tricks. No gimmicks.

"Do I have to eat these too?" I ask, glancing at her pursed lips. She nods, crossing her arms over her chest. She won't even look at me...

I shove the leaves into my pocket and tip her chin, forcing her gaze to meet mine. "I promise to do my best to keep everyone, myself included, alive. But if I do have to use these, I need your word that you won't try to bring me back. I don't want you to risk any more of your soul."

Her hazel eyes finally reach mine, searching for something there as she chews her bottom lip. It's a feeble attempt to hide the tremble, but at least she's not wearing a mask anymore. "I promise."

My hands cup her face as I lean in, pressing my forehead against hers. All the nerves and unease fade away when she's this close to me. I claim her lips in a searing kiss like this might be the last time. Savoring the moment, memorizing the way her skin feels, the way she tastes... I don't want to forget it. Not even in the next life, should it come to that. Something shifts within her and she leans into me, allowing herself to let go. I'm breathless by the time I pull away, afraid to open my eyes because once I do, everything changes.

Scarlet wraps her arms around me, clinging to my chest. "Just don't need them, alright?"

I hug her back, burying my face in her hair, and drinking her in one last time. "I'll do my best." With a deep breath, I separate from her, turning to Zephyr in the clearing near my childhood home.

"I'll get her to the ship. I promise," Zephyr says. His poor face... I press my lips into a fine line as I reach for him, turning his chin so I can see how bad it is. "I'm a doctor, remember? I can take care of myself."

That's true, but it doesn't change the fact my best friend went through all of this because of me. Luckily, the wounds are superficial and it's more inflammation than anything. "There's a special salve in my quarters. Scarlet knows where it is. Use it please?"

"I'll take it into consideration." He scrunches his nose, welting the deep purple bruises. "But I'm counting on you coming back to show me where that is.

"If it goes bad, please make sure—"

He cuts me off, holding up a hand. "I'll see that she's taken care of. You need to go."

Nodding, I know he's right. The longer we wait here, the less likely it is for us to do this and for our plan to work. "Where's Lorian, anyway? I'm surprised he let you out of his sight here."

Zephyr blinks at me a moment, then links his arm through Scarlet's. "He's on the ship. I'd planned to get herbs while I was here and he wouldn't know what he's looking for. Since Smee is indisposed, and you're here, and Nelvin..." he trails off for a moment, clearing his throat. "They needed someone to stay behind. Someone who knew how to lead."

That makes sense... He wanted to get Everbloom, and who knows who else was hurt. They might need the anesthetic now rather than later.

"Good luck," he says, patting my arm and leading Scarlet away. I start to walk away, to head toward the beach where the Crocodile is setting up camp.

"Sebastian," Scarlet calls, forcing me to turn around. "Don't die."

"As you wish, princess." I bow sarcastically, spinning on my heel as I stand up. I hate that I can't promise her anything, but I'm doing the best I can.

It doesn't take me long to reach the beach, glimpsing the white stones on the coast as they shimmer in the hell flame light. He's set up a tent on the shore, and rowboats are pulled onto the land. His ship is just offshore, and I can see the Jolly Roger looming in the distance. It's farther down the island's coast, dwarfed in comparison to his ship, but the masts are fixed and, for the most part, you'd never know she's been almost destroyed.

The salty sea air stings my nostrils, and I can feel Scarlet's unease roll through the bond as the weight of what comes next sits heavy on my shoulders. I spot Smee, sitting on the shore with her arms tied behind her back. There's a gag in her mouth and glistening streams cover her cheeks. My chest tightens at the sight; she's always been so strong... I can count on one hand how many times I've seen her cry.

The stones crunch beneath my feet as I close the distance, hands up in the air. Witches are gathered around the tent, their long cloaks hiding their wretched faces. They don't so much as flint, watching me like hawks. The Crocodile steps out of the tent, catching me out of the corner of his eye and double-taking. Whatever he was about to tell Smee dies on his tongue as a wicked grin splits his face. "I knew you'd come around."

"Well, I'm here. Let's just get it over with." I step forward, feigning surrender. My voice is steady despite the anxiety gnawing at my insides.

"What made you change your mind?" He juts his chin at me but doesn't move an inch.

"My mother did. If she believes the lengths you've gone through to get my shadow back are necessary, then I know it's the right choice. She'd never do anything to harm people on purpose."

"She was a magnificent woman, wasn't she? James never knew what to do with her. All she ever wanted was for him to stay here, yet he wouldn't give up his fleet. I am curious, though, how did you survive? I thought for sure my witches were going to pull you out, soaked through up to your eyeballs. Imagine my surprise when their spells claimed you were here. The same island as Pan's vault. Now, if that's not fate, I don't know what is." The Crocodile chuckles to himself, looking along the tree line as if he's waiting for something to pop out.

"Scarlet saved me."

The Crocodile's eyes narrow suspiciously as he mulls over my omission. "Is that so?"

"You got what you wanted. The least you could do is let Smee go." I glance at her ropes before meeting his steely gaze again.

"No can do... You see, she tried to stab me. I much prefer her as is, but she's also offered herself as a sacrifice. The ropes stay until she's in that vault. Sorry."

"Fine, but let's talk. I'll go willingly, but you have to play by my rules."

His grin turns sinister, his eyes scanning over my body, landing on the sword at my hip. "Ditch the sword first. And seeing as that cuff isn't on your wrist, I should warn you. Sapfirna doesn't play fair. In fact, she's casting now as we speak. You use even one shadow, and that ship goes up in flames." He nods to the Jolly Roger.

"Understood," I say, taking the sword off my belt and tossing it to them. One of the witches rushes forward to retrieve it. This just got a whole lot harder, but as long as the leaves are in my pocket, there's a way out if I can't get Smee free.

As I near my uncle, he holds out his arms like he's expecting a hug. I keep walking toward the tent, sparing Smee a weak smile, but she doesn't even register my presence. Her eyes zoned out on the sand. I'm dead to her... or maybe she feels bad for calling him.

Either way, I want to go to her, to pull her into my chest and tell her that I'm here, that I've got her, but I can't...

Not yet. My uncle tosses his arm around my neck like we've been best friends our entire lives.

"Now, let's have a drink, shall we?"

I take a seat at the table in the tent. It's small and foldable, but it has a whiskey bottle and two glasses on top. It's like he was expecting me…

"I knew you'd come around. My brother raised you, after all. He's the most stubborn, pigheaded man I've ever met. Clearly, he's rubbed off, but your mother was sensible. I hoped that by showing you mercy and allowing you to have one more night with your wife would get your head in the right place."

"You make it seem like I've already picked who I'm sacrificing." I cock my head to the side, accepting the glass he slides my way, but I don't bring it to my lips. I'll wait until his drink is gone first. I'm not dumb enough to get drugged.

"Well, considering Smee's on board with it, and you didn't bring your wife, I thought you had. You're welcome, by the way. Killing the elf really changed her perspective. It was great motivation."

"She's your niece." Gritting my teeth, pain shoots through my jaw.

"True, but you're my son. Your mother never knew her, and honestly, I don't think she'd question it if I said she lost the child in her womb when she got sucked into that vault. As far as she knows, Smee never existed."

Zephyr was right... He doesn't care about her in the least bit. I've got to get her off this shore. If I don't, he'll kill her out of spite if I die.

"My father died. You'll never be half the man he was." I watch my uncle down the last bit in his glass and I finally let myself indulge, letting the amber liquid burn down my throat.

"You better watch your mouth, boy. This can get a lot worse for you." His eyes blaze and I can feel the static in the air. His lightning... I'm not sure why the element obeys him still, but it does.

"How exactly do you plan to explain to my mother that you tortured her son to be with her?"

"Easy. I'm not." He leans back, fingering the rim of his glass.

"If she's truly in there, she'll have questions when you show up. She'll hate you for all of this."

"Then I'll just have to hope she can find it in her heart to forgive me. I love her, always have. You understand that now. Tell me, Sebastian. If Scarlet were to be stripped from your life and locked in an impenetrable vault, would you kill someone to bring her back? To be with her again?"

"I don't know. I'm not in that position." I take another sip.

"Use your imagination." My eyes dart away, falling on the stone sand. "That's what I thought," he sneers.

My uncle pushes up from the seat, gripping my shoulder as he walks by. "Stay here. Remember, Sapfrina will know if you use your gift. I have something I want you to see."

The moment he leaves the tent, I wait three seconds, then launch from my seat. Smee's back was to the tent wall. I can at least undo her bonds. It would make it easier to flee if she's not bound. Lifting the canvas side from the bottom, trying to be as stealthy as possible, I reach for the ropes on Smee's hands, but my hand sinks through her like she's not even there. Her image flickers back into focus and I step back, letting the canvas fall shut.

What the fuck... She's not here. It's an illusion. That's why she didn't react to me being here. She didn't see me, because someone is projecting her image with magic. Smee's somewhere else.

I start to lift the back side of the tent, ready to bolt toward the woods, but even that will end badly. I'm not sure if the blood witches can use spells on a ship as far away as the Jolly Roger, but I've seen them do some unspeakable things. If I leave, they'll kill them all. If I eat the leaves, they'll do it anyway. I walked right into his trap.

Driving my fingers through my hair, I pace the tent. There's got to be another way. Something. *Anything.*

I try to calm my racing heart, my mind reeling as it tries to come up with a way out of here that doesn't end in the people I love dying. A tsking noise sounds behind me and my spine straightens as I gasp. Part of me doesn't want to turn around.

Oh, how far I've fallen... It wasn't that long ago that I won the king's gauntlet—an event that's deemed the most ruthless bloodbath our realm has ever seen. I slaughtered and drained the life from enemy after enemy. Now, I can't kill one man. My gift is restored and I can't even use it. If the witch senses my shadows, she'll kill them. If I let him leave this tent, he'll give her the order to do so. If I eat the leaves, he'll kill them all anyway. I'm left in this box with no way out.

My hands clench at my sides, the adrenaline coursing through my veins has my body trembling, needing a release. I want to throw something. I want to break something in my bare hands. I want to watch the life drain from my uncle's eyes and ensure his soul is shredded to bits just so he can never return. I want to hear his bones snap and watch his eyes bulge as he takes his last breath. Only I can't... I'm helpless because any move I make will kill someone I love.

Filling my lungs to capacity, I slowly turn around to face him. My uncle takes one look at me and the air deflates from his body as he shakes his head.

"I hoped we could remain civil, but clearly, you have no intention of doing so. Which means we have to do this the hard way." He sets his glass down on the table and I know what I have to do. I can't let him leave this tent, but I can't use my gift either.

In a split second, I kick my foot out, smashing it into the chair. The wood splinters and cracks beneath my weight. I slide the toe of my shoe beneath the broken chair leg, not taking my eyes away from my uncle as I thrust it up, catching it in my hand. He smiles at me as I grip the wooden stake and flex my fingers.

"And what in the gods' names do you plan to do with that?" His eyes narrow into slits.

"Come find out." I shove the tablet at him, sending the glass cups and whiskey bottle to the ground. They shatter and shards fly out across the stones. The table meets his middle and he doubles over. I barely take a step before he's upright again, lifting his hand, and lightning crackles in the air. Static bolts surround his fingertips, forming a whip that lashes out towards me. I don't have time to move before it wraps around my neck and the smell of burnt flesh fills my nose.

My teeth mash together, grinding the enamel to try to ward off the pain that sears through me. But it's not me I'm worried about. Scarlet shares the bond now, and she'll feel every ounce of the pain I do. My breaths are shallow as I fight for air, desperate to get anything in my lungs, but his grip is too tight.

With a flick of his wrist, I'm yanked toward him so hard I lose my footing. His power releases me as my hands connect with the ground, and glass shoots through my palms. Wincing, I bite my lips together, smothering the cry that threatens to claw its way out of my throat.

I get one foot on the ground before his boot lands on my side, knocking the air from my lungs. My throat spasms, the pressure building in my face as I fight to breathe, swallowing down the bile that comes up.

"You thought you could kill me with a piece of wood. It's demeaning," he seethes, stepping closer.

"I don't care how I kill you, as long as you rot." Clawing my hands into the ground, I try to force my legs beneath me, but he kicks again and this time the force is so strong it knocks me onto my back. Glass digs in and I can feel the blood dripping down my flesh.

"You just don't know when to quit." He stands next to me, looking down like I'm the most pathetic man he's ever seen. I can't move as I catch my breath. I'm still recovering from drowning and being stabbed through by poisonous coral. At this rate, it makes me wish I could burn Lorian's lives.

His lightning coils around my body again, digging deep. It burns through my clothes and scorches across my skin. My muscles strain, tightening to the point that I can feel the threads within them snap as a guttural scream rips through the back of my throat. Currents slip over my body in waves, but I grip the stack and push it into the cord of power he has wrapped around me, smelling the burnt cedar as it plumes into the air. Smoke coils up, dark and suffocating, as the wooden chair leg catches fire. My uncle lets up, eyeing me like he's unsure of what I plan to do. He watches me turn over, staring up at him from my hands and knees, careful to keep the wooden piece from touching the ground.

"Tell me, do you think your witches prefer to float or burn?"

His brow furrows and I shove the burning tip of the wooden chair leg into the ground. The moonstones won't burn, but the pyrite between them will as long as there's something to ignite it. Now that I've bought enough time for the whiskey to sink deep enough, it ignites the pyrite.

I lurch to my feet, rushing forward, and slam into my uncle. I take him through a shadow with me, popping up closer to the tree line as flames explode through the tent, lighting up the boats on the shore and the witches huddled around them. They scream and run as flames lick across their skin, burning to the bone. Pebbles fly, raining down onto the shore, catching new places on fire. Every part of the coast bathed in white stones ignites, creating a ring of flames around Neverland.

My mother taught me that. It was supposed to be how we warned my father that something happened. I've only ever had to do it once, but she made sure I knew how. The fool's gold beneath the moonstone ledge runs deep and it'll burn for hours but never spread onto the island. According to her, the flames are bright enough to be seen from the Luminaries or any place between there and Solaria.

The last time it burned was the day my mother died. How fitting that it ignites again on the day my uncle does, seeing as he's the reason I had to go through losing her. It'd been my uncle's idea to take my memories and lock them away, but since I jumped off the ship, they've come back piece by piece--the good, the bad, and the worst of them being the day this fucking ring burned.

I cried as I lit those stones. My bloody hands trembled as I held my little sister. I mourned while trying to figure out how to care for an infant by myself until my father could come for us, and it took days. I had to bury our mother myself and it was all because of him, because he wanted to go see the nymphs. My uncle let me wander off because he wanted to talk to them instead of watching the boy in his charge. He's the reason they had to open Pan's vault. My uncle chose to love my mother, and it took her from me and Smee.

My fist collides with his face and I see red. The world disappears around me as I punch him, over and over, until blood coats my fingers and I have no idea if it's his or mine. It takes everything I have no to end him here and now, but I don't know where Smee is, and I can't leave her behind.

"Where is she?" I shout the words in his face, yanking my uncle up by his shirt as I straddle his torso. His eyes flutter and blood spews from his nose and mouth. His eyes are bloodshot and riddled with ruptured vessels.

"Which one?" He grins at me, flashing bloody teeth.

"Where is my sister? You better use your fucking words before I start breaking bones one by one. Where is Smee?"

"She's in the vault. You have until the moons come out to come get her, or she's dead." He coughs up blood and his face warps before my eyes, changing between a witch and my uncle in flickers of a second. He possessed her and glamoured her face... The magic is dying along with the witch. But if my uncle isn't here, then—Boom.

My heart stops beating in my chest as I look over my shoulder to find my ship burning. The ship I just sent Zephyr and Scarlet to.

"No." I breathe. No, no, no. The witch is dead when I turn back to her and push up to my feet. I bury my hands in my hair, turning to watch the ship fall apart. "No!"

The flames lick the sky, painting it orange and red as the last remains of hope smolder away into nothingness. Smoke billows out from its shattered hull and the screams of those onboard are loud enough to reach my ears. One in particular that's distinctly feminine.

Dropping to my knees, my body goes weak. My heart feels like it's been ripped from my chest, a jagged, empty pain. My hands curl into fists, and my nails dig into my palms until they bleed.

I did this... I should've eaten the leaves while I had the chance. Now, not only have I lost Scarlet, but I might lose them both. The compass to find the vault was on that ship. And if Smee is there, I'll never get to her in time without knowing where I'm going.

41

HOOK

Just as I start to stand up, to figure out what to do in order to save Smee, something massive darkens the sky. Groans of wood split the air and when I look up, I find the bottom of a ship floating above me, swooping in low and fast.

What the hell... The thought dies in my head as I spot the black sails and the skull and crossbones. The Jolly Roger.

They're alive.

The ship curves over the ocean, circling back around toward me. On the bow, straddling the mermaid's shoulders, is Zephyr with a long, coiled rope. I watch the air shimmer like a cloud of magic surrounds it... The ship is flying?

Zephyr holds his hand over his eyes, squinting to block out the hell flame. He spots me and points, yelling to the crew, "There he is! Full steam ahead!"

The roar of the crew is audible from the ground and people rush toward the rail or climb on things to get a better look at me. Sails billow, curving full of air, and

Zephyr drops the rope as they swing past me. I latch on to it, swinging in the open air.

Hand over hand, I climb, determined to reach the top. I have to know... but I can't tell what's real and what's not anymore.

My uncle has always been manipulative, but as far as I knew, he never possessed this sort of magic. His coven of blood witches has grown immensely stronger, especially if they were able to make it look like a ship was burning for this long.

The rope swings as the Jolly Roger flies, soaring above the island, but I finally make it to the top and my men hoist me over the railing.

Zephyr is the first one to greet me, yanking me into his arms. I barely get to look at him before he's coiled around me in an unforgiving embrace. I thought he was gone... His horns press against my jaw as he sobs, each heave of his chest causes the rough texture to scrap against my skin.

"I thought you were dead," he says, shoving me away. I nearly topple over the railing, but he catches me by my shirt. My eyes round as I take him in. His face is healed like the bruising never happened. However, a gnarled line of stitches cuts through his right eyebrow. That wasn't there in the woods.

"Where's Scarlet?" My heart skips, beating wildly as I look through the men on the deck, but there's not a single head of white hair present. "Where's Scarlet?" I say it louder.

"She... She jumped after you. She sank, Captain." As soon as the words leave his lips, my blood runs cold. I was so wrong... so behind.

It wasn't Zephyr in the woods. It was the fucking Crocodile, and I handed the love of my life right to him. He played me, and that's why he knew exactly what I was planning to do. I told him everything. Reaching in my pocket, I discover that the leaves are gone. He must've taken them at some point, maybe while I beat him on the beach. Closing my eyes, I grit my teeth and drag in a heavy breath. He even stole my backup plan.

"Please tell me I'm wrong, that it was you in the woods?" I step forward, the plea audible in my voice. Zephyr stares at me and the blank expression says more than words. "Fuck!" I spin and slam my hands down on the railing.

"How are you alive?" Zephyr's hand touches my shoulder gently and it takes everything I have to force the steady breaths in and out of my lungs.

"Scarlet's a mermaid," I say, and his jaw drops open. "Well, sort of. Half mermaid? Something like that." They don't need to know about the rest. "I underestimated him, Zeph... It's bad." I slide down the railing until my butt connects with the deck. The crew stares at me with emotion-filled eyes, but it's all I can do to zone out on my feet.

"How bad?" Zephyr asks, moving to sit beside me.

"He pretended to be you in the woods, so I'd give him Scarlet. He possessed and glamoured witches and made me think I saw the Jolly Roger burn to the ground with the people I love on it. If I don't get to Pan's vault by the time the moons block out the hell flame, he's going to kill them." I catch sight of Lorian coming up the companionway. "Where's Nelvin?"

Zephyr's face falls and the crew who have gathered around us falls deathly silent. So that part was true...

"Your uncle attacked him and ripped his soul from his body. He put it in this thing and told Smee the only way she'd ever see him again was to convince you to open the vault. He's trying to convince her to be a sacrifice and I think it's worked." Zephyr wraps his arm around mine, resting his head on my shoulder.

Lorian smiles weakly at us, coming to stand by the railing. "I'm glad you're alive, Hook. We thought for sure you were gone when you went over the rail. I didn't believe it when the Crocodile said otherwise. It wasn't until he took Smee and left us that I could bring myself to do the locator spell."

"Do you know how my uncle was able to project those images in my head? He made it feel so real..." I squeeze Lorian's hand the moment he rests it on my shoulder.

Lorian moves away from me, coming around it to stand in front of us, arms crossed. "I wish I knew how to answer that, but it's hard to know what he used without being there."

I turn to Zephyr, and he lifts off my arm to meet my gaze. "Is the compass here or with Smee?" Terror gnaws at my insides. Without that compass, we can't find the vault. Zephyr reaches into his pocket and pulls out the compass, handing it to me without a word. I breathe a sigh of relief, turning the cool metal over in my palm. "We've got to get to the vault."

Lorian helps me up from the ground as he nods. "In that case, we'll catch up after. Let's fly."

I nod, watching the compass's arrow spin. "How is the ship flying, anyway?" I ask.

Zephyr's expression lights up as he climbs to his feet. "Pixie dust. After you went overboard, I dug into your father's journals, hoping it would prove or disprove the Crocodile's story. Turns out, your mother saved the pixie queen during her time on the island. We stopped there first, asking for a favor."

"Of course my mother did," I say, a hint of a smile touching my life as I look at the island. I never thought I'd see the day that ships could fly...

Holding up the compass, the needle spins and Zephyr glances over my shoulder. Once it stops, Lorian barks orders, and the ship curbs to follow the compass needle. This is our one shot. We either find them, or we don't.

The Jolly Roger soars over the dense canopy of the island, her sails catching the sun's last light. It isn't long before the compass starts to twitch frantically. We're getting close.

"Take us down, Zephyr. We'll have to walk from here," I call over my shoulder. He carries out the orders, delegating to the elementals, and slowly, the ship descends. The tree limbs snap and crack as we drop, but the haul makes it all the way to the ground, held upright by the pixie dust. My men jump, sliding down ropes and using the vines from the trees to get their feet on the moss-covered forest floor, swords in hand.

We follow the compass on foot, weaving through the forest until we come face to face with a cave. A large archway rounds the entrance, carved with symbols and runes I don't recognize. The air seems to crackle, and witches pour out of the cave as if they were waiting for me.

Lorian leans in close, standing at my side. "We'll handle them, you go. Get Smee and Scarlet," he says, drawing his sword.

My pulse quickens, and I draw my own weapon as I nod to him. With a war cry, he takes off running and the crew follows. Even Zephyr has a weapon, which makes me more nervous for him than I am for the other men. Still, war cries fill the air as the men sprint toward the witches, and chaos ensues.

The clash of steel, the bright zaps of magic—everywhere I turn, there's a new threat. But I have a singular focus. The compass guides me, and with every ounce of determination I possess, I dash towards the cave.

My lungs burn as the air rakes in and out of them, scorching through my windpipe. The smell of burnt ozone floods my senses, tasting both bitter and sickeningly sweet with magic. I push my legs, forcing them to move faster as I tear through the cave. The lanterns on the wall flame alive as I near, lighting the way, until finally, I burst into an open circle of a room. In the middle is a stone pillar. The symbol my uncle showed me on his palm is carved into it. There's a round engraving on the opposite side of it, almost like a portal should be there. Runes are carved all over it and a gigantic swirl recesses into the stone.

"Nice of you to finally join us," my uncle's voice hits my ears and I jerk my head, desperate to see where it came from. To my right are Scarlet and Smee, sitting against the stone wall. Scarlet's been bound and gagged. Her eyes are swollen from crying. Smee isn't much better, but she's not secured. She's here willingly, holding the dreamcatcher in her hands.

Nelvin.

It doesn't make sense to me... None of this does. Why attack Nelvin and put him in there to convince Smee to go into the vault? He's had years to do that if he intended to use her as the sacrifice. Why wait now? Why go through the trouble of getting Scarlet too? He only needs one of them to open the vault for him to go inside and join my mother. Why go through all the effort of bringing them both here or waiting for me to love someone else?

I take one step forward and my uncle stops me in my tracks, his hands igniting with coils of jagged lines. Lightning. "Not until you open it. I would've given you a chance to say goodbye, but you've taken advantage of my mercy once already. I don't intend for it to happen again."

The chill of the room intensifies as I stand face-to-face with my uncle. My heart pounds, a furious drum in my chest, every beat calling for vengeance, for the chance to get the two of them to safety.

With a flick of my wrist, shadows twist and coil around my body as they rise from the ground like serpents, ready to strike. The darkness swirls over the sharpened blade in my hand and my uncle's gaze is charged with a similar fury, sparks of electricity crackling around his fingertips.

We clash and the ring of metal against metal sings around us. Each time my shadows reach for him, they're repelled by jolts of electricity, searing the ground where they touch. In turn, his lightning seeks me out, only to be swallowed by the abyss I summon.

With a surge of energy, a powerful bolt arcs toward me, striking my blade and sending tremors through my arm. Seizing the momentary lapse, my uncle lunges forward, driving the tip into my ribs, but I grip the metal blade in one hand, clutching it in a desperate attempt to keep it from piercing through me.

He leans in close, his menacing eyes staring into mine as he pins my body to the pillar in the middle of the room. The rune starts to glow the moment my skin touches the stone. I try to fight him off, but he pries my fingers from the sword in my hand. My uncle rips my arm above my head, smashing my palm into the rune, and the air hums like thousands of bees.

The scent of magic is pungent, and dust plumes as something starts to swirl fast enough to whip a breeze around the circular room—the portal. My uncle brings his face closer to mine, forcing me to look to the side to avoid touching him. Scarlet's wide eyes stare at me, her body jerking frantically as she tries to free herself from the ropes.

"Take a good look, son, because they're both about to be taken from you."

My mind goes blank as the realization hits me like a ton of bricks. He never meant to go inside the vault to be with my mother... None of us were going to make it out alive but him.

As the magic starts to intensify, I feel myself losing control over my body. The rune's energy courses through my veins like liquid fire, and I can hear Scarlet pleading for my uncle to stop, her voice nothing more than a distant echo.

My uncle needed Smee... He needed her to be a vessel to bring my mother back to life. My mother's body is long gone, buried in the clearing by our home. There's nothing to put her soul into without it.

Just like blood, it has to match. It can't just be some random body, but every woman passes a little piece of their soul to their children, which makes Smee capable of housing it. It also made Smee and me the only two capable of pulling my mother out of the vault. And since he needed Smee's body to put her in, it had to be me to make the sacrifice. He couldn't kill Smee—to force her soul out of her body—without damaging the vessel.

There was no promise... He needs me to get my shadow back so I can connect with my mother's soul. To guide her out, I needed the sliver she gave me at birth, something for her soul to attach to, to follow like a beacon. There's no way of knowing whether the piece is in my shadow or not, so he needed me whole first, but that would require two sacrifices. One to pull out my missing shadow and one to pull out my mother's soul.

That was always his plan... It's why he needed to wait until I loved someone else. He needed a second sacrifice. My uncle had no intention of letting any of us live. Not a single piece of it was out of the goodness of his heart or righting his wrongs. This was out of greed.

My father often alluded to my uncle's need to be better, to have everything he did, and more. My mother and father had the kind of love people can only dream of finding one day. It wouldn't surprise me if it infuriated my uncle to the point of obsession. I doubt any part of his story is true, from him claiming he and my mother were in love to me being their son. Any of it.

Focusing on my anger instead of who I fear losing, I grit my teeth and grind my jaw as he pins me harder, bending my arm into an awkward position to keep it on the rune. My lungs quiver, incapable of drawing more than a shallow breath.

The sword presses into the bones of my ribs, but the blade won't go through, not unless it twists. It's likely the only blessing I have right now, and the only thing allowing me to hold the blade in place with one hand, to keep it from sliding off to the left or right, or twisting so the flat side can pierce between the curved rib bones.

This ends here. Blood spills down my arm as the sharp edges of the blade slice into my hand, but my grip is the only thing holding the weight of it off me. He's purposely positioned the blade this way to inflict pain, but it won't kill me. The wound will be shallow, mostly skin and muscle, but my ribs can only take so much pressure before they break. Holding it is all I can do it keep that from happening, and he knows that. He knows I'll fight to keep that sword out of my body, and it's what allows him to hold me in the precarious position.

My focus is slipping, and he's just biding time until I cave. I can't keep my mind blank and off the people I love for much longer. Even a glance in their direction might be enough, and one of them will die. But he's underestimated my need, my drive, to keep them alive.

Meeting my uncle's steely eyes, I twist the hand holding the blade, releasing a guttural growl as it tears through flesh. The flat portion slips through my ribs and I let go. Without my hand holding his weight back, it plunges through my body, but my shadow is waiting for it. As the sword pierces through me, it doesn't hit the stone. It appears out of the shadow I've formed between our bodies and stabs into his throat.

My uncle sputters, releasing the sword and staggering back. I remove my hand from the rune and the portal spins shut. His hands grapple at the wound, desperate to keep the blood from spilling, but it's too late. He's not an illusion. He wouldn't miss the chance to be here in person. My uncle falls to his knees as crimson spills down the front of him and onto the dewy cave floor.

I drag in a shaky breath, my chest seizing from the pain radiating out from the wound. He's dead.

Daring a glance at Scarlet, I find her bent over, feeling every bit of the pressure and the sharpness of every movement, of every breath. It burns inside and out as severed nerves spasm. I want to go to her, to comfort her, but moving would only cause her more agony.

Hurried footsteps echo through the quiet cavern, and Zephyr and Lorian sprint into the room. They stop dead in their tracks as their terror-filled eyes take in the sight of me. Zephyr catches the movement, turning to see Scarlet and Smee. Smee hasn't even moved... She's not bound. She's just stuck—as if he placed her in some form of trance—clutching the dreamcatcher as Scarlet suffers. Zephyr drops to his knees, checking Scarlet over as Lorian rushes toward me.

"Hang on," Lorian says, his hands glowing as they swirl in front of my chest. The pain disappears, allowing me to breathe a little easier. He grips the sword, pulling it free. He yells for Zephyr over his shoulder.

"Let me get her free." There's a snapping sound as threads of rope break. "She's alright. It's just the bond."

Zephyr lands on his knees next to me, tearing away my shirt so he can see the wound. They bend me forward so he can feel where the sword exited. "Gods... You got lucky. He's still breathing. I don't feel anything that would suggest it got his lungs and it was too low to pierce his heart. None of his ribs are broken, but it doesn't mean they're not fractured. Can you take a deep breath?" Zephyr's brown eyes meet mine as he pokes and prods.

"No..." I shake my head slightly.

"But you can speak," he says matter-of-factly, pressing fingers down my neck, feeling for something there. The man has stitched me back together far too many times. I've learned not to ask questions and just let him work. "I don't think the sword hit anything important, but he needs to be closed up sooner rather than later. If air gets in the chest cavity, we're in a lot more trouble."

Lorian nods and his magic twists through me. Warmth floods through the wound, like the blade is still there, being heated by a flame. "Sorry, but it's going to scar."

I chuckle, wincing as Zephyr slides out of the way, allowing Scarlet to take his place. She grips my hand, tears running down her face. Her eyes are swollen and rimmed in red. I'd give anything to kiss it away.

"Told you I'm hard to kill," I breathe, my voice shaking as Lorian magics the wound closed.

On the plus side, having a millennium-old druid as a friend has its perks. His magic stores are expansive, having been stretched with time and practice. Where Scarlet had to use half her soul to heal me, he'll barely put a dent in his.

Tingles erupt through me as I bite back the pain, seeing Scarlet cringe as she experiences it with me. "I'm sorry... I shouldn't have had you finish the bond. I could've spared you all of this."

"Shhh. I'm not worried about me right now," she says, smoothing back my hair. I can feel the sweat beading on my brow, and I stare up at her hazel eyes as if they can give me strength.

"I love you," I squeeze out, gripping her hand tighter.

She bends to kiss my forehead, wrapping her other hand around the both of ours. "I love you too."

42
Hook

By the time Lorian is finished, I'm almost as good as new. He can't heal everything—no magic can—but for the most part it just feels like a bad bone bruise. Zephyr has been trying to get through to Smee, but she won't even look up at us or acknowledge our presence.

Something is wrong.

Lorian sits back with a labored breath and Zephyr lets out a sigh and comes toward us. I'm not sure what to do... That's my baby sister, and she's made some mistakes—mistakes that will haunt her—but she's all I have left of my family. I've practically raised the girl, even though we're only six years apart.

"I'm not sure what's wrong with her." Zephyr tosses his hands up.

It's only now that I notice how many streaked red lines pepper his skin and clothes. It's blowback from swinging a sword. Maybe he is more capable of taking care of himself than I previously thought. His hands, though, are coated from prodding at me, but for him, that's just another day in our life.

"Let me look. If they used magic, the spells should've died with the witches—assuming whoever cast it is here." Lorian groans as he pushes to his feet and crosses the open cavern to crouch in front of Smee. Placing his hands on her temples, he closes his eyes. An aura surrounds his hands, bright and shimmery. It's sort of beautiful if you can get past why he's doing it.

When the light fades away, his somber eyes glance at us. "She's not in there... That's why. Mentally she's gone. Her body remains and breathes and lives, but her mind is somewhere else."

"What about the dream catcher?" Scarlet says, gripping my hand a bit tighter. "She's been holding it, just like that, since they brought me here."

"It's possible..." Lorian takes it from Smee's hands, examining the threads. "If she is, and I try to pull her out, Nelvin will come too. The Crocodile trapped his soul in this, but if she's in there, she's at least had time to say goodbye."

"And if we don't? If we do nothing?" I ask, feeling the tear slip down my cheek and drip onto my arm. I hate this... We tried everything and I might still lose her.

"If we do nothing, this will only hold them for so long. Considering how long it's been since Nelvin died, maybe a couple more hours," Lorian puts it back in Smee's hands, standing up and pinching the bridge of his nose.

"Until the moons... It's linked to the moons. The Crocodile demanded I be here before the moons block the hell flame. My guess is he put her in there so he could torment me without her changing her mind or escaping. She's with Nelvin. He knew if she saw him again, she'd never change her mind and not go through with his plan. It'd mean giving Nelvin up and letting him move on."

Lorian shakes his head, taking a few steps closer to us. "No. If he's in there when the spell ends, his soul would shatter. There is no moving on. Either way, if he's going to be reborn, he's got to come out."

"I guess that means we're chancing it then," Zephyr says, propping his hands on his hips. "A few more hours together isn't worth Smee and Nelvin no longer existing, in body or in spirit. Her mind will return, right? Or will she be in limbo?"

"It should return to her body, yes." Lorian doesn't look at me as he says it.

"There's something else, isn't there?" I ask, using Scarlet as support as I stand up. The pain ebbs away once I'm on my feet.

"It's possible Nelvin won't return to his. The afterlife is delicate. Souls are delicate. If he doesn't return to his body, he might not keep his sense of direction." Lorian looks over at the three of us and scoffs. "Gods... It's like explaining how to steer a ship to a toddler." He clasps his hands and steps closer. "When someone dies, they have this innate drive to go to River Styx. It calls them and they just wander there. Once in the water, their soul travels through the river to the soul well, where they can be reincarnated. In Nelvin's case, his soul was trapped in here before his body died. When he comes out, he might not have this drive. He could be disoriented and if he doesn't make it to Styx—"

Zephyr cuts him off, his gaze voided on the cave floor as he speaks. "He might wander. He'll be lost."

"Yes... And lost souls don't ever move on. They wander until they forget who and what they are. Eventually, they just cease to exist." The lump in Lorian's throat bobs before he meets my gaze.

"Can we take him to Styx ourselves? We're on Neverland. It's not too far from the mainland. Could we sail there before the moons come?" Scarlet looks between me and Lorian, but my heart is too heavy to answer her.

Losing Nelvin will crush Smee as is. They might've had a weird relationship, but she loved him. Knowing that our uncle condemned his soul to the point that everything that makes him who he was ceases to exist would be devastating. Especially since she's the one who called the Crocodile to us in the first place. She'll never come back from that.

"No... Even with the ship flying, it would take too long," Zephyr says.

Scarlet shifts awkwardly beside me. She doesn't know about the pixie dust yet, but I suppose she will soon enough.

"There's another way..." I hate that I'm even thinking about this, but I know my sister. She wouldn't survive that. "I open the vault. I use her soul to get my shadow back and Nelvin can catch a ride with her in. I'm not sure what is on the other side of that portal, but at least they'll be together. Nelvin won't be lost, she won't have to live with the grief of losing him or of what happened. They both will find peace..."

Staring at my fingers, I pick at the blood caked beneath my nails. I just hope I'm making the right choice.

"Are you sure about this?" Scarlet says, cupping my cheek and dragging my gaze to hers. Her hazel eyes entrap me, and somehow, I just know it's going to be okay.

"Yes..." It's what's best for Smee and Nelvin. It's also what's best for us, too. With Scarlet's shadow gone... There's a very good chance it never returns, but I hoped it would, anyway. I didn't want her to fall apart like I did. She needed to have hope, but if it hasn't returned by now, it'll be a miracle for it to. With my shadow and our bond, she'll get to experience things the way I have through her. It'll be enough. "We need this," I say, not wanting to voice our secret out loud.

No one needs to know about her missing shadow. Not now, not ever. I'll find a witch to spell her the way my father had one do me. It'll make it look like she has a shadow if someone sees her in the light. She'll see it on the ground, and no one will be the wiser of what she's missing. It's our secret.

Tears brim, glossing her eyes as she puts together what I'm saying. "Alright."

I step up to the pillar, Scarlet by my side. It's already branded the rune into my hand, but I line it up and place it on the stone once more. The portal on the wall swirls to life, creating a sea of blues and greens and a plethora of colors that warp like a mirror. Lorian mumbles something behind me, and I can see the light cast upon the stones. He's pulling them out.

Tears stream down my face as I think of my sister. Of everything we've been through together. Her laugh, her smile, the way she used to tease me as a kid. I remember holding her in my arms for the first time and feeling so torn. She was so small, so fragile, so perfect. I'd saved her...

My mother had been gone, void of a heartbeat. Her chest didn't rise and fall anymore. I waited minutes, trying to get her heart to restart, trying to force her to breathe, and she wouldn't. I had no choice. But as I held her in my arms, something seemed right.

She was this beautiful little human who had never known pain or suffering. I couldn't help but smile at her or the way my heart was so full, even while it broke. I'd lost my favorite person that day, the woman who loved me more than she did herself, yet I'd gained someone that I could love unconditionally. I'd gained a partner in this cruel world who looked at me like I was her hero. Smee is... She was everything, and I know calling the crocodile was her way of trying to save me. She thought I was in danger.

Yet, I can't help but remember the hurt in her eyes when we were in the wardroom. I couldn't tell her what she wanted to hear, but I couldn't lie to her either. At the time, I wasn't sure how I'd choose if I was forced to pick between saving Smee or Scarlet. I don't think I'd ever have been able to hurt her. It wasn't until I stood on that ship, knowing I'd have to face that choice, that I knew what to do. Even though Smee's betrayal stung, I couldn't choose. I love them both more than anything. It's why I stepped off that ship.

I'm not sure if it was for me or them... Regardless, Smee could've burned the realm to the ground, and I'd still never be able to look past my love for her, to bring myself to take her from this world.

I just hope this is the right choice... That it's what she'd want.

Scarlet gasps, and I meet her stare, glued to something behind me. I follow it, being careful to keep my hand on the rune. Figures take shape. Ghosts almost... Their outlines hold a bright blue hue. The edges of the shapes define, revealing Nelvin and Smee, hand in hand, and my heart cracks wide open.

Smee pauses as they step toward the portal, her translucent eyes meeting mine as she smiles big. My body trembles as I bite back a sob. So filled with joy, knowing they're together, but hating that it means we'll be apart. I do the best I can to smile at her. Nelvin smirks, winking at me as if he has to poke my buttons one last time.

I snort out a laugh, wiping at the tears. Lorian clutches Zephyr to his side next to us as we watch the two of them step through. To find their own peace in whatever comes next. Together. As they disappear and the mirrored surface swirls, something darts through the surface and slams into my chest before I can react.

My body is imbued in darkness as something sears into my very core. The force knocks my hand from the pillar and the portal slams shut. The silence falls around us and the burning disappears in an instant.

My shadow... *It's back.*

43

Scarlet

We chose to stay on the island for a few days. It gave Sebastian time to be with the memories of his family and the crew a chance to rest. They buried the dead and everyone's spirits are a bit brighter now that we know Smee and Nelvin are at peace.

I think everyone can breathe a bit easier just knowing it's over.

The Crocodile is gone, so Sebastian and his crew's job of protecting the outer realm just got a lot easier. Blood witches still exist, but they won't be organized under his command anymore, and by default, my fathers. We just hope that means their terror and destruction will become a thing of the past.

Sebastian has his ship back, his captain's hat, and his shadow. I no longer have to hide my mark, and even though his men don't know about what I did to save Sebastian, they know enough. No one questions what I am since they all saw me sink, and to them, that's the most solid form of proof I could give them.

Zephyr and Lorian are as close as ever, and just happy to have things back to normal, but they—like Sebastian—still miss Smee and Nelvin. Overall, we've all found a way to make peace with our new life and have found a way to remember those we've lost along the way.

I step outside the skull house, glancing at the garden. This is quickly becoming a ritual, and I'm not sure if I should be worried or glad Sebastian is working through this so quickly. Either way, it's late and he's usually back inside by now.

As I near, I spot him slouched against the fence. It wasn't until we buried Smee that I found out his mom was buried near there, too. I guess the garden was her favorite place and he thought it'd be fitting for Smee to be laid to rest there, too. He knows their souls aren't there. They're all in the vault, but I think talking to them and pretending they are helps.

As I near, he turns toward me, opening an arm for me to curl against his side. Together, we stare at the graves. He replaced the cross on his mother's that had broken with time, but instead, there are now two names carved into the wood. Wendy and James Hook Next to it is one he made for Smee, except it doesn't read Smee. It says, Sami Hook.

My brows furrow as I stare at it. "I didn't know her name was Sami."

"I, um... I gave it to her when she was born, but when she got older, she couldn't pronounce it right, so Smee stuck."

Sebastian traps his lips between his teeth and I snuggle closer. "You don't have to sit out here. It's okay. I'm just trying to spend as much time with them as I can before we leave."

"I know," I say, catching sight of the captain's hat between the base of the crosses. They're all here... My heart breaks for him, but I can feel the peace he does settle into the bond, and deep down, I know he's okay.

"I wanted to ask you something earlier... How would you feel about living here instead of the Luminaries?"

He cranes his neck to stare at me, his emerald eyes flicking between mine as if he's not sure he heard me right. "You want to stay?"

"Not stay, as in, not sail with you, but maybe we could have this be home when we're not on the ship."

His lips tip up at the corner before morphing into a grin that flashes his dimples. "It's grown on you, huh?"

"Yeah..." I look around at the barriers, sparking in the hell flame light. "It really has, but I also know my home is wherever you are, and this place means so much to you. It's where you feel closest to them."

He nods and intertwines my fingers with his. "I'd really like that."

I stand, offering a hand to help Sebastian up. "Come on. The crew has the fire going.

He comes with me and together we join the others around the campfire, drinks in hand. The flames crackle as two dozen of us lounge in the grass with whiskey-flushed faces, telling stories of those we lost.

"Did I ever tell you about how Smee lost her ear?" Sebastian says, a smile so bright on his face I can't help but mimic it. I'm starting to understand what he meant about living—feeling—through me. With his shadow back, the loss hurts, but he's also so alive...

"I don't think so." I turn on his lap as the men chuckle and laugh so loud that it's infectious.

"Get this, Nelvin bit it off." Zephyr nudges my arm, lifting his brow.

"Nelvin? What? Why?" I quickly glance between them, needing an answer. He loved her. Why would he do that?

"Nelvin had been caught thieving, using his whole sleight-of-hand bullshit. She wanted to go with us on the ship, but she was only sixteen, and a lady. He didn't want to subject her to that, but she begged and begged. So, James gave her a test. He told her if she could find and bring him the thief that'd been terrorizing the Luminaires, she could join the crew." Zephyr pauses to take a sip of his drink, but Lorian plucks it from his hand before he can bring it to his lips. Only he doesn't notice until his hand meets his lips, and his face drops as he shoots a frown over his shoulder.

Sebastian snorts as he rests his flask against my thigh. His hand is gripped possessively around the other, and I can feel the cool metal of his rings through the material of my pants. "My sister never jumped so fast. She hunted that man down for weeks. When she finally found Nelvin, she ambushed him and hog-tied him up. He's never let her forget it."

"Ha! You're forgetting the best part," Lorian says. His eyes nearly sparkle in the firelight, the flames reflecting off their glossy surface. "She had to carry him back to the house to show James. Can you imagine little Smee, and Mr. Long Legs Nelvin slung over her shoulders as he trudged through town?"

Lorian pumps his arms, imitating how she must've looked. Nelvin was so tall. Even Sebastian had to look up to talk to him, but Smee was almost the same height as me. She couldn't have been more the five-foot-four. The mental image is staggering, but a smile breaks across my face, so wide I flash my teeth.

"Nelvin managed to bite her ear, but she jerked and dropped him, and since the fool didn't let go, it ripped it off. She got home and dropped him on our living room floor. He had her bandana in his mouth like a gag so he couldn't bite her again, but she'd hung this little pouch off it. My father opened it up and it was holding her ear. She thought we could just pop that shit back on." Sebastian sets down his flask in the grass next to us so he can wipe at his tears but is unable to stop laughing long enough to slow the flow.

"James gave him the option to join our crew and serve time for his crimes, but it took a solid year before Nelvin would be within ten feet of Smee. He only had to do three months, but he just stayed." Zephyr chokes on a laugh. "I don't think anyone ever told him his time was over. He probably still thought he was serving his sentence when he died." The group chuckles until the silence clings to the air.

"I can still hear her yelling at him for caressing her nub," someone says from the other side of the fire. I can't see their face over the flames, but the entire group laughs again, crying and holding their stomachs.

"Caressing her nub?" I ask, turning to Sebastian. It's impossible to keep the amusement out of my voice.

"Yeah, he'd always run his finger over it. He called it his love mark," he says, barely about to get the last word out like he has to swallow down the urge to laugh again.

"I heard that woman threaten to float him more times than I can count," Lorian says, talking with Zephyr's glass. "Boy, did they love each other though..."

"To Smee and Nelvin!" someone shouts, and the group echoes it, pouring one out for them.

I raise my cup and feel Sebastian stiffen. glancing over my shoulder, I find his eyes lost on the ground where my shadow is being cast by the firelight.

"Scarlet..." he breathes. "Your shadow—"

It's back!

My heart fills to the point of bursting as I crush my lips to his. His arms wrap around me tight and when I pull away, his stormy eyes stare into mine.

The crew whistles and shouts behind us. They might not know about my shadow, but I can't help but smile at Sebastian, our joined shadows mingling across the ground.

I used to think I was cursed, that the mark on my back would keep me from knowing love or be my death sentence, but it was a blessing… It led me to him—the man who loves every piece of me.

• • • ● • ● • • •

THE END

Acknowledgments

While writing this book, I had my Facebook reader group, Howler's Pub, vote and throw out name ideas for what Smee's full name would be and the most voted for was Sami, which was suggested first by Erica Lynn Switzer! Thank you so much for your input and for helping to name my character!

I also want to say a huge thank you to my husband! The poor man goes through so much while I write lol. Between helping me with our kiddos so I can hibernate in my writing nook for days on end to just riding the emotional roller coaster that I go on alongside my characters, he's there for me every step of the way. If you're reading this, thank you for being you! XOXO

My critique partner is the absolute BOMB. She's incredible, and she helps me brainstorm all of my books. Without her, I'd be crying in the corner. Thank you, Michelle, for being my muse!

Margie... How do I even begin to list all the ways you've helped me? I swear you're the Gorilla Glue that holds me together most days and especially with this book, you're the reason I'm still sane.

To my ARC and street team! You guys rock! Thank you so much for supporting me and reading my stories. Your encouragement is just absolutely phenomenal! Thank you for being you and I hope you all enjoyed the book!

Lastly, to you, dear reader. I wouldn't be able to do what I do without you—and others like you—picking up my books. So, thank you! I created this world full of characters I adore, and I hope they were able to offer a little escape from reality. <3

Cover Design by JV Arts

Map of the Seven Realms by @sekcer on Fiverr.com

Also By Amanda Aggie

THE HELL'S BELLS & DEMON DEALS WORLD
Obsidian Wings
Monster Roommate
Must Love Humans

DARK HALOS TRILOGY
The Demon Prince
Crown of Ashes
The Crimson Queen

REALM OF MONSTERS
This Wicked Fate
This Wicked Curse
This Wicked Bond
This Wicked Tower
This Wicked Kingdom

SERIAL KILLERS NEED LOVE TOO WORLD
Beyond the Palms

AMANDA AGGIE

Killer Sensations
The Hollow 47

About Author

Best known for her #1 Amazon bestselling series, Dark Halos, Amanda Aggie writes steamy dark fantasy romance. She's a wife, a mother to two beautiful tiny humans, and has a stellar caffeine addiction. More importantly, she writes choking-hazard fantasy romance that will have you laughing out loud, swooning, and biting your nails all in one sitting.

Almost all of her books take place in The Seven Realms, which she's often described as, "If Hell and Wonderland got together and had a baby." You'll find creatures of all kinds—fae, demons, dragons, witches, and more—along with morally gray villains, and steam. So, grab you some pearls to clutch and get lost in the chaos.

Check out the link below for extra goodies and places you can find Amanda!

https://linktr.ee/AmandaAggie

Printed in Great Britain
by Amazon